LOVE, BLOOD, AND SANCTUARY

Brenda Murphy
Megan Hart
Fiona Zedde

A NineStar Press Publication

www.ninestarpress.com

Love, Blood, and Sanctuary

Printed in the USA

ISBN: 978-1-64890-304-5

First Edition, June, 2021

Also available in eBook, ISBN: 978-1-64890-303-8

WARNING:
This book contains sexually explicit content, which is only suitable for mature readers, death of a major character, and depictions of blood play and homophobia.

Sanguine Faith

Brenda Murphy

Auntie, I didn't quit and thank you for everything.

Rest easy.

Chapter One

The rap on the car window rattled the glass. Laurel started and slammed her knee into the steering wheel. She cursed softly as she jabbed the window control button. The demon was dressed as a policeman. He wore dark glasses and his beefy hands rested on his thick duty belt nestled between the pepper spray canister and his pistol holster. A slight glow from a pouch near his hip was the only clue to his true identity. Huffing out her frustration at the window's lack of response, Laurel shoved open the car door.

"You okay?" The officer leaned closer and peered into her face. His feet were squarely inside the circle of salt Laurel had spread around the car the night before.

"Yeah." Laurel cleared her throat. "I'm okay."

"You can't sleep here." He gestured to the street lined with ancient brownstone townhouses and graffiti covered buildings. "It's not safe."

"I'm sorry—" Laurel wiped her hand over her face and squinted at the officer's name badge. "—Officer Sullivan, is it? I worked a late shift and didn't feel safe driving anymore. I pulled over here to catch a nap."

"Stow it. I passed this way last evening, and you were parked here. Your car hasn't moved." He leaned closer and removed his sunglasses and slipped them into his shirt pocket. "I know your uncle."

"Great-uncle." Laurel stared at his face and inhaled sharply. His eyes were light gray rimmed with red, her image mirrored in their shallow depths. His practiced glare was that of an experienced centurion. Laurel shivered under Sullivan's gaze, unable to look away from the magical enforcer. He was bound to her clan, sworn to serve and protect. Loyal to a fault, willing to die for the family. Her great-uncle had a legion of centurions, all more than willing to aid and abet his less than legal business dealings.

"Is that so? Why are you here? What do you want?" Laurel pressed her lips together and rolled the hem of her shirt between her fingers.

Officer Sullivan leaned down and spoke softly. "You're royalty in our world, Laurel. He know you're sleeping in your car?" His melodious tones seeped into her body as he used the old language, the language of secrets, curses, spells, and death.

Laurel suppressed her shudder. "My roommate kicked me out." She scrubbed her hand over her face in an attempt to hide the lie. "It was sudden."

The centurion straightened and pursed his lips. He drummed the fingers of his hand on his holster. "All right, Laurel, if that's how you want to play it. You need to discuss this with your great-uncle. If you don't, I will. I don't want to find you sleeping in your car again." He tilted his head. "You may not have inherited your family's abilities but you're still family. We take care of our own. I can't spend my nights watching you sleep, keeping watch for the Orions."

Laurel gripped her keys tightly. Orions. The hunters. So many missing. So many gone in the blink of an eye, their bloodless and mutilated bodies found months or years later. Or worse found still smoldering, their mouths open in voiceless screams. She had taken a chance last night, but after walking in on her girlfriend eyebrows deep between their neighbor's legs she had stuffed her car full of what it would hold and fled.

"I'll be safe." She lifted her shoulders and let them fall, straightening her posture before she settled her hands at nine and three on the steering wheel. "I'll talk to him today."

Officer Sullivan stepped back, smearing the salt of the circle she had spread around the car. He pointed at it, lifted his chin, and smirked. "Seriously? It doesn't work unless you infuse it with energy."

Laurel inserted the keys into the ignition. "I know." She looked away from her feeble attempt to protect herself and his smirk. After snapping her seatbelt in place, she waved at him and closed the door. She banged her hand hard on the steering wheel when the telltale *click-click-click* of a dead battery echoed in the car. "Fuck me."

Officer Sullivan opened her door. "Come on. I'll give you a lift."

Laurel chewed her lip as she looked down at her paint-stained black T-shirt and tatty jeans. "I can't go like this."

Officer Sullivan rapped on the top of the car. "Get out. Now. I don't have all day to deal with you, Laurel. And it's not worth my life to leave you here with a broken-down car." He stepped back and crossed his thick arms. "Do I need to assist you in exiting the car?"

Laurel shivered. She had experienced a centurion's assistance just once and the memory of it still woke her at night. She trembled and wiped her sweaty palms on her jeans. "Let me grab my backpack."

"Good choice."

Laurel gathered the few things she didn't want to leave in the car. After jamming her sketchbook next to her ancient laptop in her bag, she zipped the top closed and grabbed her hooded sweatshirt from the backseat before she exited the car.

"You hungry?"

"I'd really like coffee. I can't talk to Great-uncle Marcus without some caffeine on board."

"Come on, I'll buy you breakfast."

"Why'd you let me sleep there last night if you were just going to take me to my uncle today?"

"I didn't want to wake you."

Laurel glanced at Officer Sullivan walking beside her. "Thank you."

"No problem. To serve and protect. Even if it's from yourself." He held the car door open, and she slid onto the cool leather seat. She settled her backpack between her feet and pulled on her black hooded sweatshirt. The car shifted to the side as Officer Sullivan entered and levered his bulk behind the wheel.

He waited until she had fastened her seatbelt before he started the car. Laurel's gaze slid over the array of weapons lining the car. Magical weapons clipped into racks side by side with conventional firearms, their soft glow visible to Laurel.

Able to see magic, unable to wield her own power, the last female of a clan stretching back eons, unwilling to assume her role as clan leader and unwilling to produce an heir, Laurel chewed her lip as the car shot forward bringing her closer to her great-uncle's house.

Laurel shifted in her seat and drummed her fingers on her knees. "You worked for my mom and dad, didn't you?"

"I did."

Laurel stared out of the window. A familiar ache settled in her chest. There were some things even magic couldn't protect you from. The ratty buildings gave way to well-kept streets and high-rise buildings. The sidewalks were crowded with people scurrying to work and school.

"Do you think the humans ever get it? Like, do they know about us? Really get it? Other than the ones we make consorts?"

"Humans see what they want to see. If they ever understood how powerful supernaturals are, they would freak right the fuck out. And try to exterminate us. Again. All of us. Their unwillingness to see and believe is what keeps us safe." He tapped the pistol on his belt. "And this."

Laurel shuddered as the car slowed and stopped.

Officer Sullivan turned off the engine and preened in the rearview mirror a moment before he turned his head to face Laurel. "How do you take your coffee?"

"Black. Unless it's that dark roast crap. Then make it white as a virgin's wedding dress."

Officer Sullivan's loud guffaw exploded in the quiet of the car. "You got it." He left the car.

Laurel glanced at the tarnished Saint Christopher medal stuck to the car's headliner and rolled her eyes. A group of humans rushed past, small children and their adults, animated and laughing, their voices muffled by the car window. The gentle ache in her heart blossomed into full-blown longing. Laurel blinked the grit of exhaustion from her eyes, leaned back against the headrest, and rehearsed the story she would spin for her great-uncle, hoping he would listen, knowing he would not.

Chapter Two

Laurel studied the painting of her parents on the stark white wall of her great-uncle's house. Wedged in between a similar portrait of Marcus Callan and his wife, and her grandfather and grandmother, it was the only one draped in black. A fine layer of dust covered the black cloth, giving it a soft glow.

The joy on her parents' faces as they gazed at each other suffused the painting. Laurel had seen them look at each other that way every day she could remember. Her heart had bubbled with happiness when they would turn that same love-filled gaze on her. She rubbed her thumb over the edge of her empty paper coffee cup and turned away.

The worn leather couch with its overstuffed cushions called to her. She fiddled with the strings of the crocheted blanket draped over the back of it as she considered stretching out and napping while she waited for her great-uncle.

Her stomach roiled. Too much coffee, too little sleep, and too many memories in this house. She placed her cup on the table and swiped her hand through her hair. She glanced at the mantel clock. No one rushed Marcus

Callan. Laurel shoved her hands in her back pockets and perused the floor to ceiling bookshelf. Multi-colored leather-bound books with fading gold lettering on their spines filled the dark wood bookcase.

Laurel pulled a copy of *Through the Looking-Glass* from the shelf and opened it. The pages were yellowed and frail. She paged to her favorite poem and leaned against the case as she read. The nonsense words soothed her as they always did, as she read of the Vorpal blade that slew the Jabberwock. Had Carroll been one of the few humans who knew the truth?

A tap on the doorframe drew her attention. She kept her finger in the book to mark her place and turned toward the sound. A woman in a dark-blue Chanel suit stood in the doorway. Her pale-gray eyes settled on Laurel. The small hairs on Laurel's neck stood up. Another centurion. Laurel focused her energy and flexed the small bit of power she possessed to shield herself from the woman's rude attempt to probe her mind.

A hint of a smile tugged at the woman's mouth and she inclined her head. "Sorry. We can't be too careful these days."

Laurel placed the book back on the shelf before she turned to face the woman. She rested her hands on her hips. "Who are you? And why would I want to harm my great-uncle?"

"I'm Nadia, Marcus's personal assistant. He said to make you comfortable. Would you like coffee, miss? Or tea? Something to eat?" Her voice was silk over steel, gauged to seduce as well as soothe, if you were human.

Laurel huffed out her annoyance at the woman's failure to answer her question and her placating tone.

"No, thank you. And please, call me Laurel. What happened to Douglas?"

"He left, for, shall we say, other opportunities." A lethal smile curved her mouth. "Your great-uncle is finishing a business call and will be to you when he's finished. You're sure you don't want anything, Laurel?"

"No." Laurel ignored Nadia's raised eyebrow at her sharp tone. "Thank you."

"Very well." Nadia pursed her lips and gestured to the hall. "If you change your mind, my office is two doors down, on the left."

Laurel paced, her mind awash in memories and questions. She hadn't cared for Douglas. An officious toady, he had ratted her out more than once when she had been a rebellious teenager, including outing her to her great-uncle well before she had been ready to tell him she was lesbian. At least Nadia was easy on the eye. She'd have to wait to see about the rest.

*

The smell of her great-uncle's Armani cologne greeted Laurel before he did. She rubbed her nose to stifle the sneeze that hovered as her eyes watered. She plastered a smile on her face and braced for impact.

Marcus Callan was not a tall man, but he tried to be. His high-heeled bespoke boots snapped against the dark hardwood floor of the living room. Dressed in a black silk shirt and trousers that matched perfectly, his blade-thin graveyard-pale face stood out in stark contrast. His mouth contorted into what passed for a smile, his blue-tinged thin lips pulled back to expose large, yellowed teeth crowding his narrow mouth.

"My favorite great-niece, what brings you to see me." He hugged her and pressed a kiss to her cheek.

"I'm your only great-niece." Laurel stepped back, putting a half-step distance between them. "And Officer Sullivan."

"Sully is an excellent centurion. He's been with us for many years." Marcus gestured to the portrait of her parents. "I think things would have been very different if he had been working that night." He looked down and away. "Tell me what you need, Laurel, please. I want to help you."

"Nothing, Uncle Marcus." Laurel shoved her hands into her pockets.

Marcus turned and skewered her with his steel-gray eyes. "You will not sleep in your car. You are family and my responsibility. What would the rest of the clan say if they heard you were sleeping in your car? Or worse, what if the Orions found you? Don't look at me like that."

His genial expression morphed into the one that scared the hell out of everyone else in the universe but Laurel. She had been scared of her great-uncle, once upon a time, but after experiencing the loss of her parents and finding her girlfriend in bed with their neighbor, she was too numb to feel anything.

"Or what? You'll kick me out? Disown me? I moved out, remember? I don't care if I inherit any of the clan's money. None of it will bring my parents back. I'm not interested in continuing the line. Or in power. I want to make my own way."

Her great-uncle snorted. "Make your own way," he mimicked viciously. "And where have you gotten? Let me use my connections. I can get you an agent and a showing of your so-called art anytime you want. And make sure that it gets a positive review. You could be something, Laurel. Maybe then you'll fulfill your obligation to the clan."

"No. I'm not going to have you call up and lean on people to get me a showing, or representation. Not like that. And before you ask again, no, I'm not interested in a match. I'm not a brood sow, ready to pop out future supers for the sake of the clan."

"You have an obligation. You can't even give me a year of your time? You wouldn't have to marry or raise the child."

"No. That's worse."

Her great-uncle turned away, the muscle in his jaw working as he paced the room. "So, what do you want from me?"

"A job. And a place to live."

"You could—"

"No, not back here. I'm not moving back in." She rubbed the back of her neck. "I can't create here. Not with you, so you can parade every eligible clan male through here trying to get me to acquiesce to your plans. It's too much."

He pressed his lips together in a thin line and glared at her. "If you're so desperate to not live here, I have the perfect place for you. I can't keep it rented so you might as well be there." He clasped his hands behind his back. "I won't take money for rent. Let me do that, at least."

Laurel chewed her lip as she quietly calculated the balance of her bank account. "Okay."

"I know they need a bar back at Sanctuary, if you want me to put in a word."

Laurel straightened her shoulders and settled into her dependence on a man who made her skin crawl even when he was being kind. "Sure. I don't want to go back to the coffee shop." She swept a hand over her face. "I really don't want to see Alma again."

"No?" Her great-uncle pursed his lips.

"No. We're over."

"Should I say I'm sorry?"

"No. It was over for a while, last night just confirmed what I'd been worried about." Laurel crossed her arms over her chest. "So, where is this place?"

Marcus waved his hand toward the door leading to the hall. "Nadia will drive you to pick up your car and show you the townhouse. Do you need to pick up anything from your apartment?"

"A few things. And I'll need a jump for my car."

"You couldn't even summon the energy to start your car? You haven't mastered the ability to control mechanicals?" He snorted and then pressed his lips in a thin line.

"I don't have those abilities, you know this. Why do you always seem surprised?"

Marcus lifted his chin and leveled a hard glare at her. "You could. The blood of Clan Callan runs in your veins. And you waste it."

Laurel shoved her hands in her pockets. "Not just Clan Callan."

"Don't remind me of the unfortunate human dilution of our family's bloodline." He shifted his gaze to the portrait of her parents before he brought it back to her. "If you want to avoid contact with Alma, give Sully a list and he'll pick your things up for you. He'll be more than willing. I'll get Ronda to cover his shift."

Laurel scrubbed a hand through her hair. "Thank you. I'd appreciate it."

Marcus tilted his head. "I know I'm not your father, not even close, but I've always wanted the best for you, Laurel."

"I know." Laurel gave her great-uncle a quick hug. "I know."

Chapter Three

The front door to Sanctuary was set into a narrow, brick fronted building. The dimpled steel door was low-key, a dull dirty gray against the blood-red brick. A thick brass sign with "Sanctuary" etched into it was mortared into the wall next to the door. Yellow rays of energy, a hint of the world that lay beyond, seeped out around the edges of the doorframe.

Humans crowded the street next to the building, their heads bent over their phone screens with white earbuds jammed into their ears. Laurel chewed her lip and stepped out into the flow of pedestrian traffic. She clenched her teeth against the hum of magic that filled her head as she walked the narrow alley between the club and the next building.

Laurel covered her mouth and nose with her hand against the stench of urine and the faint hint of blood laced with the unmistakable scent of dark magic. After picking her way past dubious dark puddles dotting the brick path, she arrived at the side door to the club. She tapped on a black steel door with "deliveries" printed on it in yellow block letters. The heavy metal door swung open on well-oiled hinges.

"Yes?" A man dressed in chef checks and a black jacket stood in the doorway. He cocked his head sideways. "Laurel?"

"Yes." Laurel wiped her hand on her jeans.

"You don't look like him."

Laurel shrugged her annoyance.

He turned and lifted a hand, gesturing for her to follow. "I'm Bruce."

Laurel entered the brightly lit space. The receiving area was narrow. Wire shelves lined the passage. Cardboard boxes with neat printing filled the shelves. Her shoes squeaked on the floor as she followed Bruce through the busy kitchen to the front of the club.

The murmur of voices as staff scurried around setting the tables and preparing the elegant dining room for the lunch crowd created a low-level hum. Bruce waded between the tables as he led her to the bar.

He leaned his elbow on the mirrored chrome bar. "Carla?"

"Yeah?" Carla turned to face them. Her steel-gray centurion's gaze fell on Laurel.

"This is Laurel. She'll be your bar back."

Carla shifted her gaze to Bruce. "Since when?"

Bruce crossed his arms over his chest. "Since this morning. And don't act like you don't need one."

Carla shifted her stance and swept her gaze over Laurel. Her probe was ten times the force of Nadia's. Laurel pushed back at first and then, seduced by the bartender's power, she gave over, caught up in her attention. She surrendered to Carla's invasion of her mind. She flushed as Carla sifted through her memories and thoughts. The sensation of being held down, captured, and the delicious feeling of being known made Laurel squirm.

"That's enough, Carla. She's Marcus's niece." Bruce's voice broke into Laurel's thoughts and Carla withdrew.

Laurel crossed her arms over her breasts in a vain attempt to hide her nipples where they pressed against her thin T-shirt.

Bruce glared at Carla. "Get a room next time." He flounced toward the kitchen leaving them staring at each other.

Carla swept her hand over her close-cropped curls. "You okay?"

Laurel shivered. "I... It's been a long time."

Carla tried and failed to stifle her grin. "I know. Don't worry. With your looks you'll have more than a few interested." Her expression shifted to one of remorse. "Hey, I'm sorry."

Laurel frowned. "About what?"

"I didn't recognize you as a super, I wouldn't have scanned you without asking. I'm used to scanning humans. When it's supers, I always ask first, and go easy."

Laurel looked away. "It's fine. Anyone could have made that mistake. I'm not really a super."

Carla rested her fists on her hips. "You're Marcus's niece. How can you not be a super?"

"Great-niece." Laurel shrugged. "I don't know. Can you please show me what you need me to do? I've worked as a bar back before so just give me the rundown."

Carla waited a beat and then stepped back. "Yeah, sure." She gestured to Laurel's clothes. "You're okay wearing jeans and your T-shirt for today. We'll find you a uniform for later. We serve lunch and dinner. The café handles breakfast and brunch on Sunday." She waved to the rear of the dining room. "Through the glass doors is a club with a dance floor. There's a bar there as well. Jay works the bar and Kyle is his bar back. You only have to worry about me and this bar. We keep the restaurant patrons well oiled, and you'll run drinks for the wait staff."

Laurel worried her lip with her teeth. "How's tipping go?"

"We share out at the end of the night." Carla tilted her head and pointed to a locked cabinet. "This is reserved for supers. If we get mixed couples, if the super allows it, the human can be served from the special stock." She leaned on the bar and knotted her hands together. "We get a lot of humans in here. They're drawn by the hum, the power they sense. We also get a lot of supers looking to hook up with them. I keep an eye on the ones who look like they have no clue. There are rooms in the back, that can be reserved for private dining or whatever." She lifted her eyebrow. "If you see something that doesn't look or feel right to you, let me know."

Laurel relaxed her gaze and focused on the glowing doors at the end of the dining room that would be invisible to humans. Wisps of purple energy seeped around the edges and Laurel's mind filled with images of what went on behind them. "Are those locked?"

Carla nodded. "Yes." She held up a ring of old-fashioned skeleton keys and jingled them. "We keep these for show. I change the wards every day so no one gets a room without checking with me." A lascivious grin spread over her face. "I'd ask if you wanted to see one, but I already know the answer to that question."

Laurel scrubbed her hand over her head. "If I weren't fresh off a heartbreak, I'd be more than happy to let you show me a room, but I'm a bit tender today."

Carla gripped her shoulder and squeezed lightly. "Come on, I'll go over this week's special drinks and the garnishes I'll need. We have about an hour before we open."

Chapter Four

Catherine paced her attic room. The discordant strains of experimental jazz were not enough to cover the drone of the man's voice. His pompous tone grated as he discussed jazz as if he were the arbiter of all that was cool. Catherine wrinkled her nose at his bombastic tirade and praise of vinyl records as if he had pressed them himself. She slid between the gaps in the floor, waiting to coalesce into a form that would haunt the man for the rest of his poseur days.

He paused and took a sip of his drink. He lifted a bottle of bourbon from the table and held it poised over the woman's empty glass. "Another drink?"

"No. I don't think I should, Jack." The woman brushed her hair back with her hand. "I have to work tomorrow."

He fixed his gaze on the woman's breasts. "Come on, Sherry. You know you want to." Jack filled her glass, brown liquid sloshing over the side. "This is hand crafted. I found it on a trip to..."

Catherine drew herself together and revealed herself to the man. He stared. Standing behind and just to the left of the seated woman, she rested her hands on her hips.

Naked, she arched her back and raised her hands to her breasts. She lifted them like an offering.

Jack blinked and replaced the bottle on the table. His expression morphed into one of desire. He licked his lips.

"You were saying?" Sherry tilted her head at Jack.

"What?" Jack never took his eyes from Catherine's body.

"What are you staring at?" Sherry twisted in her chair to look over her shoulder.

Invisible to Sherry, Catherine blew a kiss to Jack before she rolled her nipples into stiff points.

"Nothing." He shifted his gaze back to Sherry and took another sip of his bourbon. He rubbed his eyes. "Nothing." Jack spun on his heel and glanced at the bay window looking out over the street. "Must have been a reflection." He gulped his drink before he placed the glass on the end table.

Catherine sauntered to the center of the room and then crooked her finger at him. Jack glanced at Sherry before his gaze slid to Catherine's eyes. A sly smile twisted his lips as he drew nearer to her.

Catherine held his gaze, raised one hand, and then peeled the skin from her face as one would peel an orange. She dropped the first bit of her ghostly form onto the floor and leered at Jack. His scream reverberated off the walls as he backed away. He stumbled. His arms windmilled as he tried to right himself before he crashed to the floor.

"No. No." He crab-walked away as Catherine advanced. She tore more flesh from her face and plopped it at his feet. She leaned into it then, projecting the image of blood oozing from stripped bone into his mind.

"Get away from me!" Jack kicked at Catherine.

Sherry shrieked and bolted from her chair. "The fuck is wrong with you?" She grabbed her purse and slung it over her shoulder before she ran from the room. "And I fucking hate jazz," she called over her shoulder as she ran down the steps to the front door.

Catherine flicked another bit of flesh toward Jack. He shrieked again. A dark stain covered the front his jeans and the hot smell of urine spread out in the room.

"God save me. Please. Please, don't kill me!" His voice rose in pitch.

Catherine leaned closer and placed her bloody finger over his lips. "Leave. Now. Don't come back." She blasted the words into his mind, careful to not rupture the delicate vessels feeding his brain. It wouldn't do to kill him. That was always more trouble than it was worth.

"Yes. Yes." When she let him go, Jack rolled to his hands and knees. He ducked his head and scrabbled away from Catherine. She hovered by the bay window and watched as he fled.

She pulled herself together, knitting her form back to the perfect one she preferred to hold. Why couldn't they rent this place to some quiet soul who would leave her in peace? If she had to be trapped in this monstrous house, couldn't she at least have pleasant company?

"You're so good at that. I can't scare away a mouse. Let alone a human." Manny's soft voice floated up from the basement. "Thank you. From all of us. He was talking about asking Marcus about renovating the cellar and filling in the cistern."

"My pleasure." Catherine reveled in the thrill brought about by Jack's abject terror.

His fear had spilled over and saturated her. It was always so. The moment her victims succumbed to their fear was delicious. A fine wine to be savored, although she much preferred a subtler approach, sipping her victim's fears over the weeks and months she sometimes took to rid herself of the endless string of renters.

But tonight, Jack, with his obvious plan to get Sherry drunk and seduce her, had pushed every one of her buttons, gotten under her skin as it were. She chuckled to herself at her own joke and drew in the intoxicating sensation of power. Catherine released her form and her soul passed through the ceiling, up to the attic and her room.

The stuffy, hot air of the attic surrounded her. The cloying scent of mothballs and cedar rose to greet her. A chair covered in once-white linen now yellow with age was wedged under the low knee wall that took up one side of the room. Her narrow brass bed, its mattress leaking stuffing where the ticking had split, the bloodstains on it now faded away to a light brown, mocked her.

Regarding the grim reminder of her last minutes on the earthly plane, she wondered for the millionth time since the night she and her lover had been surprised by her brother if it would have been better to surrender to the oblivion of death. The worn memory of that night wormed its way into her consciousness. The flash of the blade, Nora's screams and the way they had faded as her brother dragged her from the house, the slam of the door echoing like a pistol shot. Her soul ached as she replayed the lugubrious sounds of her last breaths as Catherine tapped all her power to drag herself to her attic sanctuary.

Catherine drew her finger along the blade she had yanked from her body while reciting the spell that would keep her spirit alive, even as her guts spilled from the wound in her belly and her earthly form died.

She shoved the kris away and it collided with her grimoire. It gouged the cracked leather cover before it clattered to the floor. Catherine rested her palm on the book as she turned her decision to stay bound to this place, to remain on this side of the plane, over in her mind. The closeness of the attic pressed around her. Immortality was much easier when you were free to wander the streets and inhabit whatever human form you desired.

Catherine picked up the kris and ran her thumb along the blade. Revenge and desire burned through her. A heady combination, it had fueled her since the night she had escaped execution and become a prisoner of the townhouse instead.

She picked up the blade and slashed the air, slicing through the waves of melancholy that roiled around her. Catherine set the blade aside and created a glamour, transforming the room into a charming attic bedroom. She lay back on the bed, resting on the rotted mattress. She pillowed her head on her hands and closed her eyes against the reality of her choice. The *scratch-scratch-scratch* of mice as they tramped in the walls searching for food disturbed her enough that she sent a lethal wave of energy toward the sound and was rewarded by the silence that followed.

Restless, Catherine left the bed and sat at her desk. She rested her chin in her hand. How long would she be able to protect Manny and the others? Their spirits were trapped in the part of the house that remained hidden from all but one. And he would never reveal it. Never release them. Marcus Callan's secrets would die when the house was renovated. Their souls would be trapped in the rubble, consigned to the pit in the basement, or scattered to the four directions and beyond.

Catherine flipped through the book again, knowing she lacked the power to send the children over to a peaceful rest. Hell, she lacked the power for herself. Without the box and the blood, they were stuck on this plane until the building ceased to exist. The high of her last victim left her, and in that space rose a fierce longing.

As much as fear fed her, she craved the sweet taste of love and adoration. Catherine closed her eyes and reached out with her mind, testing the bounds of her prison as she had every night since she had lost Nora. Hope warred with resignation. Nora had never believed as Catherine had, had never participated in the rituals, or even believed Catherine's true identity. She held little hope her lover had survived the years between them or that she would ever reverse the magic keeping her bound to the house. The townhouse would be Catherine's tomb, her final resting place as sure as if she had been buried in a proper chamber under a pyramid of stone.

Turning away from her melancholy thoughts, she opened her worn copy of the book and began to read again. Incantations and prayers she had read so many times she could recite most of them filled her mind. Catherine sorted and sifted the words and directions, determined to find a way to release the cellar spirits and herself.

Chapter Five

Laurel and Nadia stood on the gray sidewalk in front of the brick townhouse. Trimmed in Indiana limestone, wide curving stairs rose up to the faded black door. Three tiers of bay windows fronted the building. The street was scruffy, and the battered buildings around them were in various stages of disrepair. Laurel's rust bucket of a car fit in with the other late models lining the street.

Nadia removed her Bulgari Flora sunglasses and tucked them inside their case. She snapped it shut and placed it in her suit pocket. Laurel stuffed her hands into her back pockets as she surveyed the street.

Nadia peered into Laurel's face. "Would you like me to call for help?" She nodded toward Laurel's car stuffed with her belongings.

Laurel rubbed the back of her neck. "No. It's all portable. I've moved too many times to own anything I can't carry myself."

Nadia held out the keys to the building. The afternoon sunlight reflected off them and they glittered in her hand. "Has your great-uncle told you anything about the townhouse?"

"He only said he couldn't keep it rented to humans or supers." Laurel looked away from Nadia's probing stare.

"You're sure you want to risk it?"

"It's better than moving back into his house. I can't work there. It's too…"

"Safe?" Nadia spoke over her. "Full of memories?"

"Both." Laurel huffed out a breath.

Nadia pursed her lips. "This townhouse has been in the family for generations. It has been many things over the years." Her intent gaze settled on Laurel, the fine rim of red around her pupils glowed. "Inform me if any spirits attempt contact." She whispered in a voice edged in granite. "They are not for you."

Laurel stepped back. "I'm not a super, remember? Why would a spirit waste time with me?"

Nadia lifted her chin. "You are many things, Laurel, don't underestimate your worth." She reached across the space between them. "Your great-uncle asked me to link with you, for your protection. May I?"

"Yes." Laurel slid her mental shield in place as she braced for Nadia's linking. Unwilling to give up her secrets to her great-uncle's personal assistant, she pasted her most benign smile on her face as she let Nadia forge a connection between them.

Nadia cupped Laurel's chin in her hand. She tightened her grip and her fingers dug into the tender place under Laurel's jaw. "Your talents are dormant, not nonexistent. Don't waste them, and don't doubt them." She relaxed her fingers and rubbed her thumb over Laurel's lower lip, making her shiver.

Captured by the seductive web of Nadia's voice, Laurel closed her eyes.

"One day you'll find a spirit who will awaken them in you." Nadia's touch and her voice soothed Laurel.

With her mental prophylactic in place, she relaxed into Nadia's gentle mind fuck. On the sidewalk in midafternoon, after giving her permission, there was nothing she could do to resist and, in the moment, with her shields set safely in place, she didn't want to.

Nadia mapped Laurel's mind. Laurel hovered on the edges of her consciousness. Nadia pushed forward, picking her way through Laurel's mind as she wove a web of connection between them. Laurel held fast, rebuffing the centurion's efforts to push past her mental fortress, determined to keep her secrets safe from her great-uncle and his loyal centurion.

Nadia inhaled sharply and drew her hand away from Laurel's face. Her eyes were bright, and she trembled. "You're hiding something, Laurel."

Laurel opened her mouth to protest.

Nadia held her hand up. "No. It's fine. I have what I need to connect with you." Her eyes shone. Her pupils glittering black pools of promise. "I'm here for you, Laurel." Her voice oozed tenderness. "My loyalty is to you, now. We are linked. I won't harm you. If you need"—a wry smile tugged at the corner of her mouth—"or want me, for anything, contact me anytime, day or night." She stepped closer and clasped Laurel's hand and pressed the keys into them, and then held their clasped hands to her heart. "I pray you don't need me, but I hope you might find you want me." Nadia gazed into Laurel's eyes. "You're gorgeous, as promising as spring, a flower whose blooms are tightly furled, but near to bursting." Nadia squeezed her hand hard and the keys bit into Laurel's palm. "With the right tending you will blossom spectacularly."

Nadia stepped back, releasing Laurel, and held her arm out toward the steps. "After you."

Laurel shook her head to clear it of Nadia's passionate speech and the remnants of her probe. "Let me grab my backpack. No need to go up empty handed."

Nadia followed her car. "What can I carry?"

Laurel placed a large sketch pad into her hands. "This." She glanced at Nadia's Louboutin red bottom pumps. "You don't have to help, you know."

Nadia clasped the large pad of paper to her chest. "I know. I want to. I can run in these. Steps are not a problem."

Laurel shouldered her backpack. "Suit yourself."

Chapter Six

The musty smell of old carpet and bug spray assaulted Laurel's nostrils. "Great-Uncle Marcus has spared no expense I see." She spun in a slow circle and fixed her gaze on the floor to ceiling bay window. "At least it has north light. What year was it built?"

"Nineteen-oh-two." Nadia quirked her mouth. "I think he'd sell it if he didn't feel compelled to keep it."

Laurel raised an eyebrow. "Compelled?"

Nadia tilted her head and held her hand palm out. "No. Don't ask. I don't know more than that. He refuses to discuss it."

Laurel stared at the dubious plaid-covered couch and the faded maroon stain spreading over the middle cushion. The claret color flowed over the front of the sofa and ended in an irregular blotch on the beige carpet.

Laurel placed her backpack on the dusty coffee table. "Don't suppose he'd be upset if I got rid of some of this—" She gestured to the worn furniture. "I like this table and the bookshelf, but my ass is not sitting on that sofa. Or that hideous chair." She leaned down and peered at the stained couch. "It looks and smells like something died on it."

"The last tenant skipped in the middle of the night, hasn't returned my calls. And none of our skip tracers can locate him. I have a company scheduled to clean the house Thursday. If there is anything you want to keep, mark it with tape."

Laurel shoved her hand in her back pocket. "I'll have to buy a new bed. I'm not sleeping on the one Alma was banging Brittney on."

"Understandable. If you send me your specifications, I'll have one delivered."

Nadia's saccharine sweet smile of concern made Laurel clench her jaw. She turned away from Nadia. "You don't have to do that."

"I want to. Do you require anything else? I have a few other things I need to attend to for your great-uncle." Nadia moved to stand in front of Laurel.

"No." Laurel focused on the red bottoms of Nadia's shoes. "No. Is there designated parking for this place?"

"We own the block. There's a garage behind the building. The key with the orange tab will unlock the cover to the keypad to open the door. I'll email you the code after we reset it. I'll call next week to arrange a time for the company to install security cameras. Is there anything else you'd like done? Marcus has told me to do whatever you wish to the house."

Laurel huffed out a breath. "I'm not staying forever. I don't need security cameras." She shoved her hands into her pockets. "I'm broke. I don't have anything anyone would want to steal."

Nadia raised her hand palm out. "It's necessary. If you stay a month or years, it is something that should have been done long ago." She held Laurel's gaze. "And some do not seek material goods."

Laurel rested her chin on her chest and fought the urge to run out of the door. Her stomach twisted and the taste of bile rose in her mouth. Marcus would have his way. Fighting back against her overprotective great-uncle was like swimming against a tsunami. "Fine."

Nadia patted her arm before she walked to the stairs. She paused and looked back over her shoulder at Laurel. "He only wants the best for you. And the clan."

Guilt tinged with anger washed over Laurel. "I know. But we have a different opinion about what's best."

Nadia's piercing gaze pinned Laurel to the spot. "We're not always able to make good decisions about what's best for ourselves. Why not take advantage of his vision?"

"Because I have my own." Laurel straightened her shoulders and lifted her chin. "And it doesn't include following the path he and the rest of the family laid out for me when I was born. I'm not like them."

Nadia raised an eyebrow. "You are more like them than you know—or want to admit. I remember your mother. At some point, you will have to assume your role in the family. Your great-uncle has been more than patient with you. More patient than you know. You can't refuse forever."

"Or what?" Laurel rested a hand on her hip. "They'll kill me? Or let the Orions pick me up?"

"There are worse things than death, Laurel." Nadia's eyes flared red around the edges, the gravel in her voice a glimpse of the demon hidden inside the human body the centurion wore.

"Like being forced to serve a family for millennia whether you want to or not?" Laurel crossed her arms over her chest.

Nadia inhaled sharply. "We are called to serve. It is not a burden. It is our way. We are intertwined with your family in ways you can't even begin to understand because you turn away from us. Close your mind off to what is and what could be." She turned back and stepped close to Laurel, her face a breath away. "We are because you are, we exist because you exist. Never forget that. Your survival is our survival." She cupped Laurel's face, her voice shifting into the full honeyed tones of practiced seduction. "Do not consign my generation to oblivion." She pressed closer and brushed a kiss over Laurel's lips. "Please. Don't fight it, Laurel. We could be so good together."

"No. No. Stop." Laurel fought the centurion's touch and focused her energy on resisting her words and her pleading tone. "I'm not what people think I am," she choked out as she stepped back from Nadia.

"You are. The clan knows you are, as does your great-uncle. With me at your side what could you possibly fear? We could choose your mate, or mates together. Once it was done, we could rid ourselves of them."

Laurel's stomach roiled as visions of Nadia observing her coupling and then murdering the unlucky super filled her mind. "I have no desire to be bred." Laurel panted and closed her eyes briefly against Nadia's unsubtle attempt to bed her to further the clan's goals. She seized on the full horror of Nadia's suggestion and drew strength from it. "Never. I don't want you that way."

"Are you sure?" The centurion slid her hand down the front of Laurel's T-shirt and over her nipples.

"Stop that." She shoved Nadia's hand away. "And yes. Did my great-uncle put you up to this?"

"You may not have the full power of a super, but your words stab me like a dagger." Nadia's brows drew down and she clasped her hands in front of her waist. "Marcus Callan does not command my desire. He directed me to keep you alive, Laurel. There are others in the clan who don't have your great-uncle's sentimental attitude toward you. Others who believe your personal wishes are of no consequence."

Laurel balled her hands into fists. Tiny flames of blue light crackled and spread out from her closed hands.

Nadia raised an eyebrow and stared. "You won't be able to hide your abilities forever." She sniffed loudly. "I thought maybe after our moment on the sidewalk we could have had something. We could have an army of Callans as we once did. Legions upon legions who could hunt down and destroy the Orions. And force the humans to accept us." Her voice dropped to a lethal tone. "You are the key, Laurel. Let's take back our world together."

Laurel rubbed the back of her neck. "No. You're just as delusional as Marcus. That little blue light you saw? That's it. That's all I have. Not even enough juice to start my car this morning. Even if I agreed to have a child with the most powerful super you could find there is no guarantee the child would be as you imagine. Or that I would pop them out like a brood sow." She leveled a glare at Nadia. "Leave me alone. I don't want to discuss this again."

"As you command." Nadia inclined her head toward Laurel. "Is there anything else you require of me?"

Laurel's gaze settled on the furniture. "Help me move this couch and chair out of here?"

"As you wish." Nadia took off her suit coat and draped it over Laurel's backpack.

*

Laurel scrolled to her favorite playlist, and the smoky sounds of Maria McKee's "If Love is a Red Dress" filled the room. She fiddled with the receiver and moved the speakers around until she was satisfied with the sound. The acoustics of the room weren't the best, but the town home was free and right now free was good. Tips at the coffee house had been irregular and her wages had barely paid for food and art supplies. The meager tips she had brought home after her first shift at Sanctuary had promised more of the same barely scraping by existence.

After tossing a paint-splattered drop cloth over the floor, she placed her easel on it. The best thing the house offered, besides free rent and parking space, was a north facing window. Laurel had delighted in shoving the couch and chair over the balcony with Nadia's assistance. Clear of the furniture, the former living room was transformed into a studio, or what would pass for one.

*

Catherine lay on the mattress and opened her mind to the scene unfolding in the living room. She had skirted the demon's protective shield delicately, concealing her presence from the bodyguard. The woman she guarded, Laurel, was waifish, thin, her angular face drawn under thick dark brows. Her features were familiar. Catherine focused on her, observing her from a distance. Laurel had rebuffed the centurion's advances, her rage filling the space as she argued with the centurion. The lust of the centurion was palpable. Catherine indulged herself with a psychic sip of her sexual energy.

Catherine had taken advantage of Laurel's distraction and entered her mind, working her way past intricate barriers the woman had in place to secure her thoughts and emotions from the centurion's probe. Catherine rifled Laurel's thoughts and emotions seeking clues to her identity. Not human, not demon. A super. And more. So much more. And yet she kept her powers hidden. Did the demon centurion, Nadia, know their raw magnitude? And why was Laurel denying her abilities?

Laurel refused Nadia's advances and anger replaced sexual hunger as the centurion raged quietly at Laurel. Laurel held her ground and after a minuscule display of power the centurion left.

Catherine exited Laurel's mind. She disguised her energy signature and stayed hidden, following Laurel as she unpacked the small boxes she had carried in from the car. *Laurel. Curious. Why name a child after a beautiful but toxic plant?*

Working steadily, Laurel stacked several white gessoed canvases against the wall of the living room. Open crates of paints and rolls of brushes were placed next to the canvases. Laurel bent at the waist, took a box cutter from her pocket, and slashed open the top of a box.

Tossing her blade aside, she shoved the lid open and unpacked a stack of drawing pads and sketchbooks.

Over the years of watching individuals take possession of the house, Catherine had arrived at a theory of personality based on what room the renters set up first in the house. Those who valued food and creature comforts unpacked and set up the kitchen first. Desire or money drove people who set up the bedroom. They were Catherine's favorite renters, most often new lovers or those who made their living providing sexual care to others.

An infinitesimally few individuals set up their passions first. The writers who unpacked their office, stopping to scribble ideas on random bits of paper as they occurred to them. Once a woman had stopped to outline an entire novel on the packing cardboard with a marker. Catherine had hovered just out of her consciousness, fascinated by her process.

Then there were obsessive readers unpacking books and organizing their bookshelves before placing one dish in the kitchen. Sometimes, they stopped and read, letting the rest of the unpacking go while they savored words. Laurel appeared to be an artist to her core, as she unpacked her art supplies and ignored both the bedroom and the kitchen.

Waves of sorrow and frustration poured off Laurel. Deep and wide, they buffeted Catherine. Laurel had loved. And lost her heart. Scenes from her partner's infidelity filled Laurel's mind. Catherine watched them unfold, rocked by the intensity of Laurel's emotions.

Her power was unchecked, a wild surge of energy that titillated as it swirled and enveloped Catherine. The scent of her blood and energy signature filled the room, a siren call to Catherine's need. She gathered herself and stretched her hand toward Laurel's neck. *No. Not this way. No.* Catherine drew back. *She is a precious commodity. How could she not know? Or maybe she does?*

The interaction with the demon had been one-sided, that much was plain to Catherine. Laurel had allowed the centurion to believe they were bonded, while holding a part of herself back. Laurel had accepted the demon's protection although she was clearly much more powerful than the centurion. Her power was equal to Catherine's, a gift from birth if the centurion was to be believed. With education and practice her abilities would surpass Catherine's.

A smidge of jealousy seeped in as Catherine considered what she had given up in order to attain her powers, what she had done, to be as she was. Catherine shoved away the regrets that nipped at the corners of her thought. *No. No regrets. I will have my freedom. And my vengeance.* She gazed at Laurel, perhaps her pleas had been heard and this was the Goddess's gift to her. A super to free her. A partner to join her in her quest for revenge on those who had taken her lover, her life, and her eternal rest.

Laurel shoved the lid off a plastic bin and drew out an inlaid puzzle box. Dark walnut wood contrasted with light oak, the mosaic patterns on the sides and lids as ancient as the design. Laurel smoothed her fingers over the lid. Tears slid from her eyes and she dashed her wrist over her face to wipe them away as her control shattered.

The box. How on earth does she have the box? What does it mean to her? Catherine shoved away her own memories of the puzzle box and peered into Laurel's mind. She touched her pain as Laurel's thoughts unfolded like an intricate origami heart. Vivid images, a montage of Laurel's memories, spun out. A second-hand store, a lover's kiss, their hands joined as they shopped. Enamored with each other, giggling at the faint smell of sex that clung to them. The box had called to Laurel, drew her to its resting place under a layer of thick dust in a dim corner of the shop.

A swift purchase and walk home followed by her companion taking Laurel quick and dirty in the elevator. Laurel's delight in being taken so roughly sent a rill of desire through Catherine. Another image flooded Laurel's mind, the box on the dresser in a dark bedroom, a backdrop for the scene of her lover's betrayal. Laurel's resignation as she watched her lover and another, fucking in their bed. Catherine left Laurel's mind as her quiet tears flowed down her cheeks.

Drawn by her sorrow, seduced by the psychic pain rolling off Laurel, Catherine slid closer, gathered herself, and kneeled on the floor next to Laurel. Unable to resist the tug of Laurel's raw emotions, Catherine stroked her fingers down the back of her neck under the shaggy dark hair, seeking to comfort, to heal, to give her peace. A spark of energy flowed from Laurel through Catherine's fingertips as she touched Laurel's skin. She trembled, heat spread out, warming her. Even without a physical body the sensations filled her with longing. She firmed her connection with Laurel and sent sensual light along it, even as she sipped the heady taste of her sorrow.

Desire flared. What would it be like to be able to lie with her, hot skin to hot skin, legs intertwined, to have

Laurel's lithe frame nestled next to Catherine's curves? Frozen in time when women were revered for full figures, Catherine reveled in her thick body and heavy breasts. The women she saw on the street, trudging past the townhouse, seemed determined to starve off their curves instead of flaunting them.

She closed her fingers over the back of Laurel's neck, the desire to control her, to give Laurel what she kept hidden from all but a few, to be the Domme Laurel dreamed of, to fulfill her deepest fantasies surged through Catherine. Power welled up, filling her as she delved deep into Laurel's desires, flowed into her thoughts, used her energy to blot out the tear-filled memories stirred by the box. Purple light swirled around them as Catherine exposed her desires and projected her thoughts into Laurel's mind.

She drew back the curtain of reality and showed Laurel images of herself bound with intricate ropes, her head bowed as she lapped at Catherine's center. Images of Laurel's wet thighs, swollen clit, her desperate urgency to please slammed into Catherine as Laurel willingly engaged with the fantasy Catherine projected into her mind.

Laurel's engagement with Catherine morphed as they became more enmeshed in each other's minds. The sensation of Laurel suckling Catherine's clit sent a wave of pleasure through Catherine as she indulged herself in Laurel's carnal thoughts. Catherine's control slipped and her form, her essence knit together against her will, her dark fingers visible, stark against Laurel's pale skin. She collared the smooth column of her throat and bent her head, pressing her lips to the pulse that hammered under her touch.

Laurel's head jerked up. Eyes wide, she scooted away from Catherine, breaking their connection, and stood. Laurel clutched the box to her chest as she stumbled back. Catherine withdrew, dissolved her form.

A deep scowl spoiled Laurel's face as she searched the room with her gaze. "I don't know who you are, but I know you're here. Leave me alone for fuck's sake. I can't deal with anymore today."

Fear and exhaustion rolled off Laurel, and her untrained wild psychic energy flailed toward Catherine. She blocked Laurel's energy and retreated to safety behind her shields. If Laurel had been human, Catherine would have stayed, toyed with her, stoking her terror and then sipping her fear until she was drunk with it. But Laurel's dark eyes and desperate pleading made Catherine want to comfort her, gather her in her arms and hold her, drink in her pain, savor it, and leave peace behind.

Laurel glanced around the room, her pupils blown wide. A wave of want speared Catherine. The heady taste of Laurel's fear and sexual energy remained, and unquenchable desire seared her soul. She fled the space, fearful of her feelings and of driving Laurel away.

Chapter Seven

Following the flow of air, Catherine moved to the safety of her attic space. She coalesced into her form. Her body glowed with heat and energy. Catherine cloaked herself in the pent-up energy of her wants.

The first year of her imprisonment Catherine had allowed herself to feel, to remember what it was like to hate, to love, and to want. And then it had become too painful, her hope of ever being restored to her bodily form and being reunited with her lover had faded and she had tucked her feelings away into the back corner of her mind.

Laurel had shattered her control, given her a sip of desire, and now she wanted to drown in it, as she had once drowned in her lover's eyes when Catherine dangled her over the edge between fear and passion. Terror sprung up. Catherine cared. She cared what happened to Laurel. Feelings. Messy inconvenient feelings rose in her, unbidden, unwanted, unwelcome.

Catherine wanted. In the sixty years since her death, she had wanted very little other than revenge, but now she wanted Laurel. She paced the small room and savored the desire Laurel had stirred in her. Cupping her breasts, she rolled her nipples and shivered at the sensations that flowed through her.

"Catherine?"

She yanked her hands away from her breasts as fear replaced lust and she lashed out in the direction of the voice.

"Ow, stop! It's me, Catherine." Manny's voice slid into her consciousness. "Are we safe?"

"I'm sorry, Manny."

"It's okay. You mad?"

"No. I just—I wanted some privacy. I should have set wards. Sorry." She swept her hair back from her forehead before she crossed her arms over her chest. "Did you need something?"

"Are we safe?"

"Yes. I don't think she'll stay long."

"You're sad?" Manny's child's curiosity seeped into her mind.

"Yes." Catherine moved carefully in the attic as she sat at her desk, unwilling to make noises that might scare Laurel away. She had spent years perfecting how to frighten people from the townhouse. For the first time, she wanted someone to stay.

"Why?"

"I don't know." Catherine lied, unwilling to explain her desires to the boy, unsure she understood them herself.

Chapter Eight

Laurel tugged at the disgusting bedroom carpet. With both hands she gripped the edge of the rug and yanked. The worn carpet pulled free of the tack strips, scattering dust. The rank smell of animal urine floated on the air and Laurel pulled the neck of her T-shirt over her face as a makeshift mask.

The carpet was only marginally attached to the floor and Laurel pried the few staples that remained in the flooring free with her knife. With a flick of her wrist, she cut through the carpet with her blade, creating manageable strips to carry through the townhouse. After dragging the grimy carpet to the rear of the house, she piled the narrow rolls of carpet on the back patio.

The tack strips came up easily and she carried them outside. She stacked them on the bricks next to the carpet. A ragged excuse for a broom stood propped against the wall in the pantry and she carried it back to the bedroom. With firm strokes she swept the bedroom floor free of loose dust and carpet tacks.

The narrow board hardwood floor was dull gray with dirt. She located a bucket in the bathroom and filled it with her favorite all-purpose cleaner. Starting in the far corner, she washed the floor. Her knees ached from kneeling on the unyielding hardwood. The pain was comforting and grounding as she wiped the sponge over the wood, careful to not soak the boards. The fresh scent of the orange soap she used to clean the floor filled the room.

A darker area in the middle of the floor, a subtle burgundy splotch, stood out against the light oak floor. Laurel sat back on her heels and studied the stain. *Water? Wine?* She shivered and knelt to examine it more closely. She traced her fingers over the stained wood. Blood. She sensed it. *So much blood.* She rose to her feet and swiped her hand down the front of her jeans.

Laurel followed the path of blood. The faint outline of a handprint and a smear appeared as her inner vision sharpened. Smaller stains, droplet shapes led away from the larger stain. Reading the flow of the bloodstains, Laurel imagined the person had fallen, pushed themselves to their knees, stood, and then staggered from the room.

Laurel relaxed her mind, summoned her power, and focused her energy on the drops and splatters leading away from the larger bloodstain. The trail of drops morphed as her vision sharpened. The faint stains glistened bright red against the wood and she followed them to the doorway. Laurel followed the trail, unable to look away. The droplets grew smaller and more scattered as they came to the door of the attic.

Laurel clasped the glass doorknob and turned it. Locked. She reached above the door and swept her hand along the frame, finding only a thick layer of dust. She swiped her dirty fingers on her jeans as she patted her pockets. After drawing the clump of keys Nadia had given her from her back pocket, she studied them. The brass faceplate of the lock was greenish with the dull patina of time. Original to the townhouse, the attic door required a skeleton key. None of the keys Nadia had given her fit the lock. Laurel leaned her head against the cool wood of the door.

Nadia's warning of not engaging with any spirits filtered into her consciousness. Laurel shivered as memories of her earlier encounter shot through her. The sensation of the spirit under her skin and in her mind had been exhilarating. The way her fingers had circled Laurel's neck as a knowing lover would had been comforting. Her touch had roused Laurel's longing to belong to a Mistress who would cherish her, protect her, and who would torment her with unfathomable pleasure and pain.

And then I freaked, shoved her away. Will she return? The spirit had wanted her, wanted what Laurel wanted. The current of her desire as she connected with Laurel had been heady and intoxicating. Laurel had sensed no malice from the spirit, only longing as deep and as wide as her own.

This was her lair. Laurel stared at the trail of blood that disappeared under the door leading to the attic. The short hairs rose on Laurel's neck. Was it her blood that had marred the floors? Or her victim's?

Unable to suppress her curiosity, Laurel laid her cheek against the cool wood and melded her body against the door panels in an attempt to project herself through the door. A surge of raw power shot through her body, her nipples and clit reacting to the sweet pain.

Jolted, she panted and stepped back, vision hazy as purple arcs of light flashed from around the edges of the door, visible evidence of the wards protecting the passage. The scent of pine resin and cedar floated on the air and surrounded her. Ancient magic warded the door, creating a powerful fortress of protection Laurel was unable to penetrate.

Laurel blinked away the sting of suppressed tears as a tidal wave of sadness and longing pulled her down. She had lost her chance to connect with the spirit. The message was clear. She did not desire Laurel's presence. Laurel covered her mouth as she recalled the ugly words she had shouted, her blunt rejection and request to be left alone. The spirit had left her then, her withdrawal profound.

And now Laurel had no hope of connecting with her. Of finding out who She was, or if it was Her blood splattered on the bedroom floor. Laurel touched her throat. As her fingers settled over the spot where the Entity's fingers had collared her a tingle shot through her body. Laurel stepped forward and pressed her body full against the door, pushing against the wards.

Energy crackled and flowed through her, sharp and unyielding, taking her breath away. A searing pain shot through her brain and lights flashed before her closed eyes. She clasped the doorframe, standing bracing herself as she would against a St. Andrew's cross to welcome a lover's whip.

Intoxicating desire and longing kept her there, pressed against the old wood. The burning energy cords of the door wrapped around her body, arms, and legs, cutting into her flesh. She willed herself to stay centered in the pain, surrendering to the blissful peace of suffering.

Laurel reveled in the desperate sharp pain of the wards as the thorny purple vines bit into her flesh and contracted, pulling her body taut. Her blood flowed around the wounds and pattered to the floor. A deep rich ache grew in her joints and she cried out as the vines tightened, sending the burning hooks deeper into her flesh and threatening to tear her in two. Laurel closed her eyes and let her head rest between her shoulders, ready and willing to sacrifice herself, to offer all that she was to the spirit on the other side of the door.

A surge of energy cut the vines and pulled her free from the door. Her flesh closed around her wounds. Laurel's hands burned and ached, glowed where they had grasped the doorframe. She stumbled back and rubbed her forehead. A roaring filled her ears, the world tilted, and she sat down hard in the hallway. Laurel hung her head between her knees, panting.

A sharp voice filled her mind, commanded her to stand up, to back away from the door. Nadia? She had not reached out to the centurion, nor called for her assistance. A tangle of resentment rose, and anger twined with gratitude. Laurel sat back on her heels and chewed her lip. Nadia was pledged to keep Laurel safe, even from her own self-destructive desires, but Laurel was unaccustomed to sharing her thoughts and experiences with anyone uninvited.

Come away. You'll hurt yourself. Come here.

The dulcet tones flowed through her mind, cajoling her to move. Laurel stood and braced herself against the wall with one hand and moved away from the door. A familiar energy signature brushed over her shoulder, as if someone had trailed their fingers over her skin, and the small hairs on her neck rose. "You're not Nadia."

No. Don't be frightened. Come here. Aware and curious, Laurel gave in and followed the soft commands, backed away from the door, and walked to her room. The space had transformed, the floors shone with polish, and a wide bed with clean white sheets occupied the middle of the room. The walls glowed with yellow light and the bright smell of lemon surrounded her. In soothing tones, the voice directed her to undress. Laurel shed her clothes and stood naked next to the bed. The low timbred voice caressed her, touched her as a lover's voice would. Her heart stuttered. A lover. A lover who understood what Laurel needed. What she craved. A lover who craved it themselves.

Laurel let herself be guided by not-Nadia's voice, submitting to her as she imagined submitting to the Mistress of her dreams and secret fantasies. Laurel supposed this was the way a Mistress would be if she were truly Laurel's lover, not someone she had paid to act as such. A Mistress who would command her, cherish her, keep her safe the way a Mistress should. At least what a Mistress did in Laurel's dreams.

Chapter Nine

In the bathroom, water splashed from the shower head. Laurel stepped into the warm spray and ran her hands over her wet skin. Cupping her palm, she squirted lavender scented shower gel into her hand. Making a lather, she smoothed the soap over her wet skin.

Dulcet tones filled her mind. *"Don't rush. You're beautiful. Slow down. I want to enjoy this."*

Laurel lingered over her breasts, cupping them. With finger and thumbs she tweaked her nipples, teasing them into hard points. She gasped and closed her eyes against the ripple of pleasure spreading over her body.

"Very nice. You have sublime breasts. Touch yourself for me. I want to watch you come."

The honeyed voice flowed through her mind and set her nerve endings on fire. Desire welled up, leaving her skin tingling. Laurel rinsed her hands under the warm spray. She closed her eyes and smoothed her hands over her belly.

Show me how you touch yourself when you're alone.

A surge of wetness spread out and coated Laurel's thighs. The image of a voluptuous woman, reclining in a chair, her long legs stretched out in front of her crossed at the ankles filled Laurel's mind. Black strapped pumps set off delicate ankles, and shapely calves lead to thick thighs.

Her simple tan sweater set over a dark wool skirt, and her face, framed by flat ironed hair, primly styled, lent an air of clandestine wickedness to their scene as She watched Laurel. The dark eyes set deep in the woman's face glowed with a banked fire, her slash of a mouth pulled into a tight smile as the woman commanded Laurel's pleasure. Laurel braced herself with one hand against the slick tiles and feathered her fingers over her clit. She spread her legs wide, showing herself. With small strokes she circled and pressed her clit.

Fuck yourself for me. The full-throated command issued from the voice ignited Laurel's flesh.

Aching with longing and seeking solace, Laurel stroked herself to completion, fingers flicking over her fat clit, before she thrust her fingers deep. With firm strokes, the heel of her hand ground against her clit as she fucked herself wantonly. The sharp edge of the voice when She commanded her to come for her, sent Laurel over the edge and she cried out, came hard, her body clasping around her fingers. Laurel slowed her thrusts and brought herself off again. Her groans reverberated in the small space. Laurel leaned her forehead against the wet tiles as the spiral of pleasure spun out from her center. The hot water faded as the shower spray ran cold. Laurel shivered.

"Such a good girl." The voice, rich in praise, faded from Laurel's mind.

Stepping away from the spray, she wrenched the tap closed. She snatched her clothes from the floor and chided herself for lingering in the shower. The voice was gone now, abruptly leaving Laurel, and she shivered at the loss. The presence was silent, no aftercare, no way to offer her thanks to the voice.

Laurel had no opportunity to crawl to Her, to press her lips to the toes of those gorgeous shoes, and then perhaps be granted the privilege of worshiping Her with her lips and tongue, and if found worthy to be granted a taste of Her pleasure. No. The spirit had chosen to gift Laurel her attention, and now she was done. Laurel had no right to expect more. She must have others to care for, or something more pressing than aftercare for Laurel.

Tears hovered at the thought. Laurel swore and stomped to her bedroom. The glamor from before was gone, the room bare and half clean once more. Her bucket and sponge just as she had abandoned them. After locating her sleeping bag from her duffel, she placed it on the side of the room she had cleaned. She wrapped herself inside the warm silk cocoon of her bed sack and lay down on her sleeping bag.

A flaming heat covered her, filling her with warmth. A flash of recognition swept over her, a blaze of understanding and a driving need for more. Her thighs grew slick as she contemplated the lewd nature of her behavior. Laurel had willingly given herself to the spirit, allowed herself to be used by a stranger.

Burning need flared and her clit thickened again as the memories of the pain of the vines resurfaced. She pressed her fingers deep inside and slowly fucked herself, the heel of her hand rubbing against her clit as she reached out with her mind and called to the spirit, begging her to accept her gift.

"For you." Eyes wide open, Laurel spread her legs wide and fucked herself as she jacked her clit. She came with a jerk, her shoulders lifting as she curled into the sensation of her tribute to the Entity. Sated and exhausted, she rolled to her side and slept.

*

Catherine stood on the opposite side of the door and absorbed the impact of Laurel's attempt to enter the attic. Raw energy undirected was delicious and Catherine sipped Laurel's desperation as she would a fine wine. The way she reacted to the pain of the wards confirmed all of Catherine's intuition about Laurel. But then Laurel had pressed harder, risking herself to get to Catherine, offering herself, pleading with Catherine to open the door as she absorbed the energy of the ward, wallowing in the pain, promising to obey, to do anything if Catherine allowed it.

She'd intervened then, unwilling to accept Laurel's sacrifice. Assuming Nadia's voice had been easy. But after Laurel had responded to her commands, recognized her as other-than-Nadia and submitted willingly, Catherine had not been able to resist.

She had reveled in the sensations of Laurel's bath, as she had directed her to prepare for bed. Catherine had drowned in her submission and the sensations of Laurel's fingers over her pale flesh as she bathed. The warmth of the shower on Laurel's skin and then the slick slide of her clit as she had displayed herself for Catherine had been a decadent pleasure. Instead of slaking Catherine's thirst for Laurel it had unleashed a flood of longing.

Catherine had left her alone then. Withdrawn. She had sensed Laurel's sadness, her despondency when she realized that Catherine had not stayed for aftercare, that she had simply taken what she wanted and left Laurel to pick up the psychological pieces of her surrender.

She replayed the vision of Laurel's final offering. Laurel had stroked herself to orgasm, displaying herself and offering her shuddering climax in tribute. Catherine had not revealed herself but had relished her gift and the seductive lassitude of Laurel as she fell asleep.

A dark wave of guilt slithered over her. Catherine had taken without giving, left a submissive hurting as no good Mistress would do. At first when Laurel had responded to her commands believing her to be Nadia, Catherine had justified it as a way of saving Laurel from herself. But then Laurel realized she was not Nadia and had reached out to Catherine, not even demanding her name, surrendered to her, been intimate with her, with no thought to her own care and safety, so desperate was she for a Mistress's touch. Catherine had been more than willing to accept her submission.

What does it say about her? Or me for that matter, that we both could be so accepting of an anonymous encounter, so desperate to be with each other, we gave neither care nor thought of the future or the reality of our situation. Would she be like that with anyone? Or did she truly fancy me? Desire my touch and control? Or would anyone do?

Catherine experienced Laurel's wanton desire to know her flesh. The way she burned for her, her desperation to kiss Catherine's feet, to worship her with her mouth. Laurel's obsessive desire to kiss and lick and suck Catherine's most intimate parts while she begged for Catherine to spill her pleasure over her face had been intoxicating. And so overwhelming she had withdrawn from Laurel.

A bitter laugh erupted from Catherine's throat. Flesh. She had not been flesh for years, and yet her spirit knew the aching reality of flesh denied. She longed to suffer the sweet bliss of denial, have her clit thicken and swell between a lover's lips. To know the burning need of hot flesh, pleasure bordering on pain, and the ecstasy of a lover's touch. No matter. That would never be Catherine's privilege again.

After experiencing Laurel, she would never ask her to release her. Too fraught. For both of them. Even though Laurel possessed the box, it was not her destiny to free Catherine. She would not, could not ask Laurel. She would give it if Catherine asked. Laurel would willingly offer her blood, body, and soul to Catherine if she asked her. Laurel's willingness to suffer the pain of the ward vines and risk her life to show Catherine how much she wanted to serve her was hard evidence of her devotion.

Catherine lay back and rested her form on the bed. A fat mouse skittered across the floor and she stared at it, not bothering to destroy it. Disgustingly innocent, it wanted to live, eat, and reproduce. A simple life. A life Laurel craved. Catherine had seen into her fantasies. Laurel wanted to be owned, desired a total power exchange. She wanted to be loved. And she wanted a child, but not a man.

Catherine had seen other things too. Her aching loss when her parents died. Laurel's fear of being kidnapped. Her abject terror of being forced into breeding a new generation of supers. Laurel kept the extent of her power hidden away, displaying it only when she was certain no one would know, able to keep her true self hidden from everyone. Laurel lived a lie out of fear.

Bits and pieces fit into place as Catherine sorted through her experience of Laurel. Their intimate encounter reinforced her decision to never ever ask Laurel for what she wanted. Bigger things lay before Laurel and being tied to Catherine would interfere with that. No matter how willing Laurel would be, especially if she knew Catherine offered a way out of her responsibilities. Catherine would find another way to achieve her resurrection.

Chapter Ten

In her attic space, Catherine studied the puzzle box Laurel had brought with her. The container of Catherine and Nora's precious dreams of a life together for eternity and undying love had somehow ended up in Laurel's keeping. Catherine laid her hand on the box and was back in the shop in Italy where they had purchased it. Morpheus, the cabinet maker, had taken their money before he showed them the secrets of the box and its power. They had spent an hour with him learning the ways to set the hidden blade and practicing with the box's magical locks, committing the lock pattern and incantations to memory before they left his workshop.

A vision of Nora's flushed face as they hurried through the streets to return to their hotel surfaced. Catherine's thoughts spun faster as she relived their afternoon making love in their small hotel room. Her palm twitched, a visceral memory of her hand over Nora's mouth to muffle her screams as she came under Catherine's touch.

Naked and sated, the room heavy with the scent of their lovemaking, they had spent the evening writing their pledges to each other on the hotel's cream-colored stationery. The blade from the box had tasted their blood as it mingled and joined, soaking into the paper. Catherine's power and Nora's had merged.

Bonded, they sealed their future in the box, knowing when they returned from their trip their trysts would be few and far between until they could execute their plan. The chest would hold their truth until it was safe to reveal their love. They had slept, confident their secret would be safe. But even their combined magic had not protected them from betrayal.

A few scratches marred the front of the box, harsh evidence someone had tried to pry it open at least once. Catherine pushed the front frame of the wooden casket, sliding it to the left, and manipulated the sequence of panels in order, avoiding the one that deployed the blade, as memories swamped her mind. She pushed back against her dark thoughts, the burn of betrayal and memories of her last time with Nora.

The box opened and the scent of cedar rose from it. Catherine pressed a second set of tabs inside the box and then lifted its false bottom. After plucking the folded paper from the box, Catherine smoothed it flat on the desk. Nora's delicate handwriting crawled across the page, next to Catherine's bold copperplate script.

Written in blood aged to a light brown, they had signed their pledge together. A promise to love, to honor, and in Nora's case to obey. She had pledged to serve Catherine, to be her submissive. Catherine had pledged in return to honor Nora's gift, to cherish her, and to protect her.

Catherine wished for the first time in many years that she could cry as she read their vows. A second sheet of paper, the edge brittle with time, contained the words of the resurrection spell copied from The Book. Complete except for the words they had purposely left out to keep the spell useless to the unknowing.

Catherine crumpled the paper. Protect Nora. No. She had failed, spectacularly, not even able to protect herself, and had lost Nora to time and a brother's wish to protect his sister from Catherine and what he considered unnatural desires. In the years of her imprisonment Catherine had grown more powerful, able to do things she had only read of, everything except free herself from the prison of the house.

And now the key to her release lay sleeping below her. And Catherine was loath to sacrifice Laurel to free herself. She had no doubt Laurel would surrender to her if she asked, that she would lay her head in Catherine's lap and expose her neck to provide the final ingredient Catherine needed to free her spirit. But would Laurel be willing to become that which fed on humans?

Denied the release of tears, Catherine closed the box and held the paper in her hands and traveled back to that day, using her power to weave and bend time until images and sensations wrapped around her, became real. Nora's touch flowed over her skin, and then her mouth followed, taking Catherine to the dark abyss of pleasure. Real and yet not, a fever dream of desire and longing. In Catherine's daydream, Nora was real, her smile, Catherine's world, her laugh, and her kisses all that Catherine lived for until the end.

Catherine held tight to the edges of her visions, fought to hold on to what had been, to keep herself immersed in the glamour. The image of Nora kneeling before her, her declaration of love and submission on her lips, rose in her mind. A half smile played over Nora's face as she pushed back and teased Catherine. Not a bratty sub, but strong in her own desires, Nora had been willing to turn the table when she thought Catherine needed to be reminded she was strong in her own right.

A powerful super, Nora gave over to Catherine, dared to expose her neck, offered her blood, dared to bond with her and defy her clan's wishes. Nora had kissed Catherine's feet, and given her everything. They were equals in their relationship, the differences of their births of no consequence because the heart wants what it wants, family be dammed.

Catherine held the image for as long as she could, reliving it over and over until she was spent. The papers fell from her hand to the floor, and she collapsed in on herself, her spirit chiding her for her indulgence. The vision faded, replaced by the reality of open attic beams, a rotted blood-stained mattress, and a longing so deep it crushed Catherine.

She traced her fingers over the box that held the key to her existence and release. Let go? Enter oblivion willingly? She could exit the house, step into the vast wasteland of nothingness, her spirit scattered on the winds of the abyss. Catherine lifted her chin and squared her shoulders. No. She would not let sixty years of imprisonment define her four-thousand-year existence. She would escape. And then vengeance would be her joy. Her thoughts twisted back to Laurel. And perhaps love, or what might pass for it again.

Chapter Eleven

Laurel rolled the last of the living room rug to the balcony and dropped it onto the pile of dirty carpet below. Her cell phone buzzed on the table and she snatched it up when Nadia's number scrolled across the screen.

"How are you?" Nadia's voice was clipped.

"Fine." Laurel tucked her hand in her back pocket. "Why'd you call? Can't you just connect with me to see how I'm doing?" Laurel did nothing to hide her annoyance over their bond.

"I don't enter anyone's mind unless invited. Unless of course it's an emergency. I assume you slept well?"

Laurel flushed at the memory. "You tell me. Did you enjoy the show?"

"What the hell are you talking about? I don't have time to play games. I don't like you shutting me out. I'm not your enemy." An edge of frustration crept into Nadia's voice.

"I slept fine."

"You're very odd this morning, Laurel. I'm not trying to pry. But I can't do my job if you insist on blocking me as you did last night."

Laurel chewed her lip. Nadia had not even a hint Laurel had been in a tenuous position, that had she been ready to sacrifice herself for an unknown spirit.

"Sorry, not sorry. I am entitled to privacy. And if I need you, I'll call you."

"Marcus will not be pleased. He asked me personally to be your centurion, to protect you."

"That's your problem." Laurel disconnected the call.

*

The morning dragged into afternoon as Laurel continued to clean and organize her space. Her thoughts circled back to the spirit. She had kept Laurel from destroying herself, protected her, soothed her, and given to Laurel, helped Laurel find the release she had craved.

Illusion or no it had seemed real to her. As Laurel drifted off to sleep the spirit had let her psychic mask slip. She had a glimpse then, of the spirit in the attic, the soul trapped in the townhouse.

The spirit had to know, to sense Laurel's desperation, her fantasy of serving a severe Mistress, one who would push her, train her, help her in the ways a good Mistress did. Laurel needed it, needed to be someone's only submissive. She had no luck with vanilla relationships, unable to connect in a meaningful way for any length of time. She had tried, believing she would never find what she was looking for, and now, in this house, an ancient spirit was able to give her what she craved.

She called to the spirit, shouted her need, told her of the darkest of her fantasies. She had pleaded with her to return, to come back, to let Laurel in, to take control again. Laurel chewed her lip, her longing a psychic ache, mirrored by the ache in her body and throb in her clit.

As she spoke the words, she pleaded for Her to return. Laurel lowered herself to her knees, sat back on her heels, palms up resting on her thighs, and waited. A waft of cedar and pine resin filtered into her senses and Laurel sensed She observed her. Encouraged, Laurel lowered her head to the floor and begged the spirit to show herself.

*

Catherine hovered, her shields in place, keeping herself from Laurel as she watched her lithe form unload and organize her art supplies. She had been so tempted to sneak a touch again as Laurel worked. Her thin ribbed tank top stretched tight across her shoulders, and the way her jeans moved and flexed with her as she worked to tear up the living room carpet and shove it over the balcony into the alley behind the house tested Catherine's resolve.

Laurel had scrubbed the wood floor on her hands and knees. Catherine was mesmerized by her determination to clean the space. A phone call had interrupted her, and Catherine had struggled to make sense of Laurel's clipped answers to Nadia as she eavesdropped.

Laurel tossed the phone aside before she kneeled and launched into an elaborate plea for Catherine to show herself. Fear, sharp and stinging, filled Catherine. Laurel was powerful, unschooled, and wild; she had no idea of the extent of her powers but should Laurel decide to end Catherine's existence she would be hard pressed to defend against her.

What would it be like to have someone like Laurel? Catherine had known the joy of having someone as giving, as caring, as ready to submit as Laurel appeared to be. She had not dared hope to find that again, but would Laurel be willing? To be hers? To give to Catherine what she needed to live again? To breathe and love and touch, and to feel with all her senses and not just her mind?

Minutes passed into an hour. Laurel lifted her head from the floor. Fire and frustration raged in her dark gaze. Catherine observed her as she set up her easel and then with eyes closed executed a perfect sketch of the image Catherine had projected into her mind the night before. An image she had fashioned from Laurel's subconscious desires and vivid fantasies.

Laurel stood and stared at the corner Catherine occupied. Her voice strong, she hugged her arms around herself. "Are you here? Show yourself." And then softer. "Please."

Catherine withdrew, fearful of Laurel's power, pulling away from the vortex of Laurel's plea.

"Please. I know it was you last night. Come to me. Please." Laurel placed her hand on the sketch and suffused it with her energy as she continued to plead.

*

Unable to resist the vortex of Laurel's soft plea and the pull of her power, Catherine focused her energy and formed herself, allowing Laurel to see her, allowing herself to be seen. Not as Laurel imagined her but as she had been, presenting herself as a tall woman, dressed in a tailored, teal-blue, three-quarter sleeve shirtwaist dress. Cream-colored four-inch stiletto heels, curly shoulder length black hair. Her signature blood-red lipstick, perfectly applied, contrasted with her bronze skin and completed her image. She sifted through the other details from Laurel's fantasies and filled them in, morphing into a replica of the Mistress of Laurel's dreams and fantasies.

*

Laurel rose from her position of supplication. The pain in her knees fueled her anger and frustration at the spirit's refusal to return to her. She propped her largest sketch pad up, flipped open her box of charcoal, and picked out a thick piece. The vision of the woman watching and commanding her in the shower flooded her brain. Eyes closed, she applied the charcoal to the paper, the rub and scratch of the burnt wood comforting as she worked. She let her power guide her hand. A face formed, the jaw strong, a plush and deliciously cruel mouth following. She smudged the drawing with the side of her hand and softened the lines.

Laurel lingered as she drew Her shoulders and breasts, tracing the charcoal over the shapes that formed in her mind and translating them to paper. The music on her favorite soundtrack faded as she worked. Her world became the paper and image she created, as her power flowed and ebbed, guiding her hand. A trickle of desire wet her boy shorts while she worked as she relived her experience in thrall to the spirit who had guided her to an amazing orgasm without even touching her.

Laurel stepped back, opened her eyes, and studied the sketch. Was this truly the image of the entity she had interacted with? Or was it what she wanted her to look like? Laurel lifted her hand and rested the tips of her fingers on the page. She infused her command with her power. Blue light flowed from her fingertips and saturated the paper. "Show yourself. Let me see you as you are," she whispered.

A soft rustling behind her made her start and the charcoal snapped in her hand.

"No. Don't turn around. Not yet."

The voice filled her mind and she swallowed on a dry throat as the scent of cedar and pine swirled around her. The room glowed with a soft purple light.

"Please." Laurel grimaced at the whine in her voice.

"Why? You have an image of me you chose. Why spoil it?"

"You don't look like my drawing, do you?"

"Unless I'm mistaken you have drawn an image you like to fantasize about, a ready-made Mistress to get you off. A picture to hold on to while you fuck yourself to sleep."

Laurel rested her chin on her chest and her ears burned with her flush. "Was it that easy for you to search my mind?"

"Yes."

"You're powerful."

"Yes."

"What are you? Or who?" Laurel chewed her lip, worried she had offended. Her knees flexed as she considered kneeling to the powerful spirit behind her.

"You may call me Catherine."

"It's not your name, is it?"

"No. But names have power, don't they? And what do you care?"

Laurel lifted her shoulders and let them fall. "I want to know you."

"Because I can get you off?"

"It's more than that."

"Is it?

"Yes. I want to know you. All of you."

"Do you? Are you sure? What if I'm not as you imagined? What if I'm ugly as Medusa on a bad day? Or if I'm a hideous beast with sharp fangs and an insatiable hunger for flesh?"

"Then you're a hideous beast. I don't care." Laurel shifted on the balls of her feet. "Does it matter to you the meat envelope I'm in?"

"No. I was drawn to your energy."

"Why would I be different? Please. I want to see you. I have to see you." Laurel placed the charcoal on her easel, wiped her hand on her jeans, and kneeled. She grasped the hem of her shirt and pulled it over her head and tossed it to the floor. Her nipples pebbled in the cold. "Please. Touch me? Let me feel you."

A wisp of energy flowed over Laurel's shoulder and traveled down, split into two. The sensation of her nipples being thumbed made her sway toward the sensation. She groaned as her clit responded to the attention.

"So wanton. You can't help yourself, can you?"

"Not with this, you."

The energy surged around her, tightened its grip on her nipples and then closed around her throat.

"Shut your eyes," the voice commanded, hard edged and rough.

Laurel shifted to ease the ache in her clit as she closed her eyes. She clasped the fabric of her jeans to stop the tremble in her hands.

The loops of energy morphed into the sensation of fingers that dug into the tender skin of her neck and tightened around her throat.

"You trust me not to end you?"

"Yes." Laurel panted and then moaned as the squeeze on her nipples increased.

"Why?"

Laurel turned her palms up and rested them on the back of her thighs as she lifted her chin, giving the spirit access to her, signaling her willingness to be possessed. "I'm not powerless. I sense you. I know you won't harm me, hurt me." She raised her hands up and lifted her breasts with both hands. "At least no more than I want you to."

"Open your eyes."

Laurel blinked her eyes open. A woman, thick and curvy, her lips full and her shoulders wide, stood over her, the skin over her broad cheeks pulled taut. Her skin had a blue cast, the subtle shade of nonexistence. Her hair was a wild mass of jet black, and wiry curls fell about her shoulders. Her eyes fixed on Laurel's face. Black as a pit, a fine rim of red outlined them.

"You're a demon? Or a centurion? Or were?"

Catherine snorted and tightened her grip on Laurel's throat. "Centurions. Half-wit demons who allow themselves to be used. Do I look like a mindless creature to you? No. I escaped bondage when I transformed." She tapped her thumb over the pulse in Laurel's throat. "Are you disappointed? I'm not the goddess you imagined, am I? Not the wicked snow queen of your fantasy?"

Laurel rolled her nipples as she held Catherine's gaze. "No. It doesn't matter you're not as I imagined."

Catherine let her hand fall away from Laurel's throat and gestured to her breasts. "And yet you still offer yourself? Knowing what I was? Not knowing what I am?"

"And what are you?"

Catherine drew herself together and revealed her true form. "I am Entity. Devourer of Souls. Spirit and yet not. And currently bound to this place." She lifted her arm and gestured to the window. "Beyond these walls I do not exist." She placed her hand on the crown of Laurel's head. "But here, in this space, I am."

Laurel moved her hands from her breasts and lowered her head to the floor in front of Catherine's feet. "You are that which ever lives."

"I am."

"And ever loves."

"That too."

"What became of your lover?"

Catherine withdrew her touch. Laurel pressed her forehead to the floor. "Please. Don't go. Forgive me if my question was insensitive. I am inexperienced."

"She was taken from me. Put your shirt on. Enough for today."

Catherine's energy bled from the space leaving Laurel chilled. She drew her shirt over her head, hugged her knees to her chest. *Why did I push?* A deep melancholy settled in her soul. Her phone beeped, signaling it was time to get ready for her shift at Sanctuary. She rose, ripped the paper from her sketch pad, balled it up, and tossed it to the floor.

Chapter Twelve

Laurel's shift at Sanctuary had left her jangled. The first half of her shift at the supper club had passed in pleasant boredom, until she had to take over for Kyle. Her head still throbbed from the heavy bass and clove cigarette smoke that had billowed over the densely packed space. The only bright spot had been the two women, a couple who had in passing through the club left a frisson of passionate energy that lit up the room. The sensuous vibe had Laurel seriously considering taking Carla up on her previous offer of a tour of the private rooms of Sanctuary.

She thumbed through the numbers in her phone as Laurel gulped a glass of water in the dark kitchen. The number for the sexual healing service she had used in the past rolled up. Dial-a-Domme as Laurel thought of it. She could call and have a Mistress at her house within the hour, ready to give Laurel what she needed. Everything but what she truly craved. Affection. Love. She texted the number and placed her phone on the table.

Beyond the living room bay window, streetlights bathed the street in a dull yellow glow. A dark form skittered from under a car and bolted under the steps of the house across the street. Another followed, as a parade of rats frolicked in the deserted street. Laurel watched them as she sipped her water. Her phone vibrated and she picked it up to read the text asking her to call to discuss her needs. Laurel lifted the phone and dialed.

"Hello, Laurel." Mistress Madeline's sultry tones flowed from the speaker. "It's late. What do you need?"

Her voice grated against Laurel's heart. Catherine. Catherine was what she needed not this simulated experience.

Laurel pushed her hand through her hair. "Nothing. Sorry to bother you."

"You're sure, Laurel? It's been a long time. I've missed you."

"Ha. I think you've missed my money."

"Don't be cruel, Laurel. You called me."

"Sorry. I'm not in a good place. I don't want to—I'm sorry I called."

Madeline sniffed loudly. "It's three in the morning and as much as I'd love to chat with you, and then come over and spank you for you disturbing my rest, if that is not what you want, I'll just hang up now."

The click of her disconnect echoed in Laurel's ear she tossed the phone to the middle of the table, set her glass aside, and left the kitchen. In the living room she picked up the sketch she had crumpled and opened it. She clipped it to her easel and smoothed it flat, her hands smearing the lines of the drawing. Her body ached with want. Her belly taut with desire, she laid her hands flat over Catherine's image.

"Catherine. Please. Come to me. Talk to me, please." Laurel flexed her power and the paper glowed blue as she searched for Catherine.

A psychic stillness filled the space. Void of energy. Catherine was behind her wards again. Wards. Because she feared who? Laurel? A snort of laugher bubbled out and shattered the stillness. "You have nothing to fear. Please come to me."

Desperate for touch and frustrated by Catherine's reticence, angry at Catherine's refusal to appear, rage barreled through Laurel. Wisps of blue smoke rose as the paper smoldered and the edges glowed red.

Forgoing words, Laurel put psychic muscle behind her call. Focusing her energy, she lifted her hands, opened them wide, and held them out palm up. A dense ball of light gathered in her palms. She spun it, a diminutive tornado of power, and directed it toward the attic.

The dense light flowed from her hand. A funnel-shaped purple cloud of energy flowed toward the ceiling, twisted and turned, and then vanished. A bright-blue light mixed with Laurel's light, a kaleidoscope of power and energy. It danced along the ceiling and swirled together. The room glowed with technicolor illumination as the energy blended before it collapsed in on itself and formed an image.

Catherine stood before her. A cool expression on her face, tall and foreboding, she was a vision of every fantasy Laurel had ever had of a woman to command her, to seduce her, to take over and let Laurel experience and feel, and serve at her direction.

"Why do you show me this? Why not come as you are?"

"Does it matter? You summoned me, I responded to your call as I assumed you wished me to appear."

Laurel flushed and flinched. "I wanted…" She swept her hair back from her face. "Sorry."

"Sorry for wanting me? Or sorry for summoning me? Ignoring my desire to be left alone?"

"Yes." Laurel rested her head on her chest. "I'll let you go."

"No. I'm here now."

Laurel reached across the space and stopped with her hand a bare inch from Catherine's arm. "May I?"

Catherine inclined her head. "Yes."

Laurel rested her fingers on Catherine's arm, completing a circuit of energy between them. "Oh, it was you. In the shower."

"Of course, it was. Did you really think anyone else capable of giving you what you crave?"

Laurel shivered with the steel in Catherine's voice. She closed her eyes as the sensations of their previous encounter washed over her. "Why? Why didn't you let me into the attic? Let me see you then?"

Catherine moved away, severing the connection between them. "I wasn't sure you were ready. I don't like to show myself as I am."

"You've shown yourself to me, why come to me like this? Or—" Laurel swallowed bile as she remembered the trail of blood to the attic. "—is there another form you take?"

"Yes." Catherine turned her back to Laurel. "An Entity's physical form is fixed if they are imprisoned. You should know this. What kind of education did you have?"

"None, really. My parents died before I started formal training. I was deemed too weak. I was released and allowed to choose my path."

Catherine snorted. "Ridiculous. You were allowed to waste your power. Your talent is undeveloped."

"You sound like my great-uncle."

"Has no one in your family pushed you?"

"Everyone. Until my parents died. And then everyone left me alone."

"Left you alone? Or you pushed them away?"

'Both." Laurel moved closer to Catherine. "What happened? Was it your blood?"

"You know the answer to that. Use your power. Stop pretending you don't have any. Quit acting like a novice."

"What little power I have is useless most of the time."

"Because you don't want it? Or are afraid of it? Do you have any idea what I've done to attain the power I have? What I've suffered to develop what you were born with?"

Laurel flinched as Catherine's harsh words echoed in the room. "I don't want it. I didn't ask to be born this way."

"You have two choices. Use it or be used by it. Master your power, Laurel, before..."

Catherine broke off and faded from Laurel's view.

Her absence hit Laurel hard, her body craving the connection. She focused her power and searched for Catherine. She inhaled sharply and shot a bolt of power toward the spot where Catherine had disappeared. "Come back. Right now. We're not finished."

Catherine returned. "Well done. See? Not that hard to focus when you want something." She stepped closer and drew her fingers over Laurel's cheek. "Or someone."

Laurel licked her lips. "Are you real? Or have I created you?"

"I'm as real as you are." Catherine leaned close. The scent of pine resin and cedar swirled around them. She cupped Laurel's face and her dark eyes pierced Laurel's soul, pinned her in place.

Laurel fell then, into the seduction of Catherine's spirit as she held her gaze. "Please kiss me. Kiss me, Ma'am."

Catherine smiled, exposing her fangs as she leaned in and pressed her blood-red lips to Laurel's mouth. A whipcord of sensation crackled down Laurel's spine and she opened to her kiss. Catherine's voice in her mind was rich as she spoke of her desires. Laurel ran her tongue over the sharp edge of Catherine's teeth. She whimpered, caught up in the shimmering threads of Catherine's mental bindings.

Catherine broke the kiss. Laurel panted. Her hands clenched and unclenched at her sides.

"Oh yes." Catherine drew the backs of her fingers over Laurel's cheek.

The sad smile on Catherine's face made Laurel's heart squeeze tight.

"You are delicious." She smoothed her palms over the bare skin of Laurel's arms. "So tempting."

Laurel forgot herself and clasped Catherine by her arms. She tugged her close and pressed against her body. The fires of want and need flamed low in her belly. Her skin glowed and sparked with her desire. "We don't have to stop."

Catherine extricated herself from Laurel's arms. "We do. You don't know what this will cost you."

Laurel frowned. "What? Are you some kind of cosmic courtesan?"

Catherine leveled her gaze and raised an eyebrow. "Why would I need money?"

"What then? What could I have you want?"

"Blood."

Laurel drew back. "I won't kill for you."

Catherine tilted her head to the side. "I wouldn't ask you to kill for me. That's easily enough done."

"Or lure anyone here so you can do it." Laurel shivered as the light in the room faded.

"I don't need that." Catherine looked away from Laurel's face.

"Then what are you talking about?" Laurel stepped close and rested her fingertips on Catherine's shoulder.

Catherine turned to face her and met her gaze. "I need your blood, Laurel. Freely given."

Laurel recoiled. "This was all so you could seduce me to get my blood?"

"No. I..."

"You want to use me. Like everyone else."

"No. Please listen, let me explain..."

"No. So you can lie to me some more? Seduce me? Convince me that you really wanted me for myself instead of for what I can do? You're just like the rest them. Fuck you." Laurel's rage bubbled and overflowed, hot and thick as lava. Her power surged out and up and a wave of red light shot from her body and filled the room. It enveloped Catherine, the light filling her body, shining from her eyes, nose, and mouth. A shrill cry escaped her lips followed by a deep groan as Catherine's form crumpled to the floor, a rag doll of unanimated flesh.

Laurel gasped, her rage shifting to terror. "Catherine!"

The body on the floor melted into dark ooze. Bubbling slowly, it slipped through the cracks in the floor and vanished. Laurel's knees gave way and she collapsed. Her chest ached, her heart split wide. Betrayed. Again.

Laurel lay on her side curled into a ball. She reached her hand and touched the damp boards where Catherine had vanished. Hot tears flowed down her cheeks. Her rage had destroyed a spirit.

Her anger cooled, the red light faded and in its place was desolation. Laurel rolled to her back and stared at the ceiling with her hands clasped over her aching heart. She had destroyed Catherine. Destroyed an Entity who had sealed herself behind wards until Laurel had forced her to appear. Catherine had tried to protect Laurel. And what had Laurel done? Lashed out. Not even given her a chance to explain. The horror of her actions swirled in her mind and she pressed the heels of her hands to her eyelids to block the vision of Catherine's last moments. She rocked silently until she was exhausted. Too tired to move, she rolled to her side, drawing her legs up, and slept.

*

The sun rose over the buildings and suffused the room with dull morning light. Stiff and cold from sleeping on the floor, Laurel pushed herself to sitting. She wiped the dried salt of her tears from her cheeks. She touched the boards where Catherine had vanished. A telltale wisp of energy flowed from the wood. An act. An elaborate scene designed to fool Laurel as she hid behind her wards. Laurel lifted her eyes to the stairs and scrambled to her feet.

Chapter Thirteen

Laurel bolted from the room and took the stairs two at a time. Fine blue light glimmered from the edges of the doorframe. White-hot energy shards burned her palms as she grabbed the doorknob with both hands and yanked hard. The door pulled free as the wards Catherine had left in place shattered around her.

She shouldered the door aside and bounded up the three steps leading to the attic space. A rotted, brown-stained mattress rested on a brass three-quarter bed frame under the eaves. Sweat stung her eyes in the stifling attic space. She blinked and swiped the back of her wrist over her forehead.

Dim light from the single window illuminated a board atop two boxes with a small stool under it. On the makeshift desk a thick book lay open, its pages swollen and dirty. She crossed to the desk. Her puzzle box was centered on the wide board.

A shiver skittered down her spine. She had unpacked the box and placed it on the table in the kitchen. And yet it was here in the attic. She rested her fingers on top of the box and a familiar energy signature filtered up her arm. Catherine. Why would she want Laurel's thrift store find?

Alma had chided her for spending money she didn't have on a useless dust collector after Laurel was unable to open it. Laurel had ignored Alma's repeated attempts to force her to get rid of the box, and she gave up trying to explain to Alma the way the small chest called to her.

An Indonesian kris lay near to the puzzle box. The iridescent irregular wavy edge of its blade glowed with dark magic. The handle was the carved body of a demon with blood-red rubies for eyes. Laurel avoided the blade when she moved the book closer to examine it.

The pages were yellowed, the edges of the journal deckled from where the paper was worn. A series of drawings of hieroglyphs filled the page set mirrored by translations written in careful printing in Latin and then English. Laurel parsed the words as she read the spell to give the deceased the ability to breathe and have power over their enemies.

Laurel struggled to read the words and directions for conducting the ceremony. Carefully she lifted the book, keeping her place with her finger. The cracked brown leather cover offered no clues. She opened to the flyleaf. Copperplate calligraphy filled the page. Unable to read most of the words, Laurel's eyes were drawn to "Aikaterina" signed in gold at the bottom of the page. She traced her hand over the letters and an image of Catherine rose in her mind.

She turned the next few pages, filled with charts of stars and notes. Catherine's journal, her grimoire if what Laurel had seen so far was an indication. A private place for her to collect and parse her thoughts and experiences with controlling energies and forces of the world. A smattering of guilt splashed over her before she shoved it aside and went back to reading the book.

Careful drawings of plants and hieroglyphs, petroglyphs, and neat lists covered the pages. A map covered two pages. Laurel gazed at the rich colors and intricate drawings of beasts she had read about but never seen rendered so exquisitely.

Laurel opened the book to where it had been, smoothing her fingers over the brittle page. She bent over the low desk and read the enchantment again, taking time to match the drawings with the words. A dull throb in her neck blossomed. Laurel glanced at the floor. Dusty and flyspecked and she had no intention of sitting on it. Under the desk a cobweb-covered slatted wooden crate rested on its side. She got down on her knees, hooked her finger under the edge of the box, and pulled it forward.

Laurel perched on the edge of the box and read the words again out loud, more confident of her translation. She rested her hand on the top of the puzzle box. A pleasant stream of energy flowed from the box as Laurel fiddled with the pattern, pressing different points on the mosaic. She fought a yawn. The heat of the attic and the buzz of the box lulled her as she studied the charm.

A sting and then a searing sensation shot up her arm. The rippling fire traveled across her palm and up her arm. Laurel snatched her hand away from the box. A silver blade, razor thin, protruded from the edge of the chest. Cold dread prickled her skin. She lifted her hand. The slash extended lengthwise from the center of her palm to her wrist. It gaped open, edges white, before blood welled and then pulsed. Bright-red jets spilled across the book, saturating the pages, before it dripped onto the floor and sizzled where it soaked into the boards.

Her blood bloomed, flowed freely as it spurted and dripped from her arm. The pages of the book swam in her vision, the drawings and words becoming one. Dizzy, mouth dry, her power flashed and ebbed through her. Laurel clutched the edge of the desk. It shifted on the boxes and crashed to the floor.

Laurel fell to her knees, yanked her T-shirt over her head, and wrapped her hand and wrist with it, applying pressure. Fear blossomed in her chest as her blood soaked through the fabric. She panted as she curled her legs into her body. She would die, here, alone, victim of her own stupidity and curiosity.

Anger swirled through her as she replayed her brief life in her head. This was not how she wanted to leave this coil. Not this way. Alone. Never having been loved, truly loved for who she was.

Summoning what was left of her power, Laurel reached out with her mind, a frantic call to Nadia. She lay back and closed her eyes, unable to focus as her life drained away. *Will Nadia find me? Will she be able to walk through the wards? Will I be alive? Or mostly dead?* Her teeth chattered and she clenched her jaw to stop the clack of her teeth. The cloying smell of death filled the attic. A white film of frost grew and covered the room, edging closer to Laurel. Her head throbbed and she closed her eyes against the pain.

A blaze of white light illuminated the space and swept away the cold. The acrid scent of pitch and cedar resin rose and swept away the sweet smell of death. Laurel forced her eyes open and squinted to focus.

Catherine stood over her. Jet-black hair in intricate braids framed her face, eyes dark with kohl, her lips parted, fangs gleaming white in a blood-red snarl. "Fool. Why? There are safe ways to do this. You didn't have to butcher yourself."

She kneeled and clasped Laurel's wounded hand. After wrenching the T-shirt from her arm, she tossed it aside. Catherine pressed her lips to Laurel's wrist. She lapped at the blood there and drew her tongue along the cut. Laurel cried out with the connection. The cut sealed shut. Catherine's energy teemed in Laurel's body, a reprieve from death.

Catherine cupped her chin and looked into Laurel's eyes. "If you don't want this, say so now. I'll leave you and let you be. Call Nadia for you."

"No." Laurel lifted her gore-stained hand, clasped Catherine's shoulder, and tugged her close. "Please. I want this. Bind me. To you."

"Even in death?"

"Yes." Laurel grabbed the front of Catherine's shirt. The fabric gave way, buttons flew and pinged off the rafters.

Catherine pulled free from Laurel's grasp and tugged her shirt off. She took the bronze dagger in her hand, slid it across her breast, and opened a wound. She leaned over Laurel, cupped the back of her head, and held her to the cut.

Hot liquid flowed into Laurel's mouth, bitter at first and then becoming sweet on her tongue. Like honeyed wine it filled her mouth. Her body twitched. She groaned as a burning fire exploded in her stomach. She broke free from Catherine's grasp. White and red light surrounded them, swirled between them. Laurel had the sensation of falling. She reached for Catherine's hand.

"What is this?" She clutched her hand to her chest.

"Death. And life, of a sort. If you choose." She pressed her other hand over Laurel's heart.

The thudding of Laurel's heartbeat was loud in her ears as it slowed. Laurel closed her eyes and focused on the sound as it stuttered and skipped.

"I've done what I can do. You must choose now. For yourself. Not for me. Choose life because you want your soul to live. But know this. We will be bound. For eternity. This life and the next, if there is another world after this." Catherine's voice wrapped around her.

Laurel looked over the edge of the abyss that formed in her mind. "If I fall?"

"Then we are bound. Your fate is my fate."

Laurel squinted. "You're already dead, are you not?"

"Mostly dead."

"What happened in the living room when you left me? Why did you leave? I thought I had destroyed you."

Catherine cupped her cheek. "I left because you didn't want me to be there."

A green vine with bright-silver thorns grew up from the blood-red soil surrounding the abyss. The desire to climb the vine, to suffer the delicious pain of its thorns as it led her to the peaceful oblivion of death, called to her. Laurel touched a finger to the thick green vine, pricked her fingertip on a thorn, and savored the burning pain. "What will become of you if I go?"

Catherine pursed her lips. "Nothing. I will continue. As I am. On this plane. Until the house no longer stands."

"Unless another comes. Someone else like me."

"No. You are unique."

Laurel frowned. "Because?"

"Your blood is unique. Human and supernatural, a powerful combination. Most human and super children don't live long after birth. Under the proper circumstances your blood could raise legions of followers."

"Is it why you seduced me?"

"No. You would have interested me no matter what. I didn't want this. For you to have to choose me or oblivion."

Laurel closed her eyes. "It's not a hard choice."

Catherine placed her hand over Laurel's heart. "You don't have much time left in this body. You must choose."

Laurel closed her eyes, opened her arms wide, and tumbled over the dark edge into the world beyond.

*

The connection between them ebbed and flowed as Laurel waffled with her decision. Catherine waited, holding herself in check, unwilling to force her desires on Laurel. The verse was very clear. Free will and only free will would forge the bond. She wanted, oh how she wanted. Fear. Desire. Longing. And woven through all of it the barest hint of love. Catherine could grow to love Laurel.

Catherine focused her energy as she peered at Laurel's face. The heartbeat under her hand slowed and then stilled. Catherine reached out and pushed aside the thick shock of black hair that covered Laurel's forehead. Laurel's grip on Catherine's arm relaxed and her face went slack. Her mouth fell open in a last soft gasp.

The weight of her choice fell heavy over Catherine's shoulders. Searing pain wrenched a cry from her as the skin and bone of her chest split wide. Large hooks of silver pulled her flesh apart, exposing her heart. Purple light shone from her center, spilling over Laurel.

Laurel's body vibrated as the light swirled around and through her, entering her nose, her mouth, her ears. Laurel's eyes grew wide, her mouth a silent scream as the light split her chest open from the inside. The silver hooks dug deeper into Catherine's flesh as the energy bathed Laurel's heart. Catherine cried out when the vines tightened, pulling them face to face, heart to heart. Focusing on the words she had practiced so many times, Catherine spoke the charm that would bind them for eternity.

The room brightened as the purple energy surged and swelled around them. Laurel gazed into Catherine's eyes. Salvation, and recognition, as the resurrection took hold. The light faded and their wounds closed. True flesh knit around Catherine's bones. She swore and screeched as her bones and sinews formed and grew strong. She screamed long and loud as air filled her lungs.

Laurel's arms wrapped around her, holding her close, her breath coming in small puffs against Catherine's cheek. "Thank you." Her voice was rich, deep, and strong.

"You might want to wait to thank me." Catherine wiped her thumb over Laurel's cheek.

"You saved me."

"No. I gave you a choice. You saved yourself."

Laurel shifted under her. "I like how you feel over me."

Catherine sighed and leaned her brow again Laurel's head. "One-track mind."

"When it comes to you, yes. I've never had anyone I've connected with so easily." She looked away from Catherine.

"There have been others. You are not innocent, Laurel."

Laurel brought her gaze back to Catherine's face. "I've never had anyone who didn't treat it as joke or tease me about it. So many don't understand it. You are perfect for me."

Catherine hugged her closer. "As romantic as it is to lie in a drying sticky puddle of your blood, hearing how devoted you are to me, why don't we get cleaned up and continue this discussion elsewhere? Besides, I believe your would-be rescuer is on her way here."

"Nadia."

"Indeed. It seems she got your message after all."

A crooked grin spread across Laurel's face. "Timing is everything."

"You need to come up with a story that will satisfy her."

"Not the truth?"

"Your metamorphosis and binding to me are not what anyone had planned for you. Nadia is loyal to your great-uncle."

"She bound herself to me."

"No. You held your true self in reserve. You don't trust her. Not the way a super is supposed to trust their centurion. Your bond with her is smoke and mirrors."

Laurel pursed her lips. "True."

Catherine rose and stood over Laurel. She extended her hand. "Come, we need to make you presentable."

Laurel gestured to the floor. "What about this?"

Catherine shrugged. "What about it? No one will be able to cross my wards."

"I was able to."

"Nadia is not you. Nor is anyone else. Come. We don't have much time."

Chapter Fourteen

Laurel yipped as the cold water splashed over her skin. Blood and pink-tinged foam washed down the drain. The water warmed and she relaxed into the spray.

"Don't take too long, darling, unless you want Nadia to find you naked."

Laurel snorted. "She'd just turn away and hide her eyes. She's ridiculous."

"And you've never tried to bring her out of her shell?" Catherine's mocking tone made Laurel grimace.

"No. Well, other than letting her mindfuck me on the sidewalk."

"I wondered the day you moved in. I thought you were mated, or you wanted to be."

Laurel twisted the taps closed and pushed back the shower curtain. "I didn't. Not really but I knew she'd report to my uncle if I refused. And then who knows what kind of protection he would have sent me. At least he doesn't try to force me to accept one of the male guardians anymore."

Catherine frowned. "Force you? That hardly sounds like a caring relative."

"He only wants to keep me safe."

"From what?"

"The Orions."

"I'd ask you to explain but Nadia is at the door."

A loud hammering shattered the peace of the house, followed by the rasp of the lock turning and the sound of the door slamming open.

"Laurel!" Nadia's bellow shook the walls.

Catherine wrapped a towel around Laurel's shoulders. "You're on." She gestured to the faint pink stains in the tub. "I'll take care of this."

Laurel chewed her lip. "Won't she be able to tell?" She glanced at herself in the mirror.

"Do you look different to you?"

"No."

"As long as you choose to hold this shape, you'll be fine. You hid your true power before. Do it again."

The doorknob to the bathroom twisted violently. "Laurel?"

Laurel opened the door a crack. "Nadia? What's wrong?"

Nadia's eyes flared red. "What's wrong! For Asmodeus's sake! You called me, told me you were dying."

Laurel slipped out of the bathroom door and closed it behind her. "No need to swear. Do I look dead to you?"

Nadia blew out a breath. "What happened? I didn't imagine your call."

Laurel reached out and placed her fingertips on Nadia's cheek. "I'm fine. I must have been dreaming." She let the towel slip a bit, exposing the curve of her breast.

Nadia stepped back and rested her hands on her hips. "Don't try to distract me. I know you don't care for me like that."

Laurel snatched the towel tighter around her body. "Fine. I don't...I don't need you busting into my house demanding answers when I owe you none."

Nadia stepped back as if struck and lowered her head to her chest. "Right. I am only to serve."

Laurel huffed out a breath. "Stop that. I'm sorry, it must have been a nightmare. I had a rough night at work, and then I had horrible dreams. I can't always control my thoughts."

Nadia crossed her arms over her chest. "You're lying. You've been lying to me. Why don't you trust me?"

Laurel squared her shoulders and flexed her power. "Because you report to Marcus, first and foremost, despite your promises to me. You are bound to him. I know it. You know it. So cut the wounded would-be lover bullshit."

Nadia's mouth twisted into the cruel parody of a smile. "You're right." The skin around her mouth grew taut and her lips pulled into a sneer exposing her stark white teeth. "I wouldn't look twice at you on the street, but your great-uncle feels you need minding. I tried to tell him he was wasting his time. You are nothing. You will be nothing. A waste of space. A drag and smear on the family name." Her eyes glowed fiery red. "He has given me permission to do what I think is necessary to make you comply with his plans." Her body twisted and morphed.

Her suit fell in tatters as she transformed. Her muscular body filled the hallway, her hair a crown of flames framing her head. The stench of sulfur burnt Laurel's nose. "You waste my time, child." Voice full of brimstone, Nadia wrapped her hand around Laurel's throat. Her sharp claws dug into her skin. "No more playing."

Laurel inhaled and closed her eyes. Her skin burst into purple flames. The demon howled and fell back on her haunches. Eyes wide, she scrabbled away from Laurel.

"How? You've bonded to her? What have you done? You don't know. She's not to be trusted," Nadia screeched.

*

The bathroom door swung wide, and Catherine stepped through it. She moved behind Laurel and wrapped her hand around her waist, impervious to her flames. "Funny. I'm not the one who swore falsely and tried to kill my bonded charge. Isn't there a special punishment for centurions who break their vows?"

Nadia rose to her feet. Her claws flexed open and closed at her side. "Laurel. Listen to me. There is still time. We can undo this."

Laurel held tight to Catherine's hand. "No. I will not be bred like a cow."

Nadia inched closer, her hands palm up. "You would cosign your family to oblivion? And all of the centurions who have worked for you for years?"

Laurel firmed her chin. "Yes. If that's what it takes for you to leave me alone. I will not be forced to bear children or be what Marcus and the rest of those ghouls want me to be. And it's too late." She dropped her guise of flesh and stood clothed in her new form. Her shimmering skin, a gossamer veil over her energy, lit the hallway.

Nadia fell to the floor and curled into a ball, her head in her hands. She shuddered as she returned to her human form. "Finish me. I can't return to Marcus. Be merciful, please. Release me into the unknown. I can't face his torture and punishment."

Laurel laid her hand on the demon's head. "No. I've no wish to harm you, Nadia. I won't do as you ask. It's not for me to decide your fate. You chose the minute you betrayed me and pretended fidelity Go. Now." She raised her hand, wrapped Nadia in her energy, and propelled her down the stairs and out of the door.

Catherine followed her and set wards around the door. "That should buy us some peace for a while." Her brow knitted. "Marcus Callan is your uncle?"

"Great-uncle, by marriage." Laurel stretched in her power. "And that felt unbelievably delicious." A weariness settled over her. "But I am exhausted. How can a spirit need rest?"

Catherine took her hand. "Only stars come close to unlimited power, and even they eventually burn out. You are not only spirit. We both are not what we were. We are somewhat flesh, and even enchanted flesh needs rest and food. Sleep. I'll watch over you."

"You're not tired?"

"No." Catherine moaned. The rich sound echoed off the vaulted ceiling. "No. I'm too excited." She stroked her hands over her skin. "I've missed my body. I couldn't sleep now if I tried. I'm going to raid your refrigerator."

Laurel laughed. "You're going to be disappointed. I always eat at the club. Where will we sleep? I doubt Nadia will have that bed delivered now. My sleeping bag is too small for two."

Catherine tilted her head. "Sleep anywhere you want to. It's your home. And you can create any kind of space you want."

She led them up the stairs. At the top she gestured to the door leading to the master bedroom. "Imagine the perfect room to sleep in, hold that image, make it so."

Laurel concentrated a moment and then opened the door. A huge canopy tester bed occupied the room. Heavy curtains blocked the light. A tiny lamp glowed by the bed. Lush royal-blue carpet covered the floor. The heavy drapes muffled the sounds from the street below. Laurel moved toward the bed and flipped the covers back. "Seems a shame to waste this room just sleeping." She raked her eyes over Catherine's form.

Catherine lifted Laurel's hand, kissed her fingertips, and then nipped them. "Later. Sleep well, love. You'll need your strength for what I have in mind for you."

A fission of energy passed through her hand and up her arm, trailing down her body, arrowing straight to Laurel's clit. "Damn it, I'm never going to fall asleep now."

Catherine leaned close and kissed her. She clasped her shoulders and pressed her back onto the mattress. Laurel relaxed into her kiss. She swept Laurel's legs up and then tucked her into bed. Catherine kissed her cheek, her forehead, and then kissed her eyes closed. "Sleep. We have eternity for the rest."

Chapter Fifteen

"Stop moving." Laurel's voice edged into Catherine's consciousness.

"Sorry. I haven't had a real body for so long it's hard to control. Besides, you could draw me with your eyes closed, seriously."

Laurel grimaced. "I want to draw you as you are, now that I've seen you."

Catherine shifted on her chair and the drape Laurel had arranged over her body fell from her breasts. "Oh look, the drape fell. Again."

"Now you're just trying to distract me."

"Maybe." Catherine lifted a shoulder and let it fall. She crooked her finger at Laurel. "Come here. Now that I have a real clit again, I can't wait for you to suck it."

Laurel shivered. Her body trembled with Catherine's coarse words and soft command. "Yes. Ma'am."

She lay her drawing pencil aside and walked to the chair where Catherine reclined. Laurel sank to her knees and crawled to her. Shell-pink toenails peeked from beneath the maroon sheet folded over her legs. Catherine pulled the cloth to expose one long leg and the darkness between her thighs. Laurel drew her lips over her skin, soaking in the soft scent of her, and the subtle spicy scent of her desire. "Please, Ma'am, may I suck you? Suck your clit until you come in my mouth?"

Catherine leaned back and lifted her foot and placed it in between Laurel's breasts. "Perhaps. Show me how much you desire me."

Laurel stood, shed her clothes, stripping them off and tossing them into a pile. She reached between her legs and drew her fingers over the burgeoning wetness and gathered it on her fingertips. She held her glistening fingers up for Catherine to see.

"Very nice. But I think you need to show me more."

Laurel fixed her gaze on Catherine's full breasts, dark-brown nipples peaked and stood out, and Laurel's mouth watered. "May I suck your nipples? Please, Ma'am. I could show you. Show you how much I want to please you."

Catherine lifted her heavy breasts, the flesh spilling from her hands. "Come here." Laurel crawled forward and leaned in. Catherine cupped the back of her head. "Suck me. Get me off and I'll let you clean up."

Laurel bent her hand and took a thick nipple into her mouth. The velvet hardness under her tongue made her moan. Catherine's fingers on the back of her head held her in place.

Laurel swept her hands up and gathered Catherine's breasts in her hands and suckled them. Intoxicated with the scent of desire rising between them, Laurel circled the tip with flat of her tongue, licking and then drawing her fat nipple deep. Catherine's delicate groan set her on fire. Laurel applied herself to her task.

Nipping the soft skin under her breasts and then working her way back with small kisses, trying hard to pay equal attention to both nipples. Catherine's hips rocked and she pressed against Laurel, the sheet falling away. Her center was molten against Laurel's stomach.

Laurel leaned in and wrapped her arms about her waist to pull her closer. The scrape of tight curls and then the slick slide of Catherine's clit over her skin drove her. Saliva pooled in her mouth as she worked hard to earn the right to drown in the sweetness between Catherine's legs.

*

Laurel's mouth on her nipples was heaven and Catherine shifted to press more of herself between her greedy lips. The sheet had long been discarded and now the rub and pressure of Laurel's hard stomach against her clit threatened her control. Another nip and then tug of Laurel's teeth and Catherine came, her pleasure spiraling out from her center, and she crushed Laurel to her as she rocked into the sensations.

Laurel broke free, panting. "Please, Ma'am. Let me taste you."

Unable to speak, Catherine palmed the top of Laurel's head and shoved her between her widespread legs. Warm wet heat closed over her clit. She shifted and thrust her hips up, eager for Laurel's mouth. Her clit throbbed. Laurel circled it with her tongue before pursing her lips to close over it and suck. The rhythmic push and pull of her mouth swept Catherine up until the waves of pleasure took her under, swallowed her whole. She keened her release as she came again. "Fuck me, Laurel. Now. Now."

Laurel thrust two fingers in and curled them up, hit a spot that made Catherine gasp and scream as she rocked on Laurel's hand. Insatiable desire to be lost in the bliss of Laurel's mouth and touch consumed her.

"Again. Goddess, you are divine. Make me come again." Catherine panted.

Laurel growled, the vibrations rocketing through Catherine as she settled into a slow rhythm and fucked her in time to licking her clit, just enough but not enough to send Catherine over.

Her deliberate movements were exquisite torture. Laurel covered Catherine's clit with her mouth and sucked gently as she worked the hood back with her lips. When she touched her tongue to the tip, Catherine's orgasm detonated sharp and clear, her body shaking.

Laurel thrust deep and hard. Catherine curled up and over Laurel's back as she shook and trembled through her pleasure. She closed her eyes, wanting the sensation to go on forever, knowing it could not.

Laurel eased her down, slowing her strokes with soothing licks and touches of her tongue. Catherine slumped in the chair. Laurel sat back on her heels, her face wet and glistening.

"Come here." Catherine patted her lap.

Laurel curled into her arms. Catherine kissed her, savoring the taste of herself on Laurel's lips. She rubbed her hand over her breasts and down over her belly. She patted the tops of Laurel's thighs. "Open."

Laurel spread her legs. Catherine dipped into her wet heat. She slicked her fingers and spread it up and over

Laurel's clit. "Where did you learn to please a woman like that? Who taught you how to suck clit like that?"

Laurel gasped and groaned as Catherine thrust her fingers deep.

"Answer me."

"My first lover, Ma'am."

"Remind me to send her a thank-you note." Catherine teased her fingers over Laurel's clit, delighting in her loud shout as she came undone under Catherine's touch. Liquid silk spilled over Catherine's fingers as she palmed and cupped Laurel. "I hope you didn't have any other plans for the day." She stood with Laurel in her arms. "Let's go somewhere more comfortable." She cloaked them in energy and transported them to their room.

Chapter Sixteen

Catherine woke with the heavy weight of Laurel's leg draped over her thighs and stickiness between her legs. Alive, and yet not. She smoothed her hand over her belly, careful not to wake Laurel. Air moved in her lungs, her heart beat beneath her skin, and the ache in her clit signaled her desire for Laurel.

She turned her head to look at her bedmate. Her hair was scattered across her cheek, covering her sharp cheekbones. Catherine studied her as she slept, her gaze caressing her face. Laurel had chosen to be bonded, to free Catherine from her lingering half-life/half-death, even choosing to transform herself. Who were her enemies? What vengeance fueled her desire to surrender the peace of oblivion to walk the earth seeking to destroy her enemies and because of their bond, Catherine's enemies as well?

Laurel stirred in her sleep. Catherine stilled, unwilling to wake her, even as she desired to kneel over her full lips and ride her mouth until she screamed Laurel's name. After years of no physical joy Catherine wanted to drown in the sensations of sex.

Catherine pursed her lips. Marcus Callan. Laurel's great-uncle. Not a blood relative. Laurel's enemy if her words to Nadia were any indication. How much more would she hate him if she met the basement children?

She reached out to Manny, calling him to her softly.

"Yes?" Manny appeared at the bedside his forehead wrinkled. "You saying goodbye?" He turned his newsboy cap in his hands. "Are you going with her?"

"No." Catherine pulled the covers up over Laurel's shoulders. "If I do leave the house, I'll come back."

"Can you release us now?"

"Not alone." Catherine rested her hand on Laurel's shoulder.

"Will she help?"

"Why don't you ask me?" Laurel rasped. She cleared the sleep from her throat. "Who is this?" She tuned to face Manny.

"I'm Manny. I live in the basement with the others."

Laurel sat up in the bed, clutching the sheets to her chest. "Others?"

She turned to Catherine. "I'm going to need coffee for this."

Catherine pursed her lips. "Yes. I believe you will."

*

The door to Manny's world was bricked over. The faint outline of the magic sealing the tomb glowed with red light.

Laurel drew close to Catherine. "I didn't see this when I moved in."

"You weren't meant to." Catherine wrapped her arm around her waist, her presence warm in the chill of the cellar. "Are you ready for this?"

"As ready as I'll ever be." She placed both hands on the bricks and gathered her energy. The red light glowed and then faded to white as the bricks melted and vanished. A cistern stood before them, a gaping maw in the floor.

Manny stood on the other side of the pit.

Laurel looked into the blackness. She shrank back as the upturned faces of other children, their eyes glowing red, their thin bodies draped in frayed clothes, filled the pit. A wall of fear and anger washed over Laurel. Her skin tingled with the sharp cries of their gathered energy.

"Peace. Be still. All of you." Catherine's command brought stillness to the space.

"What is this place? Who are you?" Laurel's voice rose as the stench of fear and hatred flared from the pit.

Manny held his arms out wide. "They are the failed. The results of Marcus Callan's breeding program between humans and supernaturals. They were terminated when they didn't measure up to his expectations, or when he needed blood for more experiments."

"What?" A chill skittered up Laurel's spine.

Catherine held her hands up and light spilled forth and illuminated the pit and the upturned faces of the children.

"Why don't they speak?" Laurel moved further into the room, closer to the specters crowding the space.

The children opened their mouths and revealed the stumps of their tongues before their mouths opened in silent screams that rose from the mass of bodies and assailed Laurel's ears.

Manny pursed his lips. "Marcus left nothing to chance."

A burning rage built in Laurel. "How do you figure into this?"

Manny turned his cap in his hand. "I found out. Planned to expose him. Humans began investigations. Marcus made sure nothing would ever be found, sealed me in with them."

Laurel swallowed the bile rising in her throat. "What do you want?"

Manny closed his eyes. "To be free, to seek God, if there is one."

"What do they want?" Laurel gestured to the children of the pit.

Manny tilted his head. "The same, as far as I can tell. To be free of this house, to not live in fear of being entombed in this place for eternity."

Catherine settled her hand in the small of Laurel's back. "You can release them."

"How?"

"The book. And your power."

"I can do that?"

"You unsealed a wall that had been sealed and warded by your great-uncle like you were slicing butter with a hot knife and you doubt your power?" Catherine quirked her mouth.

"Get the book."

Catherine tilted her head and lifted her chin. "As you wish."

Laurel forced herself to stay in the living tomb, forced herself to memorize each child's face, and forced herself to acknowledge the evil her great-uncle had perpetrated.

Chapter Seventeen

Laurel lay on the bed, her eyes fixed on the dark fabric of the canopy. Lethargy, deep and wide, filled her. Her work to free the basement children and Manny from their tomb left her drained. Only her anger kept her awake, and under it all a sick feeling of being set up. Her great-uncle wanted her blood, wanted to breed her like an animal.

Before she had freed Manny, she had made him tell her all the details of her great-uncle's operation, needing to pause only once to vomit as he told her of his methods for attempting to create what Laurel's parents had accomplished on their own. Fueled by love, her mother had defied the clan, had married her father, and had Laurel.

Laurel worried her lip with her teeth.

"You'll hurt yourself if you don't rest." Catherine stretched out beside Laurel and placed her hand over her heart. "Let it go for now."

"I can't. I can't let it go. He's despicable, but he has never been anything but kind to me."

"That's the rub of it, isn't it?" Catherine moved her hand up to cup Laurel's cheek and tapped her thumb on her cheekbone.

"Yes." Laurel turned to face her. "You knew him?"

"I did." Her gaze slid sideways from Laurel's face.

"How well?"

"Not very. He traveled in circles below my place."

"How did you end up trapped in this house?"

"Misplaced trust. A charmed blade."

Laurel snuggled close to Catherine. "The kris in the attic?"

"Yes."

"Who?"

"My lover's brother. He considered our bond unnatural." Catherine snorted. "He was so ignorant and frightened after he stabbed me, he forgot to pull the blade free and left unspoken the words that would have truly ended me."

Laurel shivered. Her heart ached as visions of the scene flooded her mind and their shared bond flared with pain. She clutched her stomach, a dull pain in her gut mirroring Catherine's wound. She groaned softly. "Sorry I asked."

Catherine smoothed her hand over Laurel's brow. "Don't. Don't think of it." Her energy flowed over and through Laurel, sweeping the images from her mind.

Laurel fingered a thick wiry curl of Catherine's hair. The heated dark scent of pine and cedar rose from her umber skin. The signature scent of Catherine's magic surrounded her, and she settled under her touch. "Have you always been with women?"

"Are you always this curious?" Catherine's dark eyes held Laurel's gaze.

"Always. And I like the sound of your voice. So, always with women?"

"Yes. It's who I am. I've dallied with, but never been committed to a man." Catherine captured Laurel's arm and kissed the scar over her wrist. The heat from her lips spread over Laurel's body and her nipples tightened. Catherine kissed her way along her arm and then scattered kisses over her shoulder.

Laurel melted under her touch. "Stop. Please. Tell me, how does it work? How many times have you been bound to another?"

Catherine scooted away from Laurel and raised both hands palm out. "How am I supposed to seduce you when you won't stop talking? I'll give you three more questions and then that's it for tonight. We have eternity for you to ask questions."

Laurel stilled. "That's not true, though, is it? Eternity?"

"Too long?"

"No. But there have been others before me."

The weight of the unasked question hung between them. The unsaid hovered over them as the air in the room stilled.

"I've bonded twice before you." Catherine shifted her gaze from Laurel's face. "My first love struggled with her transformation. She chose to end her existence."

"I'm sorry." Laurel rose and kissed Catherine's cheek.

"As am I." Catherine knotted her hands over her stomach. "My last love was wrenched from me. Our bond broken by my near death and imprisonment. The curse placed on me severed our connection. I have no hope she still exists." She caressed Laurel's arm.

"Do you still love them?"

"I am that which ever loves. Here, or beyond I love the ones I bonded with, no matter what plane they occupy."

"How old are you?" Laurel picked up Catherine's hand and kissed her palm.

"Old enough to remember the building of Djoser's pyramid."

"And only two loves?" Laurel arched her eyebrow.

Catherine pulled her close. "Jealousy does not become you. And I said only two bonded lovers. Three now with you." She tugged Laurel's hair and exposed her throat, nipped, and then soothed the spot her sharp teeth left.

"You love me? You just met me. How can you say you love me?"

Catherine peered into Laurel's face. Her gaze locked with Laurel's. "Do you doubt my feelings? Or regret your choice?"

Laurel reached out and smoothed the lines that marred Catherine's brow. "No. I know your soul as I know my own. We're meant to be. I sensed it from the first time you touched me. It was as if a part of me I didn't even know was missing clicked into place." She brushed her lips over Catherine's mouth. Catherine cupped the back of her head and deepened the kiss. Laurel relaxed into her attention. She wrapped her hand in Catherine's hair and tugged, breaking their connection.

Laurel lifted her chin to expose her neck. "Mark me."

Catherine bit down, hard enough to bruise, stopping short of breaking her skin and Laurel groaned. Catherine rolled them so Laurel was pinned by her weight. "What do you need, my love?"

"You. Over me. Let me lose myself in you."

Catherine slid up Laurel's body. She planted her knees on either side of Laurel's head and lifted her skirt with one hand. "Like this?"

Laurel hummed and tugged her hips, bringing Catherine close. She pulled the thin silk covering her thick clit to the side and lost herself in her sweet heat.

*

"He'll come, you know. After Nadia's report to him." Catherine slathered butter over her toast.

Laurel raised an eyebrow. "I suppose you don't have to worry about what you eat."

Catherine chewed slowly. "No. And neither do you now."

"If we don't need food, what do we feed on?"

"Energy. Emotions. Blood, if we choose. Some develop a taste for it. It's more trouble than it's worth."

Laurel grimaced. "I don't even feel hungry."

Catherine tilted her head to the side. "As much as you fed on me, I'm not surprised."

Laurel's cheeks flushed a delightful dull red. "What do we do about my uncle?"

Catherine wiped the crumbs from her fingers. "What do you want to do?"

Laurel closed her eyes as visions of the cellar children rose in her mind. "I want to end him, but it feels like a betrayal of my clan, my family." A shudder whipped her frame. "What if he's still working on his breeding program?"

Catherine leaned back in her chair and folded her arms across her chest. "I can't imagine he would stop. He was obsessed with it. With power."

Laurel held her hands apart and gathered a small ball of energy and toyed with it, tossing it back and forth between her hands. "He'd freak out if he saw me do this."

"He'd force you into a breeding program. Harvest your eggs. Destroy you if you didn't comply."

Laurel sighed and let the ball of energy evaporate. "Is there another way?" She knotted her hands together.

Catherine leaned back in her chair and fixed her gaze on Laurel's face. "No."

Chapter Eighteen

The first pulse of energy shattered the doorframe of the house even as the wards held the centurion back. Laurel twisted and dodged the splinters that cascaded around her. Catherine put down her book and raised an eyebrow. "Friend of yours?"

Laurel shook the dust from her clothes. "No."

A second blast opened a small crack in the door. "Laurel? Come on, it's me, Sully. You don't have to be afraid. Come out. We know she tricked you. The family'll take care of you. Come on, Laurel. I'll get you a coffee. We can talk." The cajoling tone of his voice ratcheted up Laurel's anger. White-hot energy boiled up and out of her body. A flashing golden cloud of heat spun around her, a vortex of protective light.

Another pulse of energy pieced the door wards and stabbed through Laurel's veil of protection. Red vines of light twisted and wound their way around her body, trapping her, pulling her toward the door. Sully's grim face peered through the door. His hands were white knuckled across his weapon.

"Catherine!" Laurel shrieked. She twisted and raged against the bonds.

"Oh, for fuck's sake, I'm never going to finish this book." Catherine set the novel aside. "This is good practice. Focus on what you want. Don't be distracted by Sully's voice, or your past relationship. Use your power."

Sully growled. "Shut up, bitch. Don't listen to her, Laurel. Stop fighting me."

Laurel clenched her jaw against the pain of the red light and focused her energy. The light shifted and swirled, forming silver knives that sliced through the red light. A shrill scream sounded on the other side of the door. "Stop! Don't kill me, Laurel. Your parents wouldn't want that."

Mention of her parents tumbled her thoughts, and Laurel lost focus. The red light reknit and wound around her throat, sharp thorns digging into her flesh. She opened her mouth to scream, and the vine filled her mouth as it tightened around her throat. Lights flashed behind her eyes and her chest heaved, fighting the loss of air in her lungs. Laurel flailed, unable to summon her power. She slumped to her knees and panic set in as she was tugged toward the centurion.

Purple light flashed and swept over Laurel. The red vines shriveled and evaporated. She collapsed to her side gasping for air. A sharp scream rising in volume raged in her ears until it cut off. The sharp stench of burnt demon flesh stung Laurel's nose as stillness settled over the foyer.

"Relax, darling. You don't even need air. You have to stop thinking like a mortal. Your body can be destroyed but you can't be destroyed. Be fearless. Sentiment has no place in battle."

Laurel gazed up at Catherine and savored her transformation. Catherine's hair framed her head, a crown of intricately woven braids, and her skin shimmered and glowed beneath the azure-blue cloth that draped her frame.

Catherine extended her hand. "Get up, love, seeing you on your knees for anyone else disturbs me."

Laurel rose on shaky legs. "Sully?"

"Not a concern. But we need to prepare. Marcus will come himself now. And you must be ready."

Laurel rubbed her neck and the tender skin where Sully's magic had burned her. "I didn't think he'd try to end me."

Catherine shrugged. "To fail to bring you back would have meant his death. He had nothing to lose. If he brought your body back, he still would have met his obligation to Marcus."

*

Catherine tightened her magic about Laurel's body, the purple strands draped over her in a diamond pattern, restraining her body and energy. Her light-brown nipples were peaked. The bonds outlined her breasts perfectly. She adjusted the mirror to capture their reflections.

Laurel's eyes were closed and her breathing even.

"Open your eyes." Catherine stayed behind Laurel and held her gaze in the glass. "Now. Your task is to shed my bonds, and then—" She dipped her fingers between her legs before she brought them up to her mouth. Her tongue slid over her fingertips as she tasted herself. "Then you may have this."

Laurel panted, her hands opening and closing at her sides. Her shoulders flexed and bunched under the lines of light. "I don't know how."

Catherine landed a sharp crack on her ass. "You do know. Gather yourself. Focus on what you want."

Laurel groaned. "What if I hurt you?"

"You won't. I trust you, Laurel. Trust yourself. Or you will never be ready to confront Marcus." Catherine smoothed her hands over Laurel's breasts, tweaking her nipples before she feathered her fingers over her clit. "The moment you let go, let go of your fear, you will be more powerful than you've ever imagined. You've died in this world, what could you fear now? This bag of skin and bone is just that, it's lovely, but even if it is destroyed you will not be. Embrace it."

She jacked Laurel's clit slowly, and Laurel lifted her hips chasing the sensations of Catherine's touch. "If my body is not alive, why can I feel you? Feel your touch?" She rocked into Catherine's touch.

Catherine wrapped her arm around her waist and pulled her flush against her. "Because you remember. The sensations are etched upon your soul."

She drove her fingers deep and Laurel spread her legs wide.

"It's not real?"

"Do you remember me telling you I was as real as you wanted me to be?" Catherine kissed the side of her neck as she fucked her slowly. "We create what we want. You are capable of creating what you want. Embrace it, Laurel. Life for us is an illusion. A massive playground of what we want to be and how we want to feel."

She thrust harder and pushed Laurel over the edge and into bliss. She watched in the mirror as her face contorted into rapture, her body shaking and trembling in Catherine's arms. "This. This is what you crave. A lover's control. To surrender all. To obey my commands. Use that energy. Turn it, break free, and lick me. Show me how much you want me."

*

Catherine's command twisted inside Laurel's mind as pleasure coursed through her body. The purple bonds of light shimmered and tightened, the sensation of being restrained comforting, allowing her to thrash as she came. Waves of pleasures spiraled out from her body, taking her up and over. Her body writhed as she screamed out her pleasure. Lust, raw and unfettered longing, filled her. She needed to have Catherine in her mouth, to taste, to possess her, to give her what she had given Laurel.

Golden energy spiraled up from inside her, filled her, and she focused on the bonds, melting them gently, slipping them off. She spun and pushed into Catherine's arms. Laurel drew her stiff nipples over Catherine's skin. She kissed and licked and bit, rolling Catherine's flesh between her teeth as she moved down her body until she arrived at her heart's desire. Catherine's clit was slick and thick in her mouth. Her hands gripped Laurel's hair, tugging her close.

Laurel swirled her tongue over her, and then pressed her tongue deep. She twitched her tongue up and down, curling it, striving to hit the spot that would make Catherine moan and buck for more.

Catherine hissed her pleasure. "So good."

Laurel forged her energy into golden vines and wrapped them around Catherine's wrists. With a shift of her mind, she tugged and forced Catherine's bound hands over her head.

Given the freedom to do as she wished, Laurel gorged herself on Catherine's body, cupping and squeezing her breasts as she kissed and nibbled her neck. Catherine lifted her chin and exposed her throat. Laurel nipped harder, tasting the sweet nectar of Catherine's blood.

A deep groan rattled Catherine's chest. "Take it my love, drink freely, slake your thirst with me."

Laurel lapped and sucked, drowning in Catherine's bright blood. Each drop forged stronger links between them as their power intertwined. A whimper from Catherine echoed in the room. More. She wanted more. She held the image in her mind and a queening chair appeared. Laurel lifted her mouth from Catherine's neck and licked the spot and the skin closed over the wounds from her teeth.

Another mind shift, and Catherine was bound to the chair, her legs spread wide, her glistening center exposed.

"Yes. That's it. Take what you want, love." Catherine's eyes held Laurel's gaze. "I'm yours."

Laurel dropped to her knees and licked and sucked, gorging herself with the sweetness flowing from Catherine. Want, wild and wicked, filled her and she brought her fingers up and teased them over Catherine's slick labia. Catherine panted and groaned, held tight by Laurel's energy. Laurel reveled in the control, her ability to give Catherine pleasure, to be foremost in her mind. Laurel lifted her mouth and kissed the inside of Catherine's thighs and moved her mouth to her breasts, sucking a hard nipple between her lips.

Laurel lifted her head and stared into Catherine's eyes. "I want to fuck you."

"Do it then." Catherine's dark eyes glowed with a golden light.

Laurel stood and thrust her fingers deep and stroked hard. She bent and sucked Catherine's breasts before she moved to her mouth and kissed her. Laurel sucked on her bottom lip before she thrust her tongue deep. Catherine welcomed her, swallowing her kisses, surrendering her mouth to Laurel.

She rocked the heel of her hand over Catherine's clit as her body clutched at Laurel's fingers. Time stood still as Laurel's perfect fantasy spun out. Catherine's cries of pleasure filled the room.

With each stroke, each kiss, the scent of cedar and pine, and under it all the carnal scent of them whorled around them, filling Laurel's senses. One last thrust and Catherine snapped the bonds that held her and wrapped her legs and arms around Laurel as she shattered under her.

Chapter Nineteen

"He's coming here. Now." Her jaw was set, her shoulders rigid.

Catherine smoothed her hand over Laurel's arm. "You're ready. He has no idea how ready. You'll have the advantage. You will need to push it if you want to be free of him."

Laurel rested her chin on her chest and chewed her lip. "I know."

"He will appeal to your sentiment, raise up memories to disrupt you. You must not let him."

Laurel shuddered. "He'll use my parents. He always does."

"Did it ever occur to you that he might have been responsible for your parents' deaths?"

Laurel lifted her chin and met Catherine's gaze. "Do you know that?"

"No." Catherine's voice was soft. "But who else would have the power and connections to do it?"

Laurel scrubbed her hand over her face. "One more thing to ask him about."

Catherine clasped her hands together in front of her body. "Battle is not the time to ask questions. You need to focus. You'll need all of your power to beat Marcus." She spread her hands wide. "This and I will all disappear if he has his way. We've embarrassed him, defeated his best centurion. He's arrogant. Use that. He'll underestimate you, test you. Do not be deceived. He didn't get where he is in the clan without being cunning as well as powerful."

A dark-blue light lit the sidewalk outside the townhouse. Laurel and Catherine turned to the window.

Catherine stood directly behind Laurel and rested her palm in the center of her back. "Steady on."

A long black car rolled up to the front of the town house. Two centurions exited and opened the rear door. Marcus slid out of the car and glanced up. His eyes glowed red, the veneer of his humanness melting under their observation. His face twisted in a smile.

"You would think he would grow tired of appearing like a second-rate mobster."

Laurel lifted her eyebrow. "His look is a bit outdated."

Catherine turned to look at Laurel. "Are you ready?"

Laurel stretched her back and rolled her shoulders. "As I'll ever be."

The hiss of melting metal and burning wood announced Marcus's arrival.

"Showtime." Catherine held her arm out indicating Laurel should proceed. "After you."

Chapter Twenty

Marcus strode up the steps. "Laurel! Don't make me search for you. You won't like it when I find you if you run from me."

Laurel squared her shoulders. "I'm right here. Not sure why you're shouting."

Marcus turned the corner and stepped into the living room. "You killed Sully. That's why I'm shouting." His voice dropped to a sharp whisper. "And you forced my hand in ending Nadia."

"Sully started it, and as for Nadia, that's on you. You sent her to retrieve me like I was a child."

Marcus spread his hands wide. "So, it is true. The mouse has become a lion. Imagine that." With a quick flip of his wrist, blue light shot out toward Laurel, the strands coalesced into a net. The net wrapped tightly around Laurel and barbs hooked into her flesh.

Laurel inhaled sharply and focused on the images of the voiceless children of the pit. Her energy gathered and she shredded the net. It fell into pieces and dissolved at her feet. "You'll have to do better than that, uncle."

Marcus snarled. "Where is she? I know she put you up to this. This is not you, Laurel. We're family. She can't protect you forever."

Laurel tilted her head to the side. "The only thing I need protection from is you."

Marcus's voice dropped to a whisper. "After everything I've done for you? This is how it ends? I've only ever asked one thing of you. What would your parents think?"

A knot of pain blossomed in Laurel's chest. "No. You don't get to pull that. They would not expect me to be your chattel, breeding stock for your sick plan."

Marcus raised his head. His eyes glowed with blue light. "You have no vision. Like your parents."

"Is that why you killed them? No vision? Or because they accomplished on their own what you had been trying to force?"

A flare of blue light overwhelmed Laurel. Gooey thick strings of midnight blue covered her body. The more she struggled the tighter the bonds became. She fell to the floor. Her chest heaved as panic set in.

"I told you I wouldn't be nice. I asked you for what I wanted. Now I'll just take it."

He stepped close, leaned over her, and gripped Laurel's hair, yanking hard. "Fucking dyke. I should have ended you like the other failures." Spittle flecked his narrow lips.

Laurel's mind skittered to the images of the children in the basement, to Manny with his throat slit wide, and her parents burnt and twisted on the sidewalk. A ball of hot energy gathered in her core. It spun and gathered, whirling and twisting like a cyclone.

"It's over, Marcus." Laurel flexed her energy. Her skin glowed with purple light. Marcus's hand smoked where it held her hair.

A sharp howl escaped his lips. The purple light melted the blue goo. It puddled and sizzled around Laurel. The smell of burning flesh filled the room. Marcus wrapped his burning hands around Laurel's throat, his claws digging into her neck. "Not so easy to kill me, is it?"

Over his right shoulder Catherine appeared, the glowing kris in her hands. She raised it high, both hands wrapped around the hilt. A hum of words filled Laurel's ears as Catherine chanted while she lowered the shimmering blade. She drove it deep into Marcus's back. The point of the blade protruded from his chest. His energy vanished, his power shuttered as if by a switch, and he crumpled to his side.

Laurel crab-walked away from him and then stood.

Catherine withdrew the glowing blade. Marcus rolled to his back, his eyes wide. "You!"

"Yes. Me." She grabbed his hair with one hand and placed the edge of the kris against his throat. "Surprised? You should've taken better care who you paid to do your dirty work, Marcus."

Manny appeared and placed his hand on Catherine's wrist. "Don't."

"Why not?" Catherine's teeth pulled back in a snarl as she lifted the blade and offered it to Manny. "You want to do it?"

"Not me." Manny stepped aside. The legion of children from the pit hovered behind him, their eyes fixed on Marcus.

Marcus eyes widened. "What? No. No. End me. Do it." He clutched at Catherine's leg.

"Oh no, Marcus, I think Manny has the right idea. I'm sure they'll show you the same mercy you showed them."

The children gathered around Marcus and lifted him, their hands latching on to him as he scrabbled in a vain attempt to escape. His screams filled the room as the children bore him away to the cellar. Manny nodded to Laurel and Catherine. "Thank you."

Chapter Twenty-One

The sun shone in though the living room window and lit the space. Catherine gazed out at the smattering of people hurrying down the sidewalk. "Take me to your favorite place to eat."

"You just had breakfast."

Catherine patted her stomach. "I have spent years in this house dreaming of all the things I would eat when I had a body again. Let's go."

Catherine extended her hand and Laurel took it. The electric current of their connection flared as she led Laurel down the stairs. Laurel opened the door and Catherine stepped back.

Laurel laid her palm on her arm. "Are you okay?"

Catherine turned to Laurel. "I don't even know."

"If you're not ready, we can wait."

Catherine firmed her chin. "I'm not worried."

Laurel raised her eyebrow.

"Much." Catherine took a small step forward.

"I'll be with you."

Catherine grimaced. "Even you couldn't save me from oblivion if we've miscalculated."

Laurel drew herself up. "I would find you. Travel all the way to the depths of the abyss to bring you back."

Catherine tilted her head. "You already did."

"Would you like to check out my restaurant?"

Catherine started. "What?"

Laurel grinned. "As Marcus's only heir, I now own his share of Sanctuary."

Catherine tucked her clutch under her arm and smoothed a hand over her skirt. "Am I overdressed?"

Laurel raked her gaze over her thick curves set off by her mid-century skirt and sweater set. "Not at all." She held out her hand. "Come on. They do a great brunch. The stuffed French toast is to die for."

"Interesting choice of words."

"Not what I meant but I know you'll love it." Laurel lifted her hand and pressed her lips to her palm. "And then we can come home and work off the calories."

"You are incorrigible, now that you've got your feet under you."

Laurel kissed her wrist, her lips lighting a fire under Catherine's skin. "Do you want meek, unsure Laurel back?"

"Never."

Laurel pressed a kiss to her cheek. "Let's go."

They stepped out of the townhouse and walked down the stairs hand in hand. A few folks looked up from their phones, but most people ignored them. Catherine's long legs and quick pace had Laurel hustling to stay even with her. "Slow down, please, it's not a race."

Catherine glanced at Laurel. "I'm sorry. I almost want to run. I can't believe I'm outside."

Her giddy laugh made Laurel laugh too. She glanced at Catherine's pumps. "You can run in those?"

Catherine laid her hand on Laurel's arms. "Darling, I've destroyed armies in heels. I have centuries of practice."

Catherine glanced up as the rows of town houses gave way to high-rise buildings. "There was the most delightful deli on this corner." A frown swept over her face and she slowed her steps. "This was a neighborhood. Town houses and apartment buildings." She stopped as they reached the corner and turned in a slow circle. "There was a school down that street. And shops. Gone."

Laurel touched her arm. "This way. It's in the next block."

Catherine pressed her lips together and followed Laurel to the coffee shop door that led to Sanctuary.

*

Their brunch had not disappointed. Laurel lay on the sofa and rubbed her tummy. "I think I hurt myself eating."

Catherine snorted. "Like that could happen."

"Did you like it? Being outside?"

Catherine shrugged. "Not as much as I thought I would."

A frown swept over Laurel's face. "We could go somewhere else next time."

"It's not where we go, it's the things that are not where they used to be. The feel is different."

"Sixty years is a long time."

Catherine huffed. "I've lived centuries, but never been shut off from the world, never as a prisoner. I would change as the world evolved. I feel out of step now. I don't know if I want to stay on this plane."

Laurel hugged her close. "You'll catch up."

"I don't know if I want to." Catherine pushed back from Laurel's arms and left the couch. She paced the living room. "You don't have to leave this world. You're young. And now you have many lifetimes to explore in this dimension. I don't want to hold you back."

Laurel frowned. "You want to leave me? Aren't we bonded?"

"A bond is not a prison. We set the rules, we will always have a connection. I don't want you to stay with me if you want to stay here, if you have places you want to travel to. Or others you want to be with."

"Is this about Carla? She always flirts. There's nothing between us."

"Do you wish there to be? She is exquisite."

Laurel stepped in front of her, blocking her path, and placed both hands on her shoulders. "I want you, Catherine. I want to be with you. I don't have any interest in Carla or anyone one else. I want you. However that is. Wherever that is." She squeezed Catherine's shoulders. "We can take as much time as you need to feel comfortable in the world again. Or travel to whatever dimension you want." Laurel cupped her face. "What's the use of being immortal if I can't spend it with you?"

"You say that now. What will you say three hundred years from now? You're what? Thirty-two? How can you be so sure?"

Laurel gripped her hips and brushed a kiss over her lips before she spoke against her mouth. "I'm thirty-six and I don't know what I'll say in three hundred years. Guess you'll have to stick around and find out."

Catherine tugged her close and held tight. "Always?"

"Always." Laurel rubbed her back in small circles. "Come on, I have some new ideas for the playroom."

"The playroom? We have a playroom?"

Laurel stepped back and held out her hand. "We do now. And you mentioned a kneeling bench you wanted."

"You didn't."

"Oh, I most certainly did." Laurel walked backward toward the stairwell.

"Wait. We haven't decided anything."

"Do we need to decide now? You have a schedule, or appointment, I don't know about?" Laurel stepped up on the landing, unbuckled her belt, and stripped off her jeans. She tossed them aside before she pulled her shirt over her head and let it fall to the floor. She crooked her finger at Catherine. "Come on. We can be serious tomorrow."

"You said that yesterday."

"We have all the tomorrows we need to figure things out." Laurel's mouth turned down. "Unless—" she crossed her arms over her chest and a flush colored her pale skin. "—you're done with me?" The fear and uncertainty in her voice broke open Catherine's heart.

"Never." Catherine strode to the landing, swept her hands under her legs, and lifted Laurel into her arms, holding her close to her chest. She peered into Laurel's eyes and held her gaze. "Never, my love."

Laurel wrapped her arms around Catherine's neck and snuggled into her skin as she carried her up the stairs. The stairwell transformed into a mountain path, trees grew up thick, jeweled orchids flowered, and dark-purple vines twisted in an arch over them. A riot of color and floral scents blended with cedar and pine as their energy twisted and twined together as they climbed toward their future.

Acknowledgements

This collaboration is a result of several virtual meetings between two of my favorite people in the world. Fiona and Megan had charmed me with their published works before we ever met in person. It was a joy to work on this project together. I look forward to many more years of friendship and future collaborations. My editor, Elizabeth Coldwell's steadfast support and encouragement makes everything seem possible, and for that I am grateful. To my Con Misfits and Lesfic Sprinters, my world is brighter because you all are always there for me, thank you.

About Brenda Murphy

Brenda Murphy writes short stories and novels. She is a member of the Golden Crown Literary Society. Her novel *Double Six* won the GCLS 2020 Goldie for Erotica. When she is not loitering at her local library and writing, she wrangles one dog and an unrepentant parrot. She writes about life, books, photography, and writing on her blog, writingwhiledistracted.com.

I hope you enjoyed reading this book as much as I enjoyed writing it. For information on book signings, appearances, work in progress snippets, previews and sneak-peeks, sign up for my email list at:

Website
www.brendalmurphy.com

Facebook
www.facebook.com/Writing-While-Distracted

Twitter
@bmurphysideshow

Other NSP books by author:

Dominique and Other Stories
One

The Rowan House series
Sum of the Whole
Both Ends of the Whip
Knotted Legacy
Complex Dimensions
Double Six

University Square series
On The Square
Lockset

With Megan Hart
Soul Burn

WE CHOOSE TO

BE

Megan Hart

For everyone who loves a little bite.

Chapter One

"That's all there is to it? I thought there would be…more."

The man in front of Hadassah wore his business suit like it had been grown on him—both in its perfect fit and in the way she could not have imagined him in anything more casual. No golf tees and khakis for this guy, no way. He leaned forward now, his big hands on the tabletop, the wound on the back of his right one still slightly seeping below the gauze pad. Sweat had pearled in his hairline. His lips, chapped and raw, showed where he'd been chewing them.

It was almost always the same with these people. The same questions, the same fears, the same irrational demands. Many of them had already made their way through a plethora of fortune-tellers, psychics, tarot card readers, crystal-ball gazers, and tea-leaf interpreters before they found their way to Hadassah Batrivka's office, but invariably, they expected her to somehow put on the same kind of spectacle. Like a sideshow performance. She was used to it, but that didn't mean she wasn't also tired of it.

"That's it," Hadassah said calmly as she slipped a hand beneath the table, ready to trigger the alarm that would send Sanctuary's security rushing in to help her. It wouldn't have been the first time, but she always hated having to do it. People came here for help, and even if they deserved the rough exit, having them hoisted out by the scruffs of their necks always seemed to upset the balance of things. Ruined the rest of the day, for sure.

"Listen here, you..." Words failed him, and he became visibly smaller. Shrunken. He let his head fall onto the table as his shoulders heaved with a series of guttural cries that would have broken her heart, if this guy wasn't such a colossal piece of human garbage.

He didn't deserve her compassion, not really. He'd come to her, after all, with the desperation born of someone who'd tried every other avenue without getting the answers he wanted. But they were the only answers she had for him, and possibly unlike the others whose advice he'd sought, Hadassah could be sure that hers was accurate. At least until and unless he made some changes in his life, and he didn't seem the kind of guy to take any kind of personal responsibility for anything. It was always going to be someone else's fault. Someone else to blame. No matter what she'd told him about his part in his own destiny, he wouldn't believe her.

"But you took...you took my fucking...blood," he gasped out. "How can you read my blood and not be able to tell me what I want to *know*?"

Hadassah spoke sharply, well beyond the limit of her patience with this guy. Her fingertip stroked the call button, but she didn't yet press it. "I told you what you wanted to know. That does not mean it was what you wanted to hear."

Mr. Businessman lifted his head. His eyes were red-rimmed and bloodshot. Stubble dotted his cheeks and chin. He passed a fissured tongue over the wreckage of his lips. His fingers twitched on the tabletop. The blood had stopped leaking from the slice in the back of his hand.

Hadassah's didn't move her hand, but she relaxed a bit, now. Years of dealing with people like this guy had honed her skills in disarming a situation. She didn't need blood to read every single emotion or potential reaction.

"It's time for you to go, now," she said, still calm, her voice still soothing. Not giving him an option, but not being aggressive either.

"Do it again. Take more this time." He pushed up the sleeves of his jacket and shirt to expose a wrist encircled by a very expensive watch. "Take it from here, right from the vein. You didn't get enough the first time."

"It doesn't make a difference where I take it from. The answers are the same. And it doesn't matter if I take more," she added, "because the answers aren't going to change."

Not without some kind of changes from him, first, she thought, but didn't say aloud. She'd already gone through all that with him. How he had the responsibility for his own future, and she was only an interpreter of what she read in his blood. Clearly, he hadn't listened, but she didn't make the rules.

He stood and shook a finger at her with a trembling hand. "Damn you. Right to whatever hell will have you."

"You can find your own way out," Hadassah replied without raising her voice.

He did, stumbling a bit. His reaction to what she'd revealed to him had been so extreme that she hadn't offered him a cup of the restorative herbal tea she usually gave her clients to counteract the effects of what she'd pulled out of them. It was not the blood loss, since nobody would ever be adversely impacted by losing less than what they took if you needed your cholesterol checked. It was what she removed along *with* the blood that left her clients weak and shaky, on unsteady legs. Some took it worse than others. This guy was pretty bad off, but Hadassah didn't care if he fell flat on his face in the street and broke out all his teeth. As far as she was concerned, someone who'd taken another life on purpose deserved whatever punishment they got, and probably worse than they ever would.

"Bitch," he tossed back over his shoulder as he passed through the doorway.

Hadassah waited until he'd slammed the door behind him before she relaxed in her chair. She'd been called worse, by better people than that asshole. Still, the negative energy he'd been pushing at her for the past hour had left her in dire need of her own restorative, and she was not going to find it in the form of herbal tea.

Quickly, she put away the tools of her craft. As a hemomancer, she was immune to all blood diseases, but she put the sharp into the biohazard container anyway—her practice might be magic, but Sanctuary's rules for renting space followed all current legal and health guidelines. She tidied the remains of the alcohol prep pad, cotton balls, and adhesive bandage she hadn't even used. Her ancestors had simply sliced a vein with a thorn, a pine, a needle, or in some cases, an exquisitely honed bone, but modern times demanded updated practices.

By the time she'd finished clearing her workspace, the clock showed three in the afternoon. Never mind that "it's five o'clock somewhere" baloney, it was wine o'clock right now. Fortunately, the bar at Sanctuary was always open, and it took only a few minutes to get to it from her office.

*

"Hey, Red." Hadassah tipped a nod at the bartender.

"The usual?" asked Red, a statuesque, flame-haired witch who'd never, in Hadassah's memory, gone by any other name.

"Yes. Thank you." Hadassah settled onto her favorite seat, the one at the end of the bar, and accepted the generously poured glass of house red wine. She'd never asked what it was, a Cabernet, a Merlot, a blend, but she had a suspicion it was something special to Sanctuary. Therefore, like everything and everyone else in this place, it was unique and unclassifiable.

The first sip spread slow warmth throughout her veins, and as always, Hadassah closed her eyes to let the sensation fill her up. The liquid went into her stomach, but the alcohol, plus whatever else made this wine so special, went almost immediately into her veins. She never missed the irony that she, a hemomancer, should be so affected by something that travelled in her bloodstream.

"I'll have what she's having."

Startled, because when she'd sat down there'd been nobody else at the bar, Hadassah opened her eyes. The woman sitting two stools away wasn't looking at her, and she had not even the barest hint of a smile on her face to go along with what had to be a joke. Right? At least an attempt at one? The callout to the famous scene in *When Harry Met Sally…* had to have been on purpose, but the woman who'd said it was showing no signs of humor.

Now the newcomer stared at the sloshing glass of crimson fluid Red had set in front of her as though she'd never seen a glass of wine before. She curled the fingers of one hand around the fragile stem so carefully Hadassah wondered if she'd been recently injured. Her hands were bigger than seemed to match the rest of her lean frame, the fingers long and slender, with black-painted nails that tapered to points. They matched her black hair, pulled into a loose and tangled ponytail at the base of her neck. Even gathered that way, it fell in thick waves to the small of her back. In profile, she had strong features, including thick dark brows that furrowed now.

She was…mysterious. Intriguing. She was *gorgeous*, and Hadassah felt the stirring of anticipation low in her belly.

The woman sipped cautiously and grimaced before setting the glass back on the bar.

"No good?" Red had been watching the woman as carefully as Hadassah had.

"It is good."

"You look like you'd prefer something else," Hadassah said to capture the woman's attention.

She almost regretted it when the woman turned her full body on the stool to face her. In contrast to the glorious mess of her hair, her features were stern and fierce, neither masculine nor feminine, but not quite androgynous either. Hadassah tried to pin down her appearance but came up short. Not fey. Not witch. Not were, either, although this woman had a feral air about her suggesting something animalistic. Vamp? But no, she didn't fit that either.

Could she be...human?

Humans came into Sanctuary all the time, but they were almost always supernaturally Talented, or if not, they were in the company of a supernatural. Hadassah herself was human, although her ability to use blood for divination purposes was inherited, genetic, and therefore meant that at least somewhere far back in the branches of her family tree, something Other had been there to roost.

"No. I like. It." The woman spoke in a halting manner, almost a lilt, that suggested an accent but not one Hadassah could distinguish. As if to prove her statement as truth, she lifted the glass again to her lips and drank, gulping, until she'd consumed the entire glass.

Hadassah blinked. A flush gathered at the base of her throat as the woman licked the remnants of the red wine from her lips. Wine was only *one* of the things that soothed aches left behind from a day of reading blood.

"Another?" Red asked, her tone dry. She'd put a hand on one lush hip and was giving the woman at the other end of the bar a long, assessing look.

The woman's nod was sharp. Almost mechanical. "Yes."

"You got it." Red filled the glass with another of her signature generous pours and then looked at Hadassah, who'd barely sipped from hers. "You let me know when you need another."

Hadassah twisted on the barstool to look straight on at the dark-haired woman. "I'm Hadassah."

The woman looked like she was about to gulp down the second glass with as much ferocity as she had the first, but something stopped her. She sipped instead. She was, Hadassah realized, emulating the way she'd taken her own sip.

"And you are?" Hadassah prompted when she didn't answer.

"Thirsty."

"I mean...what's your name?"

The woman paused with the glass halfway to her lips. She put it carefully down on the bar. "I have always called myself Yael."

In addition to the accent that Hadassah could not quite place, Yael had an interesting way of phrasing things. The name itself gave Hadassah pause. As the bearer of a biblical name herself, she couldn't help feeling an immediate kinship with the woman.

But no, Hadassah thought as she lifted her glass toward Yael. It was more than the name. There was something else about Yael...something that called to her.

"Here's to new acquaintances," Hadassah said.

After a hesitation, Yael lifted her own glass. "All right."

They were too far away to clink the glasses, so Hadassah simply tipped hers toward her mouth. After another of those seconds-long hesitations, Yael did the same. The red wine had stained her lips.

Another flush teased its way up Hadassah's throat into her face. Many, many times she'd ended a session with a client by coming here to the bar, drinking a few glasses of wine, and finding a partner for the night. As far as ways to release accumulated tension went, she could have done worse to herself. Today, however, the bar was empty except for Yael, and while there was something compelling about her, there was also definitely something odd.

Not that odd was itself actually strange here in Sanctuary. The club featured this lovely bar, a fine-dining restaurant, and a cigar room, as well as several rental spaces for practitioners like Hadassah. The clientele was almost exclusively supernatural folk, or, as Hadassah liked to think of herself, supernatural-adjacent. To stand out as "different" here was no small feat, but Yael was managing superbly.

Hadassah had always had a soft spot for a mystery. "I haven't seen you around here before, Yael. Are you new to town?"

"I am new."

"Where did you come from?"

Yael blinked like a bird, rapidly and somehow sharply. "Where I had been before."

Hadassah could not stop the burble of sudden laughter that slipped out of her. "Right. Of course."

To her surprise, Yael laughed too. Her soft giggle had a bit of grit in it. Husky. "Where did you come from?"

"Me? I've always lived in the city. Born and raised." Hadassah sipped more wine, not surprised to find she was almost finished with it. She looked for Red, but the bartender had disappeared momentarily.

"Born." Yael said the word as though she were tasting it, rolling the single syllable on her tongue. "And...raised."

"Yep. I'm a real native. Not sure where I might be going," Hadassah said with a chuckle, "but I sure know where I've been."

Yael tilted her head and gave Hadassah an up-and-down look. "Does anyone know where they are going?"

"It's possible to try to find out, if they don't. I can do that."

"You're talking about fortune telling."

"I'm talking about magic," Hadassah said.

The dark-haired woman frowned and stared into the depths of her glass for a moment before saying, "*You* could tell me everything I need to know?"

"Yes," Hadassah said as a small flame kindled inside her, growing hotter. "Everything."

Chapter Two

"Sit." Hadassah waved a hand in the direction of the small table and two chairs placed toward the back of the small office space. "I'm just going to get set up."

Yael didn't sit right away. She took a few minutes to look around the room. Tapestries in vibrant colors covered the walls, giving the illusion of windows behind them, although she could tell the office was a completely interior room. Bookcases stuffed with books and other objects like goblets, bowls, and small cases lined the back of the room. A door along the back wall had been left cracked open, and through it she could see a sink. A soft scent of flowers hung in the air, without any hint of sulfur or something rotten. Hadassah didn't delve into dark magic, or if she did, she was extremely careful to hide all the evidence of it.

"Sit," Hadassah repeated, but gently.

Yael pulled out the chair and did as she'd been told. She'd been created for obedience. The instinct was fading day after day, but she didn't know if it would ever go away completely. The longer she spent inhabiting this vessel, the less she felt connected to what she was and where she'd come from...but she could only stay in this body for as long as it lasted, and humans were notoriously short-lived. At least compared to demons.

"Have you ever had a reading before? Any kind, not necessarily from hemomancy." Hadassah turned around in her chair to pull open a drawer in the cabinet behind her. She pulled out a small plastic bowl wrapped in cling wrap and added a long rectangular leather case, a bottle of clear liquid, and a small cup of fluffy white cotton balls. She put everything on the table and busied herself pulling on a pair of purple disposable gloves and then unwrapping the materials from their protective coverings.

"No." Yael hesitated, studying the process with much interest.

Hadassah studied her. "No Tarot? No tea leaves? Nothing like that?"

"No."

"Are you familiar with how hemomancy works?"

"Blood magic," Yael said. "Yes. I understand how it works. Blood is the source of everything."

It had been her source, certainly, her natural form summoned with the blood of the witch who'd called her. There'd been blood in the creation of this body she wore now too. It had been pushed from its mother's womb with blood and sweat and screams. With pain, but also joy. Yael had entered this world with blood and pain, but she had torn through the veil between realms with her own talons and teeth and suffered the agony of that birthing. If there had been joy at her arrival, it had not been her own.

"Good. Then I don't have to worry about you fainting or anything like that?" Hadassah spoke the words lightly, but with an edge to her tone that made it clear she'd had trouble in the past.

Yael shook her head. "I won't."

"All right. If you do start to feel faint, let me know right away. I have smelling salts. Also, all of my equipment is sterile and disposed of after each use. I'll be making a fairly deep wound, but due to the nature of this particular sort of magic, you'll be healed quite quickly. You should have no lingering effects. Are you ready to get started?" Hadassah reached across the table to take Yael's hand. Their fingers linked. Palms touched. Hadassah's eyebrows rose a little, and she smiled but said nothing as she released Yael's hand and turned it palm down, resting on the table.

With the other hand Hadassah lifted a small scalpel she'd removed from its protective paper covering. She used a small bottle of clear liquid and a cotton ball to clean the back of Yael's hand, tossing the used cotton into a can beneath the table when she'd finished. Keeping the scalpel steady, she once more took Yael's hand.

"It's going to hurt, but it will be over fast," Hadassah warned.

Yael had been told that before, plenty of times, and it had never once been true. The witch who'd summoned her had been arrogant, demanding, and short of temper. When she was displeased, she'd often resorted to using her magic to cause pain—at least until she'd summoned Yael to do it for her. What had started as using Yael for protection became retaliation against anyone who crossed her, for any reason at all. A person who cut in front of her at the grocery store, someone who wrote something vaguely unkind online, a clerk who forgot to give her a receipt. Any and all slights had become reasons for her to call Yael down upon them, and if Yael did not leap to obey, the witch had no problem hurting Yael in retribution.

Some demons of a different constitution might have obeyed with glee at being asked to commit constant carnage, but the witch, in her arrogance, had misread her instructional texts and refused the counsel of those with greater knowledge and power. She hadn't understood that demons, like the angels with whom they shared an origin, had a hierarchy. Not all of them had been made as warriors. Her disappointment at discovering that Yael was not the kind of soldier she desired was surpassed only by her fury when Yael had refused to continue serving her.

"You don't use any of those tools?" Yael gestured with her free hand toward the shelves of carved stone bowls and engraved silver knives displayed in velvet-lined cases.

Hadassah smiled and shook her head. "They are certainly more impressive, right? But hard to sterilize and certainly not disposable. Fortunately, I don't need all the pomp and circumstance to practice my art."

Yael thought of the witch, who delighted in the trappings of her rituals without fully being capable of controlling them. "I prefer competence to showing off."

"Me too," Hadassah said after a moment's hesitation. She gave Yael a curious look that faded quickly. "You're going to feel a sting."

The cut across Yael's hand went deep, as Hadassah had promised, but Yael had not been as ready as she'd thought. She'd taken this body from one who no longer needed it, but she'd not yet learned all the workings of it. She'd been teaching herself how to assuage the needs for sleep, food, sex...and now, she was learning the feeling of real, true pain.

"There we go," Hadassah murmured, her gaze on the crimson blood welling out from the slash on the back of Yael's hand. She turned Yael's hand over so the blood could drip into the bowl between them. "Just a minute or so. You'll be all right."

"Are you...do you offer this comfort to all of your clients?" Yael bit the words out, her jaw clenched. Once she'd been able to fully manipulate all blood, but now she could only watch it draining from her.

Hadassah glanced up with another look of faint surprise. "Only the ones who need it."

The hemomancer bent once more over the bowl and pressed the gauze cloth onto Yael's cut to dab away the welling blood, which was already slowing. She placed Yael's hand gently on the table and then cupped the bowl of blood with her own two hands and drew it toward her. Her brow furrowed.

"What do you want to know?" she asked.

"You said you could tell me everything," Yael answered.

Hadassah looked up. "Narrow it down for me. One thing at a time."

"Is there a limit to how much I can ask?"

"Yes," Hadassah said. "But I can't tell you what the limit is, only that we will reach it at some point."

"And then?" Yael wanted to check the wound beneath the gauze. The pain, as Hadassah had promised, was already fading, and she wanted to see if the cut was too.

"Then you'll have to wait until another day. Another drawing of blood. It's magic, not science," Hadassah said. "Magic is notoriously imprecise. So, start with one thing you'd like to know, and I'll see what I can do."

"Am I in danger?" The words slipped from Yael's lips like stones dropping onto glass, cracking the air between them.

If the question shocked or concerned Hadassah, she didn't show any signs of it. She leaned forward, studying the small amount of blood in the plastic bowl. She passed a hand over it. Then again, in the opposite direction. Her lips pursed as she spoke under her breath. It was not an incantation, yet the words tugged at something deep inside Yael. A sensation of fire licked along her veins and the blood flowing there. She hissed in a breath at the sting.

"Are you all right?" Hadassah looked at her.

Yael could not speak, only nod. The flesh of her hand beneath the cloth itched and burned. Alternating ice and fire filled her right down to the capillaries. Her fingers and toes twitched, tingling. Was this what every seeker felt, when asking Hadassah for answers? Or did this body react this way because of Yael's true nature?

"There is danger surrounding you, yes," the hemomancer said when Yael did not reply.

Yael closed her eyes briefly. "How can I protect myself?"

"I see the need for you to hide. Be hidden. To...mask yourself. Disguise," Hadassah corrected. "I'm not sure if that means literally or figuratively. It could mean going quiet on social media or changing your phone number. Deleting an email account. It could mean something more drastic, like moving to a new city, for example."

Or taking a new physical form, Yael thought, but did not say out loud. Hadassah again passed her hand over the bowl. Yael's hand burned more fiercely, but ice invaded her body. She blinked rapidly, unused to the sensations rocketing through her. Was this what it felt like to lose consciousness? She breathed out, then in. Her vision wavered before steadying.

"What will happen to me?"

"So, what you have to understand is that the future is not written in stone. Or blood. Your choices change what happens to you," Hadassah said.

"How do I know what are the right choices?"

Hadassah gave a small, low, and rueful chuckle. "You don't always know, Yael. That's the way life works. All I can read from your blood is what path you're on, and where it could potentially lead. No more than that. It's always up to you, in the end, what you do."

Yael's teeth chattered. She'd never felt so cold, but Hadassah showed no signs of being uncomfortable with the temperature. It was all inside her. She clenched her jaw to stop the chattering, but Hadassah still looked concerned.

"Are you all right? If you're feeling faint—"

"I'm not," Yael interrupted.

Hadassah nodded. "You can change your mind, you know. Sometimes, people think they want to know, but they really don't."

"I want to know." She *had* to know. Was the witch going to come after her? Had taking this body been the wrong choice?

"All right, then. Let me see what I can tell you."

Again, Hadassah bent over the bowl. She murmured more words, the sound of them delicate but also strong. Like the woman herself, Yael thought, studying her. Anyone who could control their talents well enough to utilize them for the sake of others had to be strong, in body, will and mind.

"This is strange," Hadassah said with a quick glance at Yael.

The ice turned to a rush of liquid warmth, flooding her. Heat rose up her throat. Into her cheeks. She parted her lips to let her tongue dip out, pressing the lower one. She tasted salt. She was sweating.

Now, Yael thought. *Now she will tell me she knows what I am and what I have done...*

"I'm sorry," Hadassah said. "I can't see anything for you."

*

Hadassah pushed her chair back, unease twisting in her chest. She stopped herself from making another pass over the bowl of blood. There was nothing more for her to discover in it and pushing for it would only end up making her sick or weak.

Unless she was actively using it to do a reading, Hadassah's magic stayed spooled inside her like a ribbon—and like a ribbon, it could tangle. In the beginning, before she'd learned how to control it, Hadassah had been untidy with her talents. They'd spilled out of her in messy, fraying threads, and she'd had a helluva time smoothing them enough for them to be of any use. Hemomancy was supposed to be like weaving a tapestry or doing embroidery—a careful, creative method of sewing together the images into a bigger picture. It had taken Hadassah years to learn how to control it, much less interpret the fleeting, shifting images she drew forth from the blood.

Even now, there were times when she hadn't rewound her spool as neatly as she should have, times when the magic she pulled from herself stretched too thin or snagged along the way, or she tried too hard to strain the limits of her talents, and instead knotted them into an untenable mess. It could take her days after that to work out all the kinks and bends before she could even think about doing another reading. If she was even more careless, she could do real, physical harm to her body.

"I'm sorry, but there's nothing to see," she said.

"Is something wrong?" Yael sounded alarmed, but at least now her voice was stronger, and she didn't seem like she was going to pass out. She sat up straight in her seat.

Hadassah forced a smile. "No, nothing like that. I warned you there was a limit to what I'd be able to see for you. It looks like we reached it sooner than expected."

There *was* more to it than that. Hadassah had never been cut short so fast during any reading, not even when she'd been apprenticing and hadn't been able to pace how much information she pulled out. But that was the way of magic, she told herself as she set about tidying up the table. Even when you'd been practicing your craft for almost your entire life, you could still be surprised by what happened...or what didn't.

"Was it something I did?" Yael asked.

"No. It happens sometimes, that's all. Magic is an imprecise talent. It's unusual not to get some sort of reading, but not impossible. You might be tired. Maybe a little anemic?"

That honestly shouldn't matter, but it was the only explanation Hadassah could make. There'd been times when she hadn't been able to do a reading because her own talents hadn't been honed enough. This was the first time she'd ever been simply cut off.

Yael stood. She took the gauze off her hand and peered at the smooth skin, marred by only the faintest line. She gave Hadassah a look. "The cut is almost gone."

Hadassah paused at that. It wasn't totally unheard of for clients to heal quickly, but she'd never had one leave her office without at least some residual wound. Yael definitely had some super in her...but what? It would be rude to ask.

"You heal fast. You might feel some tenderness there for a few more hours, so don't be surprised." Hadassah held out her hand for the gauze, which was spotted with only a few drops of blood. She tossed it, along with her gloves, into the trash can.

Yael looked hesitant, studying her hand. "Now what happens?"

"Nothing happens. You can choose to take what I saw for you and follow it or ignore it."

"What happens if I ignore it?"

Hadassah laughed ruefully. "I don't know."

"Because you didn't see my future."

Hadassah shook her head. "That's part of it. But remember what I said—"

"Yes. My choices change what occurs. What's the point, then, in trying to find out what your future holds? If it's simple enough to change it?" Yael's question was aggressive, but her tone remained neutral.

Hadassah went to the small fridge behind her desk and pulled out a bottle of sparkling water. She poured two glasses, added the sifting of restorative herbs to make the chilled tea, and handed one to Yael. "Some people believe that knowing what could happen tells them enough about what they wish could happen, or what they don't want to happen. So, they can pursue a path, or avoid one."

"But you can't ever really know, then, how those changes make a difference, yes?" Yael sipped from the glass and then lifted it to look. "Anise."

She had such an odd demeanor, but Hadassah found it thoroughly charming. If emotions could trigger alarms, a klaxon would be sounding inside her right now. Red Alert. Warning. *You're about to get way too invested in this stranger.*

Hadassah's first teacher, Regina, had told her working the blood magic didn't affect everyone the same way. Some were drawn to gluttony of food and drink. Some to frantic exercise. Some to sex. Utilizing her skills always triggered arousal; Hadassah was used to that. But sex was not necessarily intimacy or affection—at least, it shouldn't be. So why was that what she was feeling right now for Yael? An attraction, Hadassah told herself. Nothing deeper or more meaningful than that. And yet...

"I owe you compensation now." Yael reached for her black leather crossbody bag.

"No. Don't worry about it. It wasn't a complete reading." Hadassah waved a hand. She was not in the habit of giving free readings. Even if they ended up truncated for one reason or another, she always required full payment. "Are you going to be okay?"

It was kind of against the rules, unspoken as they were, to ask too many personal questions about what a reading revealed. Or what it didn't. She told herself she was just being careful, making sure that Yael wasn't going to keel over. It was more than that though. Hadassah wasn't quite ready for Yael to walk out of her office, and maybe, out of her life. She really needed to get a hold of herself, Hadassah thought with a frown.

"Are *you*?" Yael asked.

"Readings make me a little tired." And horny. "That's all. If you're feeling woozy or unsteady—"

Yael shook her head. "I'm steady."

They stared at each other for a half a minute. Hadassah drew in a breath. The tingling heat that had begun an hour or so ago at the bar had never gone away, and it surged now.

"I need another drink," she said. "Care to join me?"

Chapter Three

"I swore I'd never be like my mother, always commenting on how things had changed, or how much they were better when I was younger," the woman called Hadassah said.

They'd moved from the bar to one of Sanctuary's curving dinette tables. Hadassah had ordered a plate of what she'd called "appetizers," but which seemed designed specifically to fulfill the appetite, thus making additional consumption unnecessary. Also, they were delicious. Yael was accustomed to hunger. Demons of her kind were made for starvation. This was the first time in her eternally long life she could recall being free of that gnawing ache. It had been replaced, however, with something else. A similar emptiness, a yearning, but not for food.

Hadassah dragged a long strip of fried potato through a pool of crimson syrup and popped it into her mouth. "Yet here I am, waxing philosophic about the fact they tore down a doughnut shop and replaced it with a kombucha bar."

"It is allowable and understandable to mourn the loss of something you loved." Yael did not completely comprehend the feelings of grief, nor of love, but she knew that one often accompanied the other.

Hadassah's shapely eyebrows rose. "Very astute. You sound like you've been there."

"I have not been to any kombucha bar. I..." Yael hesitated. "In fact, I am uncertain what, exactly, is a kombucha."

Hadassah let out a trill of tinkling laughter. To Yael, who looked through the eyes of this human vessel but still saw with a demon's vision, that laughter was a swirl of blues, greens, and hints of red. Not anger, but passion.

"Well, it's a terrible replacement for homemade doughnuts, that's all I can tell you." Hadassah leaned toward Yael on the curving bench, close enough for Yael to feel her body's warmth.

Yael wondered if she was meant to also lean in. She tried it. The warmth between them increased. It was different, being in this vessel than her own true form. More difficult to respond or react. She was sensing a sexual heat coming from Hadassah, but she could not be sure how she was expected to react in response. Yael struggled with behaving human, but she was well aware that people did not simply engage in copulation as demons did, without warning, sometimes without even communication. Her former mistress had used Yael in that way... Yael forced the memory of the witch from her mind. She'd done her best to fully sever their connection, but she could not be certain nothing residual remained. Best not to test the bindings the witch had placed upon her and which Yael had so far managed to slip.

"What brought you into Sanctuary today?" Hadassah asked suddenly.

Yael allowed herself to consume another fried potato strip before replying. "It is a safe space. Shielded, yes?"

She'd been passing by in the street and seen the unassuming front doors. She'd sensed the safety within them. Too, she'd been craving something she couldn't put a name to. Companionship. Comfort. Sustenance. A respite from looking over her shoulder, certain her maker-witch would be there, even though Yael had left her miles and miles away.

Hadassah nodded. "Yes. Of course. But if you're new to the city, how did you happen to stumble on it?"

She could not admit she'd been wandering, aimless. "Good fortune?"

"It's certainly mine, I think. Or...for both of us?"

Another slow, rolling wave of sensual heat rose up between them. This body responded. Yael's stomach was full; now there was another sort of hunger to feed.

"Oh, yes. The ones like us," she said in a low voice. "Ones who want."

Hadassah made a small noise from deep in her throat. She drew in a breath. Then another. Her eyes gleamed, catching and holding Yael's gaze.

"Do you believe in fate, Yael?"

Yael could not be sure how to answer Hadassah's question. She knew the meaning of the word, but fate seemed inextricably linked to ownership of a soul—which of course did not apply to Yael.

"I do not," she said.

"What *do* you believe in?"

Hadassah leaned a little closer. She had ceased consuming the wine some time ago, and the fruity scent remained prevalent on her breath. Yael had been around drunk humans before, though, and Hadassah seemed only mildly intoxicated.

Although she had thought being in this human vessel would make a difference, Yael herself was not at all affected by the alcohol. Her belly, however, felt aching and empty. Her eyes, a little heavy lidded. Warmth had gathered low inside her, centered between her thighs.

"I believe in appetite," she said. "I believe in desire."

Hadassah made a low purring noise that somehow sent slow, swirling ripples of heat rising inside Yael's body. "What are you hungry for?"

Yael's fingers twitched. In her own form, her claws would be extending, ready to rip and rend, but this body had soft nails. Pointed, but blunt compared to her talons, even if they were painted black. At any rate, she did not wish to kill Hadassah. So, what, then?

"I would like to fuck," Yael said.

"Oh, wow." Hadassah leaned back, and for a moment, Yael thought she had misjudged. Social interactions were...difficult. But then Hadassah moved in close once more. Her mouth found Yael's, the kiss greedy but somehow soft too. Requesting, not demanding. Their tongues twisted. Hadassah tasted of sweetness, of arousal. Of something else, too, a flavor Yael could not name. The witch's kisses had been bitter and bilious... Yael drew away abruptly. Demons did not fear, but this vessel could.

"Sorry?" Hadassah's word tipped upward at the end, not quite a question, but clearly questioning. "I thought...?"

Yael slid closer on the curving bench. Her hand slipped beneath Hadassah's thick dark curls to cup the base of her skull. Her fingertips dented the flesh there. She slanted her mouth over Hadassah's, but this kiss was not soft.

Hadassah's mouth opened, and a soft moan slipped out of her. She arched her body toward Yael's. More sexual heat flowed from her, but this time, she was the one who broke the kiss.

"Do you want to go somewhere else?" Hadassah's breathy voice tickled Yael's ears.

Yael answered with another kiss. "Yes."

Chapter Four

Hadassah did not take people back to her apartment. Non-Talented folk would be likely to cringe at the sight of her altars, her vials and bottles and decanters of blood, her Velvet Elvis lined with twinkle lights. Even the supernaturals she took to bed might look at her differently—it was one thing for them to know she was a hemomancer, and quite another for them to see the blatant evidence of how she worked. For many, blood was a trigger, even when it had been collected in a bottle.

"People live here?" Yael paused outside the nondescript silver elevator doors tucked down a discreet hallway beyond Sanctuary's steakhouse.

Hadassah swiped a keycard to access the elevator. The doors opened with a genteel ping. "No. But there are rooms here."

She did not add that they were available to members only, and that she paid a decently hefty fee for the privilege of being able to use them. Inside the elevator, she swiped her keycard again and pushed the button for the thirteenth floor. The mirrored interior walls reflected the two of them into a myriad of clones, duplicated into infinity.

When the doors opened into a small, sparsely furnished lobby, she crossed the small space to the large board adorned with hooks, upon which ornately carved keys hung in rows. She tapped her keycard against the release mechanism to register which key she was taking and plucked one at random. She'd used all the rooms on this floor at one time or another and had no preference as they were all identical. Today, she picked the one at the end of the hall.

"What was that?" Yael pointed at the register box.

"It records who takes which key, in case someone damages a room, or does not return the key." Hadassah held up the key she'd chosen. "You're supposed to leave it on the table in the room when you leave, but it can be easy to slip it in a pocket or something and forget it."

"There is no attendant?"

Hadassah shook her head as she led Yael down the hallway. The silver-and-gray carpet muffled their footsteps, and she kept her voice hushed too. "No. These rooms are meant to be kept very...private."

"What if there is a problem?"

"You mean with the room?" Hadassah asked. "I suppose you could pick another key, try another room. But I've never had any trouble."

"I mean, what if someone does not merely damage a room, but another person?"

Hadassah paused. Her stomach dropped a little. "What do you mean?"

"What if someone in whom you placed your trust betrays it?" Yael's dark gaze captured Hadassah's own.

"That is the risk of engaging in sexual intimacies with someone you do not know."

Hadassah's heart thumped. "Are you planning to hurt me, Yael?"

"Only in ways you would like," Yael said in a low, husky voice. Her eyes gleamed.

Hadassah's clit throbbed. "How do you know I want to be hurt in any way at all?"

"How do you know you can trust me with your body?"

They'd reached the end of the hall and the door to the room Hadassah had chosen. For a flash of a moment, Hadassah considered turning around. Leaving. She'd regretted some choices in the past, but mostly because the women had turned out to be clingy, or selfish lovers, or entitled bitches. She'd never actually been *afraid* of someone she'd taken upstairs at Sanctuary.

But *was* she afraid, now? It had been Yael's oddness, that hint of the unknown that had appealed to her from the start. Hadassah forced herself to ask, did she truly feel like Yael was dangerous and might hurt her?

"Your heart is beating very fast," Yael said. "I can see it pulsing in your throat."

"Are you a vampire?" Hadassah blurted the words, aware she'd spoken too loud, going against the unspoken rules for using this floor. *Stay quiet. Don't draw attention to yourself, or to anyone else.* She softened her tone. "I don't have anything against vampires. I just want to know."

Yael blinked and tilted her head, her gaze clearly scanning Hadassah's face. "I've frightened you. I didn't mean to. No. I'm not a vampire."

"What—" Hadassah began, but the sound of a door opening stopped her. That was another of those rules—no lingering in the hall. It was inevitable that you might sometimes pass other guests coming to or fro, but it was forbidden to purposefully remain in the public space. "Come on."

She slipped the key into the lock and opened the door. When they were both inside, she shut the door behind them. She put the key on the small table inside the door. She turned to Yael. Before she could speak, Yael had moved in close to take Hadassah in her arms.

The kiss was gentle. Hesitant. Yael pulled away without removing her hands from Hadassah's hips.

"I do not always understand societal norms," Yael said. "I am trying. I did not mean to make you afraid. I have no intentions of causing you harm. My question was meant from curiosity, not intent."

"Are you human?" Hadassah tensed, expecting the answer to be "no."

Yael hesitated and then nodded. "I am human. Does that matter to you?"

"Not really. But if you were something else..." Hadassah shrugged. "I'd just want to know."

Yael took Hadassah's hand and placed it on her breast. "Do I feel human?"

"Very much so."

They kissed. Hadassah pulled Yael a little closer to nuzzle her neck and throat. Her tongue swept over Yael's skin before she pulled away.

"To answer your question, then, every keycard is coded to include the user's information. It registers time of entry, the room they choose, how long they stay. The rooms themselves record physical data of the people using them. The security staff are on hand at all times to make sure that everything is kept safe. But I have to ask, Yael…" It was Hadassah's turn to hesitate. "What made you think that guests of this hotel might be inclined to hurt each other?"

"A place designed for anonymity seems well-suited for those who wish to act in ways they don't wish to be discovered," Yael said simply.

"Are you doing something you don't wish to be discovered?" Hadassah asked quietly.

In response, Yael leaned to kiss her again, but this time kept her lips just barely brushing. "I don't feel shame, if that's what you're asking."

Was it? Sort of. Hadassah let her body rest against Yael's lean form. "Good. I don't want you be ashamed of being here with me."

Yael's hand slipped between them to press against Hadassah's breast. Her thumb moved slowly over the fabric of her soft T-shirt until her nipple peaked. Then she pinched it gently. Hadassah moaned.

Yael pinched harder. "You like this."

"Yes."

Yael's other hand drifted again to the base of Hadassah's skull. Her fingers dug into the tender flesh and then tangled in Hadassah's hair. They tugged her head backward, breaking the kiss. Hadassah licked her lips, taking in a breath that was not quite a gasp.

"I can hurt you, if that's what you like," Yael said. "But I don't want to damage you."

Hadassah shivered. "I like it a little rough. Nothing hardcore. We can use a safe word if you want, but I don't even really like it that hard. Kink lite, you might say."

"Kink..." Yael murmured the word against Hadassah's throat. The warm wetness of her tongue stroked along the sensitive flesh.

Hadassah shuddered. Her nipples tightened. Her clit throbbed, and when she shifted her weight, she could feel the answering pull of desire in her pussy. Slickness gathered inside her, along with the heat of need. At the press of Yael's teeth, Hadassah cried out, tensing, half-expecting to feel the pierce of fangs although Yael had said she wasn't a vampire.

The bed in this room, as in all the rooms, was king-sized. Dressed in fresh white linens. Yael walked Hadassah backward toward it and pushed her gently down, her hand still behind Hadassah's neck in support. They ended up together on the bed, legs intertwined. Bodies moving.

Yael kissed her mouth, forcing open Hadassah's lips with her tongue and stroking it deeply inside. Their teeth clashed. Yael thrust a thigh between Hadassah's own to spread her legs. Her hands and mouth moved over Hadassah's body, swiftly, without faltering. One cupped her breast. One pushed up the tiered fabric of her lightweight skirt. Yael pushed her hand between Hadassah's legs, her fingers finding the silky panties covering her bare mound.

"You're wet. I can feel it through your panties." Yael breathed this into Hadassah's ear.

Her fingers slid beyond the leg band of the panties and pushed inside Hadassah's pussy without warning.

Two fingers, her thumb rubbing Hadassah's clit. Yael's hand moved and then withdrew. She pushed up onto her knees to lick her fingers.

"You are delicious," she said.

"Take off your clothes." Hadassah pushed up on her elbow to gesture at Yael's tight black T-shirt and the matching black-and-gray patterned leggings.

Yael moved with feral grace to stand at the edge of the bed. She pulled off the shirt and then shucked out of the leggings. She wore nothing beneath, no bra or panties. Her pubic hair was neatly trimmed, but lush and thick, so dark it hinted at shades of blue. Tufts of hair beneath her arms matched. She stood with her legs apart, hands on her hips. The peaches of her breasts rose and fell with her rapid breathing, and her lips parted to allow her tongue to snake out, licking the bottom one.

"You're gorgeous," Hadassah said. "I thought it the first moment I saw you."

Yael turned her face for a moment, her eyes closing. "I am...only what I am."

"Come here."

She moved with lithe grace, pressing first a knee to the bed, dipping it. Her other knee pressed the inside of Hadassah's thigh. Yael's skin was warm. Smooth. She covered Hadassah's body with her own. Her lips found the pulse at the base of Hadassah's throat.

At the press of Yael's teeth again, Hadassah hissed out a breath, arching beneath Yael's touch. She traced the line of Yael's spine with her fingertips, lingering at the indentations above the swell of her buttocks before she cupped them. Squeezing.

"Your body…" She sighed.

"It functions," Yael answered against her neck.

Her mouth moved lower, over the swell of Hadassah's breasts. She took a nipple between her lips, tugging, sucking, and Hadassah arched again at the pleasure of it. When Yael moved down her body toward her center, though, Hadassah hesitated.

Yael must have sensed it because she stopped with her lips poised over Hadassah's clit. The soft puff of her breath eased over the sensitized flesh. "No?"

"Yes," Hadassah said. "But I want to touch you too. Taste you."

In reply, Yael gave Hadassah a long, slow lick. "Later."

She wasn't going to argue too much with that—sexual pleasure eased the aftereffects of the hemomancy, and a good hard orgasm was exactly what Hadassah needed. She wasn't trying to be selfish about it, but if Yael was willing to give without receiving, at least for now…

"Oh…oh, fuck. Yes. That. Right there." Hadassah's hips rocked. Her fingers found the thick sleek darkness of Yael's hair and dug in.

Her orgasm rose fast—it usually did after a day of client sessions, but this was different. Stronger. Vaster. When Yael slipped two fingers inside her, Hadassah writhed, bucking. She lost herself in the rising waves of pleasure that racked her entire body. Her toes curled. She cried out, first a low series of moans and then a louder, vibrant gasp as she finally tipped over the edge.

Another rush of climax ran through her, softer and somehow lighter than the first, and it took her by surprise.

Panting, she relaxed into the bed, her eyes closed, drowsy and sated. A few seconds passed before she opened her eyes. Yael was sitting on the edge of the bed.

Hadassah pushed up on her elbow and reached for her. "That was intense. Fast."

"You were ready for the pleasure. That's why you approached me, isn't it? Because you needed release."

There it was again, that distinct way of speaking. An accent Hadassah could not name, or maybe not an accent but a way of phrasing. Word choices. Something formal, almost old-fashioned.

"Do you do this a lot?" Hadassah asked.

"Fuck?"

Hadassah's breath hissed out of her with a soft chuckle. "Fuck strangers you meet in a bar, I mean."

"This is the first time for me. *You* do this often."

"I do." Hadassah studied Yael's neutral expression. Implacable, she thought. That was a good word for how Yael looked. And intriguing.

Yael stretched and stalked to the bathroom without another word. Hadassah blinked and sat up. She heard the shower running and, after a moment, followed.

Yael stood beneath the spray, her head down so the water could pound over the back of her neck. She did not look up when Hadassah slid open the glass door. Steam immediately wreathed out, swirling into eddies.

"Are you all right?" Hadassah asked.

Yael turned her head. Water sluiced over her sharp profile and dripped in rivulets off her nose and chin. Her tongue slipped out to catch some of it. Her throat worked as she swallowed.

"Yes. This is glorious."

Hadassah had taken many short-term lovers over the years, many she'd been with only once. There'd been a few mistakes. Some regrets, but only a few. She didn't want this to be one of them.

"I could join you," Hadassah offered. "Scrub your back? Or your front."

Yael twisted the faucet to turn off the water. Hadassah handed her a towel as she stepped out. She dried her face quickly. Then her body.

"I need to go," she said and handed the damp towel to Hadassah.

She pushed past her and into the bedroom while Hadassah stood, stunned and silent. After another half a minute, Hadassah heard the door open. Shut.

"Wow," Hadassah whispered. "She really just left."

Chapter Five

Yael woke from a fevered dream with the sheets tangled roughly around her ankles. Her heart pounded, and she pressed her palm to her chest, marveling at how this body worked. She had slept, even dreamed, all while her heart beat. Her lungs drew in air. And now her stomach complained with emptiness. She would need food.

Naked, she got out of bed and went to the small kitchen. The motel room was a far cry from the sleek elegance of the room Hadassah had taken her to. The sagging bed had left this body aching and sore. The shower had trickled warmish water that went cool minutes after she got under the spray. Insects scuttled out of sight when she turned on the lights. Still, it was the only place she'd been able to find that would accept the meager amount of cash she'd found in this body's wallet, and that was already gone. She had no idea what she'd do at the end of the week. In this body, she could not access her demonic glamour, could not manipulate or control humans the way she'd been able to before.

She was, as she'd assured Hadassah...human.

She hadn't planned this. Called forth from the demon realm, Yael had started her life of service to the witch without question, at least until that life had become insufferable. The witch had demanded Yael's complete obedience and forced her to harm others instead of simply protecting and defending the witch against harm. The end had come when the witch ordered Yael to kill a young woman who'd insulted her somehow.

And, taking the opportunity for escape, Yael had taken the young woman's body.

Once the soul left the vessel it was useless for anything but rot, but Yael didn't have to be human to understand the severity of what she'd done. Inserting herself inside this suit of bone and flesh and sinew had been wrong. It hadn't been her right to take it, but she'd done what she needed to so she could free herself.

She would do whatever it took to keep herself that way.

Get a job, Yael thought as she rummaged in the refrigerator for a container of leftover fast food. If she could. Humans worked for money so they could buy items, but how could Yael possibly convince someone to hire her? She had no further information about this vessel, so she couldn't really pass herself off as the woman this body had been. She had no skills she could use.

She could not stay in this vessel forever. At a maximum, she could only inhabit it for the length of time it had been allotted on this plane. And after that...what? Would she revert to her own form, be returned to the demon realm? Would she perhaps simply cease to exist? Yael didn't know.

For now, she would have to satisfy her hungers. First, with food. And later, with sex.

"Hadassah," Yael said aloud.

The hemomancer had approached Yael with purpose, unashamed. The smell of Hadassah's woman's need had been evident, and Yael had been made, after all, to serve. The sex had been different with her, and not only because of Yael's vessel. There had been more to it. A...kindness, she thought it would be called. *Consideration*. They had used each other, but it had not felt like *being* used.

Demons experienced fear. Anger. Lust. Greed. Hate. Demons were loyal only when bound to be. They did not experience human emotions...but Yael inhabited a human body now.

Yael shook away the thoughts of Hadassah. Her body needed sustenance, and this cold meat patty, its cheese congealed amongst limp lettuce and mealy tomatoes, was not going to sate her. As a demon, Yael had not needed to eat, but nor had she known the joy of food. Hunger, yes, but never satiation. It was inconvenient to be restricted by this vessel's limitations, but there was much to relish about it too. Unfortunately, the meal that had been sufficient while warm was barely suitable now the day after its purchase.

Hadassah had bought her food and beverage before taking Yael to that clean room with the glorious shower. All her needs had been met. Food. Sex. Cleanliness. Yael paced the interior of the hotel room for a bit, restless and unfulfilled.

She had no purpose.

She had only need.

From the table, her phone buzzed with a text that she ignored. There'd been many over the past couple of weeks.

Also phone calls. The previous owner of the phone had been picked up off the street, her need for drugs greater than her need to preserve her personal safety. It was likely no surprise to her friends or family that she was lax in answering her phone. It would have been better to get rid of it entirely, but Yael needed the device until she could replace it, just as she'd continued using the woman's credit card, knowing at some point it would cease to function.

She tried to ignore the knock on the door to this shabby, bare motel room, but whoever was outside refused to go away. Yael opened it. The manager of the motel peered inside and gave her a suspicious glare.

"I've paid for two more nights," she said.

"No drugs in here, you hear me? No 'guests,' either, of the paying sort, I mean. Other than you." He used his fingers to make curves in the air, emphasizing the word.

Ah, he thought she was a prostitute. This vessel might have been, but Yael was not yet. "I'm alone in here."

"Keep it that way. And if you want to stay longer than ten in the morning, you gotta pay for another night." He gave her another looking-over and then a leer. "I mean, I could be persuaded to barter..."

"Get out." Yael didn't push him, not certain what he'd do in retaliation if she tried.

For an uneasy minute she was afraid he would resist. Maybe even push his way inside. Her fingers curled into her palms, reminding her that in this body, she had no talons to use in defense. She was still strong, stronger than the woman had been when she was alive, but that didn't mean Yael wanted to indulge in violence.

To her relief, the manager stepped back and away. Yael closed the door behind him and leaned against it with her eyes closed. She took a few deep breaths, in and out, while she thought hard about what she needed to do next.

One thing at a time, she told herself. Start with the most important. Find work.

That turned out to be easier than she'd imagined. The motel was rundown and seedy, but the landscaping belonging to the office complexes flanking it on either side was the opposite. Lush, green grass. Bursts of vibrant, seasonal color. Rich, dark mulch and decorative trees. The crews tending to the areas were there every other day, too, leaf blowing or replanting or pruning or weeding.

Yael talked with the head of the crew. It took only a few minutes of conversation for him to hire her. The landscaping company didn't care that she didn't have a social security number. They hadn't even asked for one. They'd simply asked her if she could carry a fifty-pound bag of river gravel, which she could do with almost no effort, even with this body's weaker limbs. They put her to work right away. More importantly, they promised her work, as much as she could handle, for the rest of the month.

By midafternoon, she was worn out but had some cash in her pocket, and she was finally ready to head back to Sanctuary. Would Hadassah be there? Would she provide even more of a feeling of shelter, the way she'd done the night they'd spent together?

More importantly, would she be able to help Yael figure out what path to pursue for her future?

There was only one way to find out.

Chapter Six

"Wait, wait, hold on. You can't just use like, a pinprick thing? A little jab?" The woman in the blue suit yanked her hand out of Hadassah's and recoiled in her chair.

Hadassah pressed her lips together for a second before answering. She'd woken this morning with a headache and an unsettled feeling low in the base of her gut. It had been a little over a week since she'd slept with Yael, but for some reason, thoughts of her had been poking at her all day. Hadassah was not in the mood to deal with someone else's bad attitude.

"I mean," the client continued, "how much could you possibly *need*?"

"You want the answers to your questions? I need less than a gallon but more than a drop." Hadassah gestured at the small plastic bowl on the table between them. "You came to me because you wanted something. It's not free."

"Hell no, it's not free, I'm paying you!"

"What you want requires more than money," Hadassah told her. "If you're not willing to pay the price..."

"No. I'm willing. I just hate the sight of blood." The client offered her hand again, dramatically closing her eyes and turning her head.

Hadassah gripped the woman's wrist to keep her from pulling away. With her other hand, she lifted the disposable scalpel. It was nothing like the beautiful, engraved knives she had in her personal collection, but it sliced, clean and neat, the edge so sharp Hadassah knew there would be almost no pain. At least not the physical kind.

One quick slice. Blood jetted into the bowl, spattering the sides and collecting in the bottom. Thirty seconds passed, and Hadassah pressed sterile gauze to the wound with efficient movements, wrapping the client's hand quickly before she turned her attention to the crimson fluid in the bowl.

"What do you see?" the client demanded.

Hadassah shook her head, gaze fixed on the blood. "It's not like reading tea leaves. Be patient."

Hadassah passed a hand over the fluid, letting the magic inside her call to the inherent magic present in the client's blood. She breathed in. Then out. Patterns emerged, not, as she'd said, like reading tea leaves. Reading the blood was more like how she'd heard seeing auras described. Waves of color, shifting patterns. If she closed her eyes, she could still see what the blood was telling her, but she kept them open—too many freaks had tried to get one over on her when they thought she wasn't paying attention.

"Did I do the right thing?" the client asked, this time in a lower voice. Still insistent but making a semblance of respect.

Hadassah studied the blood. "I can't tell you the past. Only the future. I see success in business."

"Good."

"But failure in family." Hadassah looked up at the woman sitting across from her. "Whatever choices you made, they are affecting what happens to you moving forward."

"How do I fix it?" The woman sounded genuinely distraught. Her voice caught. She clenched her fists. Red seeped through the white bandage.

"I don't know," Hadassah answered with true regret. "I can only tell you what I see right now. But you're the only one who has the power to change what happens. You can't undo what you've already done, but you can certainly take a different path."

The woman stood. "What path should I take? Can't you tell me that?"

"I can tell you what I see for your future, but it's not set in stone. The future is fluid. Whatever you do today, tomorrow, next week, in the next minute, all of that will change what happens to you. Right now, I see money. Success. Financial comfort, it's all very clear. But I see also emptiness, loneliness, an empty house—that doesn't mean a real building," Hadassah cautioned. "It's more of your spiritual house. Your heart. You need to adjust yourself, or you're going to end up very wealthy, and very, very sad."

"I'm already sad," the woman said.

Hadassah put a silk cloth over the bowl of blood. "You can change that. If you want to. What's more important to you? Money or the people you love?"

The client didn't answer. Maybe she couldn't. Her shoulders heaved with silent sobs as she gathered her purse and jacket from the back of the chair. She gave Hadassah a long, long stare.

"Have you ever lost something you loved?" she asked.

"I don't talk about my personal life with clients."

The client tossed a stack of cash on the table. "What does your future tell *you*?"

"I've never tried to read my own future," Hadassah said, angry that she felt like she owed this woman any kind of explanation. "You can see yourself out."

Two days in a row, two consecutive clients with attitude issues. It was almost enough to make Hadassah cancel her next appointment, but justifiable outrage didn't pay the rent. Keeping space here in Sanctuary was convenient, but not cheap. Her final two clients of the day turned out to be perfect though. No complaining about the process, paid her via the cash app so she didn't have to deal with physical money, happy to hear what she had to tell them. By the time the last one left, Hadassah's mood had lifted.

She hadn't forgotten the client from earlier, though, nor her question. *Had* Hadassah ever lost something she loved? Hadn't everyone, she told herself as she tidied up her office and prepared to leave for the day. Still, the woman's question niggled at her. Pulling her phone from her purse, she quickly swiped in a number.

"Hey," she said without preamble. "I have a question for you."

Her mentor, Regina, laughed through the distance between them. "Hello to you, too, kitten. What's up?"

"What happens if we try to read ourselves?"

A long, slow sigh filtered through the phone. "All these years, and you've only decided to ask me this now? I guess it was inevitable."

Hadassah frowned into the phone. "Is it bad?"

"Bad? No." Regina laughed.

"Then what?"

"We can't read ourselves. That's all."

"When I was learning, you told me not to try it," Hadassah said, remembering how stern Regina had been about it.

"I never told you something bad would happen to you, did I?"

Hadassah hesitated, thinking back. "No, but…"

"You were always such a rule follower." Regina laughed again, but fondly. "I miss you, kitten. You haven't been to see me in ages."

"I know. I've been busy. Lots of clients…Regina, what does it mean, then, if I'm giving a reading to someone else, but I can't see anything?"

"Is this someone else a *someone else* you're involved with?"

Hadassah pressed her lips together before answering, giving herself a second or two to find the right words, and in the end, still not sure what she could say about Yael. "Maybe?"

"Someone you'd like to be involved with?"

"Maybe," she repeated. "I just met her. She's interesting."

"And you tried to give her a reading, but you couldn't?" Regina huffed a breath, and Hadassah imagined her mentor sipping from her ever-present mug of black coffee.

"I saw only a few seconds before it just went blank. Totally dark. That's never happened."

"Well," Regina said, "it sounds to me like that means it's because somehow, her future and yours are intertwined."

"That's terribly inconvenient," Hadassah said with a frown. "How is it that I've never run into this before? Even during my training?"

"You were never in love with anyone before, I guess," Regina answered.

Hadassah's frown deepened. "I just met her, Regina. Like, literally, just a week ago. I hardly think I'm in love with her."

"Not yet."

"Shit." Hadassah closed her eyes.

Regina made a sympathetic noise. "You okay?"

"I don't know. Yes. I guess so." Hadassah sighed. "How are you though?"

The rest of the conversation was quick, the way it usually was with Regina, who'd never been one for small talk. Hadassah promised to make some time to visit. Regina promised to call more often. They signed off, both knowing neither one would follow up with their promises, and neither upset about it.

That was love, Hadassah thought. Accepting each other, even with faults. She forcibly smoothed another frown. She was going to end up needing Botox for all these furrows she was creating.

Enough of that. Whatever had happened between her and Yael had happened. Whatever would happen was going to happen, no matter what, and sure, Hadassah made her own destiny, blah, blah, blah, but she didn't have to make it right this minute. Right *this* minute, she was going to have a glass of good house red.

"Red, my friend," she said as she slid onto her usual barstool. "How are you this fine afternoon?"

Red was already sliding a glass of wine toward her. "It's almost evening. But you know, it's always a good day at Sanctuary."

Hadassah sipped the wine with a happy sigh. She'd have her glass of wine, maybe two. Then she'd head home and treat herself to a long soak in a bath with a good book and some more wine. She'd order in something decadent and fattening for dinner and indulge herself totally. Because she could, damn it. Because she was a grown-ass woman who didn't need anyone else to make her happy.

"Hello."

She turned, the voice familiar although there was no reason it should be. Despite herself, her heart thumped harder. Her stomach twisted. "It's you."

"Yes. It's me. Hello, Hadassah." Yael inclined her head in Hadassah's direction. Today, she wore her dark shaggy hair piled on top of her head in a messy bun. Wispy tendrils of hair framed her face and clung to the back of her neck. Her form-fitting black top matched the black jeans and black boots. Her black-painted nails were chipped, one or two of them broken, like she'd been doing heavy work with her hands.

In comparison, Hadassah looked down at her own flowing teal skirt and white blouse embroidered with wildflowers. Her dark curls tumbled over her shoulders, held back from her face with a wide band of teal fabric embroidered with multicolored flowers. Opposites attract, she thought, and a sudden burst of wild laughter threatened to burst out of her. She quashed it, trying hard to ignore the flush creeping up her throat. Trying to pretend she wasn't giddy with glee at the sight of Yael.

"I didn't expect to see you here," she said, pressing back the giggles.

Yael shrugged. "Sanctuary welcomes everyone."

"That's not what I meant." Hadassah took a sip of wine to stop herself from blurting out something that would make her sound desperate or clingy. That was never how she'd played. She'd always prided herself on keeping things casual. Uncomplicated.

Why, then, had the way Yael left her lingered like the stink of something bad?

Shaking it off, Hadassah gestured at the stool next to her. "Want a drink?"

"Yes. I would." Yael took the seat. "Wine, the same as you have. Please. Thank you."

Red poured her a glass and pushed it across the bar before stepping back. Hadassah twisted on the stool. She raised her glass. "A toast?"

Yael stared, her brow furrowed. "Toast is bread. Not wine."

Hadassah couldn't hold back the burst of laughter this time, but she bit down hard to stifle it in case Yael thought she was making fun of her. "It is. You're right."

Yael lifted her glass, mimicking Hadassah. "Like this?"

"Yes. L'chaim." They clinked gently. Wine sloshed. Hadassah sipped, and Yael followed suit.

"You speak Hebrew," Yael said.

Hadassah nodded. "Sure. A little. You?"

"I speak many languages." She rattled off a string of words with a heavy Hebrew inflection, but she must've noticed Hadassah's confused expression, because she added, "it means, 'I have one name, but many voices.'"

"I have only one voice."

Yael studied her. "Maybe you just haven't heard your others, yet."

A witty quip rose to Hadassah's lips, but she kept silent and instead, raised her glass again. "To other voices."

They clinked. Sipped. Red poured them a second round.

"You're different today," Yael said. "Something is not the same as when we first met."

Hadassah ducked her head. The wine had flushed more warmth throughout her, but she suspected the blush heating her cheeks was more about the memory of how hard she'd hit on Yael. "I'd had a bad day."

"And today was better?"

"Much." She described the difference in clients, how performing the hemomancy always took something out of her but working with difficult patrons ended up being more draining.

She did not mention her conversation with Regina.

"And you seek comfort in sex," Yael said.

Hadassah gave a self-conscious chuckle—it was true, but she hadn't had anyone ever present it to her in quite that way. "Yes."

"It is a good release." Yael tilted her head to look Hadassah up and down. "I also think I would enjoy having sex with you again."

A short, sharp burst of laughter hurtled out of Hadassah's lips. "That's...wow. You really know how to make a girl feel special, you know that?"

Yael frowned. "You sound angry."

"I'm not *angry*." Hadassah lifted her chin, pressing her lips together to make the protest sound more convincing.

"Why are you angry with me?"

"I'm not..." Hadassah bit back the rest of her sentence. She sighed. "You walked out on me. Just like that."

"Just like what?" Yael leaned closer. "I'm sorry, Hadassah. I don't understand."

Hadassah glanced over to see Red surreptitiously listening. She trusted the bartender not to spread rumors about her, of course. Discretion of the staff and clientele was paramount at Sanctuary. Still, did she want Red knowing all her personal business?

She drained her wine and got off the stool. "This is a conversation I think we need to have in private."

Chapter Seven

"This is not where I was expecting you to take me." Yael looked around the park she'd gone to with Hadassah.

A few blocks from Sanctuary, the park was a lovely space. It featured a fountain, benches, flower-lined paths, shade trees. Yael had anticipated Hadassah would take her to one of those upstairs rooms. There didn't seem to be any place for that sort of intimate activity here at all. What, then, did Hadassah want from her?

"Can I buy you an ice cream?" Hadassah pointed toward one of the kiosks.

Yael put a hand on her belly. It was empty. Thanks to the hours she'd worked earlier, her wallet wasn't...but it could be again, soon, if she wasn't careful with how she spent the contents. "If you want to. Of course. Thank you."

Together, they ordered cones heaped with hand-scooped ice cream and took them to a shaded bench out of the way from the main path. Yael consumed hers quickly, Hadassah less so, and then tossed hers into the nearby garbage can before she'd fully finished it. Yael wiped her lips with the paper napkin that had come with the cone. She waited. There was something coming from Hadassah, she could sense it.

"Look," Hadassah began, and paused. She blew out a breath and tried again. "Listen..."

Yael laughed. "Which would you like me to do? Look? Or listen?"

"Why did you up and leave me like that?" Hadassah demanded without a hint of humor in her voice.

"We had finished what we were there to do," Yael said, but quietly. Gently. Aware that there was more to Hadassah's question than the words themselves. She hadn't known it at the time, but she did now.

Hadassah huffed and shifted on the bench. She twisted her body to face Yael's. "You didn't even ask for my number."

"Would you like me to have it?" Yael felt the square brick of her phone in her back pocket. She had no idea how long it would function without her paying the bill, but it was still working for now.

"Do you want it?" Hadassah sounded frustrated.

Yael had observed human interactions for a long time from her place in the demon realm, and she'd been witness to them from an even closer place once the witch had summoned her. She knew emotions were often not rational or reasonable or logical. Knowing and feeling, though, were two different things.

"Having your phone number would allow me to contact you without finding you randomly at Sanctuary," Yael said. "And if you had mine, you could do the same."

"That's the point, yes."

"Then yes. I would like your number." Yael pulled out her phone.

Before she could swipe the screen to type in whatever numbers Hadassah was going to share, a shadow fell across them. She looked up to see a figure silhouetted, backlit so it was difficult to see the face. It was male though. And big.

"Jackie. The fuck are you doing here? Why haven't you been answering my messages? It's been like, a couple of fucking weeks." His voice was rough. Hard. Barely restrained fury radiated off him.

Yael's stolen heart pounded. She'd run, but not far enough to avoid running into someone who'd known this body, apparently. He moved closer, menacing her.

"Answer me," the man said.

Incredibly, Hadassah got to her feet. "Hey. Buddy. Back off."

"I'm not talking to you. I'm talking to my girl."

Hadassah let out a small, surprised noise. "What, now?"

"I'm not your girl." It was all Yael could think of to say. She had no idea who this man was. She'd taken the body, not the memories.

The man took a step closer. "I told you, you'll always be my girl. Just because we broke up—"

"Back off," Hadassah repeated, venom in her tone. She lifted something toward him. "I will zap you straight to PissYourPants Town."

For all his swagger, the guy seemed at least smart enough to know when he was being faced with a legitimate threat. He backed off, hands up. "Chill, bitch."

"I might just zap you for that little endearment too." Hadassah held up the square device in her hand.

"Fine. Whatever. Call me," the man shot back at Yael as he took another few steps back before turning on his heel. In the sunlight, he was revealed to be in his early thirties. Well-worn. He cast a baleful look at both of them over his shoulder but headed off down the path without causing any more trouble.

"You're shaking." Hadassah slid onto the bench next to Yael and put an arm around her. "He's gone. It's okay."

Yael's teeth chattered. Her fists clenched. Acid filled her gut, the taste of it raw and biting on her tongue. She tried to draw in a breath but felt too suffocated.

"Hey. Hey, it's all right." Hadassah rubbed Yael's arm and pressed her lips gently to her temple.

The warmth of her breath helped ease some of the icy chill that had frozen Yael in place. Yael leaned into that comfort, that warmth, closing her eyes. Hadassah was barely less than a stranger, but she felt like an eternity of solace.

"I never…" Yael's voice cracked and broke. She opened her eyes.

Hadassah pulled away to look at her. "You never what?"

Yael shook her head, incapable of putting into words the emotions sweeping over her. She'd "never" a lot of things—never felt. Never thought. Never wanted.

Never needed.

Silently, Hadassah again embraced her. They sat together on the park bench, their hips touching. Yael sighed.

"You don't have to talk about it," Hadassah said after a few minutes had passed.

Yael twisted to face her. "We are strangers. You should mean no more to me than a stranger."

"This is true." One side of Hadassah's mouth curled downward as she fought a frown.

"And yet..."

"And yet," Hadassah urged.

Yael stood and took a few steps back from her. "What is happening with us, Hadassah?"

"I don't know." Hadassah stood, too, but didn't advance on Yael. She stood her own ground, her posture straight and tall, but her eyes and mouth soft and vulnerable. "I'm willing to find out though. Are you?"

Chapter Eight

Hadassah had not brought a lover to her apartment in so long she couldn't recall how long it had been. If Yael was judging the clutter, the clothes left piled on the chair, the dishes in the sink, she didn't show any signs of it. She looked around Hadassah's living room with interest, stopping for only a moment in front of the Velvet Elvis before turning her attention to the fake fireplace and the photos lining the mantel. She lifted a framed picture from its place of pride.

"This is you. Who's with you?" She tipped the photo toward Hadassah, who crossed the room to look at it.

"That's my teacher. Regina." Hadassah touched the frame gently.

Yael gave her a curious look. "Teacher?"

"Mentor. Guide, if you will. She's the one who helped me really learn how to harness and utilize my talents."

"Was she your lover?"

Hadassah blinked rapidly. "What? Regina? No! She would never have taken advantage of me that way. And I wouldn't have wanted her to either."

Yael put the picture back on the mantel. "I didn't mean to offend."

"I'm not offended. Just startled you'd think that. I love Regina for everything she's taught me, but she's a friend. Not a lover."

Yael nodded as though she understood and touched the framed photo next to the one of Hadassah and Regina. "Your family?"

"Yes. Mom. Dad. Two brothers." Hadassah moved closer to study the photo along with Yael. Their shoulders brushed.

"Was your mother a hemomancer?"

"No. Or if she was, she never spoke of it. Nobody in my family ever did," Hadassah said quietly. "We never do, even now."

"That must be..." Yael's mouth worked, as though she were struggling to find the right words.

"It's hard, sometimes. It was harder in the beginning, when I was young. Didn't know what the hell was happening to me. It's better, now," Hadassah said.

"Do they know about you?"

Her family knew much about her, and yet nothing at all. "Whatever they know, they pretend they don't. It's better that way. We get in touch for birthdays, holidays, things like that. The rest of the time, we live our own lives. I mean, they live their lives, and they tell themselves I'm the one who's off on her own. Living her life." Hadassah drew in a sharp breath. Old wounds. Scabs over scars. "What about you?"

"I...don't have any family. Not like that."

"A found family can be as important as the ones we're related to," Hadassah said, wondering if Yael was estranged from her family. Most of Hadassah's friends had the same sorts of relationships with their folks and siblings as she did. Loving, but distant, to protect the ones they loved from having to face uncomfortable truths. "I have a lot of people in my life who aren't technically family, but I think of them that way."

Yael looked at her. "I don't really have anyone in my life."

"By choice?" It was a bold question, one Hadassah wouldn't have blamed Yael for not answering.

"No," Yael said. "Just by chance."

Empathy pricked Hadassah's heart with a tiny thorn. "I'm sorry."

"You have a nice home," Yael said in reply.

Fair enough. There were some topics that didn't get covered until you knew someone for a long, long time. Some things were never shared. Hadassah spent her days digging into people's most personal and private circumstances, and she understood how that worked.

"Can I get you something to drink? I have red wine, but it's not as good as the house blend. I have water. Soda. Lemonade," Hadassah offered.

Yael kissed her. Her hand slid to one of Hadassah's hips. The other went to the back of her neck. The thrill of that touch wound its way through Hadassah's entire body. Her lips parted. A sigh escaped. Yael's tongue slipped inside her mouth to toy with her own. The kiss broke, but softly. Yael didn't let go of her, not with either hand.

"I'm sorry I disappointed you by leaving without making future arrangements to see you, Hadassah."

Hadassah shook her head. "I shouldn't have expected you to. It was only meant to be a one-time thing."

"But here we are." Yael kissed her again and then pressed her cheek to Hadassah's. "You brought me into your home. You must trust me."

Did she? Hadassah couldn't be sure that was an accurate description of how she felt about Yael, or why she'd chosen to bring her here. It had less to do with trust and more to do with foolishness, she thought. She thought of what Regina had told her.

"Maybe it's just fate," she said.

Chapter Nine

Demons did not deal with fate, but humans did. Which meant that while she occupied this body, so did Yael. She wasn't sure what that meant for her though.

"You told me that my own choices would change whatever was going to happen for me," she said to Hadassah, who nodded.

"That's true, at least as I've always known it." She reached to tuck a strand of Yael's tangled hair behind her ear and then let her fingers linger on Yael's cheek.

Yael put her hand over Hadassah's, holding it in place so she could turn her face to kiss the palm. "How do you know what choices to make so you end up where you want to be?"

"I have no idea. I don't think anyone does. We all just sort of muddle along." Hadassah laughed lightly.

Yael didn't laugh. "But you counsel people based on their readings."

"Yes. I mean, I try to. But I can only see what could happen. Not what is definitely going to. And," Hadassah added, "it's not my place to tell anyone what choices to make. I can only share what I see."

Before Yael could say anything else, Hadassah stepped close enough to kiss her again. Their lips parted to allow the sweet slip of tongues. Heat rose inside Yael, urging her to press her body along Hadassah's. Her hands fit just right on the swell of Hadassah's hips. Their bellies touched. Their breasts. Yael sighed out a small moan at how good it felt to touch and be touched, and at the noise, Hadassah broke the kiss.

"I love the way you taste," she whispered. "The way you feel. Everything about this, Yael, it's not like anything I've ever felt with anyone."

"I have never felt this before either." There had been sex, both in the demon realm and in her demon form, at the command of the witch, but it had always been solely physical.

This time, the kiss was fierce, but brief, and Hadassah backed away, out of reach. She drew in a breath. Hadassah turned away, and her hair tumbled over her shoulders, hiding her face.

"Did I say something wrong, Hadassah?"

She shook her head. "No. I'm just afraid…"

"Of what?"

Hadassah turned with a gesture. "Of this. Of us."

"Of me," Yael said.

"Yes. Of you. Because something that feels this good and right just can't be." Hadassah gave an exaggerated shrug.

Yael dared to step closer, hoping Hadassah wouldn't move away. She kept herself from reaching for her though. "Why not?"

"Because nothing ever is," Hadassah said.

Emotion stung Yael's throat and the backs of her eyes. The truth struggled up from her gut, trying to force its way out of her throat with words she couldn't manage to form. She wanted to tell Hadassah she was a blood demon, that this bond between them *had* to be because of Hadassah's talents pulling Yael toward her.

"You said it was fate," was all she managed to get out before her mouth closed tight against anything more.

"Fate? Coincidence?" Hadassah crossed her arms over her chest and frowned in Yael's direction. "I'm not sure I can put my faith in either of those."

"Then let's make it a choice," Yael said.

Hadassah's chin lifted, but she didn't speak. Yael moved closer, this time enough to gently pry one of Hadassah's hands from where she'd tucked it tight against her body. Yael linked their fingers, not forcing or pulling, but making an invitation she was desperately hoping Hadassah would accept.

"You tell me it's all our own choices that put us where we end up. So, let's choose this. Choose us, whatever that means."

Hadassah sighed. "Regina told me something that I haven't been able to stop thinking about."

Regina, the teacher. Did she know the truth about Yael? Had she shared it with Hadassah? "What was it?"

"I'm not sure I want to say," Hadassah told her.

"Then don't say it," Yael said bluntly, relieved Hadassah was holding back.

Hadassah nodded and met Yael's gaze. "You know what...you're right. Caution is wise but fear only holds us back from what we otherwise might pursue to our benefit. I told you I was willing to see where this went with us, and you said you were too. So, let's just do it. Let's see what happens. Let's...choose."

"Yes," said Yael, grateful, relieved, overwhelmed with another surge of those emotions she was too slowly learning how to experience and control. "Let's choose."

Chapter Ten

You were never in love with anyone before.

Regina's words echoed in Hadassah's mind again as they'd been doing over and over again for the past two months. She set her purse on its place on the shelf and opened her appointment book. It was a light day, so far, but she knew she was going to have a hard time concentrating as much as she should this morning. Too many distractions.

Five feet and approximately eight inches of distraction. Two glorious handfuls of soft breast sort of distraction. Tight belly, luscious thighs...

There was really only one distraction, Hadassah admonished herself. All of it was Yael. Since the incident with the posturing man in the park, everything had been about Yael.

She hadn't specifically asked Yael to move in with her, but essentially that's what had happened. Hadassah went off to work at her office every day, while Yael went, most days, to her job with the landscaping company, and at night, she returned to Hadassah's apartment. She hadn't moved in any of her belongings other than a toothbrush and some clothes, and even then, around the house she preferred nudity or borrowed one of Hadassah's caftans.

They'd gone through countless bottles of red wine, ordered in every variety of takeout food they'd been able to, and made love for hours all over the house.

Made love. Hadassah laughed under her breath as heat stole through her cheeks. When had she stopped thinking of it as fucking and started imagining it as making love? Somewhere around day two, she guessed, when she'd made Yael laugh so hard she cried by doing an impression of a dolphin singing a country song. Or had it been the day before that, when Yael had fed her sweet and spicy sauce from the tip of her finger?

Maybe, Hadassah thought, it had been that first moment when she'd spun around on her stool to spy Yael sitting at the end of the bar.

Maybe it had been this way from the start.

Maybe, maybe, maybe. Everything was maybe and might be and what if. She should know better than to pin too much hope to any of it. All she could do was keep making choices.

"Hello? Good morning?" Hadassah's door had eased open to reveal a woman looking around it. She took a hesitant step into the room.

She was early. Hadassah pressed her lips together against the annoyance she felt and stood to gesture a welcome. "Mary?"

"Yes." The woman didn't move. She looked around the office with wide eyes before focusing her gaze on Hadassah's. She wrung her hands.

"Do you need some time to compose yourself? You're early for the appointment," Hadassah said. "You can wait in the lounge until you're ready."

"Oh, I'm ready now. I'm all ready." Mary snapped out the answer like she was on a game show trying to win a prize.

Hadassah sighed inwardly. So much for a few minutes to herself to prepare for the day. "You can have a seat right there."

Mary nodded sharply and moved, each motion jerky and robotic, to the chair Hadassah had indicated. Hadassah hadn't yet had time to set it for the reading, so she did that now, quickly. She took her own seat across from Mary.

"Have you ever had a reading like this before?" Hadassah began the same way she did for just about every client.

"Yes. Many times."

Hadassah hesitated at the tone of Mary's voice. The woman's demeanor was not what she would have expected from someone familiar with the process. "A blood magic reading?"

"Yes, yes. I said I have." Mary waved an impatient hand and scooted her chair closer to the table. She offered Hadassah her other hand.

Hadassah didn't take it right away. Something was off about this woman. Something she couldn't identify. It wouldn't have been the first time she'd cancelled a reading before it began, based on a weird vibe. She studied Mary carefully, but she couldn't pinpoint what it was about her that felt so wrong.

"Before we get started, I like to learn a little bit about you. It helps with the reading."

This was not untrue, although Hadassah most often only needed a minute or so of assessment before she was ready to start. Most often, clients had already submitted what they were interested in learning with their online appointment forms. Some didn't, of course, the ones who wanted as much anonymity as possible. Mary hadn't, and Hadassah hadn't given it a second thought...until now.

"Sure. Ask me anything." Mary's grin stretched wide and wider, thinning her lips over the bulge of her teeth but not showing them at all. The effect made a skull out of her face, her smile a rictus.

Unsettled, Hadassah sat back in her seat. "How did you find me?"

"You advertise."

All right then, Hadassah thought with a frown. "Why did you choose me?"

"You had fair rates. You got good reviews. I place a lot of weight on the opinions of others. I'm easily led. Do any of those answers please you?" Mary cocked her head, her gaze steady and piercing.

The faintest tingle of something unusual ran a feather-light touch along Hadassah's spine, and she suddenly understood. Mary was a witch. Why would a witch require the services of a hemomancer? More importantly, why would she also be trying to work some kind of persuasion spell on her?

"You can't magic me," Hadassah told her. "It's not allowed here. Besides, I'm warded."

Mary laughed, a low, vicious chuckle. "You think your little wards could stop me?"

"I don't know if they could or not. But I know that you're not allowed to do it here, in Sanctuary." Hadassah kept her voice calm, even as alarm rose quickly inside her. The poke and prod of whatever spell the witch was trying to cast rubbed against her like barbed wire shielded with linen—protected for now, but eventually it was going to stab right through.

"Do you think I really care about the rules here?" Mary gave the room a scathing look around before focusing her attentions back on Hadassah.

Hadassah had no problem with witches, but she did take affront with entitled bitches like this one. Mary was the sort who'd wear a face covering made out of tulle during quarantine season—the sort who didn't think the rules applied to her. She slipped one hand beneath the table, ready to press the buzzer that would call the Sanctuary security team to her office. Another swell of power pushed at her, prying at the wards.

"Get out," Hadassah said. "I don't know who you think you are—"

"I know who you think you are," Mary interrupted, "and I couldn't give a single damn. What I want to know about is your new 'friend.'"

The persuasion spell encircled Hadassah like a noose, pressing at her throat. She didn't give Mary the satisfaction of reacting to it. Her fingers pressed the security button, or tried to, slipping off the slick plastic as Mary's spell made her clumsy.

"What new friend?"

Hadassah's mind raced as she tried to think of a way to break the increasing hold Mary was placing on her. An image of Yael rose in her mind, and she forced it away, unwilling to give the witch even a second's satisfaction that she'd managed to get something out of her.

"You know exactly who I mean. Don't play dumb—"

"We're done here." Hadassah finally managed to press the security button.

Mary stood and leaned across the table. Her fingers curled into the tablecloth, tugging it. Her eyes glittered as her smile pulled across her lips, twisting them. Her teeth bared, briefly.

"You have no idea what you're getting yourself into," she breathed.

The office door opened to reveal the tall figure of one of the guards, who wasted no time in taking Mary by one arm. "C'mon. Let's go. You know the rules."

Mary didn't struggle. She sneered and spat without turning her head, but Hadassah had stepped far enough away that the spittle missed her. "You think you've got yourself a fun new lay? Wait until she decides to—"

"C'mon," the guard said, shaking the witch as though she were a naughty puppy that had chewed on its mistress's shoes. "We don't allow for that sort of thing here. Keep it up, and you won't be allowed back."

With that, he forced Mary out of the door and paused to look over his shoulder at Hadassah, who nodded her agreement. He didn't close the door behind him, and so she followed him to watch. To Hadassah's surprise, Yael stood in the hallway, her eyes wide. She pressed herself against the wall, hands flat against it, to stay as far away from the guard as she could.

No. Not from the guard. From Mary.

"She's not what you think she is!" Mary shrieked, fighting the guard's grip.

The guard shook her again. "Enough! Let's go!"

By the time they'd turned the corner, out of sight, Yael had begun to shake. Hadassah went to her but hesitated before putting a hand on Yael's shoulder. She could still hear Mary hollering.

"Yael?"

Yael looked at her, the haziness in her gaze clearing into a sharp focus. "Hadassah. Do you know that woman?"

"She's...well, I thought she was a client. But apparently not. Do you know her?"

"Yes," Yael whispered in a hoarse, broken voice. "But I wish I did not."

And then, she ran.

Chapter Eleven

Yael had to get out of here. To escape. She'd been discovered, because certainly the witch would have told Hadassah the truth about Yael, who she was. *What* she was. What she had done. At the end of the hall, she stopped herself short, her mind whirling, unable to recall which way she'd entered the building. Which door? Which path?

Which *choice*?

"Yael!"

Hadassah's voice tried to turn her, but Yael could not allow herself to stop. She had to get out of here before Hadassah called a guard down on her the way she'd done on the witch. How had the witch found her? Would she be waiting outside?

Yael's heart pounded. Her feet tangled, tripping her up. She fell against the wall, holding herself up with one hand, aware that she thought she'd been running as fast as she could but that she'd gone only a few steps before finding herself frozen in place. Was it a binding spell? Was she trapped?

"Yael," Hadassah said, closer now, and the warmth of her hand on Yael's shoulder was enough to send a shudder of both longing and fear through her.

Yael sagged and pressed her forehead to the wall. Her eyes closed. She tried to speak, to explain, but only a low moan escaped her. Again, she felt Hadassah's touch trying to turn her, but she could not allow it. Terrible enough that the witch had found her, but worse that she had discovered Hadassah.

"Don't..." she pleaded. "Don't touch me, Hadassah."

"Let me help you."

Yael cringed away from the tender touch. "You cannot help me."

She had not been created for running. Facing the threat and protecting her creator had been her commands. Until she'd defected from the witch who'd summoned her, Yael had been very good at her purpose...but she'd never learned how to protect or defend herself.

She ran now though. Down the hall. Out the front doors of Sanctuary, as fast as she could, her boots slapping the pavement. She stumbled again, this time going to her knees on the rough pavement. She bruised her borrowed flesh. Something sharp sliced into the palm of one hand, and she cried out but forced herself to her feet so she could run on, ignoring the blood gushing from the wound—she wasn't afraid of blood, and even though she knew it was going to allow Hadassah to track her, she could not risk stopping. Not until she'd found the witch...and killed her.

You will never be free of me. The witch's words echoed in Yael's mind as she freed herself of the shields she'd been doing her best to maintain for the past few weeks. They hadn't protected her, not enough, and now instead of keeping herself hidden from her creator, she wanted to make sure the witch discovered her...and, rounding a corner, she did.

"You should have stayed inside." The witch stepped out from the alley and leaned against the corner of the building as casually as if she'd been waiting there for Yael all along. Perhaps she had. "They could have kept you safe from me, in there."

Yael, breathing hard, felt her hands clutch into fists she did not even attempt to open. "Why should I need to be safe from you? Why can't you just let me go?"

"Let you go?" The witch laughed incredulously. "I *own* you!"

Yael shook her head. "No. Not anymore. I won't do what you ask."

"What, you won't kill for me? Please. Look at the meat suit you've got on. You walk around in it like you own that, but you stole it. You know what you did to get that body."

"I...did not," Yael gasped.

"Semantics. In the end, she died, no matter which one of us actually did it. Do you want to go back to where you came from? Is that it? You want me to send you back to the demon realm? I could." The witch flexed her fingers in Yael's direction. "Just. Like. That."

Before Yael could answer, the witch stepped toward her. "Oh...no. You don't want to leave this world. I can smell it on you. It's as rotten as the corpse you're wearing. It's because of her, isn't it? That hemomancer. Does she know what you are? She can't possibly. Don't you know, Yael, that nobody will ever care for you the way I can?"

"Don't touch me." Yael moved a step back.

The witch frowned. "Come on home with me. We'll get you out of that nasty shell and into something more attractive. I prefer blondes."

"You hate this body because it belonged to someone you think wronged you. She shouldn't have had to die for your...your..." Yael struggled to find the words to describe what she wanted to say. "Your smallness. Your weakness."

"You're calling *me* weak?"

"If you were strong," Yael said, "you would never have needed to summon me in the first place."

The witch drew herself up as tall as she could. "You really think I'm a terrible person, don't you? Where do you get off, judging me? You're not even human. You don't deserve to be in this realm. I brought you out. I can put you back in."

"Do it, then!" Yael's voice tore from her throat in a growl as she took a step forward. "Stop making promises you can't keep!"

Magic, like the tides, ebbed and flowed even within the one who wielded it, and this witch was no different. She'd been strong enough to pull Yael forth, but she hadn't been able to maintain control. She didn't have the skill to return her to the demon realm, no matter what she threatened, and Yael saw that clearly, now. Mingled relief and sorrow warred within her—human emotions, difficult to manage and even harder to interpret.

Yael wanted to go home...didn't she?

"All I wanted was someone to protect me for once!" The witch raised her clenched fists and shook them as her voice cracked and broke. She pressed her eyes with the heels of her palms and then raked her fingers through the fall of her thick dark hair. Her shoulders heaved with panting breaths.

Of all the emotions Yael had been sorting through since she'd put on this meat suit, pity was not one she'd yet encountered. It tasted bitter, but also sweet, with an undertang of copper. Somewhat like blood, she thought.

"The fewer people you hurt, the less protection you'll need," Yael said.

The witch's laugh barked out of her, rougher than gravel. "Look at that. You put on a human body like it's a ballgown, well, I guess on you it's more like a tracksuit, and you think you understand everything about what it means to be human. You know nothing."

"I know enough." Yael took another step back.

The witch spat to one side and advanced, but Yael was no longer afraid. "What happens when that body wears out and dies? You won't go back, you know, not without the right spells to put you there. You'll be lost in the void. If you come back with me—"

"No."

"You'll regret it," the witch said, "if you're capable of such a thing."

"Yael!"

Both Yael and the witch turned in the direction of the voice. Hadassah strode toward them, her expression grim and determined. She put herself between the two of them, and the witch looked back and forth from her to Yael.

"I'm leaving. You don't have to do anything." The witch held up her hands as she backed away, but the smug grin never left her expression.

Hadassah lifted her chin in the witch's direction. "Good. Don't come back around here. You're banned from Sanctuary, by the way. I hope it was worth it."

"You're the one who should be wondering if it's worth it." The witch gestured at Yael.

Yael shook her head. Tired, now. Her heartbeat had finally started to slow, but the surge of her terror and anger had left her trembling, feeling weak. She didn't even have the voice to reply, which clearly agitated the witch, who wanted an answer.

She muttered a few words under her breath and pulled a small pouch from her pocket. She pinched something out of it onto her palm and blew it in Hadassah's direction. Yael caught a hint of lavender, a tinge of rosemary. Something that had been tangled up tight inside her released. She let out a small, strange sigh.

"She's your responsibility now. I hope you're ready for it," the witch said.

Hadassah took Yael's hand. Their fingers linked. She squeezed, her palm warm against Yael's.

"That's none of your business. Why don't you leave, now? Before you make even more of a fool of yourself," Hadassah said.

The witch's lip curled, and she tucked the pouch back into her pocket. She gave Yael another long, lingering look. Her sneer turned into a frown, her lips trembling. She opened her mouth as though to speak but said nothing. Instead, she turned on her heel and stalked away.

By the time she rounded the corner and went out of sight, Hadassah had pulled Yael closer, hip to hip, and then turned her so they faced each other.

"Are you all right, Yael?"

Yael kissed her. It was the only action she could think to take, a sign of gratitude. Of desire. She'd meant it to be brief, but it grew quickly, until Hadassah pulled away with a small gasp. Her gaze searched Yael's.

"Take me home," Yael said. "Please."

Chapter Twelve

It was all moving too fast, there were so many questions to be answered, but Hadassah was making her choices. One after the other. She took Yael home. She took her into the bedroom. She kissed her.

They tore off their clothes.

In bed, Yael devoured her with kisses, her hands roaming over Hadassah's body. She buried her face between Hadassah's thighs, drawing in breath after breath, kissing her thighs. Belly. Hips. Breasts.

Slow down, Hadassah thought, but could not bring herself to say aloud. Instead, she arched into Yael's embrace, letting the pleasure wash over her. When Yale shifted, so did Hadassah, to take her turn at lingering over the curves and lines of Yael's body. She trailed her tongue over Yael's small, perfect breasts, making sure to spend some time on each nipple until Yael writhed and gasped.

Mouth to mouth, Hadassah and Yael moved in sync. Their bodies aligned, thighs pressed to hot, wet flesh as they ground together. Hadassah had never been able to finish this way, usually needing fingers or a tongue, some more direct pressure, but today every touch, every movement seemed like...more. All of this was more. Her orgasm rose inside her fast and faster, until all she could do was let it rip through her like lightning.

Panting, Hadassah cried out Yael's name. Beneath her, Yael was shaking with her own climax. They kissed again, taking in each other's taste while both of them came.

A few seconds later, Hadassah, still breathing hard, fell back onto the bed with her head next to Yael's. They hadn't even made it all the way to the pillows, but she couldn't muster the energy now to shift. Sweat cooled on her skin, and she shivered from that or from what had just happened, she couldn't be sure.

"Wow," was all she managed to say.

Yael rolled to bury her face against Hadassah's neck, one arm going over her body. Hadassah turned her face to kiss the top of her head. Her hair was damp and smelled faintly of shampoo.

"Thank you," Yael whispered.

"You don't have to thank me."

Yael pushed up on her elbow to look down at Hadassah. "Yes. I do. You came after me. You defended me...again. You've taken care of me. It's more than anyone else has ever done for me."

Hadassah let her fingertips trace the line of Yael's eyebrow. Down her cheek, her jaw, and finally to tap her lips lightly. "Hush."

"Why?"

"Because I just came hard enough to take my breath away," Hadassah said with a small laugh to cover up her lie. "And I don't have the energy for anything else right now."

Yael shook her head. "No. Not that. I mean…why did you come after me? Why stand up for me?"

She sounded sincere. Serious. And sad, Hadassah thought, or maybe she was the one who felt sad that Yael would even have to ask why anyone would be kind to her.

"I care about you, Yael."

Yael pulled away, rolling onto her back. There was a scant bit of distance between them, not enough even to take away the warmth of her skin, but still a withdrawal. Hadassah placed a hand on Yael's belly, just below her breasts.

"You wouldn't, if you knew more about me."

Hadassah traced one of her ribs. "Try me."

"I'm not like you."

"I know that you're not a hemomancer, if that's what you mean. You're not a witch either." Hadassah paused and then traced another rib. Yael's skin goose-pimpled beneath her touch, and her nipples peaked too. "Not a vampire, not a shifter, not a were."

"No. None of those things."

"What did she do to you?"

When Yael didn't answer, Hadassah's hand slid lower, over the softness of Yael's belly. Between her legs, where her fingers sought the sensitive flesh of Yael's clit. She circled lightly, listening for Yael's intake of breath. Waited for the tensing of her body. She let her touch drift lower, over the petals of her labia, and then, only then, did she dip a finger just inside.

She kissed Yael's shoulder. "You know you can tell me anything, right?"

Hadassah nuzzled Yael's warm, tan skin. She let her tongue slide out to taste her, the salt of exertion. Her natural flavor. Between Yael's legs, Hadassah's fingers slipped a bit deeper, earning her a low gasp.

"I'm afraid...that you will be afraid," Yael whispered.

Chapter Thirteen

"Of you? How could I be?" Hadassah's voice dropped to a whisper.

Her lips tickled Yael's neck. They lay in Hadassah's bed with its clean white sheets, the soft pillows, the lightweight but warm comforter. This was what it meant to be safe, Yael thought. This was what it meant to be *happy*.

Fresh need swelled inside her, and she rolled on top of Hadassah to slide her leg in between her lover's thighs. Groin to groin, their bodies ground together. Yael dipped her head to mouth her way along Hadassah's jawline. Lower, over her breasts. She found one tight nipple and drew it into her mouth, suckling. Her mouth found Hadassah's, and Yael let the slide of her tongue open her lover's lips. She kissed her harder. Deeper.

Hadassah let out a low, greedy moan. She opened her legs wider. Her hips rolled. Yael drank in that glorious response.

"I want to taste you," she said, and before Hadassah had time to reply, Yael moved down her body to center herself at the juncture of her lover's thighs.

It was her turn to be greedy, now, using her lips and tongue to lap at the sweet honey trickling from Hadassah's warm, slick flesh. Yael parted Hadassah's folds with her thumbs, opening her to find that erect and throbbing pleasure spot. She used the flat of her tongue to stroke Hadassah's clit, over and over, and in seconds Hadassah was thrusting upward. She panted out Yael's name, and her fingers sought to tangle in Yael's hair.

Yael eased off at the last moment, blowing a gust of hot breath over Hadassah's swollen, glistening pussy. She slipped a finger inside that tight cavern. Then another. Slowly, she curled them upward, seeking the small and slightly rougher patch that would have Hadassah screaming.

"Yael!"

Hadassah's back arched. Her fingers dug deep into the bedsheets. She cried out, fierce and low. Her body tensed, released, tensed again. Her pussy contracted around Yael's fingers and bore down, gripping. Pulsing.

Before she calmed, Yael moved up Hadassah's body to kiss her mouth again. Her pussy, not quite as wet as Hadassah's but slick and slippery on its own, moved without friction against Hadassah's wetness. Yael's climax had been building inside her since the first sweet glide of their tongues against each other. Making Hadassah come had pushed her closer to the edge—but she needed a little more. Just a little bit.

Hadassah pushed a hand between them. The kiss broke; Hadassah stared without blinking into Yael's eyes. Her fingers found Yael's clit and worked it. Rough and fast and without mercy, just the way Yael craved it. She kissed her just as hard, too, so that the tang of blood filled Yael's mouth. She swallowed it and the flavor of Hadassah's breath, and she let her body give up to this pleasure she was helpless to deny.

Yael cried out Hadassah's name, at the end, and collapsed beside her. Face down on the bed, her eyes shielded in darkness, all she had to do was let herself breathe.

Breathe.

She didn't move when she heard the soft pad of Hadassah's bare feet on the bedroom floor, nor when she heard them return. The bed dipped. Hadassah placed a cool hand on the small of Yael's bare back. Yael sighed.

Yael sat. She knew she'd disappointed this woman in the past with her lack of enthusiasm for this...whatever this was that they were doing. She knew it was a combination of her inability to fully utilize this human body's emotional range and the fact that she was trying her best not to draw Hadassah into anything that might endanger her. Yet in the aftermath of yet one more amazing lovemaking session, this honesty rose simply and easily to her lips as though the words were an incantation. It *was* a kind of magic, Yael thought. What they were doing.

Yael allowed her body to loll comfortably on Hadassah's bed. The softness cradled her. She let her limbs grow heavy. Then, her eyelids. She would sleep here, in this nest of comfort, next to the woman she— she...what?

The witch had spoken often of "love." What she had done for it. What she would do for it. How she could not live without it. The witch had claimed she loved Yael and had demanded the same in return, but Yael had never been able to understand what, exactly, "to love" meant.

What the witch wanted had not been anything like this.

Beside her, Hadassah stirred in her sleep. She curled onto her side, facing away from Yael, one hand tucked beneath her cheek. Yael could not stop herself from caressing the slope of Hadassah's shoulder. Her ribs. The curving valley just below her hip and that gentle swell. She moved up close, pressing herself to Hadassah's back. She breathed in the glorious scent of Hadassah's hair. Pressed her lips to the back of Hadassah's neck. Her hand slipped up and around to cup one firm, full breast.

Hadassah sighed. Her butt pushed back against Yael's belly. Yael pulled her closer, pressing her lips to Hadassah's shoulder blade.

"Are you hungry? I'm starving," Hadassah murmured, twisting a bit to look over her shoulder.

Yael closed her eyes. "I am always hungry for you."

"I meant for something like some Chinese takeout," Hadassah said lightly, "but that's very nice to hear."

Both of them lay in silence broken only by the soft in-out of their breathing. Yael pressed her lips to Hadassah's warm flesh. She took in the scent of her, imprinting it on her memory. Eons from now, she thought, she would remember this moment.

"Whenever you're ready to tell me, I'll be here." Hadassah's slow and easy breathing hitched. Her body stiffened, then relaxed, although not to the same boneless softness of before.

"I will never forget you, Hadassah." Yael kept her voice low on purpose, not wanting to wake Hadassah.

Nevertheless, Hadassah made a sleepy murmur. "You don't have to forget someone if you're still with them."

Yael said nothing, only pulled Hadassah closer to her. They stayed that way for another minute or so, and in that passing of time Yael allowed herself to imagine what it would be like not just to remember Hadassah, but to stay with her for the rest of this life.

Chapter Fourteen

"This is why you make a list and eat before you go shopping." Hadassah laughed, ducking out of the way from Yael's grabbing hands. She held the paper list high over her head, dancing in the parking lot to keep her lover from taking it. "Hey, hey! You're going to tear it!"

"I'm putting ice cream bars on it, and you can't stop me!"

Hadassah gave up the list, still laughing, as Yael pulled her close. They kissed right there under the bright late afternoon sun, and it was as close to a heaven as Hadassah could ever have imagined. She broke the kiss, but gently, brushing her lips over Yael's before pulling away.

"C'mon. I promised you matzah balls and brisket, and if we don't get it in the oven in the next couple of hours, we'll never be ready to eat in time. Yael," Hadassah said sternly, at least as sternly as she could through giggles, "let's go!"

Yael tried to sneak another kiss but gave Hadassah a solemn face as she handed the list to her. "Ice cream bars?"

"Fine. Ice cream bars." Hadassah shook her head and linked her fingers through Yael's as they headed for the grocery store entrance.

It had been three months of this. Companionship. Romance. Bliss, if Hadassah was going to get poetic about it, and although she'd never been one for that sort of thing, with Yael it was different. Everything was, from the sex to the conversations that deep dived into philosophy, religion, politics...the rules of card games, random trivia, the way memory worked. She'd never been with a partner who'd been so much fun, both physically and intellectually, but Yael was all of that and more. Hadassah had not forgotten that there were still secrets between them. She simply made her choices, every day, and hoped they were the right ones.

"Hey, love," Hadassah said now, casually, gesturing at the cart. "Can you grab that for me?"

"You just want to watch my butt wiggle as I push it."

Hadassah arched an eyebrow. "And?"

"And nothing," Yael shot back with a wicked grin and an extra wiggle in that lush backside. She pushed the cart through the doorway, Hadassah following. "Tell me again what we're doing?"

"It's Erev Rosh Hashanah..."

"Jewish New Year," Yael interrupted, steering the cart toward the produce section.

Hadassah put a hand on the cart, guiding it toward the fruit section. "Yes. So tonight, we have a festive meal to celebrate. Including apples and honey for a sweet new year, and a new fruit too...what about a dragonfruit?"

Caught up in looking for a fruit that would be suitable for the holiday table, Hadassah didn't notice at first when the cart and Yael stopped following her. When she looked up, her easy smile faded. The older woman staring at Yael lifted a trembling hand.

"Jacqueline? Honey? Where've you been?" Her voice shook worse than her hand.

Yael looked trapped, but she managed to force a fake smile to her lips. "You've got the wrong person."

"You look like my Jacqueline. You have the same...hair. Face." The old woman gestured. "Your eyes aren't the same. But it must be you. I know you've changed, girl. The men. The drugs..."

"I don't take drugs, and you've mistaken me for someone else," Yael said, but gently. "I'm sorry."

The old woman heaved a sigh. Her eyes glittered with tears. "They told me to stop hoping, that she was gone for good. If she wanted to come back, she would. They said she ran off with that addict boyfriend of hers, but I didn't want to believe it. He might have taken her, but she didn't go off on her own. She never would've left me like that, without even a word."

Yael shifted, her expression pained. Hadassah moved to her side to put a hand over hers, both of them touching the cart. Yael gave her a grateful glance.

"I call her sometimes, but she never answers." The old lady pulled her phone from her battered purse and thumbed the screen quickly, holding it up to show that the phone was dialing.

From Yael's pocket, her phone hummed. The noise was blocked by the fabric of her jeans, too faint for the old woman to hear, but Hadassah caught the noise at once. It ended quickly, though, so fast she couldn't be positive she heard it.

"It just goes to the message," the woman said.

Yael shook her head. "I'm sorry."

With another sigh, the older woman shuffled away. She looked over her shoulder, grief clear on her expression and in every hunched line of her body, but she didn't address them again. Hadassah, stomach sinking, waited until she'd moved out of earshot before turning to Yael.

"Did you know her?"

"No. I've never seen her in my life." Yael sounded sincere.

Hadassah wanted to believe her, but that was a choice she was finding harder and harder to make.

Chapter Fifteen

Yael had to get rid of this phone. It tied her to a past that she could not call her own and worse, it tied her to the people who had known this body. The longer she was in it, the more it became hers, including subtle changes in appearance, but clearly, she was still recognizable. She had a steady job, so she could afford clothes and contributions to the household she shared with Hadassah. She certainly could buy herself a new phone.

Dropping the phone in the street as they unloaded the groceries helped by cracking the screen. Kicking it "by accident" into the path of an oncoming car completed the action by destroying the phone totally. She feigned dismay, accepting Hadassah's sympathies, and then set herself to the task of helping cook the festive meal.

Together, they set the table, lit the candles, and said the opening prayers, but the comfortable silences Yael had grown used to now felt weighted with unasked questions. Hadassah was upset, but quietly so. Whatever she was thinking about the woman they'd encountered in the grocery store, she was keeping it to herself.

Yael accepted a hunk torn from the round challah, sweetened with honey and raisins, representing more good wishes for a sweet New Year. She knew the High Holidays, of course, although she'd never acknowledged them the way humans did, with food and festivity. Hadassah had said she wasn't particularly observant, but when Yael had expressed an interest in the holiday, she'd been the one to suggest they celebrate it with the meal, the decorated table, the candles, the prayers. The rituals felt familiar to Yael, but what felt even more like a ritual was sharing them with Hadassah.

"Yael?" Hadassah's brow furrowed. "Are you all right?"

"All of this...it's just so nice." Yael drew in a breath against the sudden tightness in her throat. Emotions, so many of them. So human. The longer she stayed in this vessel, the easier it had become to take on all the elements of humanity. But she was not human, was she? Could never be? She was simply playing a part, no matter how comfortable she was.

"I haven't observed the holidays in a long time. Probably not since college," Hadassah told her. "And you're right. It is nice. My mother asked me if I wanted to come home. I told her I was observing the holiday with you."

"You told your mother about me?" Yael's throat dried at the thought.

"Yes. Not everything. Just that there *is* a you. That we're together." Hadassah paused. "Is that okay?"

She took Yael's hand across the table, linking their fingers. Hadassah gave it a gentle squeeze, her thumb passing over the back. Yael squeezed back. Their eyes met. Locked. Hadassah smiled, and a rush of nameless emotion filled Yael so fiercely that it threatened to strangle her.

"Do you want to ask me if I've ever celebrated any holidays?"

Hadassah let go of her hand to tear apart some more of the challah. She stood to dip up some steaming beef brisket smothered in tomatoes and onions, ladling it onto first Yael's and then her own plate. She added roasted carrots mixed with fruit, a dish she'd called *tzimmes*, which made Yael's mouth water. Only when she'd added some roasted asparagus for both of them did she sit and look at Yael.

"If you want to tell me, I'm sure you will," Hadassah said.

Yael poked a fork into the pile of carrots. "Do you want to *ask* me?"

"Not right now," Hadassah said quietly. "Right now, I would like to eat this dinner we cooked together and enjoy your company. And after that, I'd like to sit and drink a glass of wine with you out on the balcony and listen to the night insects, while we make each other laugh."

"And after that?"

"I'd like to go to bed," Hadassah said, "and make love with you, before we both go to sleep. Together. In my bed. *Our* bed."

Yael swallowed against the emotions clogging her throat. "And...after that?"

"I'm not thinking about anything after that right now, Yael. Okay?" Hadassah's tone got a bit of a bite to it, but she softened it with a small smile.

"Yes. Okay. This is delicious." Yael ducked her head and focused on the food in front of her.

The mood lightened. Hadassah spoke of holiday dinners she'd shared in the past with her family and seemed happy enough to be the one carrying the conversation. After dinner, just as Hadassah had requested, they toasted each other with glasses of rich red wine and snuggled close on the wicker loveseat glider on the balcony off the living room. Hadassah rested her head on Yael's shoulder. Their soft laughter drifted on the night breeze, mingling with the chirping of crickets.

Hadassah stirred and stood, holding out her hand for Yael. "C'mon. Bed?"

Yael took her hand and followed. They would make love, she thought. And they would sleep.

And then...

And then, Yael knew, she would have to tell Hadassah the truth.

Chapter Sixteen

Replete from their languid lovemaking, Hadassah had begun to doze, half-fighting the urge to sleep but still letting it tug her eyes closed. She opened them when the bed dipped for a moment as Yael pushed upward, then got off it. She bent to scoop up her discarded shirt and pulled it over her head, and Hadassah sat up at once.

"What are you doing?"

"I should go," Yael said.

"You've been living with me for the past three months, Yael. Where, exactly, do you plan to go?"

"I don't know," Yael replied in a low voice.

The urge to beg her to stay warred with Hadassah's dignity. She sat up in bed, pulling up the sheet to cover the nakedness that only moments before had felt natural and now felt like vulnerability. It was because of the old woman in the store. She knew it. But the cause didn't matter, only the effect.

"You're going to walk out on me again?"

Yael paused, her panties in one hand, and then proceeded to continue putting them on. She straightened. "I'm not walking out on you. I'm just...leaving."

"Why?" When Yael didn't reply, Hadassah sighed and let her face fall into her cupped hands for a moment before she forced herself to look up again. "You don't have to go. We don't have to talk. But it's late, we're both tired. We should get some sleep."

Yael didn't move away when Hadassah stepped closer, but her body tensed. Hadassah stopped. Her breath eased out of her in a disappointed sigh.

"Yael." Hadassah held out a hand, but Yael didn't take it, and finally, Hadassah let it fall back to her side in defeat. "Fine. Don't answer my questions. Don't give me anything. Just keep coming back around whenever you want to fuck me. I guess that'll have to do."

"You should not let me," Yael said.

Hadassah lifted her chin. "You think I don't know that? Do you really think I'm okay with letting you walk in and out of my life like all I'm good for is to get you off?"

"No. I don't think you believe that, and if you said you did, I wouldn't believe you meant it."

"There's an easy enough solution, Yael. Take your stuff with you. Leave, and don't come back around. Stay away from Sanctuary. Our paths will never have to cross again. Just leave me alone."

Yael frowned and turned away. She paced, her hands at her hips, in fists. "It will hurt you if I abandon you."

"It hurts me that you let me think we could see where this could go," Hadassah retorted, "but now you won't even give it a chance to go anywhere. It hurts that you don't trust me."

Trust. Yael shivered visibly. "You think we could be more than lovers."

"Yes. I do. We *are*."

"You think we could..."

"Fall in love?" The words shot from her lips, and Hadassah forced herself not to show any signs of regret that she'd said them. "Yes. I think so. Maybe? Who can ever know?"

She hated herself in that moment, for giving away too much of herself. It had been a long time since she'd fallen this hard and fast for anyone. Longer since she'd ever been this honest with a lover who'd been meant as something only casual. To have spat out the truth this way, in anger, like an accusation...it left a sour taste in Hadassah's mouth. And still, right now, didn't she hope against all hope that her words would prompt something, anything in return from Yael?

"I want to give you something. I want to give you *everything*." Yael's voice shook. She whirled to face Hadassah. "But I can't!"

"Why not? Does it have something to do with the guy in the park that day? The old woman?" Hadassah watched Yael's expression go as shuttered as a house preparing for a storm.

"Yes. And...no."

"You *do* know them."

Yael shook her head. "I swear to you, Hadassah, I don't know either one of them, never saw them before they approached me. Either one of them. But...they know me."

"How can that be?" Hadassah asked, frustrated with this merry-go-round of confessions only half-admitted.

"I can't tell you."

"You can," Hadassah said. "You just won't."

"I don't want to then. Is that what you want to hear?"

"Yes! I want to hear the truth. Whatever it is. If you have something in your past you're ashamed of—" a flicker. "—or afraid of?"

Another flicker, this time stronger.

"It's an excuse, and I'm tired of them. That's all. Just go." Hadassah spoke wearily. She flicked her hand toward the bedroom door. "I'd say don't come back, but I'm not sure I could say no to you if you did. So please, Yael. If you have any compassion for me at all, just leave."

"I don't know how to have compassion. I want to, but I don't understand it. I'm not like you, Hadassah. I wish I was!" Yael gave a low, miserable groan.

Hadassah steeled herself against it. Whatever Yael was going through, if she wouldn't share it, there was nothing more Hadassah could do except try to protect herself. They stared at each other, both of them miserable in the silence...but there were no words left to say. Her feelings would fade, over time, if she stopped letting herself feed them. For now, though, all she could do was wait for Yael to walk away.

"Give me a reading," Yael said suddenly.

Hadassah shook her head. "I don't want to do that."

"You have to. It's the only way I can explain to you what I am." Yael stepped forward. Her eyes had gone glittery, bright, but with excitement, not tears. Two spots of high color painted her tawny cheeks. Her chest heaved, and her fists clenched and unclenched.

"And if I do this reading, and see your future," Hadassah said carefully, "it will mean I'm not in it. Is that what you want?"

"Is that what *you* want?" Yael countered. "Would it bring you peace to know, for sure?"

Frustrated, Hadassah tossed her hands in the air. "It will mean nothing! I've told you a reading isn't set in stone. I could see what's ahead for you, proving we don't share a future, and tomorrow something could change. Or the opposite could happen. I could continue being incapable of reading you, and ten minutes after I'm finished with the reading, you could finally decide to end this and walk away from me forever."

"Or you could do a reading for me and reach into the past," Yael said.

Hadassah hesitated, narrowing her eyes. "It doesn't work that way."

"It can, though. Can't it?"

"A reading usually encompasses some information about what you've done or experienced in the past to bring you to this point, yes. But it's not the same."

"You can do it," Yael insisted.

"A person's past is so complicated and long, Yael, there's too much knowledge to go through—"

"Not for me," Yael interrupted.

"Fine." The way Hadassah snapped the word would have given any other person in the world the hint that she was anything but fine...but Yael was not any other person in the world.

She was the woman Hadassah could imagine herself loving.

"Fine," Hadassah repeated, softer this time. "Finish getting dressed. We'll do it in the living room."

She set up the tools she needed as Yael took a seat. She hissed at the slice of Hadassah's engraved scalpel. Hadassah looked at her, holding her hand over the silver bowl to catching the dripping blood.

"Hurts," Yael said. "More than it did the first time."

"What do you want me to look for?"

"Go back to when I was born."

"That's too much," Hadassah protested. "Almost three decades ago? My hemomancy talents don't work over that length of time."

"It's not three decades. It's only a few months. Look," Yael insisted through gritted teeth. "Please, Hadassah, just try."

Hadassah sighed and bent over the bowl. There *were* patterns forming, hovering and swirling. She narrowed her eyes, focusing. She drew on her power, digging deep inside herself. She expected to wade through blurry images of Yael as a teenager, a child, perhaps even an infant, if she could get back that far. But instead, she saw only Yael as she was now. As she'd been the day they met. Then, something earlier, a cluttered room, stinking of sulfur. Yael speaking to a woman...Mary. The witch. Earlier still, the images disjointed and fractured, like watching someone else's dream. Nonsensical.

A body on the floor. Yael's body, familiar even though it lay still and somehow broken looking. Eyes open. Lifeless.

Dead.

Chapter Seventeen

There is a growing pool of blood on the floor.

It leaks from the eyes, nose, mouth of the woman. Other places too. It has started to seep up from her pores. Her hair is sticky with it. Her clothes, saturated.

She is dead.

"Oh, you are a delight!" This from the witch, who coos and claps her hands and even does a joyful dance in place as she stares down at the woman she commanded Yael to kill.

Yael is drawn to the blood. She does not drink it, nor does she bathe in it. She can manipulate it, if she chooses, but in this moment, faced with what she has done, she does nothing. The push and pull of the witch's desire surrounds her, but it cannot fill her. It cannot move her.

In this form, she is little more than essence. She has a shape of long limbs, claws, teeth. She is visible, but not solid. The weight of this world presses on her but, bound by the incantations that drew her forth, she cannot go back to where she began. She is a prisoner.

The witch crouches over the sprawled corpse. She doesn't care about kneeling in the blood. She revels in it.

She pokes at the body. She laughs louder, and louder, and louder, and her glee is a stench that sends Yael reeling.

This may have been the reason she was summoned, but it is not the purpose of her existence.

"Clean this up." The witch gets to her feet, stumbling as if she's drunk.

Yael cannot. She will not. Drawn by the blood her powers spilled, her essence coalesces...and enters the body on the floor. Yael fills it with herself. In every place where once was blood, now there is Yael.

The body rises to its feet. It stumbles under Yael's hesitant and clumsy control. She stretches herself inside it, no longer what she was but something new.

And then, she runs.

Chapter Eighteen

The images had faded the instant Hadassah reeled in in her magic, but clearly Yael was in the midst of a memory. Her pale eyes had gone dark, the pupils dilated. She breathed heavily, her body tense, positioned as though she meant to flee at any moment.

"Yael?"

"What did you see?"

Hadassah hesitated. "I saw *you*. Hurt. What happened to you?"

"That wasn't me," Yael said.

"I don't understand."

"I want you to try again." Yael's voice dipped into a husky growl, nothing like a tone of sensuality. More animalistic. Chilling. Hadassah had never heard her sound that way—she'd never heard *anyone* sound that way.

"I'm not going to learn anything else." Hadassah shook her head and let the lie slip from her lips as she kept her gaze pinned steadily on Yael's. "It won't make a difference."

"That's not true. Take more. Learn more. I need you to see."

Hadassah stood and carried the silver bowl to the kitchen sink to rinse it out and wipe it clean. She sprayed the entire area with cleaning chemicals strong enough to sanitize it, to erase any signs at all that Yael's blood had ever even touched it. She kept her mind focused on the mundane tasks so she didn't have to think about what any of this meant.

"Hadassah. Please." Yael came up behind her. Took her by the shoulders. Turned her.

"I don't want to," Hadassah snapped. "You can't force it, Yael. Blood magic doesn't work that way. You can't force it, and you can't force me."

Yael drew in a heaving breath. Her eyes glittered, not with tears, but some emotion Hadassah couldn't discern. Her fingers gripped Hadassah's shoulders, pinching and hurting, but Hadassah didn't cry out or make any move to get away. Yael's touch hurt, but she'd rather feel the sting than lose that touch, perhaps their last.

"I wish you would just tell me what's going on," Hadassah said finally. Quietly. She moved closer, forcing Yael to release her grip and embrace her. "Please. Trust me."

"I..." Yael shuddered.

Hadassah enfolded her into her arms. Yael had always been lean. Strong. She felt frail, now. Somehow fragile, like a finely blown glass that would easily shatter if you tried to hold it too hard.

"Yael, I love you." The words slipped out easily, as though they'd been said a hundred times already. A thousand. If she'd had any doubts about her feelings, they vanished, now. Hadassah brushed her lips over her lover's temple, feeling the frantic pulse that beat there. "Whatever it is, whatever you're going through, you can tell me."

"Whatever I've done?" Yael asked. "Will you...love...me...no matter what I've done?"

Hadassah hesitated. "Yes. I believe so."

"What about no matter what I am?" Yael pulled away, stepping back far enough that Hadassah would have had to reach for her.

This didn't make sense. Hadassah took a step toward Yael, who moved back, her hands up in a defensive posture.

"What do you mean, what you are?" Hadassah had to force the words out of a dry throat. "You're a woman."

"I'm not."

Ice formed inside Hadassah's guts. It spread through every part of her, making her go stiff and solid, a frozen statue. If she moved too suddenly, she thought, if something were to touch her now, she would shatter into a million pieces. Irreparable.

"What do you mean?" Each word fell, solid as a stone, from Hadassah's numb lips.

"I am not a woman," Yael said. "I have taken the form of a woman, and if I could be said to have a gender, it would be female. But I am something else."

"What? What are you?"

Yael did not reply.

Hadassah's hands shook. She turned back to the sink, meaning to finish cleaning it, but found she could not. She could only grip the edge of it to keep herself steady and upright. Her knees had weakened.

"What am I, Hadassah? I think you know."

"Demon." The simple word dropped like a stone from her lips.

"A blood demon."

It explained so much.

Hadassah whirled. "That doesn't matter to me!"

"It should." Yael's voice trembled. "I can't be any good for you!"

"You *are* good for me." Stubbornly, Hadassah shook her head and moved toward Yael, who held up a hand to stop her.

Her mind raced already with thoughts of spells, incantations, the use of magics she did not understand. There had to be something, anything, that could make this work. Something that could keep Yael here, where Hadassah needed her to stay.

"I can't lose you," she said. "I won't."

Yael's shoulders hunched. Silver tears streaked from her eyes and over her cheeks. They dripped off her chin, and she swiped them away. She lifted her face to look into Hadassah's eyes, and her expression turned grim and stiff and cold.

"I stole this body."

The confession set Hadassah back a step or two, but she worked hard to keep herself from showing any disgust or fear. "There must have been a reason."

"You condone murder?"

"No, of course not —"

"Because you *love* me." Yael spat the words, her mouth twisting. Her fists clenched. "Is that what love does, Hadassah? It makes excuses for terrible acts?"

"No," Hadassah said sharply, but Yael didn't let her continue.

She paced, the air between them fairly crackling with tension. "I was made to defend my summoner against enemies. Not to take life as though it meant nothing, for any reason."

"Your summoner? The witch commanded you to kill this woman?"

"Yes. I don't know why. Something stupid and small because that's what she had become. She lured the woman to her house, and she called me forth, and I...she..." Yael drew in a few hitching, desperate breaths. She gave Hadassah a wild-eyed stare. "Her heart. She was on something, taking something that made it weak. When she saw me, she fell to the ground. I never touched her. Whatever the witch did, after, made sure she was dead. But I'm the reason."

"It wasn't your fault," Hadassah said gently, thinking of the images she'd seen in the blood.

"I killed her."

"She died," Hadassah repeated. "She'd worked her body to its limits, and it couldn't handle what she was doing to it. Mary wanted her dead, but you didn't kill her."

Yael shook her head. "That doesn't excuse my part in it. Or the harm I brought to the ones before her, the ones the witch wanted revenge on. I've been in this realm for less than a year, Hadassah, and all I have ever done in it is evil."

"That's not true. You've never done evil to me."

"I've hurt you," Yael shot back fiercely. "More than once."

It was not untrue, but still, Hadassah regretted her earlier accusations. Yael pivoted on one heel and looked at her. The anguish on her face broke Hadassah's heart more than anything else she'd ever done.

Hadassah wanted to embrace her but didn't dare. "I love you, Yael."

Those had been the right words before, but they sounded wrong this time. Yael gave a desperate, hitching sob. She turned on her heel and fled the kitchen. Hadassah ran to follow, but Yael moved so fast, with such grace—how could she not have seen this before? How could Hadassah have let herself believe that Yael was entirely human?

Because that's how love works, she thought. You see the best in the ones you love; you make yourself blind to what you don't want to see.

Except that she'd meant what she'd just said to Yael. It didn't matter to Hadassah that Yael was a demon who'd slipped into a human body no longer capable of sustaining the spirit of its owner. She didn't care about what Yael had done, had been forced to do, by the witch who'd pulled her out of the demon realm. The past didn't matter, not like the future did.

Hadassah caught up to her in the living room. Yael struck out wildly, knocking a glass vase onto the floor.

With a low cry, she bent to use the biggest shard of it to slice into the back of her hand. Crimson fluid welled up, spattering onto the floor as she stood. She held out her hand toward Hadassah.

"I am not a woman, Hadassah. I am a blood demon, wearing a stolen shell."

"I'm not afraid of a little blood."

How could she be? Hadassah had been manipulating blood since shortly after the appearance of her own monthly cycle. Blood had been her source of income. Blood had given her strength. Blood had been... everything.

"You *should* be afraid of me." Yael shuddered. Staggered. Then she turned and fled through the front door.

Hadassah's knees weakened and threatened to spill her onto the floor, but she managed to stay upright. Her breath now came in shallow, panting heaves as she tried her best to hold back the sobs. Weeping wouldn't do anything for her right now. She would not allow herself to succumb to it.

Instead, she got to work.

The puddle on the floor had already started taking on that sticky film of old blood; it wouldn't be the easiest to work with, but she'd have to do the best she could. Using an engraved silver spoon she'd inherited from Regina, Hadassah scooped up some of Yael's blood and dripped it into a matching silver scrying cup from her shelf. She hadn't used these particular tools in years—they'd been some of her first, and she'd graduated to better, but, as with the quantity and quality of the blood, she would have to make do.

She cleared her mind as best she could. Focus. Focus. Breathe. Hadassah closed her eyes. With the cup held in one hand, she waved the other over it.

You never captured the blood magic. It couldn't be forced. You had to coax it. Ease it. Many times, Hadassah had thought of it as seduction.

But not today.

Almost instantly the colors swirled and rose, twisting into the shapes and patterns it had taken her years to learn how to interpret. It was not unheard of to use hemomancy to read someone who wasn't there, but it had never been Hadassah's practice. It didn't matter, now. Nothing about her relationship with Yael had been normal.

Hadassah put forth her question, not with words, but simple desire. "What will happen to Yael?"

She held her breath. For the first time since she'd begun honing her hemomancy skills, Hadassah wished to fail. Instead, she easily interpreted the signs to see that Yael was going away—somewhere far away, to another country, or possibly, horribly, even another realm. Wherever she was going, it would be without Hadassah.

Again, she wanted to drop to her knees, to keen out her despair, but there was no time for that. Hadassah had seen something else in the blood. Something closer than the future.

She could see where Yael was right now.

Chapter Nineteen

Yael had run from Hadassah's apartment with nothing—no phone, no wallet, no cash. That meant unless she wanted to walk all the way to the witch's house, she would have to hitchhike. She wasn't worried about coming to harm from a random driver, but she hadn't counted on calling police attention to herself. When the cruiser pulled up next to her, Yael quickly shoved her hands in the pockets of her jeans and kept walking, eyes facing forward.

"Hey, Jackie. What's going on?" The cop in the passenger seat had rolled her window down, now addressing Yael.

"I'm not Jackie." She kept her gaze ahead of her, but her heart had started pounding.

"I'm going to ask you to stop for a second, let me get some ID from you—"

Yael took off.

From behind her, the blue/red flash of police lights came on as the car followed. Yael pushed this frail physical form to its limits to keep ahead of it, pumping her limbs. She drew in gasping breaths of humid, sticky afternoon air. She kept ahead of the car for a few minutes before it sped up enough to turn and come to a stop directly in front of her, one wheel on the sidewalk.

She'd misjudged her strength, believing she could clear the car with a leap, but she'd been human for too long. Instead, her battered boot toe caught the edge of the hood, smacking the hot metal and pitching her forward. Her body slammed full-length onto the hood of the police car. The officers, one male, one female, were both already out of the car.

"Holy shit, did she just try to—?"

"Yeah," affirmed the female cop. "But she didn't make it. I got her."

Yael expected rough hands to drag her from the hood of the car, but the cop's grip was surprisingly gentle. Firm, but not violent. The woman pulled Yael to her feet but supported her. She was shielding her, Yael realized.

"I got you," the cop said. In a lower voice, softly into Yael's ear, she said, "I know what you are."

After that, Yael lost the ability to discern words. She felt hands on this body she'd stolen and abused so fiercely, and she felt pain. Exhaustion. The deepest need she'd ever experienced, a desire to simply cease to exist, filled her.

Yael had never feared death. How could she be afraid of something she could not imagine experiencing? She'd never been afraid of pain either. How could something that had been woven into the very fabric of her being terrorize her?

She was afraid now of loss.

Time passed differently for demons, but her months spent as human had changed her perception of it, and of grief. Of sorrow. She mourned, now, the loss of Hadassah.

Even knowing that her leaving had been to protect her lover, Yael could not rid herself of the grinding, almost paralyzing grief. It made her stumble. It made her fall.

Perhaps death would be welcome, instead of this.

The hands holding her so tightly let her go. Yael stumbled back. The cop who'd been holding her waved a hand at her partner.

"It's not her," she said in a low voice ripe with magic.

Yael took another stumbling step away from the cops and the patrol car. The female officer pinned her gaze on Yael's as her partner moved forward. Again, the woman who'd been holding on to Yael lifted a hand in her partner's direction.

"We misidentified. This young woman is causing no harm," she said in the same pleasant, neutral voice as before.

"All right then," her partner said and got back in the car.

Yael tensed, waiting for the remaining officer to come after her, but the cop just put her hands on her hips.

"You're Mary's work. I can smell it on you. You're the demon she had bound to her?"

"Yes, but—"

The cop shook her head. "I don't need to hear it. She gives our kind a bad name. Personally, I think she needs to be brought up on charges, but she's got friends with more influence than I have. Are you all right?"

"Do you know about what happened?" Yael's voice cracked.

The cop nodded. "Heard about it, yeah. Hard to prove someone's a murderer when the body of the person she's supposed to have killed is up and walking around. Heard, too, that you'd run off from her. You're not bound to her anymore?"

"No," Yael said.

"Good." They studied each other for a moment or so. The cop opened the door to the cruiser, tossing her next words over her shoulder. "Stay out of trouble. The body you're in didn't belong to the most upstanding of citizens. You can do better than that."

"I'm trying." Yael watched the car drive away.

Her heart still pounded fiercely. *Her* heart, she thought. It had once belonged to someone else, but no more. Now, it was hers, and her responsibility, for as long as she kept it.

So, how long would that be?

Chapter Twenty

"What do you want?" The witch peered suspiciously from the crack in her barely opened door. "If you've come to kill me, you can just forget it. I've got this place warded—"

"I haven't come to kill you. I want some information." Yael pressed the toe of her boot into the crack to prevent the witch from closing it. "Let me in."

The witch frowned. "Why should I?"

"Because you owe me that. You owe *her* that," Yael added.

The witch waited another few moments before pulling the door open. She looked smaller than Yael remembered. Somehow more frail. Her hair unkempt, her clothes too loose-fitting. She smelled, too, of illness and neglect. It might have been enough to elicit pity, if Yael could have found some for her, but everything the woman had done had erased any hope of that.

"Should I offer you a drink? Something to eat? Is this a social call? I know," the witch said with a familiar, wicked smile. "You missed me. Welcome home."

Home. One syllable. A simple word that invoked complex feelings.

"This," Yael said, "has never been my home."

For the first time since Yael had been yanked from the demon realm by this woman's narcissism, the witch looked...not ashamed. But at least she looked *aware*.

"Nobody told me, Yael. What it would really be like. All the texts, all the stories. None of them said you'd be like you are." The witch gestured toward Yael with both hands as she shook her head.

Yael's chin tipped up. "I am what I was made to be. If you were not aware of it before you summoned me, that's not my fault."

"Well, it isn't mine either. It just is what it is!"

They stared at each other. Deep inside Yael's chest, a quivering curl of emotion stirred. Pity? Or at least a feeling as close to that as the witch's shame.

"We could start over," the witch said.

Yael put her hands on her hips. "No."

"Why did you come back here, then? Just to throw it in my face? I know you didn't come back to kill me," the witch said.

"I want you to send me back. I don't belong here."

The witch's expression twisted. She backed away, turning around so she didn't have to look at Yael. She went to the bottle of wine, open on the coffee table, and poured herself a glass. She didn't offer one to Yael, but she sipped from it for several long, silent moments before speaking.

"I can't."

"You have to. You brought me here, you need to—"

"I can't," the witch snapped. "Don't you get it? It's not even that I don't know how. I just can't do it. I'm not... strong enough. I never was."

Desperately, Yael pivoted on her heel, but stopped herself from beginning to pace. She held her ground, facing the woman who'd caused all this trouble. "Who can, then? You have to know someone. A colleague. A mentor."

"You'd think so, wouldn't you? Unfortunately for us both, it seems I've burned more bridges than I've crossed."

"Nobody wants to help you," Yael said.

The witch laughed without humor. "Even if they did, they can't. I brought you in, so only I can send you back. Nobody else *can* do it. I'm sorry." She said the final word as though it tasted bitter, like poison.

Yael did not believe her. "You wouldn't send me back, even if you could."

"That might be true, but I guess we'll never know, will we? Cheers. Welcome to the world." The witch raised her glass.

The gesture reminded Yael of Hadassah and the first time they'd met. That anything about this woman should remind her of the other unsettled Yael's stomach. There was no comparison. The witch was selfish, greedy, weak...

And Hadassah was the opposite of all those things.

"A hemomancer and a blood demon. It certainly makes sense. I'm sure she's been happy to use you for your extra powers," the witch said.

Yael turned away, her arms crossed over her belly. "She had no idea about that. Anyway, in this body, I'm not...I can't..."

The witch made a *tut-tut* noise and moved closer. "Well, you can blame yourself for that. I never asked you to put yourself inside a body."

"You never warned me!"

"Would you have listened?" the witch shot back. "You were so damned eager to just get away from me, you didn't care! So now, you're stuck where you are until that body dies. I'd get used to it if I were you. The longer you stay, the more human you'll become. Eventually, that's all that will be left, until you die."

Yael's fingers curled into a semblance of claws, but she didn't lash out at the woman who'd so wronged her. The witch took a step back, anyway, her wine splashing out of the glass. Her fear rose between them, palpable as a fistful of silk.

"And then what?" Yael demanded.

The witch shrugged. "No idea. Not my wheelhouse."

Yael growled.

"Changed your mind, then? Going to kill me, after all?" The witch grinned.

"I already told you, I'm not." Yael forced her mouth to stop its sneer. Her fists to loosen. "I don't want to kill anyone ever again. But I do need you to tell me something."

"Why should I do anything at all to help you?"

Yael's gaze pierced the witch's. "I don't have to kill you to bring you harm, Mary. And you know it."

It was the first time Yael had ever referred to the witch by name. It shook her, Yael could see that by the way Mary shivered. Mary gulped down the rest of her wine, but her hand trembled, and some of the crimson fluid spilled down her chin. It stained the front of her white blouse. She didn't even swipe at the mark.

"Fine. What do you want?"

"Who owned this body before me?"

Mary's eyebrows rose. "What?"

"If I'm going to live in this body until it dies, I need to know who it belonged to."

"Why?"

"Because people loved her," Yael said.

"That doesn't mean they'll love *you*," Mary said coldly.

Yael didn't flinch. "I don't need them to love me. But if I'm going to live in this body, I need to be able to *live* in it."

"You'd be better off pretending to be someone else forever. She was a thieving drug addict who couldn't get her shit together."

"If I am going to live in this body," Yael repeated, "then I will try to be better to it than she was."

"You're going to be disappointed a lot in life if that's how you go about it. Why not use up that body and take another one? It should be easy enough for you. That's what I'd do," Mary said, "if I were you."

Yael said nothing. After a moment, Mary sighed. She tipped the bottle of wine over her glass, but it was empty. She sighed deeply and looked at Yael.

"I did care for you, you know. You think I didn't, but I did."

Again, Yael said nothing. Mary's frown deepened. She set the bottle on the table with a *thunk*.

"Fine. I'll tell you who she was, but you should know something, Yael. It would be better for anyone who loved her to think she's dead than for them to know it's you inside there. Death is better than believing someone you loved has abandoned you."

Again, an image of Hadassah rose in Yale's mind. It stung. How would she make amends? Could she ever?

"You don't know anything about how to love," she told Mary.

"Oh," Mary scoffed. "And you do? I guess you think that hemomancer loves you, and you love her back?"

"I know she does. And I feel the same."

"You're a demon," Mary said with a sneer. "Demons can't love."

"This body can love," Yael replied. "So, I can too. It's just not you. Tell me who I have become."

So, Mary did.

Chapter Twenty-One

Hemomancy was strong magic, but it wasn't lasting. The images faded, leaving Hadassah shivering in the aftermath—much the way her clients sometimes felt, she realized. She'd have more compassion for them in the future. For herself right now, she made a mug of steaming tea, simmered with restorative herbs. She let the steam bathe her face as she cupped the mug. She hadn't yet started crying, but she was going to, eventually.

Yael had gone back to Mary. What Hadassah had seen felt like a confrontation, not a reunion, but it was not the purpose of Yael's actions that had put Hadassah to her knees. It had been the fact she could see what was happening at all.

Her future had no Yael in it.

It hadn't been long enough for love, she told herself. She would get over it. Move on. It wasn't the first time she'd had a relationship end before she was ready, and it probably would not be the last. She'd let herself cry for a bit, maybe indulge in some junk food and junk TV; maybe she would drink a little too much and gain some weight or take up a hobby or fuck a stranger, now and then...

Hadassah burst into racking, wrenching sobs. She put a hand over her heart, which still insisted on beating as steadily as ever, even though it was most definitely torn to shreds. Knowing she shouldn't be feeling this did nothing to stop the waves of sorrow flooding her.

"I love her," Hadassah said aloud, her voice as torn and tattered as her heart felt.

She swiped at her face and forced herself to take deep breaths. The future was not set, and Hadassah knew that better than anyone else. Her choices and actions changed her future second by second. The question now was simple: What did she have to do to change it?

Chapter Twenty-Two

Jackie Pence. That was who this body had been. The question was, who would Yael become?

With her new phone, Yael did not have access to Jackie Pence's social media accounts, but Mary was able to pull up her Connex account. It had been set to public view, and although she hadn't been particularly gracious about it, Mary had shown Yael how to search the dead woman's connexions for information about her life and family. It had been frighteningly easy to discover the name and location of Jackie's grandmother—the old woman who'd met Yael in the grocery store.

It took over an hour for Yael to get to the woman's house on foot. She had to knock loudly three or four times before she heard any motion from inside, and even then, the door only cracked open enough to reveal a suspicious set of eyes peering out.

"What do you want?"

"We saw each other in the grocery store," Yael said gently. "You thought I was your granddaughter."

The door shut quickly. Yael raised her hand to try again, but it opened before she could. The old woman stepped aside to let her in.

"You'd better come inside."

Yael stepped into a dimly lit living room that smelled thickly of dust and cat fur but was otherwise immaculate. The old woman bustled toward the kitchen, gesturing for Yael to follow. In the much brighter room, she pointed at the kitchen table.

"Sit. I'll make tea."

Yael did not want any tea, but she accepted a mug without arguing. The old woman scraped her chair legs along the floor, patterned with once-vibrant green and yellow daisies that had faded to soft grays.

"You are not Jackie," she said. "You look like her, but you ain't her. So, what are you?"

"I..." Yael hesitated.

"Never mind," the old woman said brusquely. "You've got her on like a borrowed dress, huh? I told my sister about seeing you, and she said I was losing my marbles. So did my grandson. I suppose that might be true, but it doesn't feel true."

"It's not true. I am inhabiting Jackie's body."

"So, she's dead."

"She's dead," Yael told her. "I came here to give you some measure of peace about it though. She died without pain."

That was a small lie. Jackie had died quickly, but in terror. Still, Yael was here to comfort, not to cause more grief.

"She got mixed up in a lot of bad things. I warned her she'd come to a bad end. I guess she did." The old woman peered at Yael. "I told you before. You look like you *used* to look like her, but you don't look like her now."

"Anyone else who knew her would not think so, perhaps," Yael said. "They would still believe I am her."

The old woman tipped her head to look Yael up and down. "She didn't have many who cared about her if you want to know the truth. But for your sake, I'm glad whatever trouble she got herself into, it likely wasn't enough that you'll need to worry about it. Maybe you'll do better than she did, with this life."

"I'm going to try," Yael promised.

The old woman sipped her tea, holding the mug with both hands to keep it steady. She set it down carefully on the table and looked at Yael. "I know what you are, by the way. You didn't have to tell me. There's only one thing that possesses folks."

There were more than that, Yael thought, but she didn't contradict Jackie's grandmother.

"I supposed I ought to be afraid or something," the old woman said, "but I've lived as good as I could, and if that doesn't count for anything, then I guess nothing does. Anyway, Lucifer himself was an angel, wasn't he?"

"I'm no Lucifer," Yael said.

The old woman shook her head. "I don't suppose anyone else could ever be. You're just you then. That's all anyone of us can ever be. Will you come to see me again?"

"I don't think so," Yael said gently. "It could lead to questions and trouble, don't you think?"

The old woman nodded with a sigh. "That's the truth, all right. People can't seem to mind their own business. But before you go, would you listen to me talk about her, just a bit? About what she was like before she went the wrong way. Nobody wants to remember her that way, they talk bad about her because of the trouble she got herself into, and I guess that sort of trouble is probably what led her to end up where she went. But she wasn't always like that. I'd like you to know about her, before."

"I would love to know," Yael said. "Please tell me."

Chapter Twenty-Three

By the time night fell, Hadassah had finished cleaning and rearranging her bookshelves and display cases. It had been a task she'd long put off in favor of doing just about anything else, but now her living room was not only organized and tidy, she'd been able to find and sort items that had been missing amongst the clutter for years. She'd done something similar in the half bath, the kitchen, the guest room.

She'd baked a cake.

She'd cleaned out her freezer.

She'd deep-cleaned her pores and used a facial mask.

In short, she'd spent hours focusing her attentions on tasks with lots of detail, so she'd be able to keep her mind off trying to find out more about where Yael had gone. She'd refused to allow herself a glass of wine until the final tasks had been completed, and now, although she'd been generous with the pour, Hadassah could only look at the glass in her hand. She had no appetite for it.

If not even wine could bring her out of her slump, she really must be wrecked.

The thought was enough to push a small laugh up her throat and out, but it sounded more like a sob. Hadassah put the glass on the spotless coffee table and let her smooth, fresh face fall into her hands. What was she going to do when she ran out of things to clean?

The sound of her front door opening startled her into looking up. Yael stood there, looking solemn and yet excited too. She moved from foot to foot.

"Hadassah," she said when Hadassah didn't speak. "Is it all right if I came home?"

She was up and off the couch with Yael in her embrace within seconds. No words would come out. All Hadassah could manage was a series of small, gasping sob-laughs. She hugged Yael harder, pressing their cheeks together. Then, their mouths.

Yael took Hadassah by the upper arms and separated their bodies. "Is that a yes?"

"Yes. Definitely a yes," Hadassah said.

"You're crying!"

"No," she denied, although she tasted the salt of her tears.

Yael shook her head and gathered Hadassah closer. "Please don't cry. I love you."

Hadassah shivered at the words. She closed her eyes. Hugged harder. Tighter. She buried her face against Yael's neck.

They stayed that way for some long moments, neither speaking. After a bit, Hadassah noticed that their breathing had synced. She slipped a hand between them to put over Yael's heart. It beat beneath her palm, a steady, comforting throb.

"I thought you were going back to her," she said finally.

Yael's hand rubbed her back. "I wanted to ask her some questions. That's all."

"Did you get the answers you wanted?" Hadassah pulled away to look Yael in the face.

"I got the answers I asked for," Yael said. "Even if some of them were not the ones I was hoping to hear."

Hadassah chuckled, the sound raspy and hoarse, but somehow still light. "That sounds familiar."

"Hadassah. I don't know what it will mean, exactly, for me to stay. I only know that I can't go back to where I came from, and I have no idea where I'll end up after I die."

"You and me and everyone else," Hadassah told her.

"I know," Yael added, pulling her closer, "that none of that matters, when I can live this life the best I can, and I can live it with you. Will you let me try?"

Hadassah kissed her again. "I don't have any other choice."

"We always have a choice, Hadassah. That's what I've learned from you. But I'm willing to keep making this choice, over and over again." Yael let her fingers tangle for a moment in Hadassah's curls. "I wouldn't blame you for not believing that I mean it. Would you like to do a reading—"

"No." Hadassah cut that off right away with a firm shake of her head. "I don't need to see or not see what might or might not be something for us. It doesn't matter what a reading will say. All I need to know is that we're both promising to keep on making choices. All the rest, we can figure out together."

That was how to love, she thought as Yael drew her close and kissed her once more. Deliberately. On purpose. One choice at a time.

Acknowledgements

This story would not exist without the incomparable Brenda Murphy and Fiona Zedde, two fabulous women who graciously let me tag along. Thanks are also in order to the entire NineStar team for being so wonderful to work with. You all rock!

About Megan Hart

Megan Hart writes books. Some of them use bad words, but most of the other words are okay. Some of them hit bestseller lists and win awards and some don't, but that's the way it goes. She can't live without music, the internet, or the ocean, but she and soda have achieved an amicable uncoupling. She loathes the feeling of corduroy or velvet, and modern art leaves her cold. She writes a little bit of everything from horror to romance, though she's best known for writing steamy fiction that sometimes makes you cry.

Email
readinbed@gmail.com

Facebook
www.facebook.com/readinbed

Twitter
@megan_hart

Website
www.MeganHart.com

Other NineStar books by this author

Soul Burn (with Brenda Murphy)

Promises Made by Starlight

Fiona Zedde

To my family and beloved friends who've always been there.

Chapter One

"Does it count as marriage if it wasn't legal everywhere at the time?" Izzy asked her best friend, even though she dreaded the answer.

"Not really," Taylor said with a twist of her lips. "But you just had to go back it up by buying property with her, so basically you're stuck as if you *are* actually married."

Izzy wrinkled her nose and sat back in the outdoor terrace chair, looking past Taylor's shoulder while *not* thinking about her ex-wife. Or ex-girlfriend, apparently.

Across from her at the tiny, French-inspired outdoor café, Taylor picked through her *tout le monde* salad, eating each ingredient one at a time, like she'd always done since they were kids. Now, she was devouring the black olives and making tiny sounds of pleasure with each bite.

Izzy wished she could enjoy her own food—a pair of perfectly cooked turkey and bacon sliders—especially since it would be the last restaurant meal she'd be allowing herself for a long while. She couldn't afford to splurge on this but didn't want to just drink water and gobble up all the complementary bread like her nearly empty wallet was telling her to.

At a familiar sensation between her thighs, she shifted in her seat. Soon, she'd need to change her tampon again.

The day was a beautiful one, golden with sunlight and the brightly colored spring flowers planted along the edges of the sidewalk. It was the sort of beauty she'd normally snap a photo of and upload to social media, but not today.

She had a load of problems sitting on her shoulders and they were crushing all the usual joy out of her life. When she'd inherited too much money from her grandmother years ago, she never thought she'd ever be broke, but here she was.

Now, she needed to unload the property she and her ex owned together, but apparently couldn't until she got her stupid signature on a piece of paper.

Hell.

"This is the opposite of good news, Taylor." Izzy bit her lip to stop herself from pouting. She was supposed to be a grown-up, competently handling all the so-called adult crap life was currently throwing her way.

"I know." Taylor paused with her knife and fork poised above her salad, her fresh manicure gleaming dark red against the silver cutlery. "However, I told you not to marry her in the first place. She was always sketchy to me."

When it came to other people, Taylor's instincts were usually for shit, but Izzy didn't think this was the time to bring that up. In addition to being a know-it-all with a convenient memory, her best friend was also her lawyer. Even though these days she was working for free.

"She wasn't sketchy, Taylor." Even after that last betrayal she couldn't stop defending the woman who she thought she'd spend the rest of her life with. "She's just not like any of the people you've ever met before. She's not boring."

"And she's not actually *here* either. That's the most important part of all this, isn't it?"

Pain blossomed in Izzy's mouth as she bit the inside of her cheek to stop herself from saying more. Her ex didn't deserve any kind of defense.

Although she certainly hadn't deserved Taylor's disrespect when they'd been together either.

Like Izzy, Taylor had been raised with all the trappings of wealth and the standards of their stratosphere-high society. Permed hair and straightened teeth, the best schools, summering in the Hamptons, and clubbing in Europe whenever their exclusive schools weren't in session. Even their boyfriends and girlfriends had been tailored to fit.

They had to have the same background, had to be the same shade of barely-there brown or lighter, the same conservative politics and beliefs, and ideally the same church. And, maybe most importantly, a different gender.

From the moment they met, the woman who Izzy eventually married had seemed the opposite of all that. A flash of white teeth set against midnight skin tripped through her memory and stuttered her heart.

Damn her.

Even now, three years after her ex walked out on her without so much as a note, Izzy couldn't put the relationship and that *fucking* woman behind her. She snatched up her half empty glass of water and took a giant gulp.

A flash of gilt from across the terrace caught her gaze and she jerked upright, startled by unnaturally gold eyes, burning a cold and hateful fire. The swallow of water went down the wrong way and she was suddenly coughing it all up over herself.

"Girl, you okay?" Taylor was there with her spotless cloth napkin in Izzy's face and a hand patting her back, her own face creased with worry. "Trying to drown yourself in a glass of water isn't going to get you out of this trouble."

Izzy waved her away, still coughing but at least no longer feeling like her esophagus was burning. "I'm fine—I'm good. I just—I thought I saw someone familiar."

What else could she say? That some stranger's eyes had just freaked her out? Besides, those burning eyes were already gone. Izzy couldn't even remember the face of the person who'd stared at her so intently, only that it was a guy.

"Who?" Taylor turned to look over her shoulder, rightfully expecting to recognize whoever it was, too, since, except for Taylor's law school friends and now work colleagues, they knew everyone in each other's lives.

The sidewalk was a parade of sameness, the elegant and the poised, a few hipsters who'd found their way to this exclusive part of the little riverside town thirty minutes from Manhattan by train. But no one who would provoke the kind of response Izzy just had. At least, that's what Izzy imagined was going through Taylor's mind. She cleared her throat.

"I was probably just imagining things." She dabbed at the damp spots on her blouse, glad it was only water spotting the white silk. It was one of the few things she still had from her life before. "This heat."

Taylor turned back around in her seat, giving Izzy a weird look. "As long as you're okay, sweets." She sipped her own red wine that wouldn't dare make a mess of her pale-green blouse laying just so over her elegant shoulders. "So, what do you want me to do about the paperwork? Just keep waiting for her to show up?"

"That's basically all we can do, isn't it?"

"No, that's not all, and you know it. I can put some of the firm's investigators on it, have them try to find her. After all, how many Marun Zisanus can there be in this state or even this country?"

"It's too much. I can't even afford to pay you." Even now, the thought brought a sting of humiliation to Izzy's cheeks. "I sure as hell can't afford high-priced corporate investigators."

"Don't worry about how much it costs, Izzy. We can deal with that later. I already told you, the firm's covering it and they'll barely notice the additional expense."

No matter how many times Taylor said it, Izzy didn't hate it any less.

"No, just don't do it, okay. It's too much."

"Come on, Izzy." Taylor paused to glance quickly at her work cell phone resting face-up near her plate. "Be practical."

"I am being practical. Just drop it. Please."

Her friend rolled her eyes and stabbed her fork into the pile of greenery on her plate.

Although Izzy shouldn't be counting up all the little favors Taylor did for her that cost money, she couldn't stop. She'd been independent for a few years, investing (wisely, she thought) and living off the trust fund her grandmother had left her. But now, that money was all gone.

How she lost all that money, she had no clue. One day it was there, more than enough to support her and the thriving business she'd started with her wife, and the next she was single, being put out of her apartment and then moving out of the city into a little cottage she was only *just* able to afford.

Izzy had no excuse for what happened, but she had enough pride to realize she'd fucked up and was in such a downward financial spiral there was no way she'd be able to pay Taylor back. They both knew people like that from prep school and even college, who because of whatever reason—drugs, sex addiction, or bad choices—ended up constantly going to their parents and friends for money.

Including her sister. Rose, who despite being a successful cardiothoracic surgeon had allowed her gambling addiction to rip everything she'd worked hard for out of her hands. Hooked on gambling to the point of financial ruin, she "borrowed" from friends, family, strangers, anyone who was foolish enough to give her money. Now, Rosalind lived with their parents, caught in a cycle of dependence and addiction and self-loathing that their mother was only happy to keep spinning.

That wasn't Izzy.

That could never be her.

"Everything will be fine," Izzy said and reached for one of the sliders. She was paying for these expensive little burgers; she might as well eat them. Not to mention she needed to replace all the iron she was losing from her heavier than normal period.

She and Taylor finished up the meal talking about things that barely mattered—old friends they hadn't seen in a while, plans for the summer, who got a nose job or got caught screwing someone else's husband. Despite the business reason they'd gotten together, they had a good time, laughing at the antics of their old schoolmates and swiping through the guys on the dating app Taylor just put on her phone.

When it was time to pay the bill, Taylor grabbed it up and shoved her black card in the waiter's hand.

"Don't argue!" she said and waved the waiter away.

Izzy wanted to but didn't.

After cheek kisses and a promise to connect the following week, Taylor went back to her office downtown while Izzy headed home. It wasn't a short walk, but Izzy didn't mind. Over the last few months. she'd gotten used to navigating the little town by foot instead of taking a ride share or even the bus.

With rent coming due soon, she wasn't sure she could afford to keep the place, but hopefully one of the irons she had in the fire would strike hot. Izzy adjusted the purse slung across her chest and kept walking.

Less than an hour later, she arrived at her small cottage, a duplex she shared with a neighbor she never saw, with sweat running down the small of her back despite shucking off her jacket halfway through the walk. Her low-heeled boots clattered against the hardwood floors as she made her way inside.

It was only three in the afternoon, but the shuttered windows of the cottage made it seem much later. Jacket on the coat rack by the door, purse tossed on the couch, Izzy headed straight for the bathroom. She'd made the mistake of not using the restaurant toilet before she left and now her tampon felt like it was overflowing.

Anticipating just that disaster, she'd worn black jeans. In the bathroom, she put her ruined jeans and underwear to soak and got in the shower. She scrubbed her skin of sweat and worry and blood and then let the water swirl the suds polluted with it all down the drain.

Izzy rested her forehead against the cool tiles and sighed.

For the first time since she woke late that morning, with the mists of sleep obscuring all the problems going on right now, she took an easy breath. Water flowed over her shoulders and back, splattering on the shower cap she wore and cascading over her butt and thighs, slipping between her legs.

Another sigh expanded her lungs and she felt more of her tension slip away.

It would be so damn nice just to stay there with the water washing everything away, all her cares, the blood, the anger and hurt she'd been holding on to for three long years.

But too soon, she had to get out.

Nothing in this world was free, including hot water.

Speaking of which, she had to do something to make more money before even the pleasure of taking a shower in her own private bathroom was taken away. There had to be *something* she could do. Maybe sell the last of her grandmother's jewelry that she was holding on to. After all, they were only pieces of metal and rocks. But her eyes burned at the thought of parting with those last tangible connections to her grandmother.

Tampon in, shower cap dried and put away, she left the bathroom with a towel wrapped around her mostly dry body. Still thinking about what she could do to make money, she walked through the living room on the way to her bedroom.

"Why do you want to sell the bakery?"

Izzy shrieked.

She jerked backward, arms flailing, and crashed into a corner table as her towel loosened and she pitched toward the floor. Strong hands grabbed her and stopped her from falling. Her heart galloped with fear as she backed away and slammed into the wall with a dull thud.

Wait. Wait a fucking minute.

She pressed a hand to her heaving chest, blinking hard and staring at the shadowy figure in front of her. Six feet plus of feminine sleekness in a flowing seafoam blouse, jeans, and with bare feet. Her untamed hair was a corona around her face, so thick and heavy that it rested on her shoulders, a flock of dark birds ready to take flight. And her face. Knee-weakening beauty perfected by piercing eyes that saw through everything Izzy ever was or hoped to be.

Her breath caught and her body responded to Marun's presence the way it always did, calming yet growing more agitated at the same time. The fear was gone but her skin crackled with a hungry electric current.

Snap out of it!

"What the entire *fuck* are you doing here?" she gasped out, at the same time grabbing her towel from the floor to cover herself. Her heart was still trying to beat its way out of her chest.

"I'm here to see you," Marun said as if Izzy was the one being unreasonable and not the actual woman who'd broken into her apartment.

Still dazed, Izzy wrapped the towel around herself and slid along the wall away from her ex-wife. Current wife? Girlfriend?

Her body thudded into a corner. She couldn't move anymore, could only stare at Marun and wet her dry lips.

"Telephones exist," she said finally. "My number didn't change while you were gone."

Three years.

"Why are you trying to get rid of the bakery?" Marun moved closer, eyes roaming over Izzy in that familiar, possessive way.

Izzy gripped the towel to her chest and willed her knees not to buckle, her thighs to stop shaking. Marun was back. She was here, in the little cottage, and Izzy's body was responding like it always had.

Swallowing hard, she tried to get herself back on track. "You may not notice but it's not actually a bakery anymore, just a big check I can't cash."

"Don't sell it." Marun was close enough now for Izzy to see the tiny mole high on her left cheek.

"Why shouldn't I sell it? This building is the only thing still tying us together and, from your disappearing act, you obviously don't want anything to do with me anymore." The words felt like glass in her throat.

The faint light over Marun's face shifted. Her mouth softened. Her eyes burned with an unfamiliar desperation. "Don't get rid of it. Please."

Izzy's stomach clenched, and it wasn't a period cramp. She'd never been able to resist Marun. Not when she was commanding and had Izzy on her knees doing anything to please her. And especially not when she was almost soft like this, pleading, a half-hidden shade in Izzy's living room, the living ghost of the woman who walked out three years ago and took Izzy's heart with her.

Marun.

The woman who'd called herself Izzy's wife.

The woman who'd allowed Izzy to belong to her for a few precious years.

None of that mattered now though.

"I need the money," Izzy spat in a short, resentful burst.

"You have money. I left you everything I own on this earth."

"The only thing you left me was alone."

I needed you, she wanted to shout now that she finally had a target in front of her for her anger and pain. *I missed you so much. Why did you leave? Please don't leave me again.*

But she was done begging people to love her, especially those who'd promised to stay.

"I didn't abandon you," Marun said, her voice low and softer than it was a moment before. "My plan was always to come back. When I left, you had everything, including all the money in our accounts."

Marun was lying.

The accounts were nearly empty by the time Izzy had gotten herself together enough to look. Shock and denial had her scouring the banks, hunting for proof that her wife hadn't abandoned her and taken most of their money with her.

Had the woman she loved ever loved her at all?

Tears stung the backs of Izzy's eyes, but she tried to blink them back before they fell. Her throat tightened and it felt like a vice was squeezing her chest. She couldn't do this.

"Please!" With a slash of her hand, she tried to cut off the flow of lies. "Just go. If you want to talk again, call me like a normal person and—" She swallowed the rough sob threatening to choke her. "Actually, don't call me. Talk to Taylor. She's handling everything, including the sale of that useless thing we own together."

With tears blurring her eyes, she shoved herself away from the wall and stumbled into her bedroom. The door rattled as it slammed behind her. Unable to walk another step, she collapsed to her knees and gasped in pain from the hard contact with the floor. Her towel loosened and fell. As if the physical pain shook free the other hurt inside her, the tears began to fall, hot and fast, scorching down her cheeks and dripping into her mouth. She gripped her chest, willing the pain to stop.

"Izzy. I didn't come back to hurt you." Marun's voice was just on the other side of the door, muffled by the wood.

"Then what the fuck did you come back here for?" She screamed out, slamming her hand against the door. Her palm stung, but she did it again, and again, pounding the door like an alarm drum, drowning in the pain.

"Stop. You're hurting yourself."

"Go! Leave my fucking house!"

"Okay, I'm leaving. Just—just stop hurting yourself. Please." Faint footsteps sounded across the wooden floors. The front door opened and closed.

Minutes passed. Maybe longer.

Izzy didn't know how long she stayed on the floor, but by the time she stood up, her knees hurt, her back was cramped, and the tears had dried on her face. Silence was the only thing she heard beyond the bedroom door. And, for a moment, that empty silence stabbed her deep and hurt worse than anything she'd ever felt before.

Chapter Two

Izzy went into the living room and, as expected, found Marun gone.

An undefined pain throbbed in her chest. It seemed so damn easy for her ex to leave.

After getting her trembling fingers under control, she picked up her phone and sent Taylor a text.

If you haven't already, please get the paperwork for the bakery's sale ready for her to sign.

Seconds after she hit "send," the phone vibrated with a call.

"You found her?" Taylor sounded shocked.

"No, she found me." Izzy coughed and cleared the sound of tears from her throat. "She's—she came to see me this afternoon, just now."

The sudden silence on the other end of the line was loud enough for her to hear her own internal screams. She pressed her lips together. "Say something, Taylor."

"I know this hurts. I'm sorry."

Hurt. That seemed like such a mild word from the boa constricting her lungs and her heart, making it impossible to breathe without agony.

Out of anyone else, Taylor knew what Izzy had been through when her wife suddenly left her without a word. She'd been a mess for weeks, months, and with too much of that time spent on Taylor's couch.

"I—I can't talk anymore about this right now."

"Okay. I'll get the paperwork together and call her number again."

"Thanks. I'll talk to you soon."

She hung up before Taylor could say anything else.

In the bedroom, she closed the curtains and curled up on top of the covers, the heater blasting hot air over her bare skin. With even a little bit of chill in the air, the cottage hoarded all the cool air until it felt colder in the house than it was outside. Outside the bedroom, it was freezing.

Izzy grabbed the unused second pillow on the queen-sized bed and pulled it against her stomach. During the winters in their old place, she and Marun used to cuddle in the middle of their huge bed, keeping each other warm in their drafty but perfect two thousand square foot midtown apartment.

A tear burned its way down the side of Izzy's face.

Seeing Marun again brought all the pain back as bright hot as it had ever been. For the millionth time, she wondered what she'd done wrong for Marun to leave, not just leave her, but to leave without giving any hint that the life they'd built together wasn't what she wanted.

It hadn't all been a lie, had it?

Before she consciously knew what she wanted, Izzy was on her knees in front of the open closet door and searching through the overcrowded mess for things from her old life she probably should've thrown out years ago.

Like the cigar box.

The wood was rough between her hands as she opened it, freeing the faint smell of an old perfume. Inside the box lay things she didn't have any use for.

The coffee-stained napkin from the diner where she and Marun went the night they met. A love letter with a dried African violet pressed between its pages. Her wedding ring.

Nudging aside the platinum and diamond band, she reached for a small flyer announcing an art gallery show and cooking exhibition. The paper crackled between her fingers as crisp as the night she'd first slipped it into her purse.

It came back to her in flashes. That night.

Getting dressed in her single dorm room with excitement fluttering in her belly. The black dress that hugged her from collar bones to calves, and the sky-high heels to match. She'd straightened her hair and worn it in a French twist, trying to look grown-up for the man she was supposed to meet at the gallery: her culinary school professor who'd been flirting with her for weeks.

He was French, charming, and brilliant with a cutting torch. Half the class had been in lust with him, and Izzy felt lucky he'd chosen her.

In class he was cool to her, almost too professional in a way she realized now probably hadn't fooled anybody.

In his office, it was another story. There, with no classroom between them, he'd gone to his knees to pleasure her and then begged to be allowed inside her. Izzy didn't give in. She held on to her virginity with both hands until, one day, it just seemed ridiculous to wait.

They'd planned it. For them to meet up at the gallery and then go to his apartment together. There, she'd finally give in and she'd know what the fuss was all about.

In the mirror that night, her lips had gleamed a deep red from the new lipstick. A packet of condoms sat next to her compact and a fresh pair of panties at the bottom of her tiny purse. Butterflies dive-bombed in her belly in anticipation of what she was going to do later that night. She was ready.

The gallery wasn't far away from campus so, despite the chilly night air and high heels that tortured her feet with every step, she walked there. She'd be leaving the gallery in his car anyway.

At the entrance to the gallery, a long line snaked away from the podium and the woman behind it who was stamping the hand of everyone she let in.

"That'll be ten dollars," she said when it was Izzy's turn.

Izzy dug into her purse, frantic fingers bumping against the few things inside before she realized, her cheeks hot with embarrassment, that she'd remembered to pack everything except her wallet. "Ten dollars?" She looked up from her fruitless search, snapping the purse shut. "I'm meeting someone here, the chef performing. Sébastien. Is there—am I on the guest list?"

The woman glanced down at her clipboard. "Everyone on the guest list is already accounted for."

The grumbling in the line behind Izzy turned up the heat in her cheeks. Muttering apologies, she backed out of the line to allow the next person to pass. As she backed into a nearby corner to shield herself from some of the cold, the glass doors of the gallery slid open spilling out the sound of laughter and, she imagined, the sexy rumble of Sébastien's voice.

Would he expect her to be in there while he performed? What would he do once he realized she wasn't there and waiting for him?

The questions tumbled without answers in Izzy's head. As she usually did when she was nervous, she nibbled on the corner of her thumb, teasing up the remnants of a cuticle that the woman at the nail salon had done such a good job of eliminating hours before. The smell of her deep-red nail polish teased her nose and mixed with the taste of blood as her raw finger started to bleed.

A pair of women slipped out of the gallery, one of them gnawing on some sort of meat on a stick, and stepped into the nearby alley. Their jackets looked warm.

"That chef really put his foot in it," one of them said in a Southern drawl. "The girls in there are just eating him up."

"It doesn't hurt that he's a cutie with a booty either."

They both laughed. Seconds later, the scent of cigarette smoke snaked from the alley toward Izzy. She wrinkled her nose. Then shivered from a sudden breeze.

Maybe he wouldn't be in there too long and she could just wait for him out here. It wasn't that cold anyway.

"Is your human popsicle act part of the performance for tonight?"

An unfamiliar voice jerked Izzy's attention from the gallery's entrance. A woman stood in line, dressed properly for the weather in a long and shimmery yellow dress and with a fur stole, golden and soft-looking, draped around her shoulders.

"Huh?"

The woman was *remarkable*. There was no other word for it. Her hair, a thick forest of natural coils and curls, absorbed the light and rested gently on the thick pelt draped over her shoulders. Her impressive hair framed the most beautiful face Izzy had ever seen. The yellow dress hugged her tall and lavishly curved body, showing off thick breasts, a narrow waist, and hips that begged for worship. This was a woman the term "hourglass" had been made for.

And Izzy had never thought of women as being sexually attractive before. Well, at least not outside of a television or movie screen.

The stranger's skin glowed a lustrous ebony and her eyes were sharp like a hunter's and seized Izzy as if she were prey.

She clenched her hand into a fist, tucking away her bleeding thumb. The pain from it throbbed dully but was easy to ignore under the intensity of the woman's gaze.

A smile skimmed the stranger's painted lips. "Why are you out here in the cold?"

Too flustered to lie, Izzy stammered out the truth. "Uh… I, um, I'm meeting someone here, but I—I forgot my wallet so don't have any cash for the cover." She rubbed her hands up and down her bare arms, trying to generate some heat.

"You don't need money. It's supposed to be a *suggested* donation." The woman cast a narrowed glance at the hostess who wasn't paying them the slightest attention. Her gorgeous hair fluttered like a dark dandelion in the breeze.

"Um," Izzy said again, apparently having forgotten how to speak actual words.

"Come." The woman plucked a twenty from her purse and gestured with it for Izzy to step in front of her. "No point in you standing out here looking like a sacrifice."

The heat of arousal scorched Izzy from head to toe, with too much of its fire lingering in her nipples and between her thighs for comfort. She wanted to run away from the stranger. She wanted to press closer. The contradiction made her quiver. At least she wasn't cold anymore. "You don't have to. I mean, I'll just...do something else."

"Don't be a martyr when you don't have to be, love." The woman's voice suited her body perfectly. It was lush and deep, infused with the lilting melody of an accent Izzy couldn't place.

"Oh, okay." More than a little mesmerized, Izzy nibbled on her thumb again before she realized what she was doing. She dropped her hand down at her side and stepped into the space the woman made for her, ignoring someone's mutter of objection from behind them in the line. "Thank you. I really appreciate this."

The woman waved away her thanks.

As they waited, they exchanged names.

"A pleasure to meet you, Izzy," the woman—Marun—said. She offered her hand and Izzy, in a daze, reached out to take it. A sizzling current passed between them and Izzy shivered, burned. Marun smiled as if she knew exactly what Izzy was feeling. She brushed a finger over Izzy's bleeding thumb. "Yes, my absolute pleasure."

At the podium, she offered up her twenty-dollar bill and the hostess took it, stamped both their wrists before inviting them inside. Izzy sighed with relief when the gallery's warmth washed over her bare shoulders, arms, and legs. Her skin prickled as her body returned to something like its normal temperature.

In the middle of the gallery, Sébastien held his audience as he played with leaping tongues of fire at the cooking exhibition station he'd shown the class photos of days before. His laughter was low and thrilling, his French-accented words distinctively flirtatious. Just like Izzy remembered. Just like she wanted. She should head over there and let him know she was there.

But she couldn't make her legs move her away from her savior.

"I can't thank you enough," she said, looking up at Marun. "Let me get your number and I'll arrange to pay you back. I have money, I swear."

The woman glanced toward Sébastien and then turned her back to him. "You know, if you're in such a hurry to give your virginity away, you should give it to me."

"What?" Did this woman just...?

"Your ears didn't deceive you, darling girl." Another smile. This one teasing yet with a touch of gravity Izzy couldn't ignore.

Izzy's mouth dried. Her heart thudded, wild and out of control. Mostly because she was rocked to the core by Marun's boldness yet wanted so very badly to give the woman...everything. Instead, she drew back, trying to save herself from this unexpected desire. "Do I have 'virgin' carved into my forehead or something?"

"Not there, no." Dark eyes wandered down her body, scorching Izzy like a physical touch.

Heat engulfed Izzy from head to toe, but it wasn't the blush of embarrassment. Instead, it was arousal, thigh-slickening and swift. The sensation roared through her in a way it never had for anyone else. Under Marun's intense regard, her belly tightened, her panties grew wet. She crossed her arms over her chest to hide the hardness of her nipples that had nothing to do with the cold.

Yes, Izzy wanted this strange woman, but she was also nervous. And frightened.

She willed her voice not to tremble. "I don't know what to say."

"Say you'll come home with me." When Marun lightly touched her shoulder, Izzy couldn't stop the shiver of reaction that rippled through her. "But if that's too much too soon, we can meet for coffee and just talk. You intrigue me, and I want to know everything you're willing to share."

She should have said no. She should have told Marun she wasn't willing to give just anyone her virginity. Especially not another woman. But after knowing her for only a few minutes, Izzy knew Marun wasn't just *anyone*, wasn't just any woman. And if she walked away from this heady desire that pushed her own fears and expectations far out of sight, she suspected she'd regret it for the rest of her life.

"I want to know you too," Izzy said, and it felt like a confession.

Without a single glance toward Sébastien, Izzy left with Marun. They went to a nearby café with Marun's golden stole thrown over Izzy's shoulders. There, they drank coffee and talked until the sun brushed the sky with the first traces of color. Marun listened and flirted and teased secrets from Izzy she didn't even know she had. Then, when nighttime gave way to the morning, Izzy went with Marun to her penthouse apartment on the river.

In the master bedroom's decadently large bed, Marun's touch took Izzy to a world beyond her wildest fantasies. She screamed her pleasure, clawed and begged and cried until her throat was raw and her very being was saturated with satisfaction.

That day, she skipped all her classes.

It should have felt strange—or at least *more* strange— to be picked up by a woman when she'd been at the gallery to give her virginity to another person, a man, but Marun made it seem normal. Perfect even. For two years, their entire relationship had been like that. A surreal but splendid dream.

Until she woke up one morning to find Marun gone.

It should have worried her, how effortlessly Marun seduced her and took her home. As easy as it had been for her ex to come into her life, Izzy should have realized it would be equally easy for her to leave it.

The edge of the cigar box dug into Izzy's palm as she firmly closed it. *Enough of that.* The tiny latch clicked, and she swallowed past the thick lump of emotion that threatened to choke her.

She should just throw the stupid box away, once and for all.

But of course, that's not what she did. Instead, Izzy shoved it back into the mess of a closet and stood up. She couldn't afford to let Marun's unexpected visit derail her normal routine. The night would come quickly and with it, work.

Her job at one of the most popular restaurants in town as an overnight baker wasn't enough to allow her to live and pay all her debts but she needed to keep it. And for that, she needed sleep.

With the broken promise of warm sunshine beyond her closed curtains, she climbed back into bed and tried again to rest.

Chapter Three

Nighttime. Izzy was back at the restaurant. Along with the other overnight staff, she prepped for the following day's regular menus plus the bachelorette party scheduled to take over one of the event rooms for most of the afternoon.

The women in the party sure were planning to eat a lot of cupcakes and chocolate-filled cream puffs. At least, Izzy thought as she prepared the batter for the cream puffs, she didn't have to be the one making the stripper's person-sized cake.

It was hard work, but not hard enough to make her forget about Marun and her sudden appearance in her cottage, a place her ex had never visited before.

How had Marun found her?

Why now?

Where had she been all this time?

The questions were as never-ending as they were useless. Her ex had always done what she wanted, whenever she wanted. Nothing about her was predictable or boring. Izzy should have known expecting her to stick around was a fool's dream.

By the time morning came and Izzy was getting ready to leave, her back ached from being on her feet most of the night. She was absolutely exhausted. One bright spot to her night was the voice mail message from her landlord saying he'd finally loosened and fixed the sticking lock on the door between her bathroom and bedroom.

At home, she stumbled inside, wanting nothing more than her bed. But she forced herself to take a proper shower before falling into the sheets with the lotion still drying on her skin. It seemed like no time at all before her alarm was going off.

The phone buzzed annoyingly from the bedside table. Bleary-eyed, she reached over to tap the snooze button—just once—before she realized it was a phone call, not her late afternoon alarm.

For just one moment, when she rolled over to silence her phone, Izzy felt a phantom warmth, body heat, like somebody had been lying there next to her on the usually empty side of the bed.

Shaking off the odd feeling, she groped for the answer button, not looking to see who it was. At this time of the day, it could only be one of two people. Well, only one. "Good morning, Mom."

Even though she'd told her parents about a new job that needed her to keep vampire hours, they—and her mother in particular—still called on their schedule. Meaning, she always woke Izzy up. Every day, she was grateful they still lived out in California and far, far away from her.

"Good morning, Isabella. I hope I didn't wake you."

Izzy rolled her eyes at the obvious lie.

Her mother started in on small talk about mutual friends, the charity events she was running, the continued good health of Izzy's father. Something was on her mind, but she was taking a while to get to it. Finally, at the end of a long story about a patient her sister had saved, she took a deep breath.

"We heard you were in trouble, Isabella."

Finally, there it was.

"Where did you hear that?" Izzy frowned up at the ceiling.

She'd been so careful to keep all news about her troubles away from her parents. How could they know?

"That doesn't matter, dear. You don't have to be unreasonably proud, not like when that *person* you married left you high and dry."

Izzy nearly choked on a breath. No matter how much she knew her mother was capable of, she was never really prepared for it. Back when she and Marun were together, neither of her parents approved, but her mother was the most vocal about how much she never liked them as a couple.

Every conversation with her mother felt like a blade designed to sever the ties between Izzy and her wife. Eleanor Ransom spilled her genteel homophobia all over them and pushed Izzy so far away with her surgical passive-aggressive attacks that she'd stopped visiting. Even now, years after Marun left, she only went home for Christmas, spending as little time as possible in her parents' massive house before making some excuse or other to rush back to the East Coast.

"—know you're always welcome back here with us," her mother continued. "Your father and I only want to help when you need it."

Her mother didn't sound particularly helpful. Something in her tone, something Izzy had almost forgotten in the time she'd been away from her parents, made it sound like she wanted her to fail and run back "home" with her tail between her legs.

Like Rose had.

"Everything is fine, Mom. Really."

Even though that wasn't the truth now, it would be eventually.

"All right, darling. Just remember you can always count on us to be here for you."

"Thank you." She dug her fingers into her eye sockets and tried to stop herself from screaming in frustration. "Uh, I have to get back to sleep now. I'm still tired from work."

"You know that wouldn't be an issue if you were here with us."

"I know, Mom."

"Good. Keep that in mind."

"I will."

Izzy disconnected the call and dropped the phone beside her on the bed.

Fuck me.

Who'd told her parents what was going on with her, and why? It wasn't like she confessed her financial shame to many people.

Not that it really mattered how they found out. The point was that they did know. Now, she had to do *something* to get out of this hole she'd fallen into. She'd rather end up in the poor house than in her parents' mansion filled with emotional blackmail, fake support, and conditional love.

And that meant doing something she'd been avoiding for months.

Chapter Four

"Nice suit, sis." A woman passing by gave Izzy an appreciative glance and a smile on her way past her in the bank.

Even though it was more of a nervous twitch, Izzy returned her smile. "Thank you."

The woman, who must be an intern or something since she looked so young, wasn't too badly put together herself in a slim-fitting dress in some sort of west African print. The dress, bright and cheerful in the chill of the bank, and the younger woman's unexpected compliment helped ease some of Izzy's tension. But only some.

The bank was crowded, which was probably normal for an early Monday morning. In the waiting area, Izzy signed her name on the client clipboard and took a seat. Another attack of nerves had her wiping damp palms on the thighs of her capri slacks as she looked around. Five other people waited in the seating area, including a straight couple holding hands and glancing anxiously at each other.

They were adorable and young, still wearing that dreamy look of a couple in love. Matching wedding rings gleamed on their fingers.

Probably heading for divorce in a couple of years anyway, Izzy thought and then was instantly annoyed with herself.

Throwing shade because she'd lost her own wife was just shitty. Her teeth clamped down on the inside of her cheek and she fiddled with the straps of her "business bag," a large leather purse that had all the papers she needed for this interview.

A loan.

Izzy never thought she'd see the day. She'd been literally born with a whole set of silver spoons at her disposal and had never worried about money a day in her life. Until things started to fall apart three years ago.

Now she was here at a bank, about to beg strangers for money.

You can always go home, a voice at the back of her head whispered. *Mom and Dad will take care of everything and it could be like this whole thing never happened.*

But the voice was easy to ignore. Her parents' love and rescue came with conditions she could never fulfill. It wasn't just about pride at this point, it was about survival of the person she'd become in the years she'd been away from California. She was an out, queer woman and though she wasn't dating anyone, she wasn't about to crawl back into the closet to make her mother feel comfortable.

The make-up of the waiting room shifted as people were called into one of the two offices nearby. Soon, Izzy was the only one sitting on the gray couch. Not for the first time, she smoothed a hand down the thigh of her black slacks. The matching jacket felt looser than she remembered around her shoulders, even though when she'd left the cottage earlier that morning, the mirror told her it still looked good.

She *needed* to impress these people.

After pulling a full shift at the restaurant and then rushing home to shower and change before heading back out again, she was beyond tired. Even with the homemade double espresso sitting in her belly. The leather strap of her purse slid against her sweaty palms as she gripped it, her hands spasming with nervousness.

Her gaze flicked to the loan officer's door. It was still closed.

"You shouldn't be here."

Izzy almost jumped out of her skin. "Fuck!"

Wearing a pants suit nearly identical to hers except that it was a brilliant yellow, Marun sat beside her on the sofa. Her hair was an inky cloud around her face, the perfect frame for her piercing eyes frowning down at Izzy.

"I wish you'd stop doing that." Izzy had only been a half a second from clutching at her chest in fright like somebody's Southern grandma. Her agitated pulse started to settle back down.

"Doing what?" Marun asked, that frown still all over her face, as if she didn't know exactly what Izzy was talking about.

Izzy flicked a gaze at the still-closed office doors and then over at the teller sitting placidly behind the bank's counter. The security guard was still at his post by the door. "Never mind."

That was one of the things she'd had to get used to in the first few months of their relationship. Marun would simply appear wherever she was, no call to find out her location, no agreement to meet. Izzy should've been thinking the woman had some sort of GPS or locator beacon installed on her phone or her body. But she'd always been too charmed, too excited to see her to complain.

She wasn't charmed now though.

"I can go anywhere I want," she said and tried to ignore that familiar scent of guava and lemons clinging to her ex-wife. "And I can do anything I want."

"That's true enough." Marun swept the bank with her own comprehensive stare. "But you don't have to be here doing what I think you're about to do."

Annoyance made Izzy bristle. "If you're not going to sign the papers allowing me to sell the building, then I don't have a choice."

"There are always other choices," Marun said. Her voice vibrated with an odd intensity. Or maybe the intensity wasn't odd, because she'd always had that sense of restrained power and purpose about her.

Izzy had missed it. She'd missed h— No. She hadn't missed anything to do with Marun.

One of the office doors opened.

"Isabella Ransom?"

She rushed to stand. "I'm here."

Quick footsteps took her past a frowning Marun and toward the tall woman standing in the office doorway. She stepped aside, allowing Izzy to come in before closing the door behind them.

"Thanks for waiting." Smiling pleasantly, the woman gestured for her to sit at the stiff-looking chair on the other side of her desk. "What can I do for you this morning?"

It turned out that she couldn't do a damn thing for Izzy. After nearly a half an hour of downright groveling to try to get a loan, Izzy walked out of the office with yet another rejection. She owned nothing to offer as collateral, not even the building she co-owned with one Marun Zisanu.

What other choices did she have now?

When she walked out of the meeting with the loan officer, her head determinedly held high despite the sick feeling in her stomach, Izzy was *almost* surprised to see Marun waiting for her.

God, could this day get any worse?

Marun got to her feet, easily towering over Izzy in high heels she didn't need to wear.

"Pardon me," the loan officer said to Marun. "I didn't see another name on my list for the morning. Can I help you?"

"No, you can't," Marun said, regally dismissive. "But thank you." Her hair swayed as she inclined her head to the loan officer, one in a long line of women trying to break Izzy's spirit.

"Are you going to sign the papers?" Izzy forced the words past her teeth as she walked down the bank steps with Marun right at her side. She slung her purse over her shoulder.

"That's not why I'm here."

"Then you can't help me. You're not doing anything but getting on my nerves and reminding me why I should've never been involved with you in the first place."

A rush of warmth, like the feel of sunlight abruptly released over her skin, came her way from Marun. "We weren't *involved*, we were together. We *are* married."

"We're nothing, Marun." Her ex's name sizzled over her tongue in a way she'd missed as she realized this was the first time she'd said her name since she reappeared in Izzy's life. God, was that only yesterday? "If you're not going to help me, leave me alone."

Desperate to leave Marun behind, along with all the unwanted feelings she brought back, Izzy rushed through the bank's parking lot toward the bus stop.

"Izzy, stop."

But she didn't stop. She was done taking orders from her ex. When they'd been together, she'd let Marun take control of pretty much everything, including her. She wasn't that naïve girl anymore though. For one thing, she was broke as hell and dealing with real world, adult problems.

If she couldn't get this loan on her own, she'd get on her belly and crawl toward the one decision she swore she'd never make. The dread of it spun in her stomach, swirling with the morning's coffee and the storm of emotions Marun stirred up.

Her high heels clicked furiously across the pavement.

The day was bright, unfairly golden given the ever-growing pile of shit her life was right now. Fucking spring. An arc of sunlight flashed across her eyes as she got to the bus stop, hyper aware of the woman keeping pace with her, the woman who enveloped her senses in unwanted desire and the scent of a home she no longer had.

Going to the bank, Izzy had felt a touch of optimism. Her family name was a damn good one, even if she wasn't going to throw it around to get what she needed. In theory, she was good for the amount of money she was asking for. She'd never failed to repay a debt in her whole life.

Okay, fine. So, she hadn't had much occasion to borrow money from anybody. Even the expensive college tuition had been covered by her trust fund money. So had her half of the building she and Marun had bought together on some strange whim when they'd planned the romance of their lives together, living in an apartment above the bakery they owned. Making love to the smell of baking bread every day.

But now, she was light years away from the person she was back in college, and even later when she was with Marun.

The three years in limbo had aged her.

Abandoned by her wife. All her money gone. And now, she was pleading with a bank for money while the heat of embarrassment burned in her cheeks. When the woman had turned her away, Izzy had felt a kind of relief then. At least the torture of being a beggar was over.

She was thinking too hard about the deeper humiliation to come with what she had to do next. That must have been the reason she didn't hear it at first. The screech of tires as a car jumped the curb and veered toward her.

"Oh my god!"

The scream tore her attention away from the posted bus schedule, a woman sitting inside the transparent bus stop watching with a hand slapped to her mouth, her eyes wide as dinner plates. The car, actually a huge SUV, barreled straight for Izzy. A flash of yellow appeared in front of her.

Marun.

"Don't move!" Marun shouted.

Izzy remembered this minutes afterward. Marun's hand reaching back to clamp Izzy around the waist and pull up against her while she faced the giant vehicle bearing down on them. Izzy might have screamed. She wasn't sure. Heart tripping with fear, she slammed her eyes shut and held on tight to Marun, bracing herself for the crash, and the pain.

But only one of those things happened.

A boom of sound exploded around her, and her eyes flew open in time to see the black SUV slam into some kind of invisible barrier in front of Marun, the vehicle's front end crumpling like an empty soda can in a fist. The smell of engine oil nearly overwhelmed her, a belch of heat from under the abruptly revealed hood. Then the SUV ricocheted back into the street like a giant bullet gone astray.

Clinging to Marun, Izzy could only stare in shock. The SUV flew backward, bumped up onto the grassy median on the other side of the street, and slammed into a street sign. The sign lurched and half collapsed. Metal screeched against metal as the SUV skidded against the street sign again and then, engine growling with effort, shot through the yellow traffic light and took off down the street.

Miraculously, through all this, the runaway SUV missed hitting any of the other cars in the post-rush hour morning.

Reacting to the chaos, other cars screeched to a stop as more people shouted and cell phone cameras came out.

Izzy's lungs burned and spots danced in front of her eyes. She staggered. From a distance, she heard Marun. "Breathe, baby. Just breathe for me. It's all over now." The scent of a crisp, fertile garden pulled her back from the edge of panic.

A shivery breath escaped her open mouth and the spots before her eyes disappeared. "Oh my god!"

"Are you hurt?" Marun's low voice brushed her ear.

The touch of Marun's hands on her hips loosened a storm of reactions. The most dangerous of which was a kind of calm. Her breathing evened out and her heart slowed to something like normal.

"I should be the one asking you that." Shaking, she gripped Marun's hands and then released them to touch her woman's chest, her belly, her strong arms around her. Just to confirm with her touch as well as sight that Marun was okay. That SUV could've flattened Marun. It could have crushed them both where they stood.

"I'm fine, love. You never have to worry about me," Marun said. She didn't seem afraid. Only earlier, when she'd asked Izzy if she was hurt, had there been any sort of tremor in her voice.

Now, she was like a rock.

Her steadiness was seductive. Izzy only *just* stopped herself from melting into Marun's strength and loosening the cry that had been rising in her since the day she found out her woman had left her.

But she didn't give in. It hurt, but she forced herself to pull away from Marun and her bright scent. She cleared her throat and wriggled from the grip that had never felt too tight.

"Thanks." Izzy self-consciously wiped the tip of her nose even though she was pretty sure nothing was there. "I think I'm good now."

Thank god the woman at the bus stop stopped screaming. She was on the phone now describing the incident to someone. The "Yes, girl, I can't believe it" from her side of the call made clear it wasn't the cops.

A teenage boy had his phone out, too, whirling around to film the mangled street sign, knots of frightened people, and the cars braked to a stop in the middle of the street.

"That guy must have been on drugs or something, he just jumped up on the curb out of nowhere," a man nearby chimed in.

"Yeah, and they didn't even stop when they almost killed that woman over there," another voice said.

Izzy tucked her fear-cold fingers under her armpits and stared down the street in the direction of the long-gone SUV. *She* was "that woman."

"You should come with me, love. You're still shaking." Marun made a soft, shushing noise, like she was comforting a baby or a frightened child.

Izzy bristled at the patronizing attitude. "I'm fine."

Suddenly Izzy wanted nothing more than to be home in her cottage, in her bed, recovering from her all-night work, from the bank, from all this. Although she could barely spare the money, grabbing a Lyft was the only option. The thought of staying at the bus stop so close to the street after what just happened made her shiver.

Marun stepped closer and obliterated the space Izzy had put between them. Her eyes radiated a dark comfort. "Stop being stubborn. Let me drive you home."

Izzy blamed her near-death by runaway SUV for what came out of her mouth next. "Okay, fine."

Why did it suddenly feel like she'd agreed to much more than a car ride?

Chapter Five

Of course, Marun's car was decadent and larger than life. Just like her. The cream-colored Bentley shut out the world with the firm closing of the driver side door. Inside, the car was an ocean of black and burgundy leather. It smelled new, and sweet like Marun's perfume, blended with the crispness of air-conditioning. The two-toned steering wheel, also black and burgundy, was the perfect foil for Marun's fine-boned hand. The engine started with a throaty purr and glided out of the bank's parking lot.

"Should I bother telling you how to get to my house?"

Marun slid her a smile. "I already know the way."

"Of course, you do." The seat exhaled a scent of leather and luxe as Izzy settled back to enjoy the short ride that had taken her nearly an hour by bus.

"Even with what just happened, you look good, Isabella."

She looked away from the slowly passing scenery only to be caught in Marun's intense gaze.

"Shouldn't you be keeping your eyes on the road?"

"My eyes are exactly where they need to be." Marun flicked her gaze over Izzy, but then thankfully went back to the road ahead. "At any rate, I want to make sure you're all right. Things were a bit intense back there. Dangerous." Although her words were flip, a hard gold light, as bright as the sun, briefly flared through her eyes.

That gold was familiar, and a little scary. Marun had always been like that. Lightning flashing, bright and dangerous, in a beautiful vessel Izzy always felt honored to touch and to be touched by. Marun was more than she seemed. In their time together, she'd gotten used to that feeling. Had secretly loved it.

But three years had gone by.

She wasn't a trusting and easily charmed child anymore.

She also was no longer a wife. Marun's qualities were none of her business.

"That was just an accident," she said, falling back into their conversation. "Things happen. The driver probably feels like shit about almost running us over. I'm just glad no one was hurt."

"Not yet, anyway." White teeth flashed but Marun didn't look the least bit amused.

There was something else there. A secret hidden in the corners of Marun's eyes. It had to do with the way she'd saved Izzy, somehow repelling the SUV before it crushed her. Resentment fizzled in her stomach, threatening an attack of the anxiety she normally only felt while at her parents' house. Like she was exiled from something important. Something she needed. Izzy pushed it aside. Marun's secrets weren't her business, not anymore.

And her business certainly wasn't any concern of her ex's, especially if she had no intention of signing over the building.

Izzy turned to her in the luxurious confines of the car. "What were you doing at the bank this morning?"

"I came to see you, of course." Marun rested her hand easily on the gearshift between them. "I didn't like how we left things yesterday."

Marun's fingers moved restlessly under the sun and sent the diamonds in the narrow eternity band there on fire, dispersing a rainbow of light around them.

Izzy swallowed and forced herself to look away from the ring. "You mean how you broke into my house and disturbed my peace but still won't sign the building over to me?"

"That's not quite my interpretation of things," Marun said softly. "But I am sorry I left you so hurt and upset. That wasn't my intention."

"You mean like the first time?"

Marun's hand tightened on the steering wheel. "I didn't want to leave you, Izzy."

"Then why did you?"

"I—it's hard to explain."

The uncharacteristic hesitation brought Izzy up short. Then she realized what it meant. Whatever this explanation was, Marun must think it was too complex for her little mind to understand.

She pressed her lips together. It had taken her years to get over her inferiority complex where her ex was concerned. Marun had never lorded it over her that she was obviously brilliant, richer than Izzy's parents could ever dream, and usually savagely smarter than everyone else in the room. But that didn't mean knowing these things didn't make Izzy feel some type of way.

"Explain it to me like I'm an idiot, because what you did—leaving me without a word—feels like you just left because you wanted to."

Marun's breath came out in a hiss and she looked away from the road to stare at Izzy again. "It definitely wasn't that. And don't say such nonsense about yourself, even as a hypothetical." The corners of Marun's mouth turned down and the sound of her fingernail tapping against the gearshift was loud between them. "My family is complicated. I told you that from the beginning."

She had. Back when they first talked seriously about being together, they discussed meeting each other's families. Marun mentioned that her mother knew about them but traveled a lot. Also, something about her siblings being crazy and she wanted Izzy far away from them.

"But you never said that complication would end with this." Izzy gestured to the space between them. Then she clamped her mouth shut, mad at herself for looking for an explanation when there obviously wasn't one.

Marun left because she could. That's it.

Izzy's stomach clenched hard like it just took a punch from a particularly vicious fist. No matter how many times she'd thought it over the years, the thought of Marun, the reality of her leaving, never hurt any less.

Hands clenched in her lap, she turned to stare out of the window at the passing scenery. Nope, the bushes and trees hadn't changed in the couple of hours or so since she last looked at them on the bus ride to town.

But she took the few moments to desperately get herself back together.

Being so close to Marun again brought all the old feelings back. Not just the inadequacy that had set in months into their relationship, but the want for her that always sat *just* under Izzy's skin. The desire to see one of Marun's rare smiles that was like the sun breaking through dark clouds after a storm. The need to touch her, to shut out everything except what it meant to be loved and desired and even worshiped by Marun.

No.

Only one thing was important now. And it wasn't climbing back between her ex's thighs.

From the looks Marun gave her, though, that was exactly what she had in mind. Izzy flicked a quick glance to the other side of the car, considering all her options.

Maybe, just maybe, she could get what she needed from Marun after all.

When they pulled up into the driveway, Izzy gathered her purse in her lap and prepared to get out of the car. She hesitated with her hand on the door handle.

"Do you want to come in for some coffee or something?"

With a hand still on the steering wheel, and presumably ready to put the monster of a car in gear and head back to wherever she came from, Marun gave her the *"don't bullshit me and I won't bullshit you"* look.

"Do you actually want me to come in or are you just being polite?" Her tone was light but threaded with something else.

Uncertainty?

The old Marun would never have questioned the offer, she would have just barged right in and expected everything delivered to her on a silver platter, including Izzy herself.

Strange.

Getting out of the car, Izzy just shrugged. "Make whatever you want out of it. I'm sure I have some of that Kenyan coffee you like though."

Her stomach dipped at the ghost of a smile that touched Marun's lips. So what if that small thing made her ex happy? It was just a way to get her to sign the papers, that was all.

Marun turned off the car. "In that case, I'd love to come in."

As she made her way up the driveway, Izzy was acutely aware of Marun. She walked at Izzy's side, full hips rocking tantalizingly under the brilliant-yellow slacks, her purse tucked under an arm while she made small talk about the crisp white of the cottage's paint job and the purple and red hydrangeas blooming on both sides of the porch steps.

"Come in and make yourself comfortable while I change." Hands slick with nervous sweat, Izzy hung the keys on their hook by the door and slipped into the bedroom, the repercussions of the sudden decision she'd made in the car nipping at her heels.

Was she really going to do this?

The memory of Marun sitting beside her at the bank came back to her, the dark eyes so certain, so cool and focused on her own agenda—whatever that was—despite Izzy's plea for help.

Yes. Yes, she was going to do this.

After a quick change of her clothes and tampon, then a bracing splash of water on her face, she went back into the living room. Of course, Marun had made herself comfortable. She sat on the sofa, her suit jacket discarded, a leg curled under her as she paged through one of the art cookbooks from the coffee table.

A traitorous warmth spread through her at how very much at home Marun looked there on the tobacco-brown leather couch that had been in their old apartment. It was a little too big for the cottage's doll-sized living room but, like the box hidden at the back of the closet, it held reminders of things Izzy should have let go of years ago but couldn't.

Even Marun's sweet scent, one she'd missed for so long, perfumed the room with nostalgia and remembered love. She couldn't afford to be weak though.

Marun stopped reading the book. "That's a nice dress."

Izzy passed the couch on the way to the kitchen. "It's comfortable."

"Yes," Marun murmured. "I can see that."

Her voice was like incense smoke, rising up and following Izzy through the archway separating the living room from the kitchen. The beaded curtain between the rooms brushed over her shoulders as she passed through them. With each step, she was aware of the loose drape of the dress over her body, the wide neck drooping off one shoulder and the thin cotton showing very clearly she wasn't wearing a bra. The fabric lightly rubbed her bare nipples with every breath, making them painfully hard.

Marun had always preferred her in comfortable clothes, loose and accessible instead of tight and restrictive, all the easier to slip her hands beneath to get at Izzy's skin. She flushed, suddenly overcome by memories of all the times Marun had cornered her in their apartment, fingers caressing under a maxi dress or inside her sweats, teasing Izzy with pleasure until neither of them could take it anymore and they ended up in a naked and satisfied heap on the floor.

A soft breath of laughter drew her gaze to the kitchen's entrance. Of course, Marun stood there. Watching her. Likely knowing exactly what she was thinking.

Izzy fumbled to open the cabinet door and hide her overly warm face. "Do you want it iced or hot?"

"However you want to give it to me is fine."

There was no hiding her trembling hands or hard nipples as she put the drink together, getting ice, sweet cream, and a tall glass to make the iced coffee Marun liked to drink even in the dead of winter.

"You don't have to be nervous with me, Isabella. We're way past that."

Warm breath brushed the back of her neck and she felt the light touch of hands on her waist.

"I'm not—not nervous." She bit back a gasp at the searing touch and, before she could remember this was what she wanted, a seductive and unwary Marun, she slipped away from the hands that felt too good, banging her hip into the counter in her startled escape.

Her pulse thudded fiercely in her throat and she fiddled with a nearby ceramic vase that held her wooden cooking spoons, chest aching, and waited for the coffee to brew.

She'd made the decision to manipulate Marun into signing the papers, but that didn't mean it was going to be easy. The living and breathing reality of Marun in her cottage, temptingly scented and so beautiful, weakened her knees as well as her resolve. After five minutes of her so-called plan, she was already in so far over her head that she was about to drown.

The coffee gurgled in the machine and its rich aroma poured into the kitchen.

To occupy her fluttering hands, Izzy picked up a slotted wooden spoon. "In the car, you said something about not wanting to leave me and that it's complicated—" Marun opened her mouth to interrupt but she held up a hand. "—no, let me finish. I don't know when I'll get the chance to talk to you about this again since god knows when you'll suddenly disappear again for another three years."

"Years?" Marun made a sound of disbelief. "Don't exaggerate, love. I've only been gone for..." Her voice drifted away as she looked up at the rustic calendar on the kitchen wall. "Wait. That can't be right."

The calendar Izzy put up may have been cliché, an "adorable cottages of the northern USA" spread Taylor had given her months before, but it was at least accurate. She wasn't about to let Marun distract her.

"Why did you leave, Marun?"

But her ex didn't answer. Brow puckered, she drifted across the kitchen toward the calendar. "Three years?"

she asked as if she didn't have a smart watch on her wrist and what looked like the current year's obnoxious car sitting in the driveway.

Her anger quickly clawed its way to the surface. She dropped the wooden spoon on the counter with a clatter. "You know damn well how long it's been, Marun. Don't treat me like that much of a fool." Because it hurt.

Marun grabbed her arm. "Izzy, listen!"

Izzy shook off the too-warm touch. "No, just let me finish this then you can tell me whatever bullshit you're eager for me to believe."

Pointedly turning her back to Marun, she finished making the coffee and then prepared some mint tea for herself. Coffee actually sounded more appealing, especially since she needed to be her most awake and aware self to deal with Marun, but tea made more sense. The last thing she needed was to be groggy and distracted later tonight at work.

Once everything was done, she put the cups along with some shortbread cookies on a tray and took them to the living room.

Marun trailed behind her, a silent wraith, radiating discontent.

"I didn't realize it had been so long. But dammit, I should have known." Obviously agitated, Marun dropped into the couch, her back against the armrest.

The ceramic tray clicked against the wooden coffee table when Izzy put it down. "Here's your coffee. Drink up. I made it just the way you like."

What else was there to say to Marun's madness? Three years had passed since she walked out. There was absolutely no way she didn't know that.

Marun's hands rested limply in her lap and Izzy tucked her own in the pockets of her dress, keeping to her side of the sofa.

"It wasn't supposed to be this long," Marun said. "The time..." She tilted her head back. Her thick hair quivered like a dandelion in the breeze. "I'm acting like I was born yesterday. I knew it could be like this."

"You're the one treating me like I was born yesterday." The giant mug of tea warmed Izzy's hands as she took a sip; a mint leaf swimming in the hot liquid lightly touched her lips. She wanted to scream at Marun and tell her to stop playing games, but that wouldn't get her what she wanted.

"So—" she said, resting the cup in her lap and turning to mirror Marun's pose. "—tell me, what is it that you forgot?"

"Apparently, everything about how the world works." Marun sighed and brought the tall glass of iced coffee, the thick cream and darker coffee still swirling, separately yet together, to her nose. She took a long drink of the coffee without mixing it. "This is perfect. Thank you."

"I'm glad you still like some things," Izzy said quietly. The tea, flavored with honey, was sweet on her tongue, even with the lemon juice she'd squeezed in. "Will you ever tell me why you left?"

"I will. But first, tell me why you need me to sign this paper so badly."

Izzy set the cup down on the saucer with a sharp *clack*. "Did you listen to anything I said before?"

"Yes, but it doesn't make any sense. I left you everything in my accounts. Between that and the money your grandmother left you, money shouldn't be a problem."

At the thought of just how much of her grandmother's money was gone, Izzy's cheeks burned. She should have been responsible. But somehow, it had all simply disappeared.

"The accounts were empty, Marun. I had to rent out the apartment above the bakery because I couldn't afford the mortgage, then finally had to close the business. I need to sell the building before I have to sell a kidney to live."

"If it's money you want, I have plenty. Take it. As much as you want."

Izzy clenched her trembling hand. This was the way of falling right into Marun's trap. Take the money and end up in a cycle of dependency that would break her when Marun ran off again? No, she couldn't do that. "It's not just about the money. Sign over the building to me and we'd never have to deal with each other again. You can go back to wherever you came from and not worry about lying calendars or giving me money or any of it. If you have so much cash, the bakery—the building—shouldn't mean anything to you."

If she could get this done the direct way, she'd happily throw out the seduction plan. After what seemed to be real surprise about finding out what year it was, Marun had softened. Maybe they could both be adults about this, honest adults.

"I'm not letting you sell our bakery."

Or not.

"All right then." Izzy released a sigh and sank deeper into the couch, feeling heavier now than when she first walked into the house. She should just tell Marun to get the hell out of the apartment and fuck right off back to where she came from. But though she was many things, Izzy had never been rude. "Fine. So, since you're already in my house and drinking my coffee, can you at least tell me where you've been all this time?"

"I went to find my mother."

Of all the things Izzy expected Marun to say, this was at the absolute bottom of her list. She cleared her throat. "Why?"

Under the late morning light, Marun's face was a shifting tapestry of emotion, open as it usually was only after sex. Or when she'd done something she knew was wrong.

"I needed some advice about my siblings."

"And you couldn't do that while we were together?"

"No. I couldn't. She's not easy to find, and the way can be dangerous for a huma—for someone like you."

"Someone like me?" Izzy shook her head although every part of her was getting heavy, the need to sleep weighing her down into the soft leather. "I'm not that fragile, Marun."

"My mother is a hard creature. Even steel isn't safe from her."

This was all so much shit. But it was more than she'd ever gotten out of Marun before. Even if her reasons were lies, Izzy was pathetic enough to at least want to hear them.

"Did you find her?"

"No, I didn't. But I'm still looking." Marun took the teacup from Izzy's hands and put it on the coffee table.

Wait. When did she move? Izzy blinked her heavy eyelids. The thick armrest of the couch felt good against her back, solid. With Marun's voice washing over her, she could almost pretend they were back in the apartment above the bakery, sunlight pouring in, the scent of lovemaking clinging to her skin. Marun smiling at her as if Izzy was all she ever needed in the world.

"I didn't expect to be gone so long," Marun said. "The time in your world moves so differently. No wonder you're all so fragile."

"What are you talking about?" Everything felt soft, blurred softly at the edges by sleep.

"My mistakes."

The sofa's leather under her cheek was so warm and Marun's voice was like a lullaby. This time, when Izzy's eyelids drifted shut, she didn't have the strength to open them again.

Chapter Six

When she opened her eyes again, everything felt different. For one thing, she wasn't in the living room anymore. The familiar contours of her bedroom, half-hidden in shadows, slowly came into focus. Lying on her stomach, Izzy blinked drowsily at her bedside table, the glass of water she didn't remember putting there, her cell phone sitting on its charging pad. The sheet draped over her naked back smelled like the lavender detergent she used but the comforter, a candy-pink cotton she didn't use very often because it was a pain in the ass to dry, wasn't what she'd had on her bed that morning.

Wait. Then why—?

She quickly sat up. Then grabbed the comforter before it fell away completely and left her basically naked in bed next to her ex. Thankfully, she still had her panties on.

"Don't worry, I didn't peek." Marun teased her with a weak smile.

Maybe Izzy should've been surprised to see Marun sitting in the bed beside her, her back resting against the headboard while she scrolled through her phone, but she wasn't. At least not too much.

As her heartbeat slowly calmed, Izzy dragged the comforter all the way up to her neck. She was definitely awake now. Even as she sat there, still disoriented, she realized this wasn't the first time Marun had been here, in *this* bed next to her. Yesterday, just before her mother called, she'd felt the remnants of a familiar warmth. Hints of a scent she knew.

A wave of anger flooded through her veins, making her pulse race. Then, as suddenly as the anger came, it receded, leaving her just...tired. Why was Marun doing this?

"For three years, I searched the world to find you. Now, all of a sudden, you're everywhere, like a bad penny I can't spend." She rubbed eyes that felt gritty and hot. Was this some sort of fever dream? Was she going to wake any second now and find herself alone like always? "You should've left me on the couch and gone home."

"If I'd done that, we wouldn't be talking right now." Marun put her phone down and faced Izzy. She'd taken off her intimidating high heels, leaving her feet and painted toes bare, dark elegance against the pale-pink comforter. Defying the low light, the diamonds on her ring finger flashed as she moved.

Izzy looked away from the ring. "We may be talking, but it's not like you're saying much."

Marun made a soft noise. She looked almost defeated. In the intimacy of the bedroom, closed in by thick curtains and the door leading to the rest of the house, her scent was everywhere. Izzy closed her eyes and sank back down into the bed, withdrawing a few inches to lessen the temptation to sink her fingers into the rich decadence of Marun's thick hair and pull her down for the desperate kiss she'd been craving since her wife made her reappearance. Her *ex*-wife.

"Can I tell you a story?" Marun asked softly.

"Is that why you broke into my room, to tuck me in and read me a bedtime story?"

"Not exactly, but you can consider this a bonus." Marun's eyes, moonlight bright, touched her face and the hint of skin at her throat that suddenly felt uncomfortably warm. She hitched the comforter higher until it hid everything below her nose. Marun smiled.

"So, my stubborn wife, will you allow me...?"

"Just go ahead."

Marun huffed a low laugh. Then she grew serious, her fingers fiddling with her phone that lay between them.

"Too many years ago to count, a powerful woman had nine children," she finally said.

"All at the same time? Was she Mormon or on fertility drugs or something?"

"Or something. Can I continue?"

"Of course." Izzy rolled her eyes. On her stomach, she curled up under the sheet and resettled her head on the pillow so she could properly see Marun's face. "Don't let me interrupt my own bedtime story."

Marun continued.

"Anyway, this woman who was neither Catholic nor Mormon had nine children. They were all different, all with separate gifts proving they were from a powerful family.

"They were all special, and they were all spoiled. Even more so because, although the mother wasn't Mormon or

Catholic, she really wasn't supposed to have that many, at least not at once. So, they were special, and they were always treated like they were special. No one ever told them 'no' when they wanted anything."

"Including their mother?"

"Including their mother," Marun agreed. A fleeting expression passed over her face, something with hints of sadness in it. She dropped her gaze to Izzy and, in that way she always had of piercing through any layers Izzy ever tried to put up between them, she appeared to see everything.

"Can I touch you?"

Izzy twitched at the unexpected question. "I—"

"Never mind, I can see you're not ready. I apologize."

"Wait." The covers fell away as Izzy sat up. "I'm not ready? What does that mean?"

"It means I want you back." Marun pressed her lips together, looking irritated with herself, and then shook her head. "Anyway, that's not what I wanted to say, and—fuck—definitely not now when you don't trust anything I do."

"I hope you're not blaming me for that."

"I'm not. I know what I did." Her voice dropped. "Time passes so quickly here. I don't know why I allowed myself to forget that."

"Time is time, Marun. Three years for me has been three years for you. Don't jerk me around." The words started spilling fast and garbled from her mouth, so she took a quick breath, calmed herself. "Don't play games with me," she finished.

Throughout Izzy's outburst, Marun had held herself absolutely still, just watching her. When the last words faded away, Marun reached out and Izzy jerked back on instinct. Touching was dangerous. It had been three years, but she clearly remembered that much. Marun's hand stopped, and she rested her palm on the sheets between them, just a breath away from Izzy's.

"Can I finish the story?"

She was tempted to tell her "no." To take her mother of nine spoiled kids story and get the hell out of her house. But that wouldn't get her what she wanted. "As long as you don't try to blow smoke up my ass, go ahead."

"As you might have guessed already, these children and their mother aren't exactly ordinary."

"They sound like trust fund kids and a woman who needs to know that just because you can do something, doesn't mean you should."

A whisper of Marun's normal laugh sounded in the room. "I'll make sure to tell her that."

She cleared her throat.

"The children were extraordinary," Marun went on. "Because they weren't supposed to exist and were treated like aberrations by people outside their family, they were very close. They loved one another fiercely, *savagely* even, and though there were nine of them, they didn't want to share their siblings with anybody. They kept themselves and their siblings separate from the rest of the world, especially the human world."

"*What* world?" The question jumped from Izzy's mouth although she didn't give it permission to. Her hands clenched in the sheets and her pulse thrummed.

"The human world."

"Okay. I thought that's what you said but I wanted to make sure."

This was just a story.

Yet, with each word Marun spoke, the hinges of a door long held closed were beginning to creak open. Izzy could feel it. And she was scared. Was this the door that had been closed between her and Marun all along?

Izzy's hands, tightly tangled in the sheets, shook. She curled in on herself.

Marun kept talking.

"These siblings were also jealous of each other. For many reasons, but mainly because the gifts they had inherited from their mother weren't all the same. Some were jealous in the way that children were jealous of another's toys, they wanted better than what they'd received. Others just wanted it all."

Marun's low voice faded to nothing. Izzy didn't move, only lay there curled with the loud thudding of her heart.

The bedding beneath Marun's hand dipped as she leaned just a bit closer, dark eyes with the sheen of stars seeking Izzy's. "Are you listening?"

"Yes." Izzy's throat felt scratchy.

Marun wanted something. Izzy just wasn't sure what. She hung there, a need pulsing from her in the darkness of the bedroom. It wasn't about sex; Izzy knew very well what that need coming from her felt like. This was something else. Something more. She swallowed hard, blood rushing through her veins.

Then Marun backed away.

Izzy released a quiet breath of relief.

"I have a point to this story," Marun said. "I promise."

"Okay."

"One of these privileged nine wasn't so sold on the idea of isolation. She'd been moving away from that for years. Her siblings had sex with humans but never loved them, never had children with them."

Sounded like they wanted to have sex with each other, Izzy thought but kept her mouth shut.

"This sibling loved to wander in the human world and be among them for long periods of time. Once, during her wanderings, she met someone. A human she instantly wanted and, although she thought once she had the human, fucked her fill, she would get over her, she never did. Instead, she fell in love. So, she married her human."

Marun's eyes flashed in the dim light.

Every word Marun spoke felt like she was pulling that heavy and creaking door open. Slowly revealing something Izzy wasn't sure she was ready to see. But Izzy couldn't stop listening. Her heart knocked around in her chest. To keep herself safe, to keep that door closed for just a little while longer, she could pretend she was listening to an interesting story on one of those sci-fi podcasts Taylor loved and sometimes played in the car on their road trips.

She could pretend Marun hadn't just confessed to being the *more* she'd always suspected. Extraordinary. Not human. In love.

"And did this being climb out of love as quickly as she stepped in it?" Izzy's voice shook.

"Don't make it sound like that, Izzy. The love we have isn't like a pile of abandoned dog shit on the sidewalk."

"I know what's a pile of shit around here, and the way I feel for you—*felt* I mean—isn't it." A blush threatened to catch her whole body on fire. "Anyway, and then what happened after that?"

"The brothers and sisters noticed this relationship. They started watching their sister more closely, realized she hadn't only been sleeping with a human on a regular basis, that they were actively building a life together. Which wasn't done."

"Jealousy aside, why would they even care about you—or this woman—being with a human? It's not like this human is going to pollute their gene pool. They do know two women can't make a baby together without help, right?"

The silence throbbed between them.

The creaking door between Marun's secrets and Izzy flew open.

She couldn't pretend anymore.

Izzy sat up so fast her head spun. Her shoulders hit the headboard with an audible thump when she scooted back. "Marun?"

Her ex licked the corner of her mouth, and Izzy had to look away before she found that flash of tongue unbearably sexy and offered to lick the rest of Marun's lips for her. "Actually, we—they can."

Izzy's mouth fell open. Then she closed it with a snap.

A shivery sensation in her stomach made her swallow hard and clasp her trembling hands tightly in her lap. If this was true, they'd lost the chance for so much, all because Marun hadn't been honest with her about who she was.

Her hand drifted up to her chest where a sharp ache bloomed. She was right to worry. This open door had secrets, but it also had pain.

"So, the—the sibs found out their sister was married to a human. And then what?"

"They tried to kill her."

"Excuse me?" She couldn't have heard right.

"Well, first they tried to talk their sister into leaving her human. Then when that didn't work, they tried to kill her."

"Please tell me you're joking." With a sick feeling in her stomach, Izzy recalled the dark SUV racing toward her. If Marun hadn't been there...

"I don't have it in me to joke right now." The faint light glided over Marun's face, revealing its hardened lines. "I—she tried to stop them, but they just kept coming. And it wasn't like she could kill them."

"Because they were her brothers and sisters?" Rosalind was a terrible sister, mean and narcissistic, always throwing her so-called successful life in Izzy's face, but Izzy could never hurt her.

"No, because they're more or less unkillable." The steel in her voice made it sound like she'd tried really hard to kill them.

"And that's why she left? To protect the human so her siblings would stop trying to kill her?"

"I left to get help, to find my mother so she could force my brothers and sisters to leave you alone." Marun drew a long breath and leaned closer so Izzy couldn't miss it, her switch from storyteller to confessor. "She could put a stop to everything, but I can't find her."

"In three whole years?"

"According to your calendar, yes. For me, it's only felt like a few days." She frowned. "Maybe weeks."

This part had to be complete and utter bull.

If Marun had the power she hinted at, the only reason she would disappear was because she wanted to.

Before, Marun could've told Izzy the sky was green and she'd believe it without even looking up for herself. She'd been gullible then, head over heels, and out of her mind for Marun. She wasn't that idiot anymore.

"If all this is true, why are you telling me now?"

"Because I never meant for us to be apart this long."

"So, what does that mean? You want to get back together?"

"I never left you."

A scream throbbed in the back of Izzy's throat, fighting to be set free. Three years, and this was the excuse she got? This bullshit story about murderous brothers and sisters and a mother who'd disappeared off the face of the earth?

She drew in a breath to calm herself and only ended up with a lungful of Marun's scent. It was too much. The intimacy of being in the same bed, the familiar warmth stirring in her belly by that low and gravelly voice, the dark seclusion of the bedroom. Not caring about her near-nakedness, Izzy shoved aside the covers and jumped out of bed. Making it across the room in no time flat, she snatched up her robe and quickly pulled it on while beating a hasty retreat to the rocking chair near the window.

"Marun, you left me," she croaked out. "You left and never once looked back."

"We're going to have to disagree on that point," Marun said softly.

This time, Izzy let a scream free. It was short, primal, and loud. "God, you drive me fucking crazy!"

"The feeling is *not* mutual. I've only ever wanted to love you and take care of you."

Maybe this was her chance. "Sign the building over to me then."

"No."

Blowing out a harsh sigh, Izzy sagged back into the chair. She yanked the edges of the robe over her knees. Of course, it wouldn't be that easy.

"I won't sign the building over to you. Selling it is the last thing I want. But I'll help you with whatever money problems you have."

Izzy bit back another sigh. "For the last time, I don't want your help! I just want things to go back to how they were." It has been years now and she was simply tired. Tired of being miserable. Tired of waiting for the pain of missing Marun to disappear.

"We want the same thing, love."

"No, we really don't. If we did, you wouldn't have told me that ridiculous story about *other people* who want me out of your life. You wanted me gone, just say that. The whole time we were in our play-marriage, you were the more grown-up one. Be that now. If I have a woman in my life, she needs to be a real partner, not someone with crazy excuses for not being with me."

Marun hissed in a slow breath. The sound of it was low in the bedroom, strange and nearly otherworldly because of the near-dark around them.

"Those aren't excuses." She held up her hand when Izzy drew in a breath to speak. "I have crazy siblings and an absentee mother, that's true. What's also true is, if it came down to it, I'd die for you."

Izzy bit her lip until she tasted blood.

That was all well and good but all she wanted was a partner who would tell the truth and live *with* her.

The rocking chair creaked as she leaned forward. "How do I know you're telling me the truth now?"

"Because I am."

"No, it doesn't work that way, Marun. Not anymore. You say you're some demi-god or whatever. Prove it." She didn't want that kind of proof, though, not really. What she wanted, Marun couldn't give her. Or maybe just wouldn't.

"I can't." In the space of one breath, Marun was kneeling on the floor in front of Izzy, the edible scent of her, of guavas and mangoes and papayas, drifting up from her skin. "Not without exposing you to dangerous people. If I use any of my power, my siblings will know where I am."

"That's convenient, isn't it?"

"Hardly." Marun's mouth briefly twisted, and then she put a hand on Izzy's knee, bared by the thin robe. "Please."

Izzy drew in a too-swift breath and inhaled more of Marun's scent. The palm on her knee burned into her skin and sent heat skimming into her center. She missed her so much. "No—" But her own hands were already reaching out across the space separating them, grasping Marun's arms and dragging her close while Izzy slid to the edge of the rocking chair.

She couldn't resist anymore.

She didn't want to.

Their mouths touched, and electricity sparked between them, a sharp buzz of sensation that burned into Izzy's lips. She gasped at the shock of feeling and pulled back. She met Marun's eyes and saw the amazement there, the reflection of the same longing inside her. It hurt, that kiss, but she wanted it again.

"More," Izzy whimpered.

With a rough sound, Marun gripped her shoulders, fingers sinking into her skin through the robe, and Izzy groaned into it. Opened her mouth for the slick press of her wife's tongue against hers. Firm. Hungry. Warm. Izzy sighed and her body melted, and Marun was there to be her strength, the vessel she poured her passion into.

It was like no time at all had passed since their last kiss, the familiar pleasure, the liquid heat swimming through her veins, the want settling between her thighs. Marun slid a firm hand up the back of Izzy's neck, into her hair, and cupped her head. Safe. God, she felt so safe and protected and loved. She didn't realize she was crying until she tasted wet salt.

Marun drew back and their lips parted with a sensual, wet sound. "Oh, love. Please don't cry. Everything will be all right. I promise."

Heart twisting, Izzy wrenched herself away. "No. You don't get to make promises to me. Not again."

"Isabella, I didn't—"

The buzz of Izzy's cell phone cut through Marun's bullshit and Izzy rushed across the room to answer it. Taylor's name glowed on the screen.

She cleared her throat of any emotion before answering. "Hey, woman."

"Hey, yourself. What are you up to?"

Izzy met Marun's gaze. "Nothing much. Just at home sorting through some things." When Marun frowned at her and stood up, Izzy turned her back and walked out of the bedroom. "It's nothing that won't wait."

"Good. You should take the night off and come out with me. There's a new place downtown I want us to try."

It almost made Izzy cry to turn Taylor down, but she had to. In the old days when money wasn't a problem, she wouldn't have hesitated. Exploring a new restaurant or bar would've been the perfect thing to distract her from Marun and the rest of her troubles. But she couldn't afford to take the night off from work.

"You know I can't, Taylor."

"Don't worry about how much it costs, you know I got you." Izzy winced at her friend's offer. "And get that look off your face. This is nothing like Rosalind and her leeching ways." Taylor paused. "Unless you have a gambling or coke habit I don't know about." That was where Izzy was supposed to laugh, but she just didn't have it in her right then. Her sister's bad life choices had never been funny.

"I have to work. These debts aren't going to pay themselves."

Taylor's sigh was a clear indication her patience was nearing an end. But she didn't understand. Not that Izzy expected her to. She'd never been in a position like this. Suddenly poor and being the charity case everyone expected to take care of.

"They won't pay themselves, but your parents could pay."

"No. Absolutely not!"

But Taylor kept pushing. "They already want to help you, Izzy. Come on! Don't let your pride set you up for a fall the way that ex-girlfriend of yours did."

It was like the mention of Marun summoned her from the bedroom. Her scent in the living room was all Izzy needed to know that she was there.

"Listen, Taylor. I have to go. I'd love to see you, but maybe this weekend when I have the night off."

The long-suffering sigh came again. "All right, girl. You're a pain in my ass but I still love you. Talk to you later."

After Izzy ended the call, she turned to face Marun who looked like a storm cloud in human form.

"No matter what your so-called friend tells you, we're still married." The words were dangerously low and seared with anger. "You're my wife, and I'm yours. Nothing's changed that."

Izzy ignored the hot spike of pleasure in her belly and the clear possession in Marun's tone. "I don't have time for either you or Taylor right now. I have to get ready for work."

An earlier glance at her phone had told her it was later than she thought. As usual, time with Marun had both stood still and spun ahead, the moments with her filled with an intensity of emotion that dulled her awareness of time itself and put anything else she'd ever felt for anyone to shame.

Careful not to touch, Izzy brushed past Marun on her way back into the bedroom, her heart doing sprints in her chest.

"Please see yourself out," she said to a silent Marun as she closed the door.

Trying her best not to think about what Marun's possessive words meant, or their kiss, Izzy rushed through getting ready. By the time she ran out of the house, throwing her bag over her shoulder, she'd almost convinced herself that none of what Marun said mattered.

Almost.

Chapter Seven

"You're here early." Javier, the night manager who came in an hour earlier than everyone else, looked up from his clipboard as Izzy walked past his office on the way to the locker room.

She called back to him, not stopping. "It's only half an hour."

"Well, don't think you're getting paid for the extra time." He shouted loud enough for the neighbors to hear.

Safely out of sight, Izzy rolled her eyes. He acted like he owned the place and every penny over expected expenses would come out of his pocket. "I wouldn't dare hallucinate such a thing," she muttered.

An hour later found her wrist deep in cardamom-scented dough, preparing for an East African bridal shower happening late morning in the restaurant. The women wanted traditional mandazi, fried bread Marun used to make for Izzy all the time. Although she would've liked to claim otherwise, it was slowly killing her.

The scent of the dough wrapped dangerous memories around her, brought back the phantom touch of Marun's fingers on her lips as she fed her pieces of mandazi on the balcony of their old apartment.

Marun.

Who was more extraordinary than she ever thought. Some sort of immortal, able to prevent a runaway car from crushing Izzy into the pavement. An immortal with high-strung brothers and sisters trying to kill her just for loving Marun. Even if she could look past the lie of "oh, I blinked and three years passed," was being with Marun worth the constant threats to her life?

"Are you kneading the dough or having sex with it?" Javier's voice snapped the ties of memory and yanked Izzy back to the present.

Her elbow jerked into a nearby metal bowl, splashing water on the counter. She muttered a curse under her breath and grabbed the still rocking bowl with her flour-dusted hands to keep it from falling to the floor.

"We have a schedule to keep, Ransom. Don't fuck up this early in the night." He leveled his bushy eyebrows in her direction and then, once he seemed sure she wasn't about to say anything, or go back to daydreaming, he stalked off.

Izzy bit the inside of her cheek and kept her head down, not looking up at the other four people who worked the night shift with her. Javier was an equal opportunity asshole. He didn't discriminate in who he talked shit to at any given time. One of the very reliable things about him was he was always popping up to chew somebody out just for existing.

It wasn't the first time he'd jumped on Izzy's case, and it wouldn't be the last. She kept a sigh behind her teeth and reached for the mandazi dough.

One of the other women, also wearing a full apron and hairnet, gave Izzy a sympathetic half-smile before turning her attention back to the cake batter she was mixing.

Javier was being a real asshole tonight, even more than usual. Nights like this, Izzy missed the bakery she used to run with Marun. Going at her own pace, even if that meant waking up at four in the morning to get everything ready for the day's customers. She'd never been a dick to her employees. Then again, she'd been so damn happy. Every one of those days filled with love and the challenge of making their business better and better.

Okay. Stop thinking about her.

She managed to fall back into the rhythm of work, ignoring Javier when he stopped by two more times to complain that she hadn't made the tall walk-in oven hot enough. It was total bullshit, but she wasn't invested enough to argue about it with him when he went over to the giant monster that took up a large part of the kitchen and cranked up the temperature.

Just before it was time to put the dough in, she'd turn it back down. If the huge batch of brioches burned, he'd only blame her, and she wasn't in the mood.

The street outside the bakery's large glass window was still dark, the sky obscured by nighttime, the world outside empty of most humans.

Did that mean Marun was out there somewhere?

Shut up about her already. God damn, had she always been this pussy-whipped?

Yes.

After slicing the top of the last of the raw baguettes ready for the oven, she dropped the knife to the counter with a clatter and headed over to the oven. She twisted the knob to the right temperature and then hefted the tray of raw dough to the nearly full baker's rack nearby.

A sudden bellowing voice and a shout of pain almost made her drop the heavy pan of unbaked baguettes.

The pan rattled against the edge of the baker's rack, missed the groove altogether, and slammed down onto the knee she raised in reflex.

"Dammit…"

A hiss of pain slid between her teeth.

"What the fuck was that?" someone gasped, a ripple of unease rolling through the kitchen as Izzy fought with her raw baguettes.

She righted the pan and slid it onto the rack when the swinging doors flew open with a bang. She jumped, a flash of instinctive fear swinging her toward the sound. A sizzling pop came from above her and then a shower of sparks, as a man appeared in front of the double doors.

He was massive, a beast of a man with shoulders nearly spanning the entire doorframe, all of him one huge slab of muscle. His eyes swirled with bright golden fire.

Her heart jumped into her throat as the fear turned into terror. Behind her, she heard things fall, the sound of people bumping into things as they tried to run. Fear froze the blood in Izzy's hands and feet, the breath in her lungs. She started to back away.

"You!" He pointed right at her.

Someone behind Izzy let out a squeak and, trembling with fear, Izzy almost breathed a sigh of relief when his strange eyes left her to seek out the source of the sound. "Get out!" he roared at whoever was behind her.

In that moment, the entire kitchen seemed to fill with an immense pressure. Her ears popped. Her eyes watered. The taste of fear was bitter at the back of Izzy's throat and she swallowed desperately, wanting to cry out when one of the women raced past her, feet slipping against the tile in her rush for the door.

The hydraulic mechanism of the door sighed in the silence as it slid shut.

Unkillable, Marun had said. *Shit.*

Oh my god, I'm going to die.

"I never thought it would be this hard to get rid of one little human," the man rumbled.

He moved toward Izzy, gliding in an oddly graceful way, the certainty of her imminent death a cold glow in his eyes.

"What do you want?" she gasped, backing away.

"I think you know the answer to that question." His voice thundered around the kitchen leaving everything trembling, especially her.

"Yes, but why?"

"I think you know the answer to that too." Then he was on her, grabbing her by the front of her shirt and lifting her up like she weighed nothing, was nothing.

The pain from his crushing fingers dragged a cry from her. "Let me go!" Screaming at him, Izzy thrashed and kicked her legs, gasped for air, and cried out for help. Her flailing legs slammed into something a moment before pain hammered through her ankle. Then her belly hit the steel countertop and he dragged her across its crowded surface, using her body like a rag to wipe it clean. Dimly, she heard a metal bowl fall, the splash of water, the clatter of pans hitting the floor. Desperately, she tried to grasp on to something, anything, and hold on.

Something cold and sharp bumped into her hand and she clutched at it. Pain sliced into her palm and she screamed, chest heaving, as her skin slicked with blood. It was a knife. The same one she'd used to cut into the baguette dough.

It hurt. Fuck, it hurt so bad. But she didn't let go of the knife. Even as her fingers slipped against the blade now wet from her blood.

She only clung harder to the knife as the man dragged her over and off the counter, her feet slamming into the hard floor. He was yanking her toward the industrial sized oven.

Panic clogged her throat. "No!"

Desperate and gasping for every breath, she clutched on tight to the knife blade and swung it around, plunging wildly.

Her whole body flushed with panic, the blood rushing through her veins like a storm-tossed river. She screamed, her body twisting and contorting, wild with panic.

She was fighting for her life and her adrenaline-driven body knew it.

Marun.

This was all her fault.

Izzy's throat hurt, and she realized she was shouting Marun's name as she flailed in the giant man's grip.

"Shut up. She's not going to save you." He yanked her across the floor and grabbed the oven's door release, flicked it open with no effort at all. The same lack of effort it would take him to burn her alive.

She twisted desperately one last time and struck the knife high and fast toward his face. With a liquid *squish*, the blade sank into his eye, and stayed there. He roared, a hot breath that scorched her forehead, and stumbled back, bracing a hand on the edge of the oven. His hold on her loosened, thick fingers only tangled now in the front of her apron.

She couldn't afford to stop. A wild yell vibrated her throat and she twisted out of the apron, crying out in pain when she landed hard on her butt.

"Why don't you just die already?" He crouched down to grab her again and she screamed.

"No!" Izzy kicked high, aiming for his balls with her Clarks slip-ons and gasped in surprise and relief when he actually stumbled back with a curse, a palm cupped over his crotch.

Izzy slid back across the floor, bumping into metal bowls as she scrambled backward like a demented crab, but the man was coming back for her.

"You're just making this more painful for yourself," he growled, straightening to his full height, but with his hand still on his crotch. "I don't mind that."

Suddenly, he was *right there* and reaching out for her with both hands, his fingernails transforming into sharp white claws before her eyes. Izzy's back slammed into the counter.

"Okan! Stop!"

Marun's unexpected shout rattled the kitchen. Then she was at Izzy's side, her eyes wide and terrified. And furious. Crouching low, she slid Izzy behind her and shoved out a hand glowing with bright-blue flame.

Terror clutched Izzy by the throat as she stared between the man and Marun's fiery hand. A frown carved a deep crease into his forehead while his flat gold eyes promised to tear Izzy apart as soon as he got the chance.

Tremors took her body and she clung to Marun's back, desperately happy to see her ex, and on the verge of a fucking heart attack.

"Marun, stay out of this. You should have let me take care of this pestilence years ago. You need to be with us. Our people. What you're doing with this human is an abomination."

"Fuck you," Marun spat.

Izzy heard a tremendous sound, like a colossal storm wave rolling toward land. The noise vibrated in her head, too loud, and she slammed her hands over her ears just as a boiling swell of hot blue flames shot out from Marun's outstretched hands. The fire rammed into the man, swallowing him and everything nearby. Heat blew back into Izzy's face and she whimpered in fear, ducking down behind Marun.

Then the destroyed kitchen blurred. Izzy heard a roared "Come back here!" before the familiar restaurant disappeared altogether and suddenly, they were somewhere else. Somewhere she'd never been before in her life.

Chapter Eight

Izzy drew a gasping breath as nausea roiled in her stomach and her head spun.

She only had moments to register where they were—a public bathroom, and not the one at the bakery—before Marun's face, creased with concern, blocked her sight. Her eyes, flickering with gold fire, glowed down at Izzy.

Sudden and overwhelming fear propelled Izzy backward. Gasping, she slid frantically across the dirty bathroom floor until her back crashed into the closed door of a bathroom stall. It was too much like what just happened in the restaurant. Her heart punched frantically against her chest wall and her gasping breaths were loud in the large, tiled bathroom.

"Don't touch me!"

"It's just me, love. It's okay. It's Marun. You know me, right?"

But the Marun she'd known wasn't this same creature kneeling in front of her in a strange bathroom with eyes like a whirlpool of liquid gold. Then Marun blinked, as if she suddenly realized what her eyes looked like, and the gold disappeared to become that unfathomable darkness

Izzy had fallen into years ago and never managed to escape from.

It was a superficial change, she knew, but one that made her feel better. A little.

"You know damn well nothing will ever be okay again." She drew in quick, burning breaths, her hands held out in the classic "keep away" position. Her palm throbbed with a sharp pain, but she couldn't look at it yet. Looking at it would mean reliving part of what just happened. Remembering she buried a knife in a man's eye and that had barely slowed him down. Oh god. "Marun..." Her chin wobbled. She couldn't say anything else.

"You're hurt, love," Marun said softly. She lifted a brow, a silent asking of permission.

When Izzy nodded, Marun took her hand and Izzy looked down at her limp palm, noticing for the first time that it was bleeding. A lot. Marun's fingers traced the multiple deep cuts that ran diagonally through her right palm and into part of her wrist. Cold. Her fingers were cold against Izzy's skin. "I wish I could kill that little bastard," Marun spat out, the words granite hard while her touch stayed gentle.

"Your brother is an asshole." She spoke past the tremor in her voice, her whole body shaking.

"Yes, he is." Marun's lips twitched with a weak smile. She lightly probed the cuts, and each touch made the sluggish blood start to flow again. Izzy bit back a whimper of pain.

"I'm so sorry, love." Still cradling Izzy's throbbing hand between hers but keeping it elevated above Izzy's heart, Marun slid closer. Her warmth was like a blast furnace on a winter day, washing over Izzy and sheltering her from the cold reality outside the bathroom's doors. God, she looked so clean and perfect. Nothing like Izzy did now. "Let me take care of this, okay?"

"Okay." Izzy sighed.

She was exhausted. The adrenaline from the unfair fight in the bakery had drained from her, leaving her weak and shivery. Even with the memory of Marun's strange, gilded eyes, she just wanted to climb into her wife's lap and go to sleep.

"Okay," she said again, even softer this time, and sagged back against the flimsy stall door.

At the first touch of Marun's lips on her hand, she jolted upright in shock. Her whole body went stiff and she instinctively tried to yank her hand back, but Marun's grip was strong. Fresh blood welled up from the cuts and she gasped from the rush of pain. In the stark, fluorescent light of the bathroom, she saw clearly Marun's fingers curled around her hand, the diamonds in her ring flashing, her mouth red from Izzy's blood. A long tongue lashed the blood from her palm and, though it should have disgusted her, a low sigh of relief left Izzy's lips and her spine went liquid again. Most of the pain was gone.

"What—what are you doing?"

"Taking care of you."

Through the lush thicket of her eyelashes, Marun watched her, the touch of her gaze more intimate, that penetrating look of hers sliding into Izzy, soothing and calming her the same way her tongue soothed her cuts, lapped up the blood, and stopped it from flowing.

It should be wrong. It was wrong. But Marun kept going, her tongue sweeping over the cuts in Izzy's palm in slow and deliberate licks, down to the wrist, gathering blood and erasing the pain with each touch. The pain was gone, but in its place was a different feeling. Pleasure. Another sigh swept past Izzy's parted lips and her head fell back against the door. Her eyes closed.

The sound of Marun's tongue moving over her skin was unbearably intimate. Izzy wanted more. Shuddering, she spread her fingers, inviting more of her wife's touch. Flickers of sensation lit up her body, tightened her nipples, sped her pulse.

"You should stop," she breathed, but god, she didn't mean it.

"I can't stop this any more than you can," Marun whispered into the cup of her palm, the warmth of her breath another type of salve on Izzy's flesh. "From the very beginning, your blood called to me. No matter where you bleed from, or how, when your blood spills it's like a flare across my sky. I can't ignore it now just like I couldn't ignore it when we first met. I want to heal you. I want part of you inside me." Her tongue rasped against Izzy's skin.

Marun's touch felt so good, so perfect, after what happened in the bakery. After the loneliness of the last three years. Maybe she should have taken a lover since her wife left her, she thought in a daze, maybe then she wouldn't have been so desperate for someone to touch her.

But this isn't just someone, a voice at the back of her mind said. *This is Marun.*

The woman she'd shared her virginity with. The extraordinary being she'd pined for and never forgot. Nothing felt like her wife's touch.

Deep down, she'd known nothing ever would, and left the taking of new lovers to other people.

A soft tongue slid between her fingers, teasing the sensitive skin there, dampening her panties and pulling the cotton fabric tight against her swelling clitoris.

Soon, it was over. She opened her eyes and met Marun's, licked her lips.

The familiar light in the dark eyes tightened hot lust in her belly.

"As much as I'd like to take advantage of what you're feeling right now, I won't." Amusement flickered in the glittering gaze. "Come on. Let's clean you up and get out of here."

Marun stood and, without giving Izzy a chance to disagree, pulled her to her feet.

"Oh!" She stumbled.

"The dizziness will pass. Come. The water here is nice and hot. Clean hand towels are in that basket over there."

Letting go of Marun's steadying hand and finally looking around, Izzy noticed it wasn't just any bathroom Marun had taken her to. It was obviously a public one, but each of the six stalls had real doors with gold handles. The doors went all the way to the floor, giving privacy to anyone using the toilets.

Speaking of which. "Um... I have to—" she gestured to one of the bathroom stalls.

"Sure. I'll wait right here for you."

By the time Izzy had used the bathroom and stepped out of the stall to wash her hands, she felt marginally better and gained a bit of perspective. She wasn't dead on the floor of the bakery. Marun was here. She didn't have to see Javier for the rest of the night.

The automatic soap dispenser spat a blob of foam in her palm. Her *uninjured* palm that had only the faintest smears of red from Marun's tongue.

Marun had licked her blood. And actually *healed* her. Her ex stood by the bathroom door, hands in the back pockets of her tight jeans. A pale-yellow blouse clung to her torso and showed off the ripe handful of breasts and large nipples that weren't being shy at all. Her hair, usually worn free and thick around her face, was braided back, the ends curling like delicate fronds of dark fern over her shoulders. Marun held a jacket, dark-brown leather that matched her boots, folded over one arm.

She looked so normal. So much like the woman Izzy had fallen for on that cold night a million years ago. But normalcy as Izzy knew it was a thing of the past, and even back then it had been an illusion. An ache blossomed in her chest. Not quickly enough, she looked away and carried on with the business of washing her hands.

As she searched for hand towels to dry her hands, she caught sight of her reflection in the bathroom mirror, and nearly died. Oh god. No wonder Marun hadn't wanted to have inappropriate sex with her on the bathroom floor. She looked an absolute mess. Smears of flour whitened random parts of her face and neck while the hairnet she'd had to wear for work tilted drunkenly on top of her head.

Embarrassment heating her cheeks, she snatched off the hairnet and shoved it into her jeans pocket and then quickly wiped off as much of the flour as she could.

Since sinking through the floor from sheer humiliation wasn't an option, she turned away from the mirror when she was done. "Okay, I'm ready."

With a soft laugh, Marun pushed open the bathroom door with a booted foot and allowed her to go out first. "You look fine," she said, which only made Izzy more embarrassed. *Fine* wasn't the same thing as *good*.

Izzy had only taken a couple of steps before she stopped.

"What's this place?" And how did they get here?

"A coffee shop," Marun said, like that was any kind of answer. "Come on. I see a table over there by the window."

Izzy trailed after her.

True, the place was like most other coffee shops she'd been to before. Comfortable. Perfumed with coffee. And had more than a few people hunched intently over their laptops.

Even this late at night, it was nearly half full. Low-voiced conversations hummed in the open concept space decorated like somebody's country cabin. A high beamed ceiling of dark wood crouched over a scattering of comfy sofas and wooden bistro table and chair sets.

Outside the café's wall of windows lay a garden courtyard. Old-fashioned looking hanging lanterns swayed in the light spring breeze and illuminated the few tables and benches out there. A lone woman sat at a far-off table reading something on the glowing screen of her phone.

Inside, the scent of coffee was strong and very welcome to Izzy's bruised senses.

Marun guided her to a table tucked away in a corner and draped her jacket over one of the chairs. "I'll be right back," she said once Izzy was seated.

A few minutes later, she returned with a big mug of hot chocolate overflowing with whipped cream and a cup of coffee as dark as her eyes.

"Oh, bless you!" Izzy reached for the coffee like it would save her life, and just held the warm mug between her chilled hands, savoring the temperature and the scented steam rising up to caress her face.

This wasn't enough to make everything okay, but it was close enough to normal to soothe the panic threatening to bubble up out of her throat in a scream.

Izzy took a careful sip of her coffee.

The sounds of the café eddied around them, soothing and low. Tuning out the threatening panic fizzing at the back of her mind, Izzy focused on her coffee, the strong flavor, its rich taste, the touch of normalcy it gave her in the midst of the madness she was currently living. Across from her, Marun sipped from her extra-large mug of hot chocolate like they had all the time in the world, occasionally licking away any stray bit of cream that dared to cling to her lips.

"Tonight wasn't supposed to happen," Marun said sometime later, breaking the easy silence between them. "I'm sorry."

Izzy swallowed the rich mouthful of coffee and put the mug on the table, fiddling with the white handle before putting her suddenly trembling hands in her lap. Her teeth nibbled at the corner of her mouth. As stupid as it sounded, she could've honestly gone her whole life without talking about any of this. Or, for that matter, without living it, but that horse had obviously already kicked the barn door down and run the fuck off.

"Is your brother going to try and kill me again?"

Marun sat with hands resting on the table and curved around her cup. The corner of her eye twitched. "Right now, he has no incentive to stop."

Izzy nearly choked on her next breath of air. She should have known better than to ask. "That's just fucking...great."

"My family is complicated, but I'll fix this."

Understatement of the century. *Izzy's* family was complicated. Marun's family was homicidal maniacs and women who claimed to have accidentally abandoned their wives because they didn't know what year it was.

"Okay." She blew out a trembling breath. "Tell me again what you are."

"I'm one of the Orisha." She paused and looked meaningfully at Izzy as if waiting for her to chime in with a comment, question, or denial. When Izzy didn't say anything, Marun continued in a low teaching voice like this was a conversation she'd had many times before. "We're spirits, some call us gods. Among humans, tales of us have come from the African continent, but we are and always have been everywhere.

"We are multitudes. Spirits of the waters, fertility, wisdom, storms." Marun vaguely waved a hand which Izzy took to mean "etc."

Her wife was a for real god. Or spirit.

Head spinning, Izzy reached across the table and grasped Marun's wrist, needing something to ground her. "Tell me about you. In particular."

"Ah…" Marun briefly tongued the corner of her mouth in one of those odd displays of nervousness Izzy found hard to get used to. "My domain is the heart of the blue flame," she said finally. "And blood."

Izzy's thigh muscles twitched, and she silently gasped as her body reacted, spasming deep inside, spilling more blood into the tampon she'd changed barely an hour before all the madness started at the restaurant.

"Which means what?" she asked, scared that she might already know.

"I can sense the blood connections between people. Know if they are related and how." The corners of Marun's lips curved up in an oddly self-mocking way. "I know, boring, right?" The faint smile died away. "I can also control blood. Drain it from a live or dead body, boil a person from the inside and kill them. If I want." Her shoulder hitched up in a shrug, and she curved long fingers around her cup of hot chocolate. All very ordinary. Right. "And although I don't have to drink blood to survive, I love how it tastes." Her tongue appeared again and, in the light of the coffee shop, Marun's lips looked plump and red, like she'd just had a feast.

Yes, she loved blood.

That part, Izzy knew very well. Heat rushed up her throat and into her cheeks as the memory of those times chose that exact moment to ambush her. Days when she'd been weakened in bed with period cramps, and Marun burrowed between her thighs to lick her dry and ravenously eat her to orgasm, moaning her pleasure and whispering her adoration of Izzy like she could never get enough. After months of Marun tending to her like this, her cramps had become less intense, less frequent, before they disappeared altogether.

Izzy cleared her suddenly dry throat. "Anything else?"

"Not..." Marun stopped whatever she was going to say. "Once I taste someone's blood, it can give me power over them."

And that was what Izzy was afraid of. Was her infatuation with Marun a sort of madness inflicted on her by some minor god who didn't like to be turned down? "Did you ever try to control me?"

"No, never." Marun's jaw went tight.

Izzy released a long, slow breath of relief. She clutched her coffee cup, took an unhurried sip, savoring the strong brew.

"Since the first time I took your blood, I've been more tuned in to where you are physically. When you're on your monthly cycle, I have a rough sense of your emotions, maybe not exactly what you're thinking, but the dimensions of those thoughts. That's all."

That's all. No big.

Izzy licked the hint of coffee from her lips, grounding herself in the familiar flavor, and tried not to look like the foundations of everything she'd believed about reality weren't crumbling. "So, you have all this going on and somehow didn't think to mention any of this to me before we got married?"

Marun seemed to suddenly find something really interesting to look at outside the window. When she turned back around to Izzy, her face was an expressionless mask. "Would you have still asked me to marry you if you knew about them?"

Would she have? Being with Marun was the happiest she'd ever felt in her life. She'd always been a happy child, despite her parents trying to make her into someone she didn't want to be. She'd simply left them behind to live the life she'd wanted. She'd found that and more in New York. Meeting Marun, falling in love with her, was the icing on the cake.

With Marun, she was the best version of herself. One that was well-fucked, well-fed, knew exactly what she wanted out of life, and how to get it.

She'd also been in danger of being murdered by her psycho brothers and sisters.

"Honestly, I don't know." Marun flinched at that but Izzy forged ahead. "You could've at least given me the choice."

It was incredible, the changes in Marun she'd seen over the last couple of days. Unreal. Being a fire-eyed demi-goddess aside, Marun had shown more emotion, more warmth and vulnerability, than Izzy had ever seen when they'd been together.

Now, her ex toyed with a used napkin, long fingers clenching and releasing around the badly wrinkled paper. She stared down at the smooth wood of the table like it held the answers to every question she'd ever had.

"That's fair, I suppose," Marun said with a twist of her mouth. "Nobody wants to go into a marriage expecting to be threatened with death by their wife's family. I... I just wanted you so much, and I didn't know if I'd lose you if you knew the whole truth." A frown made the barest wrinkle in Marun's brow, but she didn't look up from the table. "By the time you asked me to marry you, I was so gone for you that I couldn't think straight. We were so happy, *I* was so happy, that it was easy to forget about everything else. But then, one of my sisters told me I had to give you up one way or another. I didn't want to. I couldn't. Finally, after living for so long, I realized for the first time what love was like." Shock rippled through Izzy's body and she couldn't hold back her gasp. Marun finally looked up, her eyes uncertain. She shrugged. "That's when I knew I had to find our mother and get her help to make things right."

Her mother. Okay...

But Izzy was still focused on what Marun said before.

There had never been any discussion of feelings. Things had simply *been* between them. Every time they touched, Izzy reached a level of intimacy with Marun she never thought possible. All Marun had to do was look at her and she was transported to a place where nothing mattered but the two of them. There had been no need to discuss what they meant to each other because it had always been obvious. They were happy. They loved each other. Nothing else mattered.

Now, with the word out in the open, so raw in Marun's low and compelling voice, Izzy realized how much she'd actually wanted to hear it.

Love.

How simple. How normal. But they'd never said the word to each other. They'd just been so sure it had been there between each of their breaths. At least Izzy was.

She and Marun had connected from the first moment they met. They'd known each other intimately, shared secrets in their quiet bedrooms. But they never actually *talked.*

Izzy sat back in her chair, stunned.

Didn't the experts all say communication was the key to any successful relationship? If that was true, it was a miracle she and Marun had survived together as long as they had.

"We really don't know anything about each other, do we?"

"That's not true. We know everything that's necessary," Marun said, hotly. She grasped for Izzy's hands across the table but after only a brief touch, Izzy pulled back. Her fingers were cold. The corners of Marun's eyes turned down. "You know I can't stand the beach, that my favorite color is yellow. I know you'd rather starve than ask your family for help and subject yourself to your mother's homophobia and your father's passive acceptance of his wife's bad behavior. We know everything that's important," she said again.

But they both knew that wasn't true. Izzy picked up her coffee but only held the heavy mug in her hands, needing something to ground herself.

"If that's true, why don't I know who or what you really are?"

A charged silence throbbed between them. "You know now."

"Only because your family tried to kill me. Why did I have to lose you for three years to find out such an important thing about you?" Izzy shook her head. "I know the answer to that. But that's my point. We bleed our feelings all over each other, but we don't communicate like real people. What we had wasn't sustainable."

The sound of Marun swallowing was strangely loud in the half-full café. "You know, I thought I had all the time in the world to tell you everything and to make you understand about my life. But then, I left to try and fix everything and just ended up losing three years of us along with your trust. I'm sorry. That's not what being a real partner is about. You deserve better." Marun licked her lips and reached out, her palms up on the table. Instead of taking, she was waiting for Izzy to reach for her.

Because all she'd been waiting for during these years was to have Marun back in her life, Izzy reached out. A crackle of energy flared between their fingers and Izzy flinched, expecting it to hurt. Instead, a warmth flowed from her wife's hand to hers. She gripped Marun tight.

"You can't do this to me again," she said. "I wouldn't survive it."

"I won't. I wouldn't survive it either." The dark eyes shimmered with what looked suspiciously like tears. "I'll do anything to make this right between us. I'll talk." Those eyes flared wider for a moment, like suddenly something occurred to her. "I'll even sign the papers so you can do whatever you want to the bakery. I'll do whatever you want. All I'm asking is that you give me a chance to make these three years up to you. To love you the way you deserve."

Triumph surged through Izzy. Finally. A promise to sign the papers. But the victory tasted like ashes on her tongue. The prize she really wanted was much more valuable than that.

Marun's ring dug into her own finger and Izzy looked at it properly for the first time in three years. The diamonds were still as brilliant as the day she gave the band to Marun at their wedding. She thought about the matching band she still kept in the cigar box and, despite all she'd been going through with money, could never bring herself to sell.

"Take me home," Izzy said.

Chapter Nine

Izzy and Marun left the table hand in hand. Joined palm to palm with the glowing heat between them that warmed Izzy with every step. She'd missed this.

As they walked through the café, she realized there was no real front door. The door with the bell above it led into the fenced, lamplit courtyard. Marun led her past the café's counter to a set of wide double doors with ornate looking handles. The doors were pushed open as they approached and a tall woman, white haired and with glowing pale eyes, stepped past them, giving them a nod of acknowledgment.

"Stay close," Marun murmured and held her hand tighter. "It's crowded tonight."

What?

No sooner had the thought come than a thud of music overwhelmed her. Loud, sensual, vibrant. Startled, she jerked her head to look behind her at the double doors slowly drifting closed to hide the coffee shop.

No way could this music have been playing the whole time they were in the coffee shop and Izzy didn't hear it. But this wasn't a party that just started. At four in the morning, maybe five, the crowd was still peaking. All around them, gorgeously dressed and undressed people leaned into one another, talking or laughing, dancing where they stood or on the packed dance floor nearby. The scent of sweat and perfume and clove cigarettes teased Izzy's nose. Voices rose and fell in conversation while the music poured over them. Izzy felt the deep bass of it in her chest. Melodic. Intense. Throbbing like a desirous heart. Although she wasn't in the dancing mood, the beat tugged at her hips.

"What's this place?" she shouted at Marun who kept walking, gently pushing her way through the thick crowd and keeping Izzy close behind her with their linked hands.

"This is Sanctuary." She didn't shout but Izzy still heard her loud and clear.

"Is this a coffee shop or a club?"

"Yes." Marun smiled back at her. "And much more." She gestured to a long wall that held several evenly spaced doors. "Meetings rooms, sex club, restaurant. And those are just the parts I've seen."

Sex club?

Izzy narrowed her gaze at Marun through the gloom broken now and then with flashing strobe lights. Did she come here for sex when they were together?

A pretty man with glitter all over his bare chest pushed past them, apparently in a rush for the dance floor, shoving hard into Izzy. When she stumbled, he gave her a smile of apology and a shouted offer of a free drink she could collect later. His boyfriend or whoever squeezed Izzy's arm as he passed, laughing, too, and then he followed in the shimmering boy's wake. "It's a madhouse tonight," Marun said and swept her into the heat of her body.

With her skin thrumming from their renewed contact, Izzy clung shamelessly.

It wasn't long before they tumbled out into the cool early morning air and onto what could have been any New York City side street. Outside the thick metal door of Sanctuary, the city was quiet. Not even a police siren sounded to break the dark tranquility.

Izzy shivered from the sudden temperature change and, in search of warmth, shoved her hands into her jeans pockets. It was colder now than it had been when she'd gone into work earlier that night. Her shoulders felt tight, hiked up as they were nearly to her ears. "Do you come here a lot?" she asked, hoping she was being subtle.

The amusement on Marun's face said she wasn't. Her wife shrugged off her leather jacket and held it for Izzy to slip into. Warm leather that smelled like verdant, growing things enveloped her. A sigh left her lips without permission.

"I did come here before, yes," Marun said, and managed to look only a little smug. "But not since you and I have been together. Since it's a safe place for people like me—people who aren't quite human—it used to be a kind of home away from my family. Now, you are my home."

Before Marun had even finished talking, hot emotion clogged the back of Izzy's throat. Declarations like this had hooked her to Marun from the very beginning. Words that hummed with poetry and meaning Marun dropped between them in the midst of the most mundane things. There had never been any doubt about how Marun felt, but Izzy did wonder if those feelings had come and then left with the tide of passing years.

Now, she knew they hadn't gone anywhere.

"Tell me about your family," she said to Marun.

They walked through the night toward the cottage. Izzy was in no hurry to arrive. It was just good to walk beside the woman she had always loved, their destination far away yet inevitable, the truths and words that mattered bare between them at last. Their footsteps fell in sync, and words flowed easily between them as if the three years apart had never happened.

"We're different," Marun said. "Mother has always been the rebel in her family, and she encouraged us to be the same. But after a long time, it just felt like we were fighting against each other."

"I *wish* my sister would try to tell me what to do with my life," Izzy said with a low laugh, thinking about Rose who had too many problems of her own to be lecturing anybody on how to live. "It would be a short ass conversation."

They walked for what felt like no time at all, passing through the city, under bright streetlights, through parks. The sky slowly brightened.

"My mother is still worshiped by many, but they don't know about us. We have been lost to stories and to time, the nine of us who, the last time I read, were supposed to have died in some sort of accident or deliberate homicide, which happens among us from time to time."

"I thought none of you could be killed." Izzy frowned.

"Well, it is difficult but, if there's one thing living all this time has taught me it's that *nothing* is impossible."

"I'll remember that next time I see your brother."

Marun laughed. "That's one thing I have always loved about you. Your ability to make me laugh, even about the most serious things."

"Your whole life is so serious, no wonder you want to keep me around."

They arrived at the cottage when the sun was just beginning to come up. "Oh damn, I left my purse at the bakery. It has my keys in it."

"Don't tell me you don't have a spare key stashed here somewhere. You were always doing that at our old apartment. No matter how many times I told you how dangerous it was."

Izzy sidestepped the question. "And who would have dared to break into our place, where an actual superhuman with flames shooting out of her hands lives?" She climbed the short steps and picked up the tiny fake turtle squatting to the left of the welcome mat. The spare key was inside the belly of the turtle, right where she left it.

"Very secure," Marun said, rolling her eyes. "Obviously very secret."

"It's so obvious, no one would ever think to look there." The door opened with a click and Izzy stepped inside.

For a moment, she thought she smelled a staleness, one that wasn't there before, but it had only been a few hours since she left. Then Marun stepped up behind her, gently crowding her.

Izzy jumped. "God, your cheek is cold." Then she remembered and felt like a selfish ass. "Shit, I have your jacket. Of course, you're cold." She grabbed a handful of Marun's T-shirt and dragged her inside before shutting the door.

"I'm fine. Don't worry about me. Temperatures don't affect me like they do you." Smiling in that subtle way of hers, Maran allowed herself to get tugged into the house anyway, and she stumbled against Izzy, their bodies bumping together, once then twice, in the coolness of the living room. The faint stale smell of the house disappeared beneath the perfume of Marun's natural scent.

"You always smell so amazing. Why is that?"

"Because you want me to."

Hands still caught in the fabric of Marun's T-shirt, Izzy looked up into smiling dark eyes. The pulse fluttered in her throat. "That's a genuinely weird answer. How can what I want affect the way you smell?" Izzy leaned into her wife, aware that the long night was catching up with her, leaving her thoughts a little floaty while her body felt electrified and far too wired to sleep. "Are you trying to get mysterious on me now that I know your biggest secret?"

"Never," Marun said. She lazily ran a thumb along Izzy's jaw and Izzy shivered deliciously from the sensation. "Don't you ever notice that when you say you like or want something, it appears in the house, or you're suddenly in a position to get it?" She spoke in the present tense, as if their time apart never happened. "I would remake an entire world just for you, Isabella. Including myself."

Izzy drew in a sharp breath.

That was both flattering and frightening. The words also conveyed a depth of feeling, a tenderness, that Marun had only ever expressed before with her body, and with the things she did for Izzy.

"Then let me smell the real you, not what you think I want."

"Of course."

The scent around her, of citrus and tropical fruit, slowly bled away, leaving the barest essence of green and fertile things, the light perfume of a forest after the rain.

It was wilder than the smell she'd always associated with Marun, not sweet at all. She liked it.

"How's that?" Marun's hand slipped under the jacket Izzy wore, cool and firm between the leather and her thin T-shirt.

"It's...it's good. Really good," Izzy said and cursed that her voice came out sounding so weak.

It was small, this thing with Marun's perfume, but it led her mind toward larger doubts, as if she didn't have enough of those. Was that what they'd been all this time— a relationship built on illusions? Izzy started to pull away but, with an arm around her waist, Marun snared her back.

"What's wrong?"

"I..." Should she even say? No, fuck it. They were supposed to be talking to each other now. Izzy took a breath. "Since the beginning, I've only ever wanted you. The real you. Not a curated idea of what you think a lover—my lover—should be. Is any part of the woman I married real?"

Cool hands gripped Izzy's. "Everything between us is real. This thing, it's just perfume. Something humans do all the time to make themselves more appealing. That's all. Nothing more. No more trickery than that."

She didn't want to believe it. She shouldn't. There were so many lies between them.

"I may have kept things secret in the past, but I've never lied to you," Marun said. "Not about my feelings, not about anything."

Her fingers were light now, this time underneath the shirt and directly on Izzy's skin. The contact sped her pulse and she leaned into Marun and her wild, beautiful scent. "Earlier you said we didn't know each other. I wanted you to be wrong, but in some ways, maybe you weren't. We talked the night we met, but it wasn't an exchange like it should've been. I was so captivated by you that I just took in everything you had to give, asking for more and more. And maybe we just got used to things being that way, me taking and you giving."

Agreeing would be easy, but it wasn't true.

"No, that's not what I meant. You've always given. Maybe yes, we didn't truly exchange life stories, but don't suddenly paint yourself as the selfish one here."

Damn, wasn't she supposed to stay angry at Marun for all the lies? And now here she was defending her, against herself.

"So, what do we do with this?" Marun asked softly.

Izzy bowed her head, rested her forehead against the soft slope of Marun's shoulder. Her place of comfort, a place she'd missed. "We don't have to do anything right now. I just want to breathe you in and stop—" She let out a breath. "—stop thinking."

She just wanted to feel something good.

The soft hand under her shirt swept over her back, making slow and sensual strokes on her skin that made her quiver and accelerated the thick pulsebeat she already felt between her thighs. She licked her lips.

"Can we go to the bedroom now?" Even to her own ears, she sounded breathless and desperate.

"Whatever you want, love," Marun said.

No. Izzy didn't want it to be like that. She wanted this only if it was something they both wanted. If it only came from her, then it wasn't theirs to have, it was something she was doing to Marun, and they had never been like that. They had always been synchronicity and mutuality, desire meeting desire, love meeting love. And that was what she craved now.

She met her wife's eyes. "Do you want me?"

"What kind of question is that?" Before Izzy could answer, Marun put a finger to her parted lips and the light touch sparked a flash of heat Izzy felt down to her toes and every place in between. "I *always* want you. The moment I laid eyes on you, shivering in your little black dress outside that gallery, I wanted you. A craving for you took hold of my appetites and nothing's been the same for me after that. Since then, all I did was wait for your desire to catch up with mine."

Izzy caught her breath and released it in a trembling sigh. "Then show me."

If there was one lesson she should have learned from having Marun in her life it was never to give Marun any kind of challenge. A light flared to life in her love's eyes, golden and warm.

"I love you, Isabella." Marun slid that warm hand down her back again, and lower, to cup her ass through the thin jeans in a blatantly possessive way.

It was as if Marun was reminding her of this love, reminding her of her feelings, before she tore Izzy apart in a way that might seem to negate that love.

Her breath shivered as she drew it deeply into her lungs. She was ready.

Between that moment and the next, it felt like they moved from the coolness of the living room into Izzy's bedroom. The curtains were open, inviting in the blush of dawn from the backyard. It was like the first night and morning they were together, when they stayed at the little café until sunrise and then walked across the city, drunk on each other, before ending up in Marun's penthouse apartment. In her bed.

Now, a cooling breeze slipped through the open window to wash over Izzy's face.

"I missed you so much," she confessed.

"I know. And I'm sorry." Warm breath teased her lips and she gasped in pleasure at that light and stomach-tightening sensation.

Had she always been so sensitive there?

Anchored at Marun's waist, her fingers flexed and dug into warm skin through her T-shirt. No, not warm, Marun was so hot, and all Izzy wanted was to burn from her love's touch.

Seeking, she stretched her neck for the kiss she desperately needed. Their lips met and she moaned at the perfection of it.

God, it had been so long.

Light touch, soft flesh, a huff of breath, and the heat of them coming together at last. A groan slid from her, desperate and probably too loud for what was just a simple kiss, but she didn't give a damn. This was what she'd been waiting so long for. This connection. This heat. This woman.

Gasping, she dug her fingers into Marun's shoulders, stretching up onto her toes, and hungrily kissed back. Their tongues met and explored as, groaning deeply, Marun dug her hands into Izzy's ass and lifted her up, helping her to wrap her legs around Marun's waist.

She'd been starving, and now here was all the food she could ever want, spread out to her in a smorgasbord.

"I missed you," Izzy gasped again, closed her eyes to better savor the wild lust running rampant through her body and leaving heat and wetness in its wake. "I missed us." She tightened her legs around Marun, squeezed her thighs and held on, her center wet and clenching around the tampon she wished wasn't there. Not today when she wanted to feel everything without the distraction of her period. As tempting as it was to let Marun feast on her the way they were both used to, something inside her held back.

For now, though, this was enough. The sensation of Marun against her, hot and whispering in her ear, hands digging into her ass and ratcheting up her arousal to the next level. She'd always had a thing for when Marun grabbed her ass like that, something about the sure and firm way her fingers dug into her flesh went straight to her clit and made her lose her mind.

"Do you remember when I used to fuck you standing up?" Marun gasped against her ear, and the glowing ball of desire growing in Izzy's belly became a bright star, a meteor threatening to immolate her from the inside out.

"I loved how you grabbed my shoulders and spread your thighs wide like you were opening your entire world just for me." Her hot breath panted into Izzy's neck. "We can't do that here—"

No, they couldn't. Every wall space in the bedroom was taken by the too-much she'd packed from her old life.

"—but when we have the space, I'm going to do that again, my sweet wife." A warm hand wormed between them, caressing Izzy through her jeans, pressing into her clit in long and firm strokes while Izzy sucked on Marun's tongue and moved sinuously in her sure grasp, hunting for friction against her hard, tingling nipples. "Fuck you hard against the wall and make you scream my name, slide down to the floor and eat your hot pussy after making you come." Izzy shuddered and bucked even as she and Marun swayed, a tower of arms and legs and desire, toward the bed. "Would you like that, love?"

All Izzy could do with the only brain cells she had left functioning was moan. She grunted as they tumbled onto the bed, Marun on her back under her, Izzy crouched over her lap and leaning back to yank her own shirt and bra off.

"Ease up, love." Marun sat up, using her stomach muscles alone, to wrestle with the buttons of Izzy's jeans. "I want this off too."

Yes.

She moved back enough to shove off her loose jeans, underwear, shoes, and socks, and by the time she got back to the bed, Marun was already splendidly naked against the pale sheets, and reaching up for her.

"I can't go slow." Izzy moaned as thumbs brushed across her nipples. "I want you too much. You made me wait too long."

"You don't have to wait any longer," Marun rasped.

She flipped Izzy over on her back and Izzy let loose a soft scream of surprise at the sudden move and immediately groaned from the stroke of fingers between her legs, unerringly against her thick and wanting clit. Izzy felt it then. A gentle tug on her tampon string. But Marun, after meeting her eyes to read what was there, only moved it out of the way before leaning down for a devouring kiss. Their mouths slotted wetly together.

She flushed all over, groaned into the kiss, hips moving in time to the stroking fingers, as their breasts heaved together. Her mind swam, her senses hyperaware of everything happening between them, the electric connection of the places they touched, the gasping sounds they made in the room, moaning into each other's mouths while her body felt every place the sheet touched her back, her ass, her spread thighs. And Marun, a beautiful wall of heat at her front, firmly circling her clit. Izzy's belly tightened. The heat flashed through her. She'd wanted it hard and fast, but suddenly it was all too much. Izzy tore her mouth away from Marun's.

"I can't—" She gasped, her hips still moving, the fireball of pleasure flaring through her.

"Don't worry, love. I've got you. It's okay." Fingers pinched her nipple, tugged. Her thighs shook. "Come for me. I'm right here."

At Marun's low command, Izzy's entire world went supernova. Pleasure blazed through her, white hot and incinerating. When she resurfaced, she had no idea how many minutes later, she was a rag doll in the bed, twitching and gasping for air.

With her whole body still tingling, she reached up to touch Marun's face, to trace the seductive outline of her lips, exhaustion tugging at her limbs. "God, I feel so selfish." Muscles pleasantly weak, she pushed herself onto her elbows, clumsily kissed Marun's mouth, and clasped her full breasts in her hands, scoring the thick nipples in her palms. "Let me take care of you now."

Marun smiled down at her, started gently pushing Izzy's hands away. "It's not a tit for tat, darling. I wanted to please you, and that's exactly what I did." The gentle smile took on a bit of smugness. "I did please you, didn't I?"

A slow flush worked its way up Izzy's chest into her face in a tingling wave. "You know you did."

"Good. That's all we need to do for now."

But after waiting for so long for her wife to come back, there was no way she was going to let sleep come without tasting the ambrosia between Marun's legs. Izzy pushed aside her fatigue.

"Sure, baby," she said, and then grabbed the curling ends of Marun's braided hair and dragged her woman's mouth back down to meet hers.

"You're tired, love," Marun protested against Izzy's mouth but she went down easily enough on her back at a light touch. Now that she had her there, Izzy's appetite flared with a rush of moisture over her tongue.

"I'm not too tired to make love to you," she murmured.

Thick breasts the size of juicy, East Indian mangoes quivered under her hands and then her tongue. The stiff peaks hardened even more in her mouth and she groaned with pleasure, sucked, and fluttered her tongue against the delicious flesh. "Not after I've been dreaming about this moment for years. Even if I wanted to kill you at the same time."

The soft thighs fell open with the grace of butterfly wings, and Marun watched her, eyes hungry and dark, a hand touching Izzy's hair. With the revealing of her hot center, the rough hair there matted from the thick stream of her arousal, the knee-weakening scent of her floated up and flexed Izzy's fingers into the thickness of her thighs. Delicious. Marun looked absolutely edible, the aroused petals of her sex, the aggressive thrust of her big clit, bigger than Izzy's and the perfect size to suck and drool all over.

"You say the most romantic th—oh!"

Izzy smiled into the wet thatch of Marun's sex and then she was done smiling as she was swept away by the scent of the delectable flesh under her tongue, the smooth thickness of her clit, and the clench of her fingers in Izzy's hair. Her noises. Low moans. And the slow circling of her hips clasped in Izzy's hands.

Izzy moaned as her arousal came rushing back, new moisture flooding between her own legs, with the motion of her head between the warm clasp of Marun's thighs.

She moaned into the hot flesh and pressed down into the bed, fucking her hips into the mattress but trying to ignore her own desire to come again so she could pleasure Marun.

But if the noises her wife made were any indication, her pleasure wasn't even a question.

"Look at me, baby. I want to see your eyes while I fuck your beautiful mouth." Tremors shook Marun's thighs. "Open your eyes for me, love." A gasp and slow thrust against Izzy's mouth. "Please." Marun pushed her question home with a rough grip in Izzy's hair.

Weakened by desire and the slick sounds of her tongue working between her love's thighs, she opened her eyes with a flutter of her lashes, drugged by pleasure.

"That's it, baby. That's it. I love your mouth on me. Having you right here between my legs is like coming home. No one else belongs here but you. No one." Marun's hips bucked and her head flew back, but still she kept her eyes on Izzy's, the star-like depths capturing Izzy's attention like she had no intention of ever letting go. "I love you, Isabella," Marun gasped, moving her hips harder as Izzy basically just held on and kept her tongue moving. "I love you so much, baby."

A powerful breath rushed from Marun's wide-open mouth and her center clenched against Izzy's lips. Released, and tightened again. All the while, her eyes stayed wide, stayed with Izzy as the tremors of completion racked her body, fluttered the muscles of her thighs against her cheeks. Izzy didn't stop moving her tongue, couldn't stop her own frantic motion against the mattress. Then she was coming again, a wild burst of bliss.

With her breath coming in uncontrolled gasps, she lifted her head to reveal her smile.

"Yeah? You love me?"

Izzy gasped when Marun yanked her up until they were lying face to face, heart to heart.

"Yes," Marun said softly. "I love you."

Their kiss was messy, slick, and salt-flavored. Eventually, their movements slowed and Marun drew back, her eyes drowsy and heavy-lidded.

"And I'll never stop. No matter what."

Chapter Ten

With the sun slowly creeping through the window and Marun's light caress over her naked back, Izzy fell asleep. It wasn't a plan. It wasn't even a conscious decision. They were talking about the past, turning over things that happened between them that had seemed so simple then but now had layers of meaning.

When Marun had walked Izzy to class one afternoon and they ran into Izzy's professor and would-be boyfriend. His scowl in their direction. Then the next time Izzy had seen him, he'd scurried to get away. Marun had apparently scared the French accent out of him a day before with a flash of her gold eyes and threats to neuter him if he so much as looked at another student.

The hesitation Marun had shown when Izzy, giddy with excitement, had asked to marry her. "I didn't want my family to kill you" was more than the excuse anyone needed not to join their lives with someone else.

Even at the bank days before, the SUV that nearly crushed Izzy into paste before Marun stepped in and basically punched the two-ton vehicle into the street.

"And I've been looking into it," Marun whispered as she lay against the sheets with Izzy hovering above her, their hands joined together and resting on Marun's belly. "You didn't mismanage your money, my sister made it disappear."

Izzy gaped down at her wife, her mouth opening and closing like a landed fish. "But—but that's not fair."

If she'd expected anything from these homicidal maniacs it was that they would just go straight for bodily harm, not force her into bankruptcy and destitution. That was worse than nearly getting shoved into a hot oven.

"Are you sure about that?" Marun asked when Izzy voiced the thought out loud. "My siblings and those like them have learned a lot during their time on this earth. Killing someone is quick and sometimes too easy. Driving them to live with no money and no resources is a slow death. Stress. High blood pressure. Losing your pride. Being forced to beg." Marun's jaw tightened, and anger flashed through eyes gone gold. "I should've figured it out when you first told me there was no money left."

Weakened from the shock of it, Izzy flopped down at Marun's side and shook her head. "Oh my god…" The jagged teeth of anger snapped closed around her throat, stealing her breath. But seconds later, relief came. This meant she wasn't as shitty at life as she'd been thinking these past three years.

"I'm sorry, Isabella." Marun gathered her closer, and Izzy went, draping herself over her love's chest. "You'd think with all this power comes a certain responsibility, but for many of us, it just makes us act like vindictive children."

Tender fingers trailed down her back, a soothing caress that soon drooped Izzy's eyelids. Despite her surprise and anger at how some random spirit-gods had ruined her life, she tumbled into a deep sleep.

Chapter Eleven

"Get out."

The pillow under Izzy's cheek was growling. She lazily batted at it, mumbled for it to be quiet, but it stirred and the sound only grew louder. Reluctantly, she opened her eyes. Dammit, she was comfortable!

"Isabella Courtney Ransom! You should be ashamed of yourself!" She jolted upright in bed at the unexpected sound of her mother's voice. In her house. Not on the phone like she should be and was easiest to deal with.

Standing in the doorway of her bedroom, her mother scowled at her and then threw that pissed-off look over her shoulder at someone else. "You told me she wasn't really in trouble. Did you know about this?"

A glance past her mother told her it was her father wandering through the living room.

"Wha—?"

Izzy's hands were way ahead of her sluggish brain, though, and scrambled to grab the sheet and pull it over her bare breasts at the same time as Marun, apparently her growling pillow, sat up, too, but didn't bother with the sheet. She faced Eleanor Ransom with a glower that her mother returned with interest.

"I should have known you had something to do with this!" Her mother pointed at Marun.

"For fuck's sake," Marun hissed. The bedroom door slammed shut, powered by an unseen force.

"What did you just do?" Izzy stared from the closed door to Marun's furious face. Finally, her brain caught up with what was going on.

Her mother was here, in New York.

Fuck.

"Try not to burn your mother to an annoying crisp where she stands?" Marun muttered something in a foreign language that sounded a lot like a curse and left the bed to sort through the pile of clothes they'd left discarded on the floor last night. "All I had to do was sleep with you again for your mother to show up? If only *my* mother was that easy to summon," she grumbled, separating a pair of jeans from the pile and holding them up to eye level.

Summon?

"I'm not sure about yours but my mother isn't a demon."

"That you know of," Marun shot back. Instead of putting on the jeans, she frowned down at them.

"Stop." Shower. Izzy needed a shower right now. A quick sniff of her pits confirmed that decision. Plus, she was pretty sure her whole face smelled like Marun's snatch.

She rushed to get out of bed and then gasped when her legs tangled in the sheets and she stumbled, almost falling face first onto the floor.

"Take it easy, love." Marun was instantly there, hands on Izzy's hips and still wearing nothing but a frown.

Izzy scowled back. "Easy for you to say, that's not your mother waiting out there." She planted a quick morning-breath kiss on Marun's lips before darting for the bathroom.

But when she came back less than ten minutes later, Marun was still naked, but this time lounging on the window seat in the sun. Izzy nearly tripped over her feet. She stood there drooling, wishing her parents were anywhere else but outside her bedroom door.

Marun lay stretched back on her braced arms, her face turned up to the sky while the sun poured like gold over the luscious fruit of her breasts, delectably curved stomach, thighs, and the ripe dip between them. Moisture swam over Izzy's tongue and she swallowed hard.

"Shouldn't you get out there to see what your parents want?" Laughter teased through Marun's voice. Her eyes were closed, and she didn't move from her sun-worshiping sprawl.

Izzy licked her lips, realized that she was walking toward her wife like some sort of lust-struck zombie, arms already reaching out to touch.

"You're a little evil, you know that?" she muttered.

"It's nothing you don't know already, Isabella."

Izzy stuck out her tongue and changed her path. At her closet, she dragged out the floral jumpsuit she used to wear all the time in college. It was loose, comfortable, and easy to get in and out of.

"Oh, I remember that." Marun turned to watch her, head cocked to one side while a faint smile played on her lips. "Does it still have that tear in the crotch?"

"No, I fixed it, thank you very much."

Marun laughed. "Too bad."

"Ass." She left the bedroom to the music of her wife's laughter. At the sight of her mother's sour face, all sense of lightness drained out of her like air from a pricked balloon. Izzy closed the door behind her.

Her mother started to say something but suddenly her father was right there.

"Izzy girl!" He grabbed her up into a fierce hug that overwhelmed her with the smell of pipe smoke and black tea. "We were so damn worried about you. I'm glad you're all right."

Confused, she hugged him back, though she had no idea what he was talking about. But as she pulled back to get a proper look at him, she saw the dark circles under his eyes. It looked like he hadn't slept in days. If he'd been that worried about her, he could have just called.

"Of course, I'm okay, Papa. You know I've been right here this whole time." But maybe she should have made the effort to talk to him more between her mother's badgering phone calls.

A frown puckered his forehead. "What are you talking about? You haven't actually been missing?"

Missing? "What are *you* talking about, Papa?"

But her mother talked over her. "I told you she was all right, Trevor." Her mother put down her teacup with a sharp *click*. It looked like she'd found her way to the hot water kettle and put together what amounted to a full tea service and set it up on the coffee table. "That *woman* probably took her off someplace and she forgot all about her responsibilities to everyone else."

Her mother's snide reference to Marun instantly triggered Izzy's defenses and pushed everything else out of her mind.

"Mom, that woman is my *wife*." She stressed the last word with a savage bite and crossed her arms over her stomach.

"Don't be ridiculous, dear. I doubt whatever ceremony you two indulged yourselves in was even legal." Her mother glanced back at the closed bedroom door and sneered, a delicate baring of her perfect teeth.

Sharp words crowded Izzy's tongue, ready to fly at her mother like daggers, but the light squeeze of her father's hand on her shoulder stopped them. "I know, my girl, but it's not worth it."

Anger tightened its vice around Izzy's throat, and she choked out a breath.

Her father squeezed her shoulder again. "Come tell us what happened to you. It doesn't feel like we're on the same page here." With his comforting warmth pressing against her side, he led her to a chair.

"I don't understand," she said.

"You've been gone for more than a week, Izzy," her father said. "How could you do that without telling anybody where you were?"

A week?

A twisting feeling of nausea took her stomach. "No. That can't be right." The chair squeaked under her as she sat forward. "I went to work at the bakery just a few hours ago."

Then she remembered the stale smell of the cottage when she'd first walked in. The curtains and windows in the bedroom had been open, too, and she hadn't left them that way. At the time, she wasn't sure but...

"Did that woman drug you or something?" Her mother's gaze sharpened. "Like your father said, you've been missing for over a week. The police are looking everywhere for you. According to them, you left your purse with your cell phone at the bakery and just disappeared into thin air after some sort of violent confrontation."

"One of the girls who works there swore you'd been killed by some crazy man the police haven't been able to locate," her father said, his voice husky with emotion. "I'm so glad she was wrong."

"The security cameras had all been blown out and the footage completely destroyed."

Every word was like a blast of ice down Izzy's spine. She shivered and her teeth snapped together, biting down hard on her tongue. "Show me—show me your cell phone. This can't be right."

A cell phone appeared in her line of sight, her father's. He tapped the screen and the time appeared. The day of the week. The date.

It had been nine days since she last walked out of her front door.

"No. That's not possible. I was just at work last night and walked back home this morning." But Marun had told her again and again about losing time. That this was part of what it meant to be a demi-god. Or whatever identity Marun claimed.

Her father put his phone away and pulled up a nearby footstool to sit next to Izzy. Grateful for his closeness, she gripped his hand.

"Last night, Isabella? No." Her mother dismissed what she said with a scornful sniff. "Your father and I got on a plane the same day the police called us. We stayed in town for a few days with Taylor, worried sick about you, then had to rush back home when your sister had an emergency. A real one."

"When your neighbor called to say she saw you come back home early this morning, we got on the first flight back out here."

All this had been going on while she and Marun were talking—and other things—for just those few hours? It seemed incredible. Impossible. But her parents were here, talking about a long week of worry. Her father's hand, grasping hers like he was never going to let go, was trembling and cold.

"I—I'm sorry." What else could she say? Izzy squeezed her eyes shut as her world spun and she sagged back into the chair.

"Izzy!" From what seemed like a long distance away, she heard her father's voice, felt a cold touch on her face.

This was what it had been for Marun. One moment, walking out of their apartment and the next, separation and disaster.

"Isabella!" A sharp voice brought her abruptly back. She opened her eyes.

Marun knelt in front of her, forehead creased with concern, the scent of Izzy's coconut body lotion drifting from her skin. The curving ends of her braids painted trails of wet over her shoulders left bare in one of Izzy's sarongs. "Are you going to make me break out the smelling salts like in those ridiculous English romance books you love?" she gently teased.

"Stop..." She weakly pushed at Marun's shoulder although that didn't move her wife even an inch. "I'm fine, just a little surprised by everything, that's all."

Her father stood behind Marun, warily watching the two of them.

"Good." With a gentling smile, Marun touched Izzy's cheek, her jaw, and the wet-feeling corner of her mouth. Izzy drew in a breath of surprise when Marun's finger came away smeared with blood. She hadn't realized she was bleeding. Meeting her eyes, Marun licked away the red, allowing Izzy to see the stripe of it on her long tongue. When she swallowed the blood, Izzy only felt loved.

"This is all your fault," her mother said from the sofa, pointing her teacup at Marun like it was some sort of weapon. "Don't act like you're so very worried about her now."

"Unlike you who can't so much as pretend a little concern?" Marun stood now with a hand on the back of Izzy's chair.

"There's no need for that, young lady," Izzy's father said. "My wife shows her care in her own way."

"Through neglect and homophobia?" Marun shot back. "That's a new one for me, and I've been around for a while."

"Don't presume to know anything about my relationship with my child!" Izzy's mother snapped.

"I'm not presuming anything. If you cared half as much about her as a person instead of the version of her you can control, she wouldn't avoid you as much."

This was getting out of hand.

"Marun, that's enough. It's okay." Izzy fought off the last of her dizziness to stand up. "Mom, Papa. Please, stop attacking Marun. She hasn't done anything but keep me safe."

"Safe?" Her mother sounded like she was choking on one of her clotted cream scones. "She probably dragged you off to some orgy and that's why you lost a whole damn week. She's a bad influence. I've been telling you that ever since you brought her home."

"A week?" Marun looked as surprised as Izzy felt a few minutes ago.

"Yeah, that's how long we've been gone."

A soft curse left Marun's lips. She reached down for Izzy's hand and Izzy grabbed on tight. "I'm sorry, love. I feel like I'm losing control of everything."

Izzy shook her head in denial but before she could say anything, her mother jumped in.

"See, I told you it was her fault." Tea sloshed over the edge of the teacup as her mother aggressively pointed it at Marun. She spat out a genteel curse as the tea spilled over her hand and the wrist glittering with an unfamiliar diamond bracelet and her favorite Cartier watch. "She probably kidnapped Isabella and dragged her back here to lie for her because she was worried about the police finding out what she did." Her voice shook with anger, rising and becoming shriller. "We should call the police and have her arrested."

Seeing her normally ice-cold mother losing her cool was tilting this whole morning dangerously into the realm of the surreal. Not that discovering she and Marun had been gone for over a week instead of a few hours made the morning seem any less crazy.

"You should make up your mind, Mrs. Ransom. Am I a kidnapper or depraved orgyist ready to drag your daughter with me to hell? I'm afraid you can't have it both ways." Marun's voice was a barbed whip lying uncoiled between them and ready to strike. She stood as still as an ice statue, but only an idiot would mistake her look for calm.

Although it would be kind of fun to watch, the last thing Izzy wanted was for Marun to verbally eviscerate her mother. If she thought their relationship was a mess now...

"Mother, there was no orgy and Marun didn't kidnap me."

"Then what happened, Izzy?" her father asked softly. "We want to know why you were missing and, more importantly, the police do too."

This was a mess. Couldn't Marun use her bad-ass goddess powers to make all this go away? She threw her wife a look of desperation.

Maybe they could just tell her parents the truth and leave it at that. Having them know she'd been accidentally swept out of the normal stream of time by a minor Yoruba deity was way better than them thinking she'd been off having a gang bang in a crack house somewhere.

She grabbed Marun's hand. "Baby, could you—?"

Just then, the doorbell rang.

"Oh good." Her mother put down her teacup and headed for the door. "That should be Taylor. I called her on our way here. Maybe she can talk some sense into you."

But it wasn't Taylor at the door.

Instead, it was a woman Izzy had never seen before. She stood, poised in the doorway, tall and imposing, like an onyx statue come to life. Her bald head glinted in the morning light and, with her blood-red lips and the simple white dress glowing against her perfect skin, she seemed too beautiful to be real.

For an electrified moment, the woman's eyes found Izzy's and her lips curved up into a warm smile. Then, of course, her mother had to ruin it. She turned a confronting stare to the stranger. "Who are you?"

The woman ignored her. "Hello, my darling daughter." She looked straight at Marun. "I see you still haven't managed to solve your little problem."

Chapter Twelve

"Iya," Marun finally said after a loaded silence. "You came."

"I did." The woman swept an arm wide, a regal gesture that incredibly, Izzy's mother obeyed, stepping aside to allow the woman's electric presence into the house.

Instantly, the too-cool temperature of the living room gave way, warming to become more comfortable and inviting. And was that...was that the smell of roses?

Izzy swallowed the sudden lump in her throat. This was her. The mother Marun had been searching for. The god. Was she anything like her son who'd attacked Izzy the moment they met?

Fear darted down her spine.

But Marun's thumb brushed along the back of her hand, instantly calming.

Right. Standing around with her mouth hanging open like an idiot wasn't going to accomplish anything. It certainly wouldn't save her if the woman decided to attack.

Izzy squeezed her love's hand and stepped forward.

"Hi, Ms. Zisanu. I'm Izzy. Can I offer you something to eat or drink?"

Approval shone in the woman's eyes.

"That's very lovely of you, my dear. And please, call me Iya." For some reason, that invitation issued in the woman's warm voice which held the same accent as Marun made Izzy blush with pleasure. After her mother's reaction to Marun, she had half expected any relative of Marun, especially her mother, wouldn't like her either. Not to mention the homicidal greeting of her brother. With the grace of a feather on the wind, Iya floated over to where Izzy stood. Her hands on Izzy's cheeks were light but warm, her eyes glowing with a comforting flame. "I can see why my darling Marun chose you. Your blood smells sweet."

Izzy darted a nervous glance toward her parents and a smile jerked across her lips. She probably looked like she was having a seizure. When Iya stepped away and gave her some breathing room, she couldn't hide her sigh of relief.

"What's going on here?" Her mother, thankfully oblivious, had closed the door on the now empty front porch and was getting riled up again. The jewelry on her wrist clicked in her agitation.

"Ellie, hush. Let's go make some more tea. Mine is cold." Izzy's father took his sputtering wife by the elbow and towed her into the kitchen.

Iya tilted her head, a motion like a curious cat, and then waved a hand in the direction of the kitchen. A shift in the atmosphere rippled the fine hairs along Izzy's arms. Her ears popped.

Marun probably didn't notice any of that, she was so busy staring at Iya like she was some sort of apparition.

"I can't believe you're actually here," she said to her mother. "I've searched everywhere for you."

"Not quite everywhere, darling." Her mother smiled, a faint movement of her red lips that seemed to say more than words.

"You didn't want to be found," Marun said with certainty. Though her face reflected the same calm sea as always, her disappointment was thick in the air. Overcome with the desire to comfort, Izzy took a step in her direction, and then forced herself to stop. Whatever this was, it didn't concern her.

"Not exactly," her mother said in response to Marun's statement. "I was waiting for you to find the solution for yourself."

"But *you're* the only solution."

"That's not true, and you know it." Light arching in from the windows glinted on the silver hoops in Iya's ears as she clicked her tongue. "All right. Let's answer this question once and for all."

The sound of her voice had barely died away before the empty space next to her burst open, like fabric ripping, and sparks flashed out, a mini-fireworks display with none of the noise.

"Iya, don't do this!" Marun stepped in front of Izzy to face whatever Iya had called up.

Izzy couldn't stop watching, even with the panic clawing at her throat and threatening to rip out a scream.

Izzy gasped and backed away as two figures emerged from the swirling chaos of sparks, fixed in place like they'd been in the middle of something when Iya yanked them into Izzy's living room. A reclining woman with thick hair like Marun's, the details of her face lost in silhouette. And the man who'd tried to kill her at the bakery. Despite Marun's protective height between them, his metallic eyes immediately fixed on Izzy.

Her knees trembled and she nearly lost her shit.

Something was familiar about the young woman who was suddenly in her living room. Her bikini-clad body glistened like she'd been snatched from the side of a pool or beach. After a quick visual sweep of the room, she took a single step forward. Izzy flinched, but then the girl stopped, bumping into an invisible barrier.

Anger bared the girl's teeth. "Iya, what's this?"

"It's all right." Iya rested a hand on Izzy's back, but if that touch was meant to be comforting, it had the opposite effect. Izzy jerked away from her and stumbled back. "My children won't hurt you," Iya said.

"How can you be so sure?" Izzy hated that her voice shook, broadcasting her fear. She wanted to run but knew she wouldn't make it very far. Already, the man's eyes were focused on her, she could feel them burning into the side of her face.

"I'm sure." Iya waved dismissively.

"I'll make sure of it," Marun said.

The space the pair emerged from sparked one last time and then returned to normal, nothing behind it but the living room wall. A flush of scent, like the air after a lightning storm, filled the room.

The man straightened from his half crouch, his eyes still burning into Izzy. "Did you bring me here to finally finish off this human?" His voice was a rumble of thunder that shook Izzy to the core. He flicked a dismissive glance around the room before once again pinning Izzy with his stare.

Fear cooled the blood in the veins, dried her mouth, but she wouldn't give him the satisfaction of backing away.

In a rush of movement, her clothes rustling in the wake of her own breeze, Marun stepped toward her brother. Her hands glowed with blue fire. "You will *not* touch her."

But he only laughed. "Oh, really. Who's going to stop me?"

Bright mischief lit up his face like they were fighting over the last piece of pie, not Izzy's potential death.

Okan. She remembered his name now.

Izzy looked between them, too stunned at their interplay to be scared just then. They were acting like little kids, she thought, and wasn't at all surprised when Marun shot a glance toward her mother who had sat down in the chair Izzy left, legs crossed, and watching her children with an indulgent smile.

Murmurs of conversion came from the kitchen, Izzy's parents probably discussing whether to make coffee or tea for this round of drinks, and Izzy froze, her fear rushing back in a wave of goose pimples over her skin. What if her parents came back out just then? Marun's brother almost killed her. What would he do to her parents? She had to warn them. Protect them. Something.

Izzy took a step toward the kitchen.

"Be easy, Isabella." Iya made a soothing gesture. "They're safe in their bubble and have no idea what's happening in here. To them, we're just having an ordinary and very boring conversation."

Izzy wasn't convinced.

She swallowed down a lump of fear.

"By my word, they have nothing to fear from us." Iya held Izzy's gaze, waiting.

"She'd never break her word, Izzy," Marun said, still squaring off against Okan though her hands were now by her sides. "My brother, yes, but never her."

"Okay." Slowly, she felt the fear for her parents bleed away. "Okay." Now she could focus on the monsters in her living room.

"Iya, why did you bring Okan and Asaa here?" Marun asked.

"Because we need a resolution to this strife," her mother replied as if it was perfectly obvious.

"There is no strife." The young girl, Asaa, frowned down at what she was wearing—a string bikini with bare feet—and flicked a hand down her front, turning her poolside get-up into a cropped top, jeans, and heels. Her hair, worn in a massive puff on top of her head like a crown, stayed the same. "Marun shouldn't be with the *human*." Her sneer turned Izzy's way. "She knows that. We all do. I don't know why she's surprised that Okan is acting the way he is." She jerked her head toward her brother who, other than his glower and new homicidal threats, hadn't moved since his sudden appearance.

As Asaa talked, every movement of her expressive mouth showing contempt, Izzy realized where she'd seen her before. The bank. That day she'd gone begging for a loan.

Nice suit, sis.

Had this psycho family been watching her all along? Izzy shivered.

She tuned back into the conversation in time to hear Marun say, "It's my life, and I've chosen Izzy to share it with me." Marun spoke evenly and slowly, like she was explaining something to a particularly dim child. "It shouldn't be any of your business."

"*Shouldn't be* is for fairy tales," Asaa snapped with a scornful look. "You're not a baby, Marun. Like all of us, you grew up knowing the rules." With a rude suck of teeth, she turned her back on her sister. "Iya, you should enforce the rules and tell her to leave the human alone."

"Rules? No, my darling. You and your brother have always been too possessive of each other and your sister. This has nothing to do with the rules."

Asaa was obviously shocked. She looked at Okan who hadn't stopped staring at Izzy and giving off his murder vibes. With hands on her hips, she tracked her gaze from Izzy to Marun.

"Whether it's about rules or tradition, you don't belong with her, Marun. It doesn't even make sense to form that sort of attachment to a human."

"We just fuck them and run, that's it?"

Asaa rolled her eyes. "Don't act so above it all now that your little 'wifey' is watching. For centuries, you were more than okay with the 'fuck and run.'"

"And now I'm not," Marun said. "Change happens."

Izzy felt her careful glance, gauging to see how she would take this. But that was Marun's past. She wasn't going to hold it against her. It wasn't as if Izzy had expected Marun to be a virgin like she was when they met.

"At any rate," Marun continued. "You and Okan may want me to give Izzy up, but I won't." She slipped a hand around Izzy's waist and pulled her closer, and Izzy melted.

No one had ever chosen her so completely before. A rush of warmth suffused her, and she held onto Marun.

"Then give up what makes you one of us," Okan snarled, apparently done with listening to everyone else talk. "Once you do that, you can be a human like her and stay with her. Whatever you do would no longer concern us."

He said the *human* the same way someone else would say *cockroach*.

"Exactly. Give her up or give us up. Those are your choices. You should've known that when you started this farce of a relationship."

Before Izzy knew it, her mouth flew open and words came out of it. "Excuse me?" Scary or not, this bitch was just plain rude.

Then her mind tracked back to what Asaa said before.

Give us up.

No one should have to choose between their family and the person they loved.

"No," Izzy protested. "You can't ask her to do that!"

Though Marun lightly squeezed her waist, the rest of the family ignored her.

"I came to you for help." Marun faced her mother. "But if this is what you want me to do, give up my family so I can have a love I deserve, the kind of love that you had with my father, then I'll do it."

It felt like all the air rushed from the room. Marun's family looked shocked. Izzy figured she probably did too.

"You're willing to give all that up for her?" Asaa asked.

"I'm not giving anything up. I'm gaining the life I want."

No, this wasn't supposed to happen.

Even back when she'd made the choice to move away from her family and love the way she wanted, Izzy had felt cracked down the middle. Her mother was homophobic and controlling. Her father was mostly passive. Her sister had her own problems and rarely made time for her. But they were still her family. Moving to the other side of the country felt extreme and painful, yet necessary. She still kept some connection with them. Had even needed it.

And now Marun had to give up everything, every tie with her family just to be with her. No, she couldn't allow that.

With her heart a frantic drumbeat in her chest, she turned into Marun's warmth, pressed a hand meant to comfort against her love's belly. She felt Marun tense up, the muscles of her stomach hard and twitching. Izzy half expected to feel an electric shock run through her at the intimate contact. But nothing that dramatic happened, just the firming of muscles under soft skin, an additional tension and a sure sign of Marun's unhappiness.

"Please, don't throw your family away for me," she frantically whispered. "It doesn't make any sense when we've been apart for so long and you didn't even notice the time had passed. Keep your relationship with your family. You'll miss them more than you ever missed me."

Marun's eyes flashed a deeper gold than Izzy had ever seen them and a look that was alarmingly like desperation tightened her lips. "You're mine," she rasped in a voice filled with pain. "And I'm yours. Finding you at the gallery that night was like discovering the other part of my heart I never knew was missing. I can't leave you again. I won't." She swallowed, a sound painfully loud in the ensuing silence and, with Izzy still in the loose circle of her arms, turned to her mother. "Iya, I'd rather give up everything I was born with than abandon her again."

"Done." Iya stood, the power pouring from her, invisible but potent enough for Izzy to feel it.

The power seemed to gather around Marun for the space of a single, throbbing heartbeat. Golden light pulsed from her skin and she stood there, calm and accepting. Izzy watched, breathless. It didn't look like it hurt.

"But, Iya—?" Asaa looked frightened.

"Your sister has made her decision. It is as she wills it. Marun no longer has god-power, and you both will leave her and her woman alone." Iya tipped her head toward each of her children. When they nodded back and dropped their eyes, she waved her hand, banishing Asaa and Okan to wherever she'd snatched them from.

The atmosphere in the room immediately lightened and Izzy felt like she could breathe more freely again. She hadn't even realized how difficult it had become.

"Thank you, Iya," Marun said.

"Don't thank me, daughter. I imagine you'll regret this very soon. Being a human is no easy thing."

How would she know? Izzy frowned at the god, but kept her mouth shut.

As if she'd read Izzy's mind, Iya shook a finger at Izzy, and then turned to her daughter, the two of them standing so close that Izzy should have felt uncomfortable, but strangely didn't. "I'm heartened you came to this decision on your own. Since you haven't been truly happy in a long time, I was trying to be a good mother and allow you to create your own path. You've had an eternity to be happy, maybe all you needed was a shorter life and the right companion by your side." She shrugged, an elegant movement that, in Izzy's eyes, brought her closer to being human.

Long fingers drifted up to Marun's cheek, and Marun closed her eyes, seeming to savor her mother's touch. For a moment, Izzy envied her. She looked so much at peace. Then the moment of jealousy was gone, and she was just happy for her love.

"Isabella." Izzy startled when Iya turned her exclusive attention her way. The god's eyes were dark, none of the gold of her children. Just a universe of unforgiving starlight and centuries of wisdom. "Take care of my daughter. If you don't, I know where to find you."

Then she stepped back, real amusement shaping her carmine lips, eyes flashing with humor. Izzy wasn't amused though. "Good luck to you both," Iya said, just before she disappeared.

Seconds passed.

Maybe even a minute.

Then Izzy's breath came out in a gasp and she sagged into Marun. "Wow—that was—wow."

"I know." Marun's breath brushed her neck and she held Izzy tight. "I'm sorry you had to deal with that. I told you they're a little intense."

"You and your understatements." She exhaled a laugh into Marun's throat, relief and exhaustion and the draining away of fear still making her body shake.

A clacking sound, the beads between the kitchen and living room separating, lifted Izzy's head. Her parents came cautiously into the room. Her mother looked a little calmer than when she left, while her father just looked apologetic.

"So," he said, looking around the living room. "What did we miss?"

Chapter Thirteen

"What was that all about, Isabella?" Her mother, a cup of tea in hand, stepped from behind her husband's broad back and swept a frowning gaze around the living room. "Where did that strange woman go?"

"She went back home." Izzy indulged in one last cuddle with Marun before turning to face her mother. With the intensity of Iya's visit, she'd forgotten all about the sour attitude her mother had brought with her, but now it all came rushing back.

She felt Marun step up behind her, wind a long arm around her waist. Her warm breath puffed against Izzy's ear.

"A little rude of her, isn't it? Not even saying goodbye to us." Her mother shot a gaze toward Marun. "But I suppose I shouldn't be surprised since she's *your* mother."

"Okaaaaaay." Izzy's limbs felt like jelly and all she wanted to do was curl up with Marun and go back to sleep. But she couldn't ignore this. She squeezed the arm Marun had around her waist before the tension she could sense in her wife's body ended in an explosion of words her mother couldn't handle. "Can you give me a few minutes alone with my parents?"

"Of course," Marun said quietly.

"You can say whatever you're going to in front of her, Isabella. It'll spare you telling the story twice."

"Mother, I'm trying to be tactful here, and you're not helping."

"Ellie, just listen to the girl and let her have a say in her own home. Please."

Izzy stared at her father. He was defending her?

She loved him and knew he loved her, but she couldn't begin to count the number of times he'd let his wife stomp all over Izzy with her words while he just rustled a newspaper in front of his face like none of it was his concern.

"I'm going to take a shower, love." Marun's touch snapped her out of her mini-shock. Her wife started to walk away but Izzy clung to her.

"I'm glad you're here." She squeezed Marun's waist, inhaled her rich scent. A wave of feeling, warm and grateful and blessed, rolled through her. "Thank you for loving me."

"Not loving you was never an option," Marun brushed the backs of her fingers against Izzy's throat and Izzy nearly melted, her eyes falling closed as peace flowed over her like water from a tropical sea. "From the moment I saw you, I was yours."

When an uncomfortable cough came from one of her parents, she opened her eyes, a blush warming her cheeks. Marun ducked her head and stepped back. After a nod to

Izzy's parents, she slipped into the bedroom and closed the door behind her.

"Well." Her mother huffed. "That was some display."

"Ellie." The censure was plain in her father's voice. "Let our child enjoy her happiness." He gave Izzy a gentle, if slightly apologetic, smile.

Again? Was she living in some kind of alternate universe?

Apparently, her mother had the same feeling of disconnect. "What's been going on with you lately, Trevor?"

"I'm realizing I can't leave the parenting of our children only up to you. I've been more of a husband than a father these past few years, and I'm starting to wake up."

A narrow-eyed glance from his wife didn't seem to faze him. He took a seat on the couch and, looking at his wife, patted the space next to him and waited until she sat down, her tea arranged fussily in front of her, before giving Izzy his full attention. "Now, what do you want to say to us, Izzy girl?"

Good question. She needed to stop staring at her father like he was an alien and just open her mouth. Izzy drew a steadying breath. "I love you both very much."

Her mother looked startled at her admission.

But her father only nodded, his eyes sad. "We know, darling."

"But it's been hard."

Her father nodded again but her mother sat up stiffly. "How *dare* you?"

"Just let me finish, okay." She took another deep breath and drew courage from what Marun had done, something she'd thought about doing ever since she discovered that loving women, and one woman in particular, was what she was made for.

"It's been hard because your love for me seems to always have conditions to it. That hurt me, and I don't want to hurt anymore." Her hands shivered with cold even though the room itself wasn't that chilly, not after the warmth Iya left behind. "Marun is my wife. She's not going anywhere. And—and I'd like for you to accept us as a couple, and me as your queer daughter."

There. She said it.

Izzy felt like a giant jumping bean had replaced the heart in her chest. She pressed a hand there, trying not to hyperventilate.

"But that woman abandoned you," her mother said after a moment, voice rising. Her father's hand landed gently on his wife's knee.

"She didn't," Izzy said. "I know that now."

Her mother started to say something else, but her father spoke over her. "We support you, Izzy. And we love you, no matter what you do or who you choose to be with."

"Trevor! Don't speak for me."

The leather of the sofa sighed as he turned to his wife. "You've been speaking for me for years now, Eleanor. It's time I spoke up for myself, and it's time I spoke up for our children."

Izzy's mother squirmed. Her face contorted and her chin wobbled a little. "I really don't know what's come over you, Trevor."

"The police said our girl was missing, and probably dead. When the officer was talking to us, I thought of all the ways I could've been there for Izzy but wasn't. Now, for whatever reason, I'm getting another chance. I don't want to squander it." He faced Izzy. "I love my child, and I want her to know that while we're both alive."

Fighting the tears was a lost cause. They ran a scalding path down Izzy's chin. "Papa."

Then, her father was holding her to his chest, and she breathed him in, the scent of pipe tobacco and the wool of his sweater vest. "I love you so much."

"I love you, too, sweet girl. Don't ever forget that."

He produced a handkerchief from somewhere and wiped her face, kissed her forehead. "I think we can all agree this has already been a very intense day, yes?" His chest vibrated under Izzy's cheek as he spoke. "We all need to breathe a little." Sniffling, she nodded, feeling protected by him for the first time in a long while. "Come see us at the hotel tomorrow," he continued. "Maybe we can have one of those fancy brunches the kids love these days. Bring your wife."

"Mom?" Izzy turned to look at her mother who clutched an empty teacup to her chest like it was some sort of anchor in a world suddenly turned upside-down.

Her mother cleared her throat. "Your father and I need to discuss some things but you and your wife"—she choked on the word—"should come meet us for a bite in town. It's the least you could do after making us worry so much."

Well, that was better than nothing. "Okay. I'll let Marun know."

Her father hugged Izzy again. "I think we'd better get going and leave you and your young lady alone." Izzy nearly smiled at the word *young*. "We'll call you in the morning. Okay?"

"Okay, Papa."

On the way out of the door, Izzy's mother gave her an awkward hug. "See you tomorrow, Isabella."

When the front door closed behind them, Izzy collapsed against it, heaving a breath of relief tinged with just a little hope. Did she think her mother would suddenly stop being a raging homophobe overnight? No. But getting her father back in her life was a gift she never expected. Fresh tears threatened.

The bedroom door opened with a gentle creak and she looked up to see her wife walking toward her through a sheen of tears she didn't mean to let loose.

"Oh! I'm such a blubbering mess." She gasped out a sob in the fragrant shelter of Marun's throat.

Had she always been like this, with tears ready to fall at the tiniest hint of emotion?

"True. Good thing I like the taste of your tears." Marun smiled down at her, starlight eyes warm with affection.

Izzy choked on a burst of unexpected laughter and clung, sighing, to the only woman she ever loved.

Chapter Fourteen

Izzy fell onto the couch, her knees still trembling from the visit of both her and Marun's families. She felt lighter though. Better.

At the other end of the couch, Marun put Izzy's feet into her lap.

"So." Uncertainty plucked a discordant note in Marun's voice. "Do you still want me even though I'm human like you now?"

Silly woman. She cracked an eye open to peer at the woman she loved.

"To me, you were a god or whatever for only about five minutes. Are *you* okay with it? That's the real question."

A sharp pain behind her breastbone had Izzy abruptly sitting up on the couch. What if Marun resented her for losing her godhood and her family? That would kill their love faster than any disappearing act.

Carefully watching Marun, she chewed on the edge of her thumb. "I never wanted you to give up anything for me."

"I gave all that up for myself. I'm just lucky I get to have you too."

Izzy still couldn't quite reconcile it. "They're your family—"

"Yes, and nothing will change that. I may not be able to claim godhood anymore, but the bonds of blood are strong. We'll definitely be seeing my mother again, maybe even the others too."

Oh, that didn't sound like a threat or anything. Izzy gnawed harder on her thumb and the raw flesh brushed against her thumb, already tasting vaguely of blood. "That's great?"

Marun laughed and her eyes lit up like the morning sky. "It's perfect. With me being a human, you're safe and we can be together. The only thing that would make it not worth it is if you don't want me."

Izzy made a rude noise. "Seriously? That night at the gallery sealed my heart to everyone but you. You're inside me, and nothing will ever get you out."

"That sounds painful, and a little bit kinky." Marun adjusted their position so that they were lying down and Izzy was on top of her, their faces only inches apart.

She took Izzy's hand and kissed her palm, the raw edge of her thumb. The brush of her breath against her skin was as comforting as it was arousing. Izzy curved her hand around Marun's jaw, stroked behind her ear. Her thumb, bleeding sluggishly now, moved against Marun's lower lip, stained it red. Marun sucked it into her mouth, tongue lazily moving over raw skin, soothing it.

Apparently, she was still into that.

"So, we're going to be okay?" Izzy asked, already feeling the answer, twinned with the warmth of growing desire, in her belly.

An image appeared in her head of the building they'd owned together. The building they still shared, thanks to Marun's stubbornness. The two of them standing at one of the loft's windows overlooking the early-morning street while the scent of fresh-baked bread drifted up from the bakery below. In the daydream, Izzy stood in the circle of her wife's arms and Marun pressed a kiss to her temple whispering, "I love you so very much."

The vision tasted real.

"Yes, we're going to be okay," Marun said softly. "And we're going to be happy."

Izzy believed her.

About Fiona Zedde

Fiona Zedde was born under the Jamaican sun but now makes her home in Spain. Since getting the writing bug, she's published around thirty books and short stories, mostly about black queer romance, including the Lambda Literary Award finalists, *Bliss* and *Every Dark Desire*. Her novel *Dangerous Pleasures* received a *Publishers Weekly* starred review and was winner of an About.com Readers' Choice Award for Best Lesbian Novel or Memoir.

At this very second, she's probably writing another book, and it has 100 percent chance of having queer romance and queer women in it. Her pseudo-healthy obsessions are French pastries, English cars, and Jamaican food.

Email
f.zedde@gmail.com

Facebook
www.Facebook.com/fiona.zedde

Twitter
www.Twitter.com/fionazedde

Website
www.FionaZedde.com

Also from NineStar Press

Soul Burn by Megan Hart and Brenda Murphy

A mistress, a werewolf, a screenwriter and a shapeshifter walk into your heart in these two sexy paranormal stories of love and redemption.

Shifting Flames

Shunned screenwriter Eve Perez has something to prove. Shut out of the industry after a scandal, she's ready to do whatever it takes to climb back to the top, even if it means working with notoriously difficult author Celeste Quon.

Reclusive best-selling author Celeste Quon is adored by a generation of fans, but would they love her if they knew her truth? Under pressure from her fans, Celeste agrees to bring her best-selling novel to the screen but on her terms.

After a freak spring snowstorm strands Eve at Celeste's home she discovers Celeste's incredible secret. Amid their fiery attraction should she let their relationship burn out, or surrender to the flames of their desire?

The Fire Inside

For Clara, crafting pain into pleasure is her job. For Selena, it's her salvation. When submissive Selena hires Clara as her Domina, it seems like the best of business arrangements. But when their emotions infiltrate what was meant to be only professional, both women are rocked by the possibilities that their relationship might be changing into something... more.

Selena has given her submission to Clara for months, but faced with the idea of giving her heart, she runs. Loving Clara means revealing her secret, the one that sent her seeking pain in the first place, and it's a risk Selena can't take.

Clara, confused and terrified by the glimpse she had of Selena's true self, can't keep herself from wanting more. And, as Selena's Miss, she's not afraid to demand she be given the chance to take it. Snowed in at Clara's mountain cabin, the women must face the truth about themselves and about each other.

Can true love grow from a business relationship, and can it conquer even the darkest of fears?

Connect with NineStar Press

www.ninestarpress.com

www.facebook.com/ninestarpress

www.facebook.com/groups/NineStarNiche

www.twitter.com/ninestarpress

www.instagram.com/ninestarpress